THE LUXURY OF TIME TRAVEL

CHRISTELLE LUJAN

For my Family

BOOK ONE

*T*he sign hanging over the front door squeaked on rusty hinges that London could hear from inside the house.

Readings $45 was hand painted onto a wooden board.

London scratched her arms as the cheap red velvet dress she was forced to wear tugged at tiny hairs. She leaned on the arm of the couch and waited to receive her mother's first client.

"Can't I just wear my regular clothes?" London asked.

"The pageantry is part of what they pay for." Ruth repeated this every time her daughter asked if she could be relieved of her position in the family business.

A knot twisted in London's stomach when she heard the knock. She opened the door, sunlight streaking into the house, and all she could see was the silhouette of her mother's next client. Frail and narrow, Mrs. Matthews seemed more likely to be blown into the house than to walk. Her ability to move was slowed by the cloak of sadness that hung on her shoulders. London had only ever met one other person who had lost a child, but from what she could tell they all bore the same open wound.

Mrs. Matthew's blonde hair shone in blazing juxtaposition to the dark pit buried beneath her ribs. The first time she'd been in their home, her voice barely audible when she'd spoke the words, "I didn't know where else to go," London thought she might be sick. The petite woman emitted an anguish that sucked all the oxygen out of the room. But after years of seeing her sob into Ruth's arms, London had learned to smile gently in the face of incurable agony and deliver the speech her mother expected of her.

"Please enter, Mrs. Matthews. Allow your heart to open and your mind to clear as Madame Ruth prepares herself to reach into the beyond."

London choked on the next line as her classmate stepped into her living room behind his mother. Gable Matthews had gotten tall over summer, and the sudden squareness of his jaw made his round glasses look like they had landed on the wrong face. He seemed as uncomfortable to be here as London felt. The small, outdated living room seemed to swell to accommodate the influx of anxiety and agitation Gable carried with him.

London skipped the second part of her speech about "trusting in the power that lead you here" and just directed the mother and son to a pair of chairs tucked under a small round table. She darted behind a curtain that lead to their kitchen and wished for a meteor to strike her house.

Mrs. Matthews was a regular visitor, practically a staple in the Riley home, but she'd never brought Gable with her before.

London's mother came and stood beside her at the kitchen sink, fastening an earring and humming some undefined melody.

"Everything all set?" Ruth asked.

"They're out there," London said. "Do I have to let them out at the end? That boy goes to my school."

"Oh, don't be so dramatic. All you have to do is open a door. I promise it won't be the end of the world."

Ruth either didn't see or chose to ignore the exaggerated eyeroll. Instead, London got a kiss on the cheek, loaded with red lipstick, before watching her mother's auburn hair disappear behind the curtain.

It usually took an hour or so to complete a reading. In the meantime London wasn't allowed to watch TV, so she grabbed a book and tucked herself into a chair on the back porch. She was unable to focus on the words as they glided by in incomprehensible repetition. The sound of the front door slamming relieved her of her attempt to read. She traced the noise around the house and found Gable throwing a rock into her driveway. She couldn't tell if he had tears or sweat running down his cheeks, but his face was reddened and his brow puckered. London lingered in the shadows, now fully aware of her ridiculous costume, her unkempt brown curls, and the hairs between her eyebrows she'd been meaning to pluck for weeks. She tried to inch her way back toward the patio, but the gravel under her feet cracked in an unforgiving chorus that made Gable jump.

"Oh, hey," he said, snorting in a rattled breath.

London could feel sadness and anger rippling off him in equal, quivering waves. She could also detect a memory of his sister. It bled into her mind, fragmented images of an outgoing little girl, eager to grab the attention of her older brother.

She forced herself to stay in the moment by responding with a weak, "Hey." He didn't add anything, but London felt stuck in a conversation nonetheless. "Are you okay?" she asked.

"Me? Yeah. I'm fine. No offense, but I don't believe in any

of that." He pointed at her house as if it were quarantining an infectious disease.

"It's not for everyone," she said, trying not to defend or condemn her mother.

"Tell my mom that," Gable said.

"Are you—" London tried to change the subject, but her mother was calling her name in a whispery yell from the back door.

"I've got to go," London said.

Gable gave a slight two-finger salute. She considered saluting back, but returned a meek wave instead, dashing to the back porch and nearly slipping as she rounded the corner.

"Please go see Mrs. Matthews out. Hurry, hurry."

London entered the room, panting a little from her sprint, and held out a hand to Mrs. Matthews to see her to the door. The beautiful but broken woman bit her bottom lip like a child and attempted to straighten her back before falling into her sullen slump again.

As always, Mrs. Matthews pushed an extra five dollars into London's hand.

"Thank you for coming, Mrs. Matthews. May Madame Ruth's light carry you home safely," London said.

As she held open the door, she noticed Gable wasn't in the driveway anymore. She felt relief that he was gone—but also a twinge of disappointment.

Her mother's arm squeezed her across the shoulders. "See, that wasn't so bad."

"I don't want to do this anymore."

"We could work on expanding *your* abilities."

"I really don't want that," London grumbled.

The only thing that sounded less appealing than being her mother's eager sidekick was taking on some of her own clients. Her abilities only offered her insight she didn't want to have. Tapping into someone's subconscious gave her access to all the parts of a person's emotions they were trying to forget or ignore or didn't even know existed. Who would want their buried truths laid out before them? No one, as far as London could tell.

At least Ruth had access to a client's full spectrum—what they were thinking, what they were feeling in the moment, their memories, even what they were planning on doing within the near future. That was a useful ability people should pay a lot more than forty-five dollars for. All London could offer a client was a piece of them that was buried beneath their façade.

Besides, anecdotal proof had led her to realize that being a psychic's daughter made you strange. Being a psychic's understudy would be a social disaster.

Ruth looked at her daughter with pity.

"London, you get to choose your life. Just understand that if you don't own these abilities and get to know them, they'll be your undoing."

*G*able was doing everything he could to keep his eyes planted on the road. His knee bounced and his hands were clammy, but his mother made little effort to hide her tears as they drove home.

"I didn't mean to upset you," she muttered in between sobs.

He stared silently out the window, not wanting to soothe her.

"I think if you embraced the reading instead of getting scared, maybe you'd feel some relief," she added.

"I'm not scared. That psychic stuff is just a load of crap."

"Madame Ruth has a true gift, Gable. And she's using it to help me heal."

"Mom, her name is just *Ruth*. And she doesn't have special powers. She's just taking your money and telling you what you want to hear."

"That's not true," his mother said in a sterner voice than he expected.

"Whatever."

They didn't speak the rest of the way home. Gable felt

anxious as he considered the possibility that psychics were more than just counselors with a con-artist twist. He loved science and math—things that had tangible and testable elements. If a person could just reach inside another and pluck information out to the tune of forty-five dollars, what did that mean for the order of things?

Just because Ruth had guessed a right answer—or done some research to find it—didn't mean she had anything real to offer. In Gable's opinion, what his mother needed was to move on from death, not go back to visit it again and again.

And what about London? He cringed at the idea of her living with that fraud and working like a magician's assistant. The girls at school talked about her like she would infect them if they stood too close, but standing there in front of him, she seemed too normal to actually believe in what Ruth was selling.

When Gable and his mother got home, he didn't even stop to greet his father. Instead, he sought out the one thing that tethered him to the world: chemistry.

*A*fter she was relieved of her duties, London hopped on her bike and headed down a dirt road to Taryn Trainor's house. Her best friend earned that title because they both happened to be the only girls from their school who lived in the dusty, manufactured homes in the south part of town. She also happened to be London's only friend to speak of.

Taryn's father answered the door and pointed to the garage on the side of the house without offering even the remotest greeting. The smell of cigarettes and too many days at work without a shower billowed off him. London had only been inside her friend's home once. The severe lack of ordinary maintenance hadn't seemed to bother Taryn. She'd stepped over engine parts and shuffled away adult magazines like they were ordinary household knick-knacks. London's face must have carried a look of horror or disgust as they waded through the mess because she was never invited in again. As she rounded the corner to the garage, Taryn slapped a bicycle helmet on London's head.

"What the hell?"

"Shh, just let it happen," Taryn urged.

The helmet was plugged into something that looked like a car battery. Another perk of being each other's only friends was that London was frequently the guinea pig for whatever invention Taryn was tinkering with at the time.

"I'm gonna die."

"Don't be stupid," Taryn snapped.

Taryn flipped a switch and tossed her hair as if both movements were crucial to what she was doing. Her machine started to whir and hum, and a vibration pulsated on London's scalp.

"Anything?" Taryn asked.

"What's supposed to happen?"

"Just give it a minute."

London's eyes darted around the garage. She was certain that at any moment she'd be electrocuted. Then, all of a sudden, a warm, tingling sensation crept up her legs. For a second she thought she might pee her pants. The machine began to smoke and sputter, and London ripped the helmet off.

"Well?" Taryn asked, her eyes glittering.

"What is it?"

Taryn began to laugh uncontrollably. "I call it an Orgasmagraph!"

"A what?"

"It's supposed to give you an orgasm. Did it work?"

"Ew, no," London said.

"Don't be such a prude. You didn't feel anything?"

"No," London lied, a hum still lingering in areas she didn't care to admit.

"I'll make some tweaks."

Taryn was always crafting some sort of device out of scrapped parts from her father's auto shop. She'd made small motors that could make her bike go faster. She rigged a set of earrings to trigger a barely audible alarm when her dad was coming toward the garage.

Her most recent infatuation was London's least-favorite phase so far. Taryn recently had a sexual awakening that made her fully aware of phrases like *G-spot*, *strap-on*, and *Tantric sex*—all things London had to do her best at guessing what they were. On nearly every occasion they were together, Taryn found some way to insert innuendo. When London would stare back blankly, unsure of what she was talking about or how to respond, Taryn would giggle and call her a "baby" or a "virgin" before crinkling her nose up at her like an adoring pet owner. London couldn't tell if Taryn was just reading an absurd amount of *Cosmo* or if she'd actually been experimenting with some of her admirers at school.

"Why would anyone want that machine?" London asked, already regretting the question.

"Oh, Londy, you're so cute and innocent."

London shriveled under Taryn's pity, angry at failing to ascend to the level of maturity her friend had reached. In an ordinary relationship, London would simply read the person and get an understanding of why they were behaving a particular way, then act in accordance with their desires. With Taryn, though, her entire subconscious was unreachable because her internal dialogue was entirely in Korean. Her mother had immigrated two years before getting pregnant with her daughter. From the little information Taryn spoke about her, London knew she virtually never spoke English, either because she couldn't or didn't want to. So as a little girl, Taryn's first language was Korean. She quickly learned English once hitting school age, but her internal dialogue remained in her mother's tongue. In fact, it may have been the only thing left of her mother for Taryn to cling to.

"Guess what?" London asked. "Mrs. Matthews was over again today, and she brought Gable with her."

"Oh, yeah?" Taryn asked without looking up from her device.

"Yeah. He seemed really sad and upset."

"Oh, God, you didn't try to fix him, did you?"

"What? No!" London had grown used to Taryn's direct way of speaking, but it still stung a bit when it was pointed at her. "No, I mean we talked for a second, but I didn't do anything about it."

"Good. You know that weirdo shit isn't going to fly this year."

London twisted her foot into the ground, well aware that her "weirdo shit" wasn't exactly flying already.

It had been almost four months since her last outburst. And while she wanted nothing to do with the world her mother lived in, she couldn't always suppress her ability to read a person's subconscious.

Walking down the hall she knew Julie Master's was always sucking in her stomach as a trained reaction to her mother pinching her waist throughout childhood. London could sense the unflappable confidence that came with Paul Thompson being the best-looking guy in school and the gem of his family. She thought she could almost hold Mrs. Jacob's sadness over the death of her brother in her hands, despite the forced smile the teacher showed everyone else. From every corner of her life, London could hear the whispers of people's pain and pleasure. Whether they knew it or not, each person carried with them a massive depository of memories and experiences and habits that made them act and speak a certain way. For some, the effects of their subconscious were obvious to them. For others, it was a truth they buried deep and stored away.

She had tried to describe it to Taryn once.

"It's like a car. Most people see tires moving and someone turning the wheel. But I can see the drive shaft and the engine and the spark plugs and even what's in the trunk."

While Taryn just shrugged and went back to whatever she was doing, London had deeply wanted her friend to understand that there was this secret system in charge of every human being. Most couldn't see their own inner workings, let alone anyone else's. But she could see and hear the cacophony of life experiences that pushed a person's actions to the surface, and it was terrifying and tragic and beautiful.

When she was seven, an old man bellowed at her to get out of his yard. Most kids would have been scared and ran, but London stood and looked at him as reels of a broken marriage and children moved across the country played through her thoughts. She stood staring at him and started to cry, her heart aching for his sad, lonely life. She remembered wanting to hold him and say she was sorry, but the man threw an empty beer bottle into the rocks and told her to "get" before she got the chance.

Most of the time, London held what she saw inside. But on rare occasions, she felt overwhelmed with the urge to act. Last year, when Jerry Daniels had been getting pummeled by three members of the football team, London's heart had filled with volcanic fury. She could feel his abusers blood lust, each tied to some petty, macho need to claim their alpha status or a cowardice duty to fall in line with their friends. What was worse was Jerry's agony and fear. The only son of a single mother, he'd never even seen a real fight. Nor did he have the skills to hold his own during an attack. As the boys began beating him, lifelong wishes for a dad he never met flooded his mind. And London's. All of a sudden and without thinking about it, as if someone had been remote-controlling her, she flung herself into the fight. She covered Jerry with her body, took a punch to the ear, and screamed in a single and unbroken note until all that was left of the action were dozens of eyes staring and mouths gaping.

As the football players backed up and London pulled herself off her frightened classmate, even Jerry looked at her like she was a lunatic.

It wasn't the first time London's attempt to aid someone in pain had gone awry, but it was the most public occurrence. Most people, despite what they may say, don't want to be cared for. They prefer to wallow, alone and hidden.

Throwing herself on Jerry had earned her the official title of *freak* by anyone who didn't already call her that. Those who were members of the upper echelon of high school popularity spread rumors that London must be in love with the class geek. More sympathetic peers guessed that her mother beat her, which was why she couldn't stand to see it happen to someone else. Even some teachers prodded her with questions like, "London, should we be worried about you?"

London had wanted to scream, "Maybe you should be worried about the people doing the beating!" But instead, she just said "no" and hung her head deeper on the walk to her desk.

"Can we go to Fud's tonight?" London asked.

"Uh, I guess. Why?" Taryn questioned with a raised eyebrow. "You never want to go there."

"I don't know. I just don't feel like being at home. My mom has clients until late, and I'm really trying to get out of working."

"Okay, Madame London."

"I hate it when you call me that."

"I know. That's why I do it, dumb-dumb. Now come here and put this helmet back on."

"Pass."

London got on her bike and kicked back toward home. If she told Taryn that the reason she wanted to go to Fud's was she thought Gable might be there, her friend would have shown no mercy. London had never been in as close proximity to Gable as she was today. He was in all advanced classes at school—classes London would never have been able to keep up with. He was also in honors clubs and on student council. He had friends. A lot of them. Not just one person who derived most of their pleasure from teasing him, which was all London had. When she'd been within a few feet of him today, his feelings had poured over her in a torrent. She just wanted to feel that again—his emotions like crashing rapids over jagged rocks. She wanted that rush.

4

*G*able had been in his room for seven hours, thirteen minutes, and forty-seven seconds since coming home with his mother. He always started a timer when he began working. His father had bought him a shot clock hoping he'd be some sort of basketball star one day, but Gable only used it to count his working hours. Being tall does not a basketball player make.

He hit Stop and jotted the time down into a spreadsheet. He'd read that if you dedicated ten-thousand hours to any one task that you could achieve mastery in it. He'd been working on his hypothesis for nearly fifteen-hundred hours so far, and though he didn't feel anywhere near mastery, there was some gratification in watching his hours tick up toward his goal.

What Gable wanted was simple, in theory. He wanted to be able to make happiness a sustainable state of mind. If someone was having a good day, he wanted to elevate it so it was the best day of their lives. Conversely, if someone was sunk into sadness, he wanted to be able to lift them out. Not with narcotics, which were littered with side effects, or anti-depressants that only dulled feelings. That sort of medical science was criminal in Gable's mind. What he wanted was to be able to find and enhance the parts of the brain that make humans feel happy in the most ordinary sense. He wanted to bottle what a great song or piece of chocolate could do for your mood and then increase it by a thousand.

To start, he had experimented with foods and vitamins in an attempt to hijack joy via the digestive system. He would binge eat avocados, black beans and salmon hoping to flood his body with the right chemicals. Dozens of foods and nutrients can help boost endorphins, serotonin, oxytocin, and dopamine—all the "feel good" chemicals. But boosting those chemicals wasn't the problem. Keeping them up was. As a part of every human's survival instincts, the limbic system will kick in during moments of perceived threats and flood the body with cortisol. Gable hypothesized that, while that may have been useful in caveman days and perhaps in times of war, the ordinary human didn't need such frequent takeovers of the survival instincts that flood a person's systems with stress-inducing chemicals. Happiness, he felt, should be obtainable more often and for longer stretches.

What started with overindulging in nutrient-rich foods and vitamins, which his parents simply chocked up to obsessively healthy habits, evolved into the actual development of his own chemical compounds. He spent an excessive amount of time with his chemistry teacher and late nights on the Internet studying everything from pharmacology to holistic medicine to psychedelics. He never ceased to be amazed by what he could learn and buy online, spiraling into sleepless nights of educating and ordering.

The first twenty-seven versions of his compound did little more than make him sick to his stomach. Too much of even the best chemicals can cause an overdose. The problem, he found, was with ingesting his super-infused substance.

Inevitably it would get metabolized and the cortisol would come flooding back into his system to fill the spaces where "happy chemicals" once resided.

On the twenty-eighth attempt, he made a taffy. It was meant to be chewed continually, not swallowed. This way it could release the perfect combination of Iron, Magnesium, Omega-3s and other nutrients in a steady stream that could keep a person elevated for longer stretches of time. He spent seven blissful hours gnawing on his creation, feeling over-joyed at his accomplishment until his jaw ached to be relieved.

He knew he couldn't expect people to chew flavorless gum all day, but he felt he was onto something. Something he was finding it harder and harder to tear himself away from.

"Gabe." His dad knocked at the door. Gable clenched his jaw. He preferred his full name, but his dad could not resist using the sportier nickname.

"Yeah?"

"Can I come in?"

"Sure."

"Hey, your mom's not feeling so good." He threw a ten-dollar bill on Gable's desk. "Are you good to fend for yourself for dinner tonight?"

"Yup."

"Thanks, champ. Don't worry about your mother, she'll feel better tomorrow. She just needs a rest." His dad spread a practiced, thin-lipped smile across his face. His long legs took up too much of his body, and his hips thrust forward under the bend of his awkward height. He was too tall to be pitiful and too pitiful to be an imposing figure, so Gable felt little need to show restraint when he was feeling agitated by having his focus broken.

"What she needs is to stay away from 'Madame Ruth,'"

Gable mumbled, using air quotes when he teased the psychic's name out of his mouth.

His dad left the room—maybe agreeing, maybe not. Daryl Matthews never let on how he felt about his family's crumbling foundation or his wife's failing mental health or the empty, untouched room next to Gable's. He just kept going to work, making sure everyone was fed and, in their beds before he went back to watching whatever game was on at night. The most harmless man anyone could ever meet, but no one to aspire to be like.

Gable stuffed the ten dollars into his pocket and sniffed at the collar of his shirt. *Good enough,* he thought as he misted something called "Field of Steel" onto his shirt from an aluminum can. The sting of the masculine fragrance tickled his nostrils and clouded his glasses for a second. He wiped the lenses on a cloth meant only for that purpose, and then grabbed his skateboard to get to Fud's. He'd already messaged his best friend Derek to meet him there in fifteen.

5

_T_aryn had insisted on coming over early to get ready before going to Fud's. So when they arrived at the burger restaurant, London was reluctantly wearing a black spaghetti-strap shirt and a pair of blood-red pants. She had resisted Taryn's attempt to slap a pair of platform heels on her but was unable to escape a noxious cloud of perfume.

When they dismounted their bikes, London began to tug at the top and bottom of her shirt in a futile attempt to cover the exposed skin on either end. Taryn strode a few steps ahead of her, making London look like a kid sister she'd had to drag along. Her eyes skimmed the collection of people, but she couldn't spot Gable's golden-brown hair. She could, however, feel the swirl of emotions emanating from her classmates as their eyes landed on her. Mixed in with the smell of burgers on a grill and fries in oil was a peppering of thoughts and feelings and memories. In crowds, when she wasn't focused on one specific person, the internal landscape of the people around her would pellet her mind with fragmented readings.

She could pick up that a girl, perched on the hood of a car

in the parking lot was jealous of Taryn. There was a waiter mentally reciting some sort of financial mantra that helped him tolerate clearing ketchup smeared plates from the table. A small child danced around her parents, the tune of a nursery song playing in her mind.

London did what she always tried to do when the noise around her was overwhelming and she counted every step she took until they reached the order window. Taryn bought them both a side of fries and Diet Cokes.

"We're not going to eat a burger?" London asked.

"God, no," Taryn shrieked. Apparently eating real food was just another social faux pas London was unaware of. "Londy, I swear, every time we go somewhere it's like you've never been around other humans."

The restaurant consisted only of a kitchen and an order counter, the seating was made up of weather-abused picnic tables in a dirt lot. Umbrellas bleached from the unrelenting sun drooped lazily above half the tables.

The crowd mostly consisted of teenagers and twenty-somethings looking for a cheap meal and a place to gather. London recognized a lot of the people from school. There were girls sitting on top of tables and boys shoving each other around in a playful, energetic buzz. She had to force herself not to stare and not to read as individuals caught her attention.

Taryn found a spot on the curb outside of the commotion to eat, sip, and watch the crowd. She sunk her fries into ranch dressing and poked fun at the classmates around them through mouthfuls of greasy potatoes. "Did you hear that Julie Master's hooked up with Chase Kyle in the racket ball courts at school?"

"Yeah. He's not even cute," London said in a poor attempt at gossip.

"I know!" Taryn snorted. "But she's kind of a chubsters, so I guess it makes sense."

London winced, knowing how insecure Julie was about her weight. The poor girl spent almost every waking hour counting calories and reminding herself to suck it in. London wished she didn't know that, but she had two of her most boring classes with Julie, and so her mind would wander to the emotions pouring out of those around her.

"Do you think Gable and Derek will be here?" London asked.

Taryn's mouth teased into a smile that turned her narrow, black eyes into mirrors. "Why do you ask?"

"Because I know you like Derek," London said.

"Mmm-hmm," Taryn hummed. "I can text him and ask."

Neither Taryn nor London could afford a phone. More than half of their classmates were properly cell-phoned by now, but there was no way Ruth or Taryn's father would fork over the cash for such a luxury. Taryn, however, had managed to rig an old calculator with two-way pager parts and a flip phone antenna she swiped at the mall, making an ugly but functional device capable of sending text messages that were fifteen characters or less.

"You can text him if you want to," London said, forcing a nonchalant blankness onto her face.

Taryn showed London her screen that said, "U coming?"

The two girls waited in silence for a reply, taking synchronized sips of Diet Coke.

"Yep. Almost the—" The message cut off at the fifteen-character limit, but it was enough to know that at least Derek was on his way.

"Well, that should make you happy," London said.

"And you too... Derek never goes anywhere without Gable." Taryn drew out Gable's name like a lullaby.

London sucked ice-cold air through her straw, trying to ignore Taryn's taunting.

The girls could hear Gable and Derek's skateboards scratching on the pavement before they could actually see them. Gable was considerably taller than his friend, but both had an impressive, triangular shape to their shoulders. Derek kicked the back of the board and grabbed its front with a single, fluid motion. Gable rocked his board under his foot as they ordered something from the window. Taryn and London watched as the boys brought food to a picnic table. London felt a twinge of envy over the fact that they were apparently allowed to eat a real meal.

Taryn crinkled up her nose at London and grabbed her by the wrist.

"What are you doing?" London asked.

"Giving you what you want, baby."

London shook her wrist free from Taryn and followed her to the picnic table near the center of the patio. She felt panic rising up in her throat, but knew it was better to walk over on her own two feet than to have her braver friend drag her.

Derek looked up from his basket of chicken and smiled a flirtatious and confident grin at Taryn. Gable glanced up from his burger and then did a double take when he realized it was London standing in front of him for the second time that day. London could feel Gable growing uncomfortable. He had a bubbling urge to flee.

"Hello, boys," Taryn said. Her black hair moved across her back in a single sheet. London had never met her mother, but Taryn always said that she got her best features from her. *I'm an Asian goddess on the outside like my mom and redneck garbage on the inside like my dad,* she'd always say when someone raised an eyebrow at her often foul mouth.

Regardless of some of the dark and twisted things she'd

say at a moment's notice, most guys still seemed pretty taken by her small frame and large lips.

"Hey, ladies," Derek replied, looking only at Taryn. Gable offered no greeting.

"What are you guys up to tonight?" Taryn asked.

"Just this," Gable answered before Derek could say anything.

"Oh. Well, we were thinking of going to the lake. It's a full moon," Taryn said.

London watched as Derek elbowed his best friend. Gable scowled and Derek murmured, "Come on, man," under his breath. To the two of them, he added, "We're in."

London's stomach collapsed in on itself. Going to Fud's was one thing. It was easy to ride her bike home from there. If they were going to the lake, though, she'd have to get in a car, and then she'd be stuck there until someone wanted to take her home.

"I don't think I want to—" London started, but Taryn cut her off by poking two fingers in her ribs.

"Great! Who's driving?"

"I can take my brother's car," Derek offered. "He's camping with his friends this weekend."

They walked their bikes to Derek's house, and London resumed counting her steps. She counted to avoid the sensation of Gable's dread. She counted to escape Taryn's butterflies. She counted to avoid Derek's borderline pornographic thoughts.

One-hundred thirty-seven, one-hundred thirty-eight, one-hundred thirty-nine...

"London!" Taryn yelled. London snapped out of her counting spell to catch Taryn giggling and looking confused.

"What?"

"Get in the car. You're riding bitch with Gable." She winked and squeezed her shoulders up next to her ears.

When London slid into the back seat, Gable was nestled up close to the car door, putting as much space between them as possible. She pressed her lips together into a non-smile that made her cheeks pucker.

Mercifully, Derek turned up the music loud enough that talking wasn't an option. London saw Taryn slide a hand onto Derek's lap. She wondered if her friend learned that move in an article titled "Ten Ways to Turn a Guy on in the Car." London tried to picture any version of herself where she might be confident enough to do that with a guy but was unable to find one. She sucked in her stomach so that her pants and shirt connected to cover her midriff.

When they got to the lake, the foursome stumbled through some brush and rocks until they could see the glow of a large fire. A dozen or so other people from their school were standing around it. Some held on to red plastic cups, others dangled cigarettes from their lips or between their fingers as they chatted.

Gable kept enough distance so that no one could mistake him for coming with London. Taryn hooked a hand around Derek's elbow and let him drag her toward the center of the party with London following a few feet behind.

She watched as Taryn wrapped her freshly glossed lips around a clear bottle and wince when the amber liquid hit her tongue. A girl from London's English class let out a "whoo!" in Taryn's direction. London drifted to the outer ring of the bonfire crowd. Orange light painted her kneecaps, her back was dipped in darkness. The subtle slosh of the lake lapped behind her, but she couldn't see the water. Gable sat opposite her, fidgeting with something in his hand that London couldn't make out.

There was something toxic in the air. London could almost taste a lingering sourness, and like a trained blood-hound, she got up to find its source. She ducked out of the fire's radiance and into the moonlight. She could hear rocks shuffling and could sense the feeling of a predator lunging onto prey. She was afraid she might stumble onto a coyote eating a rabbit—it was sometimes hard to tell the difference between animals and humans when they were experiencing primal emotions.

London tripped over cloth. When she picked it up, it felt like denim, but it was too dark to tell. She squinted into the unlit desert and whispered, "Hello?"

No sound was returned, but she inched closer to the feeling that had drawn her out. "Is someone out there? Hello?"

She could hear scrambling beside her, and when she looked down, all she saw was a pair of exposed breasts.

"What the hell, freak?" a boy's voice lurched near her. As her eyes came into focus, she could see it was Chase Kyle, bare bottomed and on top of Julie Masters. "Get out of here!"

"Oh, my gosh," London said as she tried to stumble backward away from them.

It was too late though. Chase was pulling on his pants and following her toward the party. London could feel Julie's relief over no longer being pinned beneath the crooked-nosed man-boy, but she didn't try to stop him from coming after London.

When London staggered back into the firelight, Chase was only inches from her and the commotion made everyone turn.

"I caught her creeping on me and Jules in the bushes," Chase yelled and pointed.

"No that's not—" London started.

Chase had one of the least complex interiors London had ever come across. She didn't spend a lot of time with him, only in passing at school and in this moment, but she knew his primary motivation was always to fight. At home, he fought with his father and brothers. At school, he was constantly on the attack. And in this moment, as his chest expanded and contracted with rage, he was readied for battle again.

"Who the hell brought this freak to my party?" Chase continued.

The crowd's reaction was in direct opposition to Chase's. Everyone, especially London, was in flight mode.

No one volunteered an answer, and Taryn hid behind Derek, knowing she'd be the obvious suspect.

"Whoever brought her needs to get her the hell out of here."

The heat of the desert, even at night, closed in around London as Chase tossed her a final warning look that said, *I better not see you when I come back out.*

London headed for the car. Chase disappeared back toward the lake and Julie. As she passed party go-ers who were slowly moving their thoughts back to their friends, she could hear them commenting from within on what had just happened.

What's wrong with her?

Why is she even here?

What was she doing spying on them?

Questions no one was brave enough to ask out loud. Just accusations they kept buried beneath false sympathy.

London heard Taryn yell, "Gable, go check on her."

"What?" she heard him reply as she made her way toward the lot where all the cars were parked.

She was sitting in the dirt with her back against a tire when Gable approached. She hadn't expected him to follow Taryn's instruction. He leaned up against the car door, still keeping a measured distance.

"I wasn't doing what he said." None of Gable's subconscious was accusing her of anything, but she felt the need to defend herself. "I'm not a creep."

"I know," he replied.

She still felt ashamed.

"Chase is a dick. Everyone knows that," Gable added.

Silence hung on the stars. She was perfectly comfortable not speaking, but Gable fidgeted under the quiet. "Why'd you even go out there?' he asked.

"Does it matter?"

"I guess not."

More silence.

"I thought she was hurt," London answered after feeling his tension rise at the lack of conversation. "I just wanted to make sure she was okay."

"Why would you think she was hurt?"

At this, London felt hot tears pour over onto her cheeks. She wasn't going to tell Gable that she could feel pain. That she could smell the mustiness of shame radiating from the desert. That all she wanted was to not care about how other people felt, but that she was drawn to it anyway. A magnet lived deep within her belly, pulling her toward hurt people who didn't want her there. She couldn't tell him about how, when she sat next to Julie in math, she could reach in and pluck out the memory Julie carried everywhere with her, the one where Julie's mother told her, "your baby fat will fall off eventually." She couldn't tell Gable that she felt Julie's failing self-esteem tied to the very moment by the lake. That she knew Julie was letting that beast of a boy climb on top of her because she thought it was the best she could do, even though she hated the feeling of his alcohol-tainted breath on her neck. London couldn't say any of those things, so instead, she cried.

Gable readjusted his stance half a dozen times and then held something out to London.

"Here," he said.

"What is it?"

"It's kind of like gum."

"Kind of like gum?"

"Yeah, just chew on it like gum."

"Well, what's in it?"

"It's hard to explain. It'll make you feel better."

"Oh, thanks, but I don't do drugs."

"No, it's not drugs," Gable said with a little growl. "Look." He took a bite of the chewy, tan wad between his fingers to show her it was safe. "Just try it."

She took the offering and placed it in her mouth. After turning it over with her tongue a couple of times, she felt like the tears on her face were reversing their way into her eyes and she chuckled. The air went out of her lungs and the tense agitation in her shoulders relaxed.

"What is this?" London asked again.

"It's something I made."

"Why do I feel so good?"

"That's what it's supposed to do," Gable answered. "I'm working on a compound that makes people feel...better."

"Better than what?"

"Better than whatever it is they were feeling before."

"Well, it's nice, but why would you want to make something like that?"

"Would you rather still be feeling shitty?" Gable snapped.

"No."

"I just think the world would be better if instead of people being depressed and stressed and anxious and angry and sad, if they could just be...better."

London tried to blot out her ability to feel Gable's heart drifting toward his mother. She shut her eyes and tried to focus on the tasteless taffy in her mouth and the feeling of relief washed over her again.

"It's pretty cool," London admitted.

"Yeah," Gable agreed.

Gable collected Taryn and Derek and drove everyone back to his friend's house. Taryn and Derek mauled each other in the back seat, while London allowed her eyes to close up front. The taffy began to toughen with each chew and London tried to remember the last time she felt this light. When she opened her eyes, the dark desert sky had transformed into a blinding beach. She jolted, as if an electrical pulse had been shot through her body. She closed her eyes again and opened them once more to find herself seated in a marijuana-scented car next to Gable. She blinked twice more, but nothing changed.

"You alright?" Gable asked as her head whipped around the vehicle, looking for evidence of her momentary trip to the beach.

"I think so."

When they got back to Derek's house, Taryn trailed after him, but London grabbed her back to head for home.

"Thanks," she said to Gable, pointing to the chewy substance between her teeth. He nodded and she pedaled away.

When she got home, the lights were out in her house and her mother wasn't there.

6

*S*chool was starting in thirty-four minutes. London grumbled at the idea of confronting her classmates. By now, most of them would have heard about how she'd almost fallen on top of Julie and Chase's naked bodies during the desert party.

She could only imagine the whispered words that would be floating on the air.

She's just curious because she's a virgin.

I bet she has a crush on Chase.

Maybe she has a crush on Julie.

London let out an audible shriek and threw her hair into a sloppy ponytail. Curly fly-away hairs brushed her ears. Makeup Taryn had applied the night before left an ashy shadow under her eyes. *I look like someone who'd creep up on a pair of lovers in the desert,* London thought to herself.

A frozen waffle burst from the toaster, offering her the tiniest bit of sweet comfort. When she stepped outside, she was surprised to hear a voice coming from the front patio.

"London!"

"Gable?" London asked. His honey-colored hair turned

upward in the places where he had slept on it. His clothes, usually ironed straight, were wrinkled as if they had been pulled from a basket in a hurry.

"I'm sorry to come over like this, but is your mother home?"

"Umm. No, she's not."

"Shit."

"What's wrong?"

"My mom was hoping yours would be available. She had a rough night and won't talk to any of us. She just keeps demanding to see Ruth."

"I'm sorry," London said. "She didn't come home last night. I'm not sure when she'll be back. I can let her know you came by."

Gable swept his hands through his hair. London was afraid his chest might explode onto the pavement; waves of pain were pouring out of him. He cursed internally and she could sense him puzzling out what to do.

"Is it true that you can do it too?" Gable blurted out.

"Oh, I, uh…what do you mean?" London said.

"You know. What your mom does?"

"No, I'm not like my mother. I can sense some things, but I don't know how to help anyone." London shrugged apologetically.

"I've seen you. Last night, even. You just seem to know things and be in places where people are hurting."

London felt caught off guard by his attentiveness and wished she'd made more of an effort over the years to mask her reactions to people in pain.

Gable's eyes were pleading and panicked.

"Maybe I could just come talk to her," London offered.

"Yes. Please. I wouldn't ask if I felt like there was any other option."

Gable had his mother's car and so London rode quietly in

the passenger seat, trying to mentally prepare for whatever it
was she'd gotten herself into. She tapped her toes inside her
shoes and bit the skin around her nails. Ruth would not be
happy if she found out what her daughter was doing. Any
time her mother had caught London testing her powers on
unsuspecting strangers, she warned that using an ability she
hadn't yet learned to control was dangerous territory. But
London didn't feel as if she could say no to Gable. Something
had split open inside him and all London wanted to do was
patch it up.

When she entered the Matthew's house, London felt a
chill rush into her veins. There were newspapers scattered
on the kitchen counter and the blinds were all drawn shut. A
smell was trapped inside. It wasn't necessarily foul, but it
made her eyes water like she was engulfed in the cloud of
powerful cleaning agent. Gable led her down a hall. Daryl
Matthews was sitting in a heap on the floor with his back
against a closed door. He scrambled to his feet and gave his
son a panicked look. Gable just held up his hand. There was
an odd role reversal that transpired between them, as if
Gable had assumed the parental position.

He knocked on the door Daryl had just scurried away
from. "She's here," he lied.

The sound of Mrs. Matthews wrestling around in the
room filled the silent hall. London assumed she'd locked
herself in a bathroom or her bedroom. The door creaked
open and Mrs. Matthews peered into the hallway, never
making eye contact with her son or husband. She began
shaking her head with epileptic intensity and saying "no, no,
no." She was not happy with Ruth's substitute. As she was
about to slam the door shut, London wedged her foot in the
opening and grabbed the fractured woman's hand.

"Please, Mrs. Matthews."

No one was more surprised by what was happening than

London, but she couldn't imagine just walking away and leaving the two men with the tornado churning in that room.

Mrs. Matthew's eyes darted for a second and then she opened the door just enough for London to slide in. The door slammed behind her and she was shocked at the sudden brightness. This wasn't a bathroom or a shrouded master bedroom. It was a little girl's room. Bursting with pink accents and stuffed animals. The tulle curtains were open, and the morning sunlight bounced off the glittery décor. Mrs. Matthews looked like a black-and-white portrait inside a candy shop. Her hair and makeup likely hadn't been tended to since she was last at London's house, and the robe that hung on her shoulders was unseasonably thick. It appeared to be the only thing tethering the woman to the ground.

"Darling, where is your mother?" she asked with practiced, but crumbling patience.

"I'm not sure, Mrs. Matthews."

"This is my goddamn hour of need," she snapped. "And I've kept a roof over both your heads these past few months."

London wasn't entirely sure what she meant by that, but now wasn't the moment to inquire. She knew she was unequipped for this job, but she had not expected to find the feeble but typically polite Mrs. Matthews in such an agitated state.

In an effort to stall, London traced the room with her eyes. She could feel the love that had gone into every item selected for this perfect, rosy little space. "Abigail loved this," London said, gently running her fingers over a small caboodle smeared with makeup. Mrs. Matthew's internal attention was drawn to her late daughter's favorite items, making it easy for London to pick them out.

Mrs. Matthews caught a gulp of air in her mouth.

London opened the lid to the plastic box and plucked a

lipstick from the jumbled mess of half-used items. "This one. It was her favorite?"

Mrs. Matthew's anger eased and her sorrow returned. Despite the frazzled ponytail and disheveled jean and t-shirt combo, the air around London shifted and her mother's voice, or something like it, started to stream out.

"Happiness is a strange thing," London continued. "We're always looking for it but have such a hard time living in it when it's here. That's what my mom always says at least." Her confidence was slipping.

Mrs. Matthews sat on the edge of her daughter's bed and London joined her. She took the broken woman's hand in hers and began rubbing her index finger in an unfamiliar pattern on the woman's palm. Mrs. Matthews burst into tears, and London began to realize that the pattern wasn't random at all. She'd been spelling Abigail over and over.

"She used to do that," Mrs. Matthews said. "It's been five years. Abigail would be turning twelve this month."

"She still is turning twelve, Mrs. Matthews," London said. "Maybe not in the way you would have imagined, but she's still here. I still feel her in the way you love her. She and Gable have the same eyes."

Everyone knew what had happened to Abigail. It wasn't a special story, but a heartbreaking one, nonetheless. The Matthews had a pool in their backyard. Their children learned to swim at a young age according to one of the local news articles she read. For some reason, while her mother made lunch, Abigail snuck into the backyard to go for a swim. No one heard the screen door open. No one heard her drag the chair over to the pool fence. No one heard it unlatch or detected the small sound of her splashing into the water. Abigail dove in "as she had done a hundred times," but this time her head hit a step as she went in. She lost consciousness and drowned in minutes. As Mrs. Matthews cut the crusts from her sandwich, Abigail died.

Reporters called the Matthewses' experience "a tragic tale of doing everything right." Abigail wasn't a latchkey kid, and Maggie and Daryl Matthews weren't drunks. The child was capable of swimming but had a terrible accident.

London let Mrs. Matthews collapse onto her shoulder and cry. She held the grown woman as if she were an injured child and let the tears wet her shirt. For a few minutes, London could have sworn that Mrs. Matthews was asleep.

When she lifted her head there was a disorientated panic on her face, like when a person wakes up and doesn't know where they are.

"Where did she—? I was just holding her…"

"Are you okay, Mrs. Matthews?"

Margaret looked around the room and then let her ribs sink into her stomach as she slouched further into herself. She removed something from her mouth and put it in a wastebasket. Inside, Mrs. Matthews mumbled, "I had her. She was here. Why couldn't I just look up?" Her exterior seemed to be recovering, though, as her back straightened a little and she wiped hair out of her face.

London wasn't sure how to exit.

"May I open the door?" London asked.

There was a lingering darkness she could feel right at Mrs. Matthews's core, but London assumed that would always be there. There was no cure for losing a child.

Mrs. Matthews shuffled her socked feet toward the door. London led the poor woman out of the child's bedroom by her elbow. When the two made their way into the hall, Daryl and Gable released a synchronized sigh of relief. Mrs.

Matthews collapsed into her husband's arms apologizing in hushed tones as he led her into another room, closing the door behind them.

Gable stared at London for a while without speaking. His face was tired and heavy, but his eyes still had their trademark brightness under his wire-framed lenses. London looked to the door, hoping to break his uncomfortable gaze. Instead, he grabbed her by the shoulders and pulled her into a hug. London's arms dangled at her sides, paralyzed from shock. She allowed her eyes to close for a moment but couldn't remember if she moved another muscle in those brief seconds. When he broke their connection, London's heart was beating so hard she felt certain Gable could hear it.

"We should probably get to school," he said. "I'll drive."

She nodded and followed him out.

The car ride to their high school was as quiet as the one to the Matthewses' home. Gable didn't ask what London had said to his mother. He didn't explain what had driven Mrs. Matthews so far over the edge this time to begin with. He just drove with an expression that was somewhere between relief and intense focus. London peered out the window, wondering what her mother would have thought of her actions today. Would she have been proud or angry that London had dove into something she'd been bitterly unprepared for and came out more or less on top?

The engine cut off and the two of them sat there for a moment.

"Thank you," Gable said. "For what you did for my mom."

"You're welcome."

"Please don't tell anyone."

"Don't worry. I won't."

London grabbed her backpack off the floor and left the car. Gable remained behind. Maybe, after everything, he was still leery about being seen with the school creep.

7

*L*ondon could only focus on the events of the morning. Despite all the different elements, her mind continued to drift to the way Gable held her in his hallway. If she focused on that scene, she could feel her whole body transport back to it. This wasn't a memory or a vivid daydream. She could feel each of his fingers on her arms. She could smell the slight remainder of toothpaste on his breath. She could hear Mr. Matthews starting the tub for his wife in the background. She felt more in that moment now than she had during the actual experience. It was as if she'd tethered herself to that specific instant and was able to toggle her mind between being there and being in class.

"Ms. Riley. Ms. Riley!"

London's eyes flickered open. She hadn't even realized they were closed, but now her math instructor and his pointy nose were just inches from her face.

"Am I boring you?"

London sat up a little straighter in her desk and this seemed to satisfy Mr. Johnson enough to convince him to walk away. She hadn't been sleeping. In fact, she'd felt more awake seconds ago than she did now. A few of her classmates were staring at her. Chase flipped her off when they accidentally made eye contact. All London wanted was to return to the loop where she was able to occupy that moment in the hall with Gable, but her focus was breaking.

The day was more than half over, but as she stepped into the hall to go to lunch, a rush of horror raced into London's skin. Something poisonous was in the air, like an exterminator had just coated the entire school with toxic chemicals. People were whispering and covering their mouths. Even teachers seemed to be involved in the gossip.

She couldn't seem to tap into a single thread of information that was responsible for the sudden shift in mood, but it was infecting people one by one. It was fiercely contagious— as one person knotted with anxiety whispered to the next, it spread.

Though the sun shone without mercy, a shadow was settling in on the campus. Groups of friends would circle, pulling out their phones and darting looks around corners in search of a monster London couldn't identify.

The clips coming out of everyone she passed didn't make sense in the collective story.

Karen Davenport was telling herself to text her mom.

Mark Barber had a memory of a funeral playing like a tape in his mind.

Mr. Franklin was looking for someone but moving too fast for London to be able to tell who it was.

London's eyes swept the walkway for the only person who was her own source of information.

Taryn came up on London so fast that their bodies collided. Her eyes looked even wilder than usual.

"Did you hear?"

"Hear what," London asked.

"Gable! Fucking Gable's mother is dead."

London couldn't possibly have heard that right.

"What?" London asked. "No, that's not right. I just saw her this morning."

"What do you mean you saw her? She came to see your mom?"

"No, I went to see her," London said.

"Why the hell did you do that?"

"Taryn, she's not dead, that's impossible."

"Gable was pulled out of second period today. The principal came and got him herself, and everyone was saying how weird it was. Gable's never in trouble."

"Get to the point!" London screamed in a panic.

"Well, you know how Ashley Douglas's dad is a doctor? He told Ashley that Mrs. Matthews had been brought in and that she overdosed on like sleeping pills or painkillers or something and that she freaking died. She wasn't supposed to tell anyone because doctor confidentiality and whatever, but Ashley is a gossipy bitch so of course she told everyone."

Taryn continued to ramble about how it was "so sad" and how "Mrs. Matthews was nice, but it's not *that* surprising."

London swallowed the excess spit filling her mouth, desperate to avoid throwing up. Her mind raced through the infinite number of ways this could be her fault. She shouldn't have gone over there. She shouldn't have said any of the things she said. She should have just left when she felt how devastated that household was. Where the hell was her mother?

"I have to go," London managed to wretch out.

"Wait, what?" Taryn asked.

London didn't bother answering. She walked past the front gates of school and started to run home. The air in her lungs burned and she couldn't tell if her tears were from heartache or the speed of the wind hitting them, but water raced passed her cheeks and toward her ears.

When she reached her driveway, she found a gray sedan parked there. Her feet skidded to a stop in the gravel. The first thought that occurred to her was that someone was here to arrest her. Could she actually get in trouble for what she did this morning?

She opened the front door and Ruth was standing there with a rigid, wiry man in a suit. He looked like an FBI agent, or at least how London pictured one would look based on what she'd seen on TV.

"Mom?"

"London, what happened?"

Her mother's face made it clear that she could immediately detect the panic and anxiety in her daughter. She pulled her by her arm into the next room.

London looked over her shoulder at the man they left behind.

"Is he here about Mrs. Matthews?" London asked.

"What? No, why would he—" Ruth Riley's eyes got big and London knew she was starting to see the events of the day unfold. Her mother had always described her abilities as a series of pictures being flung onto the table. *The heavier the emotions, the sharper the images,* she once said.

"Oh, my god," was all Ruth could muster and she pulled London against her chest. London burst into tears.

"This isn't your fault. London, do you hear me? This isn't your fault. This is mine. I'm so sorry. And I'm so sorry I have to do this right now, but we have to go. We have to leave."

8

The more he tried to sit up straight, the easier it was to choke back his tears. At his sister's funeral he was younger, and waves of emotion had pummeled him throughout the entire ceremony. He could remember people gasping in terrified sorrow at his uncontrollable state.

This time, he would be strong. Steady. Level. Gable didn't want people to think he was cold, but he refused to give even a sample of the storm that weathered beneath his chest. Grief was useless. He wanted to *do* something. He wanted to fix shit for a change. So he wasn't going to cry. He wasn't going to come apart. He was going to dig in and do for other people what he couldn't do for his mother in time.

His dad hung his head, the only sign of life was a lazy hand resting on Gable's knee. Gable desperately wanted to return to his lab, where he'd cloistered himself since they left the hospital. Something was wrong with the compound. Terribly wrong. And only time and attention could fix it.

There was a small part of Gable that had expected London to be at the funeral. He hadn't seen her in the week since his mother's suicide, but he hadn't seen much of anyone. Some family members brought food and people from church came to clean the house, but other than Derek, no one from school came by.

Couldn't London read what was inside him? Could she possibly even detect that he wanted to speak with her if he concentrated on it hard enough? He didn't know how any of it worked, but if she actually had psychic ability, she wasn't directing it at Gable.

He felt stupid as he tried to push the idea outward, hoping she'd be drawn in like a mouse to a trap. He imagined the aroma of his pain would entice her until her feet left the ground and her body floated to his house. What had she said to his mother? What had his mother said to her? London Riley was one of the last people to speak to his mother before she killed herself and he needed to know what those words were.

He had questioned his father mercilessly. The guilt of the interrogation still lingered, but he hadn't worked up the nerve or the time to apologize.

His badgering hadn't even led anywhere helpful.

"Did she say anything after London left?"

"Nothing important. She was just sad," his father offered. Gable got the sense he was trying to avoid hurting his son.

"Not all sad people kill themselves, Dad! Tell me what she said."

"I asked her if the tub was warm enough. She said yes. I asked if she needed anything. She said, 'No, thank you.'"

"That's it?" Gable pushed.

"When I was leaving the room she was just saying, 'She was here. I felt her. She was here.'"

Gable had stormed out of the room. He felt pity for his father, but also overwhelming irritation. His dad should have stayed in the room. He should have asked her what more he could do. Gable also felt a measure of guilt for having gone to school feeling happy that he'd "fixed" his mother. There was no undoing what she'd done, but with some real information he might be able to dissect it better. He wanted to roll it over and study it from all angles, but the one person with answers had vanished.

After the ceremony, Gable drove to the Riley home. He stood under the sign on the front porch:

Readings $45

He wasn't exactly sure what he would say to London if she answered. As he pounded on the door, the tension in his chest grew tighter. He banged again with no answer.

"London! Ms. Riley!" His voice cracked under the strain of his heartache. He cleared his throat and shoved it all down. "Ms. Riley, London! This is Gable Matthews. I need to speak with you immediately."

Sweat was already forming at his temples and he knocked again. He pounded the door until his hand vibrated and then he pounded some more. His knuckles began to bleed as he slammed them into the paint-chipped wood.

"Please, somebody answer," he spoke, without yelling.

Every day after school he returned to their home. He searched for footprints or tire marks. Dust gathered in thicker heaps on the windowsills and the welcome mat blew into the corner of the porch. Gable placed a rock in front of both entrances to see if they were moved, but day after day his trap remained undisturbed.

On the eighty-seventh day, he got up the nerve to break into the home. He smashed a window in broad daylight using a chair that had been left behind and crawled past shards of broken glass. His shirt caught and an edge sliced his shin, but he pushed into the home. It was musty with absence.

The one time he'd come here with his mother, they

entered the front door and the only room he saw was intentionally adorned with expensive-looking fabrics, unusual figurines, and an overabundance of candles. Arriving through the back of the home he was able to see it for what it was: a neatly kept but sparse, small space dedicated only to functional needs. There were no frames or carefully selected decorations. Just baron walls and unfilled floor space. He had always carelessly associated living in poverty with being dirty, but the home was spotless except for the dust that had settled because of the lack of movement in the home.

The only way he could discern the difference between Ruth's room and London's was that one bed was larger than the other.

He searched Ruth's room, hoping to find evidence of a plane ticket purchase. Was it juvenile to hope for a map with a big circle drawn around a city name? The closets and dresser drawers were empty.

In London's room he laid down on the bed and tried to imagine what she was thinking the last time she was there. Did she feel guilty about what happened to his mother? Did she even know? Was she hiding from him or was it just some horrible coincidence that she left around the same time his mother died? The truth was, he didn't know London or Ruth at all. So why they left or where they were going was something he might never be able to answer.

All he knew for sure was that the Riley women were gone.

BOOK TWO

9

*T*he main rooms at AION had massive circular windows that served as a looking glass into the surrounding desert. London was grateful for the expansive view, even if what she was looking at was a barren landscape of dust and shrubs. When she leaned against one of the windows she could pretend that there was nothing between her and the rest of the world. She could convince herself that she had the same freedom as anyone else.

"London, focus please," her mother urged.

She was twenty-six years old and her mother's voice could still snap her to attention. Taryn lipped *focus please*, in mock exaggeration. London was on her fifth reading of the day and her tolerance for other people's thoughts and memories was wearing thin. Taryn's patience was always thin.

A woman with large brown eyes stared nervously at London from across a table, while Taryn fiddled with the buttons of a machine nearby. Ruth was poised in an angular red leather chair that looked like it had been dyed to match her hair. The young woman's name was Fatima and she was one of a dozen AION candidates that London was expected to vet that week. Taryn pushed away Fatima's hair with militant precision, hooking the nervous prospect up to a machine that looked like a ham radio and an iPad had a baby. Two wires were fastened to Fatima's temples by round white circles. The machine—which Taryn referred to as "Clair"—whirred to life, and Fatima jumped as gears clicked and a tingle crept in around her hairline.

"Is it supposed to do that?" Fatima asked, rubbing the baby hairs that were standing up on her forehead.

"Yes, it's supposed to do that," Taryn responded, offering no comfort or eye contact that could leave the young woman feeling reassured.

"Just try to relax," London suggested. She was always a yin to Taryn's yang. The soft to her hard. The weak to her strong. The self-conscious to her confidence. Sometimes London wondered if there were any two people more different in the world, but fifteen years of friendship had proven over and over that what they had worked, even if it was just the result of a lack of options.

"Clair" was the invention that landed Taryn a place at AION. Everyone had to earn their spot. The 860-acre stretch of high desert that housed a futuristic fortress contained marvels that went far beyond architectural splendor. James Todd took over ownership of the oddball Arizona commune five years before London and Ruth were brought there. The compound had one purpose. A purpose James had been consumed with since he was young. There were thirty-seven people living in the maze of rooms at AION, each with specific talents that drove toward James's mission. Named after the Greek deity of unbounded time, the name was a nod to his driving motivation and an acronym that stood for Arizona's Institute of Neurotransportation to the few people in the world who understood what that meant.

When London and her mother had arrived ten years earlier, James tried to explain his intentions with the enticing prose of a politician. London could remember sitting in his office, a traumatized and confused sixteen-year-old with no tolerance for his pageantry. He had the squarest jaw she'd ever seen and tar-black hair that was slicked in place to hide any evidence of his natural wave. His face was shaved so close it gave him the illusion of boyishness even though he had to have been in his forties. But the most unsettling part about him was his eyes. So blue they were almost clear, they were impossible to look away from even if eye contact made London antsy.

"The human mind is capable of so much more than we can imagine, London," he'd said to her without any context when they'd first arrived on his estate. "You and your mother are some of the rare people who know there is an unseen connectedness that lies within our consciousness. It's how we think of someone just moments before they call us. It's the gut feeling that kept some people from getting on their planes before 9/11. It's the thing that's allowing you to try to read me now."

London could remember being in shock that James was able to detect her intrusion on his mind.

"How do you know I'm trying to read you?" she'd asked.

"I've worked with a lot of psychics over the years. You learn to get a sense for when someone is trying to get in. You also pick up a few tricks of your own that help to keep your thoughts private when you choose." London was getting nothing from James. Like her mother, he had an ability to keep her out. "What was I saying?"

"You were talking about consciousness."

"Right. Our consciousness is like an infinite stream, and each of us is a tiny whirlpool in this great stream. Now tell me, what is the difference between the water in the stream and the water in the whirlpool?"

"None, I guess."

"Right. And could the water from one whirlpool intermingle with that of another whirlpool?"

"I guess so."

"Exactly. I think this is a way we can explain you and your mother's gifts. You are simply two whirlpools who have found a way to navigate the stream. You can enter and leave other people's minds. You can reach someone who is deceased or see events that haven't yet come to pass. You can navigate the stream because you were born with an innate awareness that the stream exists. Are you following me?"

"I think so." London's gawky teenage body had shifted in her seat as his celestial eyes bore down on her. His posh office inside the futuristic community she and her mother had just rolled up to was by far the strangest place London had ever been. Without the comfort of her abilities, she'd felt exposed as he twisted words into riddles that seemed to have no destination.

"What I want to do is give other people the ability to navigate the stream. Ordinary people like myself should have just as much opportunity to explore as anyone else. And extraordinary people such as yourself can pave the way for even more conscious mobility."

"I still don't understand what it is you do here. Or what my mother and I are doing here."

"Your mother and I go way back. Did she tell you?"

"She mentioned you two were friends when you were younger."

"Friends. Confidants. Partners in crime. Explorers." He'd let out a nostalgic chuckle. "What I learned from her was that your kind has a boundless ability to see into the consciousness of others—past, present, and future. In very rare cases, we've found that people like you and Ruth can also see into themselves, travel back and forth within their own consciousness. Seeing things through their childhood eyes and through the eyes of their older selves. And in even more unusual cases, you can physically relocate where your whirlpool is in the stream."

"What does that mean?"

"Well, London, in layman's terms, I'm talking about time travel."

London had snorted at that, but James's face remained unmoved. He'd stuck a hand in his pocket and stared as she shifted from entertained to uncomfortable, and that was when she'd begun to feel an opening in the room. James allowed her to read him and as he unlocked the gates on his memories and knowledge, and London had felt a flood of panic. She saw years of obsessive research that had led to this moment. Countless experiments, hundreds of interviews, and travel to countries she didn't even know existed in search of answers. At his core was a truth James was unflappably certain of: time travel was real.

"I have invited you and your mother here to be a part of a team I'm building. I already have six members, but we need more. From what I understand, you two are in a bit of a financial bind. I also heard of your classmate's mother. I'm very sorry you were in any way involved with that." London had felt her stomach drop as thoughts of Mrs. Matthews returned to her mind. "I can offer you both sanctuary and security, and all I ask in exchange is to study and develop your talents."

London had chewed the skin next to her nails. She'd tried not let her knee bounce too much. "My mother has already agreed to this hasn't she?"

"I told her I wanted to make sure you were comfortable with this arrangement, as well. I would never want you to feel forced into this." His tone was soft and assuring, but she had still felt unsettled.

"I don't think we have a choice, Mr. Todd."

"There's always a choice, London."

Nearly a decade later London was still at AION, and with each passing year it felt less and less like a choice. She and her mother were outcasts during her childhood, but after years of living in isolation, toiling away at the mysteries of time travel, and having never been traditionally employed or even earned her diploma, where was she supposed to go if she chose another life? She didn't even know people outside the walls of AION. So instead of leaving, she stayed, desperately hoping that their team would unlock a piece of the puzzle, be generously rewarded, and she could retreat to a beachside cottage away from people and readings and James Todd. To date, though, there were only minor advancements and so they added more and more people to AION. Each new member was a fresh rush of hope for James, fueling his enthusiasm for work that often felt stagnant.

One of London's jobs was to read each candidate to see if there were any indicators that they'd be a benefit to the mission. Clairvoyance wasn't among her abilities, but she could assess someone's history and dig through their memories for evidence of a good fit.

As sweat began to form on Fatima's forehead, London waited for Taryn to give the signal that "Clair" had calibrated and the reading could begin. Taryn's machine helped amplify a person's consciousness. In essence, it took psychic ability and put it into a machine. For the average person, Clair could make some basic psychic ability possible. The machine would whir to life and grainy images would appear on a digital screen that reminded London of some of her first readings as a child. For naturals like London, the machine helped bring the reading into high definition. The invention was one of AION's most prized possessions, and Taryn had gotten the technology halfway there before she even moved onto the compound.

There were no free passes into AION. Taryn got in on her own brilliant mechanical ability just three years after London's arrival. Being London's childhood best friend was merely a coincidence, though James regularly explained there was no such thing.

Now Taryn gave London a thumbs up, letting her know she could begin. So she dove into her standard line of questioning, knowing already that Fatima wouldn't be admitted.

10

"*N*ame?"

        "Gable Matthews"

"Age?"

"Twenty-seven."

"Occupation?"

"Pharmaceutical assistant."

"Why are you here?"

"What do you mean 'Why am I here?' You people told me to come here. You've hacked my computer. You've been following me. I've gotten handwritten letters."

"I don't mean 'here' as in this place. I mean 'here,' like in the universe."

Gable was seated in front of the largest window he'd ever seen. Circular and astounding, it didn't make sense to him how the wall could stay standing with glass as a main feature of its structural integrity. The woman sitting across from him looked barely twenty and had the attitude of a person who didn't have anything going on, but was still bothered to be kept waiting.

"What's your name?" asked Gable.

"I'm Beth."

"Beth, how about you tell me why I'm here *physically*. And I'll think about telling you why I'm here universally."

"That's not how this works."

He nodded his head and rubbed his hand over a sloppy, stubbled beard. Had it been two days or three since he last shaved?

"It's been three days since your last shave, and I don't really think this pertains to my line of questioning."

Gable pulled his head back and narrowed his brow.

"How did you—"

"You are not here to ask me questions. I'm here to ask you. Can we continue?"

"Fine. Why am I here? I guess I'm here by random coincidence. I was one of millions of sperm who managed to become a person. I was born into a normal family who had abnormal things happen to them. I'm just a regular guy."

"What is your purpose?" Gable rolled his eyes and checked his watch, but Beth was unrelenting. "You have an answer to my question. It's right there on the tip of your tongue. Now why don't you find your balls and say it out loud, Sugar."

Gable was taken aback by her sudden turn from irritated professional to tactless antagonist.

"I want to be a man who makes things happen instead of lets things happen to him."

"Great. Now that wasn't so hard was it?"

Beth flipped a switch that was fastened to the table, and a cheery-looking man removed from Gable's temples the circular stickers with wires that ran to a machine Beth simply called 'Claire' without ever explaining what it did or why his head itched furiously as soon as it turned on.

"Come with me, Mr. Matthews," the man said, and Gable left Beth sitting at the table without a salutation.

. . .

Gable entered a blatantly modern and expensive office where the décor was so stark it was hard to process all the details. There was a fish tank the size of the average flat screen embedded in the wall. Inside there were only white fish surrounded by white coral. The desk was see-through, made entirely of glass. Gable thought about how easily it would get smudged and that whoever's desk it was must have a full-time cleaner wiping it down every hour.

"Gable," a deep voice greeted him from behind a spire-shaped marble statue. He was relieved to find the man wasn't also dressed in white.

"Hello, Mr...?"

"You can call me James."

"Great, hello, James. Are you the one who's been stalking me?"

"I prefer to look at it as admiring up close."

"You hacked my computer."

"Well, not me personally, but someone on my staff, yes."

"Why are you following me?"

"What do you know about consciousness, Mr. Matthews?"

The irritation lingering from his moody interview was now escalating into full blown anger. "What does anyone know about consciousness?"

"Well, here we know a great deal actually. I'm more curious to hear your take on it as an underground neuro-chemist."

Underground neurochemist was a nice way of putting it. Most would describe Gable's work as mad science. Mixing and testing compounds in his apartment, some of the chemicals stolen from his day job where his co-workers treaded carefully around him. It wasn't his intention to come off scary or crazy, but that was the way most people reacted to him, and he'd given up on changing their minds.

"As far as I can tell, consciousnesses is an external factor that we humans all process differently through our own identities. It's unbridled reality, and our brains are a cage that traps a sliver of that reality into a more digestibly sized piece."

"That. That right there. *That's* why I've sought you out. You have an understanding of consciousness that very few people outside of my little community are capable of."

"You brought me here for my beliefs?"

"No, Gable, I brought you here because of what you created based on that belief."

James sat coolly on the couch with his hands folded on top of his knee. There was no detectable embarrassment or shame for the ways he'd invaded Gable's life. In fact, he seemed more proud of his access to information than regretful of the violation on Gable's privacy.

"Describe to me what Compound X is." James had a way of speaking that implied he wasn't told no very often.

"You seem to already have the answers."

"I want to hear it from you." James stared with a placid serenity that implied he'd wait all day for the answer.

"When I was young, I was obsessed with the idea that if our brains could create our reality then there should be a way to uncreate it. If we were inescapably sad because of the way our brains processed information, then why couldn't that information be processed in a positive manner? If it's just neurons and chemicals that tell us to be heartbroken, then why couldn't we just change the formula and feel better?"

"An interesting hypothesis for a teenage boy."

"My mother suffered from depression. I wanted to help her."

"Pursuits of the heart are the most admirable ones out there."

"Is that what this place is? A pursuit of the heart?"

"AION is many things for many people. Continue," James insisted.

"My early attempts consisted of flooding the brain with positive hormones. It was a rudimentary effort at best. The compound would insight a momentary euphoria, followed by a crash. Anyone who took it would feel great, but the effects wore off fast. That iteration had...catastrophic results."

"You're referring to your mother's suicide?"

Gable cleared his throat, attempting to choke back the rising bile that came with any conversation regarding his mother. It was disconcerting to hear anyone talk about her, but to have a total stranger link his compound with her death was like a knife wound to the gut.

"I don't know that I feel comfortable telling you anything else before you give me some answers as to why I'm here and why you know so much about me."

"Fair," James said with a soothing smile. "London Riley was also there on the day of your mother's passing." Heat shot through Gable's system, and he suddenly questioned whether or not he was dreaming. "London is one of my residents. We've heard about the events that transpired that day."

"She's here? That's impossible. I've spent years looking for her."

"We pride ourselves on our security, Gable."

"What is she doing here?"

"As I'm sure you remember from childhood, she and her mother are exceptional individuals. Like yourself. I pride myself on having an eye for exceptional talent."

The information overload was getting to be too much for

Gable to handle. He rubbed his sweaty hands on his jeans and looked out the window for answers.

"Are you going to get to the part where you tell me what you want from me?"

"Gable, when you and London combined her natural abilities with your first compound, something that most would consider unbelievable happened. You sent your mother back through time using her own consciousness as the vehicle. London opened the door and set the GPS with her reading, and you sparked the ignition with your compound. It's something we've been trying to replicate for years, with no success quite matching what you two achieved as teenagers."

"Success?"

"Pardon my poor choice of words—I do understand the subsequent calamity. However, the actual event was perhaps one of the most remarkable discoveries in history. Our mission here, Gable, is to open up the pathways you two stumbled upon for anyone who dares to venture into the next plane of our existence on this planet. Mankind was not meant to live out their whole lives in this linear, day-to-day fashion. We're meant to transcend the bounds of time, and consciousness is our roadmap."

Gable rose to his feet, no longer able to maintain his energy while seated.

"So, let me get this straight. What you're saying is you want to use my compound to let people time travel through their minds?"

"Through their minds. Through the minds of others. At some point, we hope it isn't even bound by the mind and memories of an individual."

"You're out of your fucking mind," Gable said as he stormed toward the door. Just before his hand reached the knob, James surprised him once more.

"Your father is sick."

Gable spun around, unhinged and fed up with the invasion on his life.

"That's enough. I don't want to hear another word."

"AION is quietly funded by very powerful people who want this discovery to happen but can't compromise their own reputations by attaching their names to such an unusual project. We have the means to make our members and their families' lives easier. Better. All we ask in exchange is for the opportunity to help you expand on what you've already created in secret. We know you had a recent breakthrough. For the sake of your history with London we were trying to avoid tapping you, but we've hit a dead end. We need your compound and, while I could just buy it off of you, I'd rather have your mind involved in the process so that no one gets hurt in this pursuit. In exchange, I can get your father the treatment he needs and supply you with a real laboratory that allows you to climb mountains you haven't even begun to imagine."

Gable began to realize that he'd walked into this place never having a choice. James had prepared a long time for this conversation, and it only led to one place. There was no reason to ponder the offer. He had been trying to find a way to save the last of his family, and now the answer was being served up on a silver platter.

"How can I be sure any of this is real? Or that you'll go through with what you say you're going to do?"

James pulled out his phone and showed documentation that his father had already been registered with a cancer treatment hospital Gable could never have afforded.

"As for believing that any of this is real, you already do. Otherwise, you would have never gotten this far onto my property."

James led him to the door. A cheery-eyed woman whose

desk sat outside of James's office stood up and smiled. It was the first normal exchange since he arrived.

"Mr. Matthews, I'm Myra. I'll be working with you on all the details of your move to AION."

James's office door clicked shut and all the light from the window disappeared with it. In the cramped space where Myra sat, claustrophobia set in and Gable knew there was no escape.

11

*L*ondon and Beth were two of AION's most capable psychics, so they typically sat in adjoining rooms, rattling through interviews. If one of them missed something in a candidate, the other could usually pick up on it. They had equal but opposite talents that served the process well.

On this day, however, London had been asked to conduct her interviews in another building, and something unsettling was working its way into her sight. She couldn't quite put her finger on it, but there was a familiar and ominous presence lurking in the area where she knew Beth was.

"Hook me up," London said to Taryn as she was dismantling Clair to stow away in a padded metal suitcase.

"What? No. I'm almost done putting her away."

"I'm getting something, but it's not coming through. I need a clearer picture."

Taryn's thoughts raced through her head in indecipherable Korean. London could tell she was irritated but, as was always the case, couldn't understand why. It's possible to pick up on tone in just about any language, but that was all she ever got from her friend's internal dialogue. Part of her liked it that way. It meant she could have a regular relationship with her. At least as regular a relationship as anyone could have with Taryn.

"You're a pain in my ass," Taryn said as she reassembled her machine.

Taryn had created at least two dozen iterations of Clair, but she only ever kept two around: whichever the latest model was and the first prototype that had won her a spot at AION. The latter looked like a taser attached to a dog leash compared to the sleek, chrome version she had with her now. The first invention was kept on a shelf in her room as a trophy to mark her achievement.

Taryn's commitment to James's mission went beyond loyalty. It bordered on fanaticism, something London could never quite get on board with, but she understood it from Taryn's perspective. For those without an innate ability, seeing what the psychics on the grounds were capable of was all the drive they needed. It was both unsettling and alluring to know what psychics could do. The possibility of being able to do it themselves was the ultimate prize. Taryn named her machine "Clair" with the hopes that one day it would have all the same abilities of a psychic: clairvoyance, clairaudience, clairsentience. A machine built for translating consciousness in all its forms. It could showcase some rudimentary images and would also emit a scratchy collection of conscious thoughts that sounded like what comes out of a child's toy walkie talkie, but its best use so far was in how it enhanced psychic ability in those who already possessed it. A feature that gave Taryn more irritation than pride.

"It's not meant to make you more capable," Taryn would lament to London as she tinkered with it in her workshop. "It's meant to help people like me get on your level."

London was indifferent to the rants. She wished the machine would work in the way her friend hoped so that other people would realize how inconvenient it was to live with everyone else's thoughts and memories racing through your own head.

Taryn licked the sticky pads that were connected to wires and slapped them onto London's head.

"Gross," London said.

Taryn chuckled, apparently pleased that she could at least disgust her friend while being inconvenienced.

The machine hummed to life. London much preferred when her subjects were the ones hooked up to the machine. It amplified just the individual's thoughts and made the reading so easy she barely had to concentrate. But when it was placed on her own head, the entire world around London erupted, and she had to weed through the muck like listening for someone calling your name at a concert. She tapped her foot and pushed past Taryn's unreadable contemplations. She closed her eyes and tried to use sight and sound to pinpoint the source of anxious energy that had been haunting her for the last hour.

As if leaving an open field to enter a tunnel, she began to narrow in on what she was looking for. There was a stormy quality to the feeling. A brewing that was distant, but familiar. Then, like a brick to the head, the image of Margaret Matthews came into full focus. She was there. On campus. Not her as London knew her the last time she saw her, but a more ethereal version. Her spirit had wandered onto AION, but it hadn't gotten there alone. It followed someone.

"Fuck. They promised."

"What?" Taryn asked.

"Gable Matthews is here."

The foreign conversation inside Taryn stopped and there

was only silence. A choppy memory of Gable's teenage face flashed in Taryn's subconscious.

London ripped the pads off her head and threw them onto the table.

"Where are you going?" Taryn asked.

"To find my mother."

*M*yra led Gable down a narrow hall to a small apartment. He had to duck to walk through the door, but once inside, the space was no smaller than his current apartment. A modest kitchenette stood next to yet another large window.

"Lots of windows here," Gable said. He was a little embarrassed by how unintelligent he'd sounded since arriving at AION, but it was hard to reconcile all the information he'd been presented with.

"Yes. Good for clearing your mind, don't you think?"

He couldn't imagine having a clear mind in this place.

"Do you live here too?"

Myra blushed. Standing next to a bed made it sound like a proposition more than a question.

"I do. I'm one of the AION Originals."

"AION Originals?"

"Some of us were still living here when Mr. Todd took over. He informed us of his mission and asked if we wanted jobs. Eight of us stayed. We do things like maintain the grounds, prepare meals, paperwork, act as test subjects."

Gable raised an eyebrow at that. "This place has always been about finding the future," she reassured.

Myra showed him a place where he could put his things, though he didn't have any. He didn't come here knowing he was staying. She pulled out a stack of documents and set them on the two-person dining table.

"What's this?" Gable asked.

"An NDA. I can only take you beyond this point if you sign it. Should you choose not to, I can walk you to your car."

Gable seriously considered walking out that minute. He could find his father treatment. Maybe not five-star accommodations, but something suitable. It was crazy to throw away his life and join some desert cult.

"Why did you stay?" Gable asked.

Myra squeezed her cheeks up under her eyes. She had untamed curls and no makeup on, but the freckles on her face and the way she bit her lip before each sentence made her seem genuine and reliable.

"This is my home."

It was hard for Gable to imagine anyone calling this place home, but he hadn't lived in a place that felt like home since he was a kid, so what difference did it make?

"Are we allowed to leave once we move in?"

"Of course," Myra giggled. "This isn't an insane asylum."

That seemed an odd reference considering he had to be at least a little unstable to believe the things James told him and opt to become a member of his ward. He signed his name without so much as scanning the materials.

"Perfect," Myra said, stacking the papers and sliding them into a manila envelope. "Care to meet some of the other members before you go home to pack?"

Gable shrugged as if it didn't matter, but his insides were exploding at the idea of being face to face with London Riley again.

---

*L*ondon rapped on the door of her mother's suite. She
had the best living arrangements in the complex.
Isolated, extravagant, spacious. The only other
person housed anywhere near her was James, conspicuously
located on the hill above her so, London assumed, he could
always look down at Ruth, keep an eye on her. London
jiggled the knob and found that it was locked.

Shit.

As London turned to walk down the steps, she nearly ran
into Siobhan Murphy. A serious woman, her sharp features
always carved into an intense scowl. She was one of the few
people who was at AION before London and Ruth arrived.
At first, London was terrified of her. Though she was only in
her mid-thirties now, she came across with an authority that
demanded respect and fear. She was someone who had been
through something and that's all London knew for sure. Her
hair was always tied up in a slick bun. Her fingers, long and
brittle, were clasped in front of her at all times. The readings
that came off of Siobhan were jolted and confusing. Memories flashed that didn't match what London knew about her.

A child would sometimes dance through her mind, but she made no effort to share who he was.

But as the years went on, she became something of an older sister to London, comforting her when Ruth would vanish for a couple of weeks at a time, listening to her as she daydreamed about living anywhere but here. Siobhan rarely offered insight or advice, but she never stopped London from saying what she wanted to say. There was little to no internal dialogue for London to read, either. Siobhan seemed to be living in the present most of the time, only thinking about what was right in front of her.

"Have you seen her?" London asked. Siobhan tilted her head to one side. "Perfect. So you already know why I'm here. Because she knew I would come, and she decided not to be here on purpose?"

"She felt this was information you should spend a little time with on your own."

"Of course she did. God forbid she ever deal with me head on."

"She's trying to let you grow."

London drove her fingers into her hair and shook her wavy locks, the crackle of mousse and hairspray bristling in her ears.

She felt scattered, so homing in on exactly where Gable was on campus was difficult. He was everywhere in her mind. The past, the present, inside her memories, racing through her internal dialogue. She saw the look on his sixteen-year-old face when he believed she had healed his mother of her incurable sadness. A pull at her stomach began tugging her toward that day, so she shook her head like there was a wasp inside and squeezed her temples with the heels of her hands. *I need a drink*, she thought.

·   ·   ·

Her friends usually gathered on a balcony that overlooked an unused pool. At night she could hear the bats dive and swoop just after the sun set, when the sky was an oyster gray. There weren't any city lights so the stars quadrupled in number. The misfits of AION, whom London had grown to love, would drink wine in mismatched chairs, thinking of days from the past and ones in the future, agreeing that if they just kept working, either could be reached.

Taryn and Beth were already tucked under the same blanket on an oversized recliner. Miles sat across from them, twisting a corkscrew into a bottle. He had arrived a little over a year ago. He wasn't psychic, nor had he invented some miracle pill or magic machine. What he was was a hell of a good hacker and a time-travel savant. As he would tell anyone who was listening, he'd seen every movie, read every book and researched every option out there. He didn't seem to have a complicated past that demanded fixing, he just adored the idea of time travel, and one day he went down an internet black hole that landed him inside James's private email inbox. When the security system finally notified James of the intrusion, instead of having Miles arrested, he brought him to AION to serve as his permanent in-house hacker. Now he was used to identify other potential members and discoveries that lurked in the underbelly of the online world. Though he was referred to as the Head of Research and Development for the sake of optics, it was easy for London to read him and understand his role was more along the lines of "dig up and uncover."

His dark hair was parted perfectly to one side and an overeager beard tried desperately to cover the bottom half of his face. When he spoke his eyebrows bounced, and London could feel just how genuinely joyful he was to be here. He had been a geek obsessed with time travel for most his life, and AION was the first place he'd felt true belonging. The gentle repetition of his emotions felt like a carousel to London. Melodic, steady, and content. Occasionally, on nights where the wine flowed too freely, London would sleep with him. She could tell it hurt his feelings that she never wanted more than a casual, late-night romp, but she had nothing more to offer him.

As she approached the group tonight, a memory of Miles scrolling through Gable's personal information flashed in his mind.

"Oh, I see," London said. "That's why you've been avoiding me."

Miles gave her a sheepish grin and she could hear him think the words, *It's my job. It's nothing personal.*

"Feels pretty personal if you felt the need to keep away for the last week."

"It was more like a quarantine. James knew I wouldn't be able to keep you out."

"You and James are conspiring against me then?" London asked.

"Oh, fuck off, London," Taryn spoke up. Not to defend Miles—the two of them never got along. He was too chipper for her surly moodiness. "No one is conspiring against you. Everyone was trying to protect you, princess." She scrunched her nose, a Korean rant prattling on inside her mind.

"Protect me?"

"Babe, if he wasn't going to accept, then there was no reason you had to be involved," Beth answered for Taryn.

"So does that mean he's accepted?" London asked.

"Of course he did," Taryn replied. She held out her glass to Miles, but kept her gaze locked on her best friend.

"I suppose you knew too?" London asked.

"I knew first, actually." Taryn tilted her head, daring London to get angry. At least once a week she would give London good reason to spit in her face. But she also had a way of making London feel more at home with her than anyone else in the world. Their relationship was as complicated now as it was when they were girls. Always a push and a pull.

"How did you find out?"

"Come on, Lond-y, you know I've been hooking up with the admissions clerk." Taryn had a rotating roster of partners, none of which ever ascended into a relationship. Most of whom she never even referred to by name. While everyone knew everyone, Taryn was dedicated to keeping them anonymous. "I was just trying to spare you worry if it was unnecessary."

"You should have told me."

"Yeah, but I didn't," Taryn said, sipping her wine as a signal that the conversation was over.

Silence pierced the air as Beth and Miles held their breath, hoping the inquiry would die out before they were called onto the carpet. An alert on Taryn's phone broke the silence. As one of her side projects, she'd created a sensor that could detect someone coming toward their balcony. Not just *that* someone was coming, but who that someone was. She had recently managed to map and track consciousness. Like a fingerprint, everyone's mind carried a unique stamp. She'd managed to process that, create a sensor and attach it to an app of her own making. Taryn was brilliant and had an inexhaustible work ethic that often made London feel useless and insignificant.

Hypnotize by The Notorious BIG began playing on Taryn's phone and the group knew Dennis would be rounding the corner any minute. Taryn turned up the volume and held the phone up as if it were a homing beacon for her unrivaled favorite member at AION.

"Big Daddy D!" Taryn yelled even though he was only feet away.

"Tiny Tits T!" Dennis yelled back.

He was the only one who could out shit talk Taryn and for that, he was the entire group's hero. Maybe it was because he was the oldest. Maybe it was because he had the confidence of a well-built black man who had taken much worse than a mouthy 26-year-old mechanic had to offer. Either way, their banter was entertaining and he could always be counted on to throw Taryn over his shoulder and cart her back to her room when she'd had enough, but wouldn't admit it.

Dennis was one of the first recruits to introduce significant progress to the work they did at AION. He was a forty-two-year-old physician whose work with psychedelics was unprecedented and also unsanctioned in the hospital where he'd performed his tests. He was making leaps and bounds in the field of consciousness research, but when a subject experiencing a bad trip attempted to hurl themselves through a plate-glass window, Dennis was arrested and stripped of his license to practice medicine. He also lost his wife and son in the deal, but he gained AION. No one was ever quite sure how James managed to bail out many of his members from their legal troubles, but everyone assumed with enough money just about anything was possible.

Dennis continued his work and AION began to see major progress. For a long time, London's experience of a person's interior was foggy and clipped, blurred with partial details and the imperfection of an individual's own memory. Under the influence of Dennis's concoction, London's abilities awoke and with each dose she gained skills. What was once a single sentence pulled from someone's recollection of a tragic day in their childhood was suddenly minutes-worth of a conversation and interactions that London could repeat with shocking accuracy. The drug had its downsides—mostly a wicked hangover that would take three days to recover from. Eventually, it was no longer used in testing, and Dennis began to oversee development of other people's compounds rather than creating them himself. But the change it had made to London's abilities had a lasting impact. Once a door was opened, it didn't close.

"You know, I still don't love that your phone can smell me approaching, T," Dennis said, swaying his hips to Biggie Smalls as if he had no choice.

"It doesn't smell you," Taryn said with a giggle. "It picks up on your special snowflake little consciousness. It doesn't take a genius to code an alert to match it."

"I'm still not convinced you didn't microchip us all," Miles said with a snort.

"If I did you'd never find yours. It's tucked behind your balls, which you don't seem to use."

Miles just rolled his eyes. He was so used to Taryn's attacks that they barely phased him anymore.

Siobhan snuck up to where they were seated without a word. She didn't have an alarm. Taryn had been told to keep James, Ruth and Siobhan off her radar. She sat in a green corduroy chair just close enough to be a part of the group, but barely close enough to hear anyone. The silver moonlight drew a line down the center of her face, illuminating her pale skin on one side and leaving the other in a dark shadow. London handed her a glass of wine, but didn't force her to engage in even a basic greeting.

"So, how are you feeling about it, London?" Beth asked. She never shied away from heavy emotions or personal questions. Everything was on the table as far as she was concerned. Precognition was her strength, not clairsentience. Beth couldn't easily read emotions like London could. However, she could see into the future. Her ability was as untamed as she was. Sometimes she would get visions of something months or years in the future and talk about it like it was a preview at the movies. "Oooh, I can't wait for that," or "That didn't look good at all." She rarely gave any context and pretty much everyone had learned to ignore her commentary on the future. In other circumstances, her consciousness would enter the body of her future self, something she coined a "mind leap," which was accepted as common vernacular amongst AION residents for the relocating of one's consciousness. Her eyes would close and she'd be still and silent. If she was standing when it happened, she'd often collapse onto the floor. So on the days she said her mind was feeling "squirrelly," she'd ride around campus in a wheelchair she'd bought at a thrift store and spray painted pink.

"Well, Beth, I don't feel great," London said, sarcastic and edgy. "Please tell me you've seen into the next couple of days and that I get hit by a bus before Gable moves in."

"Sorry, babe. You're going to be alive and well for quite some time."

"In that case I'd like to be drunk."

"You don't want to see him?" Taryn asked. "You're not even a little curious?"

An image entered London's mind. Taryn and Gable, sitting in the dirt side by side as teenagers. She didn't understand it and knew better than to ever ask Taryn about any glimpse into her past that showed up.

"I'm curious about why, of all people, we had to bring him in. I'm curious about where my mother is as all of this is coming out. I'm curious why I am always treated like a child."

Taryn shook her head. "If it's good for the mission then how you feel doesn't matter. He wouldn't have been brought here if he wasn't onto something."

London stuck her nose in her wine glass and let the sting of cabernet flush her mind clear with each inhale and subsequent sip.

"I guess if I'm honest, Beth, I don't feel much about him coming here. And that's what scares me. Usually I get a sense, for better or worse, during times of change. But I can't pick up anything. It's like Gable coming here has created this massive black hole that we're all at the center of, and I can't get my mind around whether him being here is going to be extraordinary or catastrophic."

"Maybe it'll be both," Taryn said, barely loud enough for anyone to hear.

Dennis broke the tension as he often did. "I have an idea for a test, if you guys are up for a little 'out of bounds' exploration tonight."

That perked everyone up. AION was built for the purpose of discovering time travel, but James's rules were rigid. He'd regularly remind the members that if anything got "out of hand" and the authorities were brought in, they would all be screwed. It was essential that they follow safety protocols while in the labs and for experimentation to happen in slow, deliberate iterations. "The smallest change could introduce a breakthrough or unimaginable chaos. We have to always be treading lightly toward the finish line," he'd say.

But for a bunch of rebels already prone to breaking the rules, the tight guidelines within the lab didn't always feed their need for wild leaps of discovery. In the evenings, behind closed doors, they would push the bounds of what was accepted in the daylight hours. And that was when the magic happened.

able was embarrassed at how little time it took him to pack. He didn't own much of value. Not because he couldn't afford knickknacks or a full set of dinnerware, but because he never saw the point in stockpiling aesthetic items for just himself. His one bed one bath wasn't necessarily a bachelor pad, either. It was immaculate, and he had storage bins that organized everything from his bathroom products to his refrigerator. Still, realizing there wasn't a single framed picture or saved concert ticket made him feel empty. *Most people wouldn't just drop everything and move to the desert with a bunch of strangers. Only a weirdo who lives like a serial killer,* he thought.

There was something drawing him to AION though. More than James's elusive promises. More than the allure of confronting London. Something more primal and intuitive, like an animal being lured to water. It felt like a matter of survival. He couldn't explain why, but as soon as the option was on the table he couldn't conceive of any other plans or destinations.

In a large suitcase he packed most of his clothes. In a

duffle bag he stored his best sauté pan, a hand crank pasta maker that was his mother's, and half a dozen books. That was it. At twenty-seven years old, these were the only material things that meant anything to him.

Gable had been given three weeks to get his affairs in order. In that time, his father had become a patient of one of Arizona's finest oncologists. Gable made an effort to visit him every few days. Each time he had a Styrofoam takeout box full of chicken wings. On the third trip he also brought a bundle of balloons. He wasn't sure what his dad was supposed to do with the balloons, but a hospital room without any flowers or cards made it seem like the person inside was unloved, and he didn't want that for his dad. For all the things his father wasn't, he was a kind man who never hurt anyone and he didn't deserve to look abandoned.

"Hey, Pops." Gable held out the bouquet of balloons like a tramp clown. His face downturned to match the atmosphere in the room.

His dad feigned a chipper tone. "Gabe, my boy."

"How you feeling?"

"Right as rain. These nurses are nice ladies." He pulled the sheets up to his waist, covering his shrinking belly.

"I'm glad you're being taken care of."

"This place seems pricey. You sure you can afford it?" His dad never wanted to inconvenience anyone. It was the one line he drew.

"Don't worry about it, Dad. I told you I got a new job."

"Yeah, yeah. That's right. I'm very proud of you."

His dad popped open the box of wings and the smell of hot sauce mixed with the sterile hospital environment in a swirl of competing scents. As he licked his fingers, Gable worked up to the question he'd come to ask his father.

"If there was a way to go back and stop Mom from doing what she did, you would do it, right?"

His father cleared his throat in the textbook Darryl Matthews way. An old man's tick that was meant to buy him time before he had to speak. His eyes dropped from the game on TV for the first time since Gable walked in and he dabbed his lips with a napkin. Gable began to regret the question. He shouldn't burden his sick father with hurtful "what ifs."

"If there was a way to go back, I wouldn't stop her. I'd stop Abigail from getting anywhere near that pool. That's where it all started. Your mother would still be alive and well if I had just installed a latch on the back door that your sister couldn't reach."

It was perhaps the most honest thing his father had ever said. They almost never talked about the women they had lost. Occasionally they would accidently reference a memory that included either his sister or his mother, but more often they kept the topics safe: sports, weather, work.

"It wasn't your fault, Dad. Neither of them were your fault."

The gentle man who had aged beyond his years took a deep breath in and the wrinkles in his forehead deepened. "One day, when you're a husband and a father, you'll understand that you can never untether yourself from your wife and your children. They become a part of you, and whatever happens to them echoes inside you forever."

With that, he returned to watching the game. Gable had no response. Just awe for the man he always assumed existed on the surface of the world, but who actually ran deeper than he could have ever imagined. Before his chest could tighten any more, Gable stood and kissed his dad on the forehead.

"I'll come visit again soon. It might take a while. I gotta get settled into my new job, but I'll check on you."

"Call on Sunday?"

Gable nodded and left the room, his heart pounding in his chest and cheeks colored with emotion. At his car, he took five deep breaths and let the hot sun bake away any tears that could threaten to spill over. His apartment was packed, his father was settled. The only thing left to do was move to AION.

ondon's oddball collection half-drunk friends piled into her and Taryn's co-living space. They repressed laughter unsuccessfully, each engaged in their own little jokes. London clung to Siobhan's elbow, in part to stabilize herself and also to avoid falling into the common trap of letting Miles into her bed. He was talking with Beth in a desperate attempt to appear aloof, but London could tell his thoughts were focused squarely on her. An image of one of their recent romps dancing through his mind.

"Okay, Big Daddy, we're all here. What's the idea?" Taryn asked Dennis.

"When you guys were kids, did you ever do the thing where your friend squats down takes deep breaths and then they stand against a wall while someone pushes on their chest to make them faint?"

The room was silent. Apparently, it was just Dennis who had spent his youth suffocating friends.

"You all were a bunch of lame ass kids. Well, I was thinking, what if we had L do a reading while a subject was strapped into Clair, and then we fainted them out and see if we can get a time leap?"

"I hate to be the naysayer, but even if that works, what good would that do? We're just supposed to go to James and say, 'Time travel is possible, but you have to choke the person out?" Miles asked. The wine had made him loose-lipped and brave. London tried to resist her attraction to him.

"Some people like that," Taryn chimed in.

"I was just thinking it might replicate an NDE."

"A Near Death Experience happens when someone's brain is shut off. When their heart stops. Not when they go to sleep for a second because of a party trick," Siobhan interjected. The group was in a pessimistic mood.

It actually isn't a bad idea, London thought. People who had brushes with death regularly reported transcendent experiences. Many AION members suspected it tapped them into raw consciousness.

"London thinks it might work," Beth blurted out. "You want to volunteer, mama?" Beth was the queen of pet names. She almost never completed a sentence without adding a cutesy term of endearment.

"Sure," London shrugged. "I'll go." She would take any distraction from the impending run in with Gable Matthews.

"Let's do it," Taryn said. She reached for Clair. Next to it on the shelf, as always, was her first version of the invention. The prized possession she insisted no one touch. London knew she pictured it in her mind often, even dreamed of it in her sleep. When London was able to see into her friend, seconds worth of intense anxiety rushed through her any time she was near the machine. London didn't know why she kept it. It seemed like a source of darkness. If she believed in that sort of thing, she might even call it evil. But there it stayed, perched like a vulture over her roommate's bed.

"If London is going to be the subject, then I'll do the reading," Beth volunteered.

London felt the buzz of her wine and the rush of anticipation like she was about to take off on a rollercoaster as Taryn went to work attaching the apparatus to her head. There was a thrill and a terror to traveling. She had relocated her consciousness into the past dozens of times, but only occasionally found herself in the position where she could operate her past body. Each of those times she had been too nervous about changing anything, so she made every effort to do what she guessed her former self would have done. She preferred being an observer and simply reliving her memories with a fresh set of eyes. She marveled at just how imperfect memory was, often seeing things she didn't recall and gaining a new perspective. That was enough, she thought. No one needed to make changes to their past. Gaining knowledge gave you the chance to improve your future, without any risk. Still, she was willing to push forward with AION's mission because it was the only purpose she'd ever been given. The only importance the world held for her. Without it, she was no one.

"We're calibrated," Taryn announced. "Ready to go when you are. Dennis I'm assuming you're performing the fainting trick?"

He nodded and Beth sat down in front of London.

"I want you to take a few cleansing deep breaths, honey," Beth asked. "You've had a lot happen today, and if you don't clear out the muck you're going to end up somewhere you've been with Gable, and I'm not sure that's a good idea." Beth and London were pretty evenly matched when it came to telepathy. It served as a solid tool for travel. A psychic with this ability was able to help provide an objective look into someone's consciousness. Everyone was a liar. Especially when it came to their own beliefs and feelings. Having an external observer helped to get someone on track to travel to a specific destination. Without a psychic telling you what to focus on, the traveler's muddied mind could go shooting off anywhere in time.

London felt her face heat up and hoped no one else could see her flush.

"It doesn't help to clear my mind if you're all focused on Gable," London said to her crowd of friends. She could feel all of their questions and concerns. Even Taryn was giving off something that bordered on distress. Taryn was many things, but empathetic wasn't one of them. She tried to shake off her own thoughts and those of everyone else.

"Now I want you to focus on where you'd like to go," Beth instructed. "Maybe try picking a fairly innocent day.

London flipped through her history like a card catalog, looking for some place to land. On the Clair's screen, images of waves appeared.

"I've got it," London said.

Beth rubbed London's forearms like she was trying to warm her up. She always said physical contact helped her connect better. Everyone was silent, both in the room and in their minds, focused on the task at hand. Siobhan leaned on the counter; Miles lounged in London's bed as if it were his own. The others were playing their role in the experiment, waiting for the reading to begin.

"It's warm," Beth started. "Not like Arizona heat. More humid. The air is salty. I can taste it in my mouth. Your mother, she keeps singing a song." Beth began to hum and London recognized the tune immediately. It was *Wonderwall* by Oasis. Her mother had been obsessed with it for an entire summer, playing the CD over and over.

"I know the song," London said.

"Perfect, doll. Sing the song in your head to stay focused, and Dennis is going to step in and do his thing."

"London, I'm going to have you squat down with your head between your legs," Dennis instructed. "I want you to take ten really big breaths. When you stand up, I'm going to push on your chest."

"Are you sure this isn't just a ploy to get your hands on her boobs?" Taryn asked, squinting her eyes in fake judgement.

"Don't be jealous just because London's got 'em and you don't," he returned without skipping a beat.

"Will someone catch me if I fall over?" London asked. Miles got up too quickly and stood at her side. She hadn't intended it as an invitation, but if it kept her from waking up with a concussion, it was fine.

"Ready?" Dennis asked.

"Ready," London said.

"The song, keep the song in mind," Beth reminded.

London bent over and began breathing heavily. When she stood, she was light-headed, and the sudden force of Dennis's large hands only seemed to spiral her further. She continued with the lyrics playing out in her mind and everything darkened.

The first sensation to fill her mind was the sound of her mother's voice.

"London, hand me a soda."

London flinched under the brightness of the sun and newness of her location. The 26-year-old woman looked down at her seated body to find, nestled in sand, haphazardly painted toes that led up to knobby knees covered in fine, never-shaved hair.

"Hello...Little Miss," her mother called, using a nickname London had almost forgotten. "A soda, please, from the cooler."

London looked to her left. Beside her was a cheap, foam cooler. She plunged her hand into the ice and retrieved an off-brand lemon-lime drink.

Ruth's red nails popped the top and she offered London the first sip. London shook her head, still a little disoriented. She shook her head again, realizing that she could produce movement. She hadn't just mind hopped, she was in the driver seat of her ten-year-old body. She could feel the chill of the ocean breeze, raising the goosebumps on her skin. She was aware that her adult body was on the floor of her room while her mind was sixteen years into the past, but she felt calm.

London dug her heels into the sand again and again, uncovering darker, wetter ground with each pass.

"What time is it?" London asked her mother, for lack of a better conversation starter. Her voice was small and pitchy, but the words had originated from her grown up mind.

"I don't know, baby, I left my watch in the car," Ruth said. "Got a hot date?" She nudged her young daughter playfully.

London took a deep breath and smiled at the scent of suntan lotion and seaweed. She didn't just want to come here because it was a beautiful day on the beach. She had always suspected it would have been a good time to ask about her father. There was something so intimate about that vacation, but at ten, she had been so wrapped up in sandcastles and ice cream it hadn't even occurred to her to ask. She had spent the months following that trip waiting for another opportunity to ask about her absentee father, but none came. The subject was brought up in random, poorly timed ways in the future, but none led anywhere productive. Her mother hardly ever gave her more than a first name and brush off about how it didn't matter anymore.

"I'm really glad we're here, Mom." She didn't want to hurt her mother, and the question that followed likely would. "I know you don't like it when I ask, but can we talk about my dad?" the adult London asked her mother, more confident and unflinching than a child would have.

Her mother took in a deep breath and seemed to hold it in her chest for a long time.

"John," Ruth said.

"You've told me his first name. Who was he?"

Ruth looked at her daughter with suspicion. "He was a man I didn't know for very long. He was kind and sweet, but we couldn't be together."

"Why not?"

London couldn't tell if her mother was sad or angry. Her lips remained in a straight line, but her eyes were set on the distant horizon. She let rows of waves crash without a word. With her adult abilities she could detect that her mother was softened and sad.

"He died, Little Miss."

London's heart sank and it took her by surprise. This wasn't much of a surprise. She had always assumed he was dead, but tears poured over her lashes anyway.

"Did he know about me?"

"No."

London's tiny chin quivered. She was beginning to feel guilty for ruining this beautiful day. Her follow up questions seemed unfair and suddenly unimportant, so she stayed quiet. Ruth rolled over onto her stomach and let the sun sting her back. London walked her tiny body down to the water's edge and let the tide bury her feet. The adult London knew that this was a much better delivery than the original fight that led to this revelation, but her younger self would never know that relief. She let her tears fall until they dried and stiffened on her cheeks. As she turned to walk back to her mother, he eyes opened on her present-day apartment.

· · ·

Everyone in the room looked a little uncomfortable.

"Well?" Taryn asked.

"It worked," London said with a breathy sigh. "I feel like I was there a lot longer than usual." The problem with travel is it was always fairly brief. Thus far, a person might be unconscious in the present for hours, but typically would only experience about thirty seconds in the other timeline. It wasn't a lot of time to make a difference, and it was just one of many problems they were trying to solve at AION.

"No shit?" squealed Taryn. "Well, Denny, guess we've got to go around and choke people into the past. Tell us everything, London."

"Oh, give her a damn minute, T," Dennis urged.

"I'm good," said London.

"Are you sure?" asked Miles.

"Yeah, why?"

"You were crying pretty hard," Beth said.

"Oh." London felt a little embarrassed. "Did I say anything?"

"Just, 'Did he know about me?'" said Beth.

"I'm alright," London repeated. She felt dizzy and a strange stream of consciousness washed over her. She could remember two histories. One where she simply sat on the beach with her mother, wishing she had the courage to ask about her dad, watching other kids play in the sand with siblings and longing for one too. And another version, the one she'd just changed. It was the first time she'd ever deviated from a memory. Neither event felt more or less real. They both held as much space in her mind, as much truth. From what she could decipher, her younger self was never aware she'd been overtaken and diverted. London couldn't remember feeling like she'd been possessed or manipulated from within as a child. She processed it as a sudden surge of courage followed by regret.

In the days following her faint-induced travel, London wrote her experience in a journal:

How do any of us really know where our thoughts and our impulses come from? Maybe intuition and bravery and instinct are another version of our own consciousness taking over. Who hasn't done something wildly out of their comfort zone and looked back in woeful admiration, wondering how they summoned the nerve? Moreover, who hasn't done something terrible and wondered what they were thinking that made them act so egregiously? Are we all already living in a world where past and future versions of ourselves are manipulating the choices we make?

As the days and weeks passed beyond her travel, her memory began to blur. When she'd think about that day, the details of the original events grew harder and harder to grasp. Like a dream at first wake, all the events were defined and tangible immediately following the travel, but the further away she got from the event the less she could hold on, until the only evidence left of the original timeline were the notes she had taken. The change she made cemented itself in her mind. The original event disappeared as if it never happened. Because it never did.

16

*G*able sat in the driver's seat for thirty minutes before turning off the engine. There was no going back, yet he was having a hard time moving forward. He stepped out of his car, and within seconds someone was flagging him down. A wide-chested man offered a comforting wave. Gable approached and shook his hand.

"I'm Dennis Locke," the man said.

"Gable."

"Nice to meet you, Gable. You freaking out yet?"

Gable rubbed the back of his neck and tried to hold in a manic laugh. "Is it okay if I say yes?"

"Honestly, it would be pretty damn weird if you weren't at least a little freaked. I remember walking up that driveway. But you only really do it if you have no choice, so you might as well lean into the weird and get comfortable there."

"How do you fit into all of this?"

"Don't worry, man, we're going to go through all of that."

They walked up a long stretch of concrete steps. There were people milling about on the grounds. One man was tending to some unruly shrubbery with clippers, another was doing some kind of metal work. A woman in a floral dress stood and waved at Gable. He recognized her as Myra, the woman who had shown him his living quarters and had him sign an NDA. He returned a stiff wave, suddenly aware that everyone was watching as he made his way through the campus.

"Lots of eyes," Gable said.

"New members don't show up every day. It can be a bit of an event."

Gable kept his head down but scanned for the one person it would be most startling to see.

"You won't meet anyone of major consequence until we've had something of an orientation, so you can relax."

"Are you…"

"Psychic? No. I'm a scientist, like you. You just wear your stress all over your face, and I'm very close with London Riley so it's no secret why."

The tension in Gable's shoulders relaxed. He was relieved both by the news that he wouldn't be having an accidental encounter with London and by the revelation that Dennis couldn't read his mind. Perhaps there would be at least one other sane person in the asylum with him.

Gable and Dennis arrived at a room that said *Laboratory* on the door, but when they entered, instead of a sterile environment, it looked more like a green house. Plants hung from the ceiling and spilled over onto countertops. The tables looked like they were made of hand-crafted wood rather than a hygienic laminate.

"This is the Laboratory," Dennis said, with his hands held out. "It's where the fun stuff happens."

"Doesn't look like any lab I've ever seen."

"No, it doesn't. But this isn't a place like you've ever been before."

"No shit." There was something comforting about Dennis. Gable felt like he could speak freely.

"I'd like to explain to you what we've achieved here so far. Where we're hoping to take things, and how we think you can help, if you're ready to hear it."

"Please."

"Do you need a water?"

"No, I'm fine." Gable was desperate for more information. Maybe even validation that he hadn't totally lost his mind.

"The first thing you're going to have to wrap your science-filled brain around is that psychics are real. And that what they are capable of is just as scientific as what you create in a pharmacy. I know you've seen some of this in action, but like anyone else in the scientific community, you're going to be tempted to poke holes in psychic ability. You're going to be focused on how 'it can't be real,' and you're going to waste a lot of time if you concentrate only on that."

"So, I'm just supposed to take everyone's word for it?"

"You're going to see enough that you won't have to. I'm just warning you not to get fixated on it. That's not what you're here for. If you need some scientific backing to ease your mind, you can check out IONS."

"IONS?"

"The Institute of Noetic Science. They have folks there that have been researching psychics for decades. It goes far beyond anecdotal proof. Trust me."

"Then for the sake of moving forward, let's just say I accept that psychics are real."

"Excellent. Now, psychics have a wide range of abilities and it shows up differently in each of them, just like athletic ability. Some people are born fast, others have to train. Some people are strong while others are nimble, you get what I'm saying?"

"I think I'm following."

"What we've found is that the best of them, we're talking the Michael Jordan's of mind reading, are not only able to read consciousness, but relocate it. They are best known for using the skill to see into other people—their memories, their emotions, even their thoughts as they are happening. But if they turn that ability inward on themselves, which takes a lot of time and practice, they are able to occupy their own body at different points in their life. Now, this isn't time travel in the 'hop into your DeLorean with Doc Brown' sense, but these highly connected individuals are at least getting a front row seat to other points of their life, both future and past, depending on their skill set."

"Where does the science come in then?"

"What most people don't understand about consciousness and the human brain is that our brains aren't what is creating consciousness. Our brains are filtering it. Based on what James told me, this is a theory you have also stumbled upon, yes?"

"My work has led me to believe there is more to the human mind than gray mush firing signals," Gable conceded. Anyone who has taken magic mushrooms would have to at least embrace that possibility. Like anyone else in college, Gable had his fair share of experiences.

"Well, you're right, my friend. But you may not know just how right you are. Psychics are simply people with a natural ability to dial back that filter. And in very rare cases, turn it off entirely. We've seen clairvoyants, mediums, and telepaths retrieve incredible amounts of information on others as well as themselves. What this place seeks to do is find the absolute pinnacle of their abilities and then, using other scientific methods, try to turn those abilities on in people who aren't born with it."

It was a dizzying amount of information. Gable was regretting not taking a glass of water when it was offered.

"Why is James so obsessed with making this happen? It's one thing to buy into it. It's another thing to build a mini-city around it." Gable was waiting for the catch. There had to be one. James was too slippery and smart to just explore without reason. Gable didn't buy that he would just build a team for the sake of elevating humanity to a higher state.

"James believes in something called Divine Travel. While all levels of transporting consciousness are a goal here, we are reaching for the ultimate peak."

"And what is the ultimate peak?"

"We have people who can relocate their consciousness and just observe the world around them through a former or future version of their physical self. We are just starting to reach a point where some of our more advanced psychic members are actually able to take over operation of their own bodies during this experience. We're talking about an ability to actually make changes in the past. Speak, move, fight, flee. The implications of that are astounding enough. But James says that there is an even higher level to reach. One that defies even my own beliefs in physics and the material world."

Dennis kept pausing for dramatic effect. Or maybe it was to give Gable a little time to process. It was a theatrical way of speaking that James also practiced, but it was frustrating and added to the feeling in Gable's gut that this whole thing was a magic show.

"Divine Travel, as James describes it, occurs when someone has completely untethered themselves from the constraints our minds put on consciousness. According to him, it's when a person is able to relocate their entire physical form, mind and body, to another point in time. Poof." Dennis snapped his fingers. "Real, genuine time travel. Being in two places at once. Going anywhere and any *when* in time, regardless of the traveler's own history. We're talking back-to-kill-Hitler shit. Legit time travel."

"You've seen it?" Gable had nothing but skepticism for this revelation.

"No, but James has. And it's the finish line we're all hoping to arrive at."

"Why, though? Surely you've all considered the ethical and global impact a power of this magnitude can have, right? I mean, money markets would immediately crash because every person would try to go back and pick the winning Powerball or invest in Google or something. Add to the fact that crime would run rampant because if you screwed up and left evidence, all anyone would have to do is go back and cover it up. Governments would topple. The entire history of the world could be unmade over and over."

Dennis smiled a knowing grin.

"And what if the opposite happened?" Dennis asked. He was calm, as if he'd been expecting this exact reaction. "What if instead of the world crumbling into chaos, we had an infinite opportunity to fix it? Parents could save a child from being killed in a crosswalk. New technologies could be brought into the past that would keep our skies from being polluted and our ice caps from melting. Assassinations of great people like Martin Luther King Jr. and JFK could be stopped."

"And don't forget you could kill Hitler."

"And, God willing, we could kill Hitler!" He spoke with the enthusiasm of a preacher. "Gable, none of us know where exactly our choices will lead. You could step onto an airplane and be dead within the hour. Or you could let someone merge into your lane on the highway and prevent an eight-car pile-up. We're all just existing in this chronological way that leaves everything up to chance. What AION offers, and what psychics already know, is that reality is much more pliable than this straight arrow our species has been walking for centuries. The next phase of our evolution is to embrace the fact that time isn't linear. We weren't meant to just keep trudging forward into the darkness. Will mistakes be made? Of course. We're already making mistakes right now. AION is about second chances."

"How do you know that psychics aren't already doing this? That they haven't already changed things and made them worse." As much as he tried to resist it, a memory of the day his mother died flashed into his mind.

"We don't know. We also don't know if they've already made it better."

"Your optimism is a little hard to swallow."

"Eh, you'll get used to it." Dennis let out a roaring laugh and clapped Gable on the back.

For the next three hours Dennis and Gable flipped through the files of all the people on campus, reviewing their abilities and what they had achieved. Dennis's work wasn't all that different from Gable's. He believed that psychedelics were just one of the ways in which a human's natural psychic ability could be awakened or expanded. It was rudimentary, he explained, but they had witnessed some powerful break-throughs in both psychics and ordinary individuals. For one member, she claimed it stopped her urge to smoke entirely. She reported that the experience opened her up to a greater respect for her body. In some of the psychics, it opened up an entirely new ability.

"Gable, from what I understand, the compound you've created is also meant to destabilize some of the limitations the brain puts on the mind?"

"I don't know if that's how I would have described it. My

intention was to limit our ability to perceive things nega-
tively. If hormones and chemicals can tell us what to feel,
then we should be able to manipulate or lessen their impact
in order to decrease the level of pain or anxiety or depression we're experiencing. That was the theory at least."

"And yet, what you created was so much more."

"Was it? So far it has had little to no positive impact."

"Your compound is an opener. I've had the chance to
study some of your journals."

"My stolen journals you mean?"

"Yes, those." Dennis gave a smile that in no way apolo-
gized for how the information was obtained. Everyone at
AION seemed abundantly comfortable with the institution's
methods for acquiring data. "What 'openers' do is create a
hole in the protective shield that keeps raw consciousness
out. It's like puncturing the side of a submarine. It doesn't
even have to be a large hole to let water in, but once it's
opened, there's no closing it while you're submerged."
Dennis took a deep breath and made unflinching eye contact
with Gable. "Before I show you these last three files, I want
you to know I'm very sorry for what happened to your
mother. I lost my mom when I was young too, and there's no
amount of whiskey that can quite fill that void. I apologize if
the things we're about to talk about hit a nerve, but as you
may have already figured out, it's hard to keep a secret
around here."

Dennis flipped over three folders of different thicknesses.
Paper-clipped to the front of each was a photograph. One of
Taryn Trainor, one of Ruth Riley, and one of London Riley.

17

*W*hen Ruth returned to campus, London could feel her arrival immediately. She wasn't always able to read her mother, but there was something distinct about her presence. It was like the ability to detect when rain was coming. Everything shifted around London in an unmistakable, atmospheric swirl of sensory details. The smell of wet grass, a melodic hum in her ears, a warmth that swept over her skin even on the coolest days.

She raced to meet her mother at her suite. As she raised her hand to knock, the door swung open. Ruth had already turned away from the entrance and was walking into her living room, expecting London to follow without so much as a "hello."

"Where have you been?" London asked, following suit and skipping the greeting.

"Away."

London received a flash of an image. Cleopatra Hill.

"You were in Jerome?" London asked. Jerome was the small mountainside town where Ruth was born and raised. It was rife with quirk and in the recent decade had become a must-see tourist destination. Ruth, however, had only disdain for the place that "held her captive" during her youth.

Ruth spun around to face her daughter. She wrapped her arms around London and rested her cheek against her ear so that the words she spoke were muffled. "When are you going to talk to me about how quickly your abilities are progressing?" Ruth asked.

London took a step back from her mother and tried to clear her mind of any recent memories.

"Why were you in Jerome?" London asked.

"I went to see your grandmother."

The only thing Ruth Riley hated more than the town she came from was the woman she came from.

"You never go see Grandma Nancy."

"Well, she's an old bag and who knows how long she's got. Seems wrong not to at least pop in on her every now and then." Ruth poured a sparkling soda over ice and spoke of her mother's failing health as if it were a shop closing in town.

London didn't buy the reason, but internally, Ruth was reciting a rhyme in irritating repetition—a tactic she had used to keep her daughter out her whole life.

Little Miss,
> *you must resist*
> *the urge to go exploring.*
> *When you hear,*
> *my feelings clear,*
> *it's best you start ignoring.*

"Ugh, make it stop," London begged. "I can't listen to that rhyme one more time. I'll stay out."

"I'm not sure you're able to anymore." Ruth stared for a moment. "You had another mobile travel?"

London had barely said more than a handful of words, but already her mother knew everything that happened since she left. They constantly fought over the hypocrisy of Ruth reading London but hating it when the tables were turned. The last thing London wanted to talk about was her after-hours testing. She wasn't here for that. She had one purpose for this visit.

"How could you let him do it, Mom?"

Ruth sipped her soda, leaving a lipstick mark behind on the glass.

"I don't make the decisions around here, London."

"James does anything you say."

"That's not true at all."

"You should have fought him on this. How am I supposed to be around Gable Matthews?"

Ruth handed London a piece of chocolate. It was the number one thing they had in common. Both had no ability to resist something sweet. London unfurled the candy wrapper and popped the chocolate into her mouth between exaggerated sighs.

"There was no way for you to avoid it. At some point, you were going to have to face what happened. You can't hide here forever."

"Hiding? Is that what I'm doing here? I distinctly remember being dumped at this place without much of a choice."

"When are you going to learn?" Ruth shook her head.

"Learn what?"

"That you always have a choice. And that our choices are the only thing in the world that matter."

"You're just dodging the conversation."

Ruth crunched some ice between her teeth. She looked down her nose into her glass.

"London, Gable is destined to be in your life. I've seen it since before I even met Mrs. Matthews."

London's chest tightened. Ruth never revealed anything about the future. She had a strict policy against it, in fact.

"What does that mean?" London asked, trying to be careful not to spook her mother.

"Nothing has ever been more clear or unclear to me. Gable is a part of your future, there is absolutely no denying that, but there's something dark about his arrival. He is a part of your journey, London, but you have to be so careful. Use every ability at your disposal. Do not let your guard down."

London didn't know what to make of the information. She was astounded by how forthcoming her mother was being.

"Why are you telling me this?"

"I'm just doing what I've always done. Trying to protect my daughter." Ruth kissed London on the cheek and walked her to the door. There would be no more conversation on this matter. London wasn't sure she could handle it even if there was more to be said.

Beth met up with her in the middle of campus. She was in her wheelchair, apparently anticipating a rough day where her mind could skip out on her.

"Is everything okay?" Beth asked.

"I don't know."

"Do you want me to try to check? I'm already in my chair."

"No, it's fine. I don't think I could handle any more information today."

"Alright, babe," Beth bit her lip, making her look ten years younger. "I hate to be the bearer of bad news, but it's time for the intro."

"Is there any way I could get away with skipping it?"

"I seriously doubt it."

"Taryn always skips these things."

"Yeah. But she's Taryn."

London got behind Beth and pushed her chair toward the amphitheater. It served as the area where James would deliver news to the members on the occasions where he needed to address the whole community. Introducing a new member was one such occasion when these gatherings would take place. Every member was expected to attend and with less than fifty people on campus, any absence was obvious. Taryn was the one exception. She had long since established that if she was busy working, she wouldn't break concentration for anything or anyone. So, as London rounded the corner with Beth, she was surprised to see her friend perched on a concrete step, her elbows leaning against the seat behind her. London parked Beth near the exit.

"I'm going to go sit with T," London told her. Beth nodded and waved to Taryn.

"You actually showed," London said, scooting in next to Taryn. She smelled like weed and lavender.

"I couldn't resist the chance for a high school reunion." Taryn was cool and relaxed on the surface, but her insides were wrought into a tight ball.

"I'm not ready for this," London admitted.

"It's happening anyway."

James stepped onto the stage and flashed the small crowd a smile. Dennis stood a few feet behind him, relaxed with his hands in his pockets as if he was waiting in line to order a burger. Siobhan took a seat in the front row next to Beth. Miles looked around the theater and London made every effort to avoid eye contact with him.

"Hello, everyone," James said. He didn't need a microphone to be heard, but he had one anyway. "It feels like it's been a while since we all gathered here. Thank you for coming." He slid a hand down the front of his shirt; his energy was confident. "As many of you know, we're welcoming a new member into our community. I'll get to that in a moment, but first I wanted to say just how proud I am of the work being done here. I know how tirelessly you have all dedicated yourself to our mission. I know how exceedingly hard you're exploring the unknown. Nothing goes unnoticed."

"Yeah, that's because he has cameras installed all over the place," Taryn whispered.

James began singling out members for their recent achievements. "Michael recently developed a method for tracking a traveler's destination." One of the IT guys, a quiet, thirty-something waved his hand at the acknowledgment. "Beth here," James pointed to where she was seated, "has astounded us with some revelations about the future of AION. There are amazing discoveries on the horizon, I assure you. And then Taryn—nice to see you could take a break and join us." She snorted at the callout. "Taryn has been developing a bridging technology for Clair that will enable one of our natural travelers to extend their ability to another. We're hoping this is a big leap forward in creating opportunities for those of us not born with the skill to travel."

"I didn't know you were getting so close with that?" London said under her breath.

"I'm not getting close. I've already done it." She looked London in the eye, something alarming flashed inside, like an airhorn. London jumped as if someone had snuck up behind her. Taryn frowned and turned back toward the stage. "Alright, alright, let's get on with it, James," Taryn shouted.

London's heart was still pounding. For a second, she forgot what it was they were waiting for.

"Right, Taryn, thank you. Without further ado, I'd like to introduce our newest member of AION, Gable Matthews."

A man stepped out from behind the curved concrete wall. There was assuredness in his stride, but he kept his gaze fixed nervously on a distant point. Still, London could see that set behind round, wire-framed glasses were the eyes she had spent nearly a decade trying to forget.

Though his face had acquired stubble and his height continued upward, there was no denying that that man was Gable Matthews. London had to fight the urge to flee from her seat. It took only seconds for his eyes to meet hers. It happened so fast, as if he'd been looking for her. He held her stare for a few moments before blinking and turning his attention back to James. The pounding in London's heart turned into a freight train. She was suddenly faced with an unrelenting torrent of images pouring into her mind. Visions she couldn't quite understand zipped in and out of her peripheral. Train car after train car of information. It was as if she was standing too close to the locomotive. Everything flashed by so fast that she couldn't perceive any of the visual or auditory details.

It wasn't until Taryn shook her shoulder that she was able to break free of the onslaught.

"James is asking you to stand," she said, trying to pull her to a standing position.

Taryn, Beth, Siobhan, an AION Original named Ryan, and a former Army medic named Amelia were already standing. Everyone's eyes were turned toward London, waiting for her to stand up. Everyone's except Ruth. She stayed dead-still facing the stage.

London stood and accidentally made eye contact with Gable again.

"Great. Gable this will be the team you're working with. Dennis will be leading your efforts. Everyone else, please help make Gable feel at home. I hope you all join us for a family dinner under The Vault. Thank you again for taking time out to welcome our new member."

James returned the mic to its stand and disappeared in the direction of his office. Dennis put an arm around Gable's shoulders and led him off the stage.

"Well," Taryn said. "At least you didn't make a total ass of yourself."

London was sure she might puke. Even though Gable hadn't shot her where she stood, which she felt was a feasible possibility, she couldn't imagine things ending up much worse than they did.

"Something weird just happened," London's head seared with a migraine and she pinched the bridge of her nose. "Gable being here is really bad."

"Maybe for you," Taryn retorted.

"How am I supposed to work with him? It's bad enough that he's here, but my mother didn't mention I would be teamed up alongside him."

"Did you see James's face? Gable has something big. What if this is *the* breakthrough? Get over yourself for once and get on board."

"I shouldn't have to do this."

"You could leave."

Taryn never tempered her delivery. It was always just one hit after the next. She wasn't wrong though. London could leave.

18

*D*ennis walked Gable away from the stage. He pointed to where the dinner would be held and then let Gable excuse himself to his new living quarters so he could freshen up. As soon as the door closed behind him, Gable felt himself begin to hyperventilate. He opened a window, but the warm air that poured in only added to his increasing blood pressure. His hands began to tingle, and he pumped his fingers to try to stop the sensation.

He went to the bathroom and splashed water on his face. Then rifled through his suitcase until he found the bottle of Xanax. He popped one on his tongue and, scooping water from the sink into his mouth, washed it down.

For years he dreamt about what he would say to London Riley when he saw her again. The questions he would ask. The interrogation he'd conduct to get to the bottom of what she had said to his mother. There was a plan always resting in the back of his mind, but he hadn't prepared for being on a stage when that moment came. He hadn't prepared for her hair to still be in wild locks that danced around her face. He hadn't prepared for the look of terror in her eyes when she saw him. *What does she have to be so scared of? She isn't the one who lost something that day,* he thought.

He was expected at dinner within the hour, but eating was the last thing he could imagine doing. Was it already too late to get in his car and go?

A knock came at his door. He wasn't sure who it could be, but he felt certain he wasn't ready for company. Gable used the bottom of his shirt to wipe off the water on his face. When he swung open the door, he was surprised to find Taryn Trainor outlined by the setting sun. Little about her had changed. She had a couple more tattoos and a lot less makeup on than she'd worn as a teen, but she hardly looked a day older.

"Gable Matthews," Taryn said.

He wasn't able to form words. The whole day had already been so strange and he couldn't think of how to react to another human being.

"Good to see you too," she continued, shoving her way passed him. "It *has* been a long time."

"Sorry. Hey, T. It's really good to see you."

"Is it?" she raised an eyebrow. "You look like you've seen a ghost. You know there's people around here who can actually do that?"

"So I've heard."

"Well."

Gable waited for her to follow up with a question. Instead, she sat in a chair as if he had asked her to come there.

"Well what?"

"What the fuck are you doing here?"

Gable could see adulthood hadn't softened any of Taryn's edges. She was still audacious and unflinchingly cavalier.

"James made it pretty clear, I think. My compound has a role to play in…all of this." He couldn't say it. He couldn't admit he had come to a place where people believed they could invent time travel.

"Oh, and you're just all about this *Twilight Zone* life?" Her eyes rested along the top of her lids. She stared at him through her lashes without blinking. She was toying with him the way she used to taunt his football player friends in high school. She dragged her index finger across her collarbone. Crossed and uncrossed her legs to punctuate a question. Smiled, but not out of happiness.

"Why are you here?" he asked.

"I'm a refugee."

"I mean why did you come to my room?"

"God, you're tense. I just came by to say hi. And to get a few things straight."

"A few things straight?"

She came to a standing position and got so close to Gable's face that he could smell a hint of cinnamon rolling off her tongue.

"Listen to me, Gable. You don't tell London a thing about us, you hear me?"

There was an uncomfortable lack of space between their bodies. Just as he was ready to take a step back, she began listing her demands.

"You don't tell her about my dad. You don't tell her about my first machine. And under no circumstances do you tell her about us. You can't even think about it."

"T, I don't—"

Before he could protest, she cut him off again. "Don't call me T. Call me Taryn or Ms. Trainor."

"Are you serious?" He risked a smile only to realize this was no joke to her. "Okay, okay." He agreed even though he didn't understand any of it.

"She can get in there." Taryn tapped his forehead. "You have to try to keep her out."

"How am I supposed to do that?"

"Get a song stuck in your head. Meditate. Keep your mind focused on the here and now. Don't drift into memories or emotions, especially your sad, sad past." She grabbed his prescribed anti-anxiety medication and shook it. "Maybe double down on your dosage. Trust me, you don't want her rooting around in there. Whatever she finds, she'll use."

Taryn lifted herself onto her toes and kissed his forehead in an unexpected gentle gesture that was more confusing than anything she had done since walking into his apartment. She popped her gum in a symphony of crackles as she left the room.

"See you at dinner," she said, closing the door behind herself.

It had been almost eight years since he'd last spoken to Taryn. After his mother died, she was the only one who didn't seem to care about his tragedy. He was allowed to be himself around her. Not the poor boy who'd become a motherless only child within the span of a few short years.

When London and Ruth Riley disappeared, there were only two people who were invested in figuring in where they had gone: Gable and Taryn. Gable was desperate for answers, and Taryn had lost her only real friend. On one of his daily visits to their abandoned home he spotted Taryn sifting through their mailbox. Much like she had in his apartment, she hit him with a gruff question.

"What the hell are you doing here?"

"I was coming to see if anyone was home."

"No one is home. No one is going to be home. They're gone." She flipped through coupon books and credit card offers before tossing the junk mail into a dusty trash bin.

"So why are you here then?"

"It's quiet. It's close to my house. It's none of your damn business," she said.

He remembered turning to leave as if he'd just found the property guarded by a Rottweiler baring its teeth.

"Sorry," he said, not really sure why he was apologizing.

"I didn't say you have to go."

From then on, without a conversation or any plan put in place, they began to meet at the deserted Riley house every day after school and sometimes on the weekends.

It was hard to get to know Taryn, but slowly they formed a friendship. The only one either of them had at the time. He learned quickly that Taryn had two modes: quiet and moody or terrifyingly open. Some days she'd scratch at her arm and pace without a word of explanation. Other days, she'd clobber him with information he didn't know how to process. Ill-equipped as he was to be a confidant, he appreciated that Taryn seemed to have so many problems of her own she had no time to worry about his. He liked that she was messed up even if he hated himself for thinking it. So he'd lend an ear whenever she felt like talking.

"What's with the shiner," he'd asked once, assuming for some reason that she had gotten in a scrap at the mall.

"I couldn't fight my dad off last night."

His seventeen-year-old self sat in stunned silence. Taryn stared off into the dirt as if she just told him what the school was serving for lunch.

He didn't know what to say to her then. He didn't immediately understand what "fighting her dad off" meant. To this day, he still wasn't exactly sure what to do with the knowledge of Taryn's abuse.

For over a year and a half the two met at the same place. They never acknowledged each other at school, but a friendship formed that neither of them could deny. For a long time it was the only thing Gable could look forward to. It was the only time when he felt like he could exhale. She would never admit it, but he knew Taryn felt it too. Occasionally she would unleash a laugh that was so unrestrained her upper lip would tuck into itself and disappear.

It wasn't perfect. At least once a week he would say something that would piss her off and she'd leave, usually with her middle finger in the air and her backpack slung over one shoulder. But no matter how mad she seemed, she always showed up the next day. Until she didn't.

The rumors were so scattered and so inconsistent it took almost a week before he could get any of the details straight. Emergency vehicles had shown up at Taryn's house late on a Tuesday night. Mr. Trainor was taken to a hospital nearby where he lay in a coma for reasons no one could quite confirm. Taryn spent forty-eight hours at the police station before a lawyer showed up, put her in a car and took her away. She left, just like everyone else. The only goodbye he got was a copy of her favorite movie—*Heathers*—left on his doorstep. Inside it was a note with a quote from the movie that read, "Chaos is what killed the dinosaurs, darling." Nothing more. Not even her name signed to it. Less than a year later, Gable's father showed him a brief and unemotional obituary for Taryn's father. No funeral ever came, and if Taryn returned to retrieve the ashes or settle anything with the house, she didn't stop by to see him. She just stayed gone until the day she'd knocked on his apartment door at AION.

19

*L*ondon wanted nothing more than to opt out of the "family dinner." Conspicuous as it would have been, the backlash from bailing felt like it was worth putting off seeing Gable again for one more day. She would be forced to join him and the rest of the team in the Laboratory the next morning, so why appear for the meal? She lay in her bed, wishing the night would move on without her

"You're not planning on skipping out are you?" Taryn asked. She had stopped in at their apartment to change shoes, and as she unlaced her boots, London saw a memory of Gable and Taryn laughing. She thought it was in the front yard of her own childhood home, but the scenario didn't make much sense to her.

"Did you and Gable spend time together after I left?"

She felt tension flood back into Taryn's emotions, but her consciousness remained coded in an incoherent stream of Korean.

"No. He and I lived as monks in silent solidarity after you left."

"Would it kill you to just, for once, answer a question?"

"Would it kill *you* to stay the hell out of my head?"

London pulled a pillow over her face, trying to physically stifle her ability to read Taryn with a feather-stuffed barrier. Her mother wasn't wrong, her abilities were growing more intense and more vivid. Even in her hard-to-read best friend things were getting clearer. London didn't want to see every little thing any more than Taryn wanted to show her. She emerged from trying to smother herself when she felt Taryn sitting on top of her, legs straddling her on each side.

"Ugh," she grunted under the slender but still full-grown adult weight pinning her stomach.

"Look, Lond-y, you can hide out here if you want, but nothing is stopping tomorrow from coming. Except maybe this..." She pressed the pillow down over London's face again and held it there just a second longer than London was comfortable with. She sat up, inhaling sharply, but giggling with unhinged surrender. Taryn had unusual methods for shaking her out of a funk, but they typically worked. London reached her hand out for help up, but Taryn smacked it and bolted out the door without her. London took a minute to look in the mirror. The pillow incident had smeared her eyeliner and her hair frizzed at the top. She pumped lotion in her hand to remove the makeup and smooth her ends. All eyes would likely be on her, and she didn't need to look like she was falling apart already.

When London approached The Arch, the herbaceous aromas of roasted meat hit her nose. Even though they were outside, the 60-foot half dome trapped in the smells of dinner. A dozen eyes fell on her within seconds of her arrival, and she felt her mouth run dry. There weren't many secrets here. She grabbed a plate of food and headed for a small table toward the outside of the crowd where only Siobhan was seated.

Gable wasn't there yet. If he had been, she believed she would have felt it.

"Hey," London said, looking around as if she was wanted by the police. Eight table setups were scattered about and the members pooled into the same groups they spent all day working alongside. She didn't need any gifts to read the tone of the room. Everyone was trying to hold regular conversation while quietly hoping for a show. Only a few of her close friends had specific details about what had happened between Gable and London, but everyone knew there was a history there. Like any place confined to a small area and a select group of people, word spread quick. Add the fact that a large amount of AION's population was also psychic and it didn't leave much to the imagination. She wasn't sure what they expected her to do. Grovel on her knees in apology? Demand answers from James? Faint over the weight of her own past? She was just hoping she'd manage to swallow a bite or two of food and leave before Gable came anywhere near her.

"Nothing bad is going to happen tonight," Siobhan said. As always, her words felt carefully chosen and minimal.

Siobhan was highly valued at AION, but what exactly she was capable of remained unclear even to London.

"I don't think something bad is going to happen. I would just rather not deal with this publicly."

"So deal with it privately."

Siobhan's entire focus was on the conversation the two of them were having. No other memories, emotions, or distractions were traveling through her.

"You mean confront him alone?"

"I mean speak with him like an adult."

There was no condescension in her advice. Just direct, unapologetic observation.

"I don't even know what I'd say to him."

"You could just start with hello," a man's voice said. A quiver ran down London's back, as if there were a spider in her shirt. Gable Matthew's was standing over London with his hand in one pocket and a serene look on his face. Instead of a freight train filled with screaming memories, he had a staticky air about him. She'd experienced it before with people she knew to be on anti-depressants or other mood-altering medication. It was something of a relief that she wasn't being bludgeoned with Gable's internal thought process, but the icy emptiness gave her nothing to go on.

"Hello," she said, trying to clear her voice of any shake.

"Can I have a moment?" he said to Siobhan, who stood and left. Around them the other members had gone quiet. Gable slipped into a seat with his back turned to the crowd. "London, you and I have a lot to sort out. And we will sort it out."

Heat flooded into her face. She didn't know what she was expecting him to say, but diving right into it wasn't anything she could have prepared for.

"Right now?" she asked.

"No. Right now we have an audience. And tomorrow we'll have a job to do. I just didn't want you to misinterpret my professionalism as water under the bridge. You will give me an explanation for what happened that day. I will have all my answers. And if I'm fully satisfied, I'll leave. If not, I will continue this charade until you decide that I am owed every last bit of information I ask for." He was working hard to be stern and commanding, but London could still see the boy she knew even with the layers of manhood caked on top.

"I'm not trying to keep anything from you, Gable. That was never my intent."

"Well, you sure didn't make any effort to reach out in the past ten years, either. Not even a condolence."

Before London could apologize, Dennis was striding

toward them. Gable looked over his shoulder and stood to shake his hand.

"The two of you finally crossed paths, I see," Dennis said cheerfully.

"Thought I'd take advantage of the chance to reconnect with an old friend while I waited for you," Gable said. His smile was fake and his tone didn't give away any of the harsh under currents that had just transpired between the two of them. "I suppose I'll see you in the morning," Gable said, walking away from London.

As he and Dennis headed toward the food, London watched him walk away. He had the faintest spirit trailing behind him. Mrs. Matthews didn't speak in her post-life state. She just followed her son close by, her translucent head never looking up from her feet.

The years had built London Riley into a monster in Gable's mind. She was a fraud who had manipulated his mother's mind on the day of her death and held her hand as she marched toward suicide. Afterward, she had abandoned him without a word. Left him to hold all the blame. While he knew he had some responsibility in the events of that day, he needed London to be a vicious creature unworthy of trust or sympathy.

Instead, he found himself face-to-face with a completely ordinary woman. There was no pentagram tattooed on her wrist. No voodoo doll sticking out of her pocket. In the regular world, he might have bought her a drink at a bar or asked her what book she was reading on an airplane. He had delivered the lines he'd rehearsed in his room nonetheless. He'd established that he would be in control of what they spoke about and how. And as they both separately headed to the Laboratory, he tried to return to his resolve. This place meant nothing to him. It was a way to get his father quality care and answers to the only questions that mattered. What did London say to his mother on that day? What did she say to London? And if she was in fact psychic, why didn't she see the horrible mess they had gotten themselves into?

Maybe it wouldn't change anything, knowing the truth. His mother was gone and there was no way to fix that. If he could just be cured of his guilt for bringing London to his home that morning, perhaps he could have a normal life one day. One where he didn't wake up in the middle of the night, sweating, with his mind racing out of control. Maybe he could have a wife or a kid without being certain he'd lose them too.

The heat of the day was already creeping into the morning. Sweat started to form under his collar. He'd pressed a pair of slacks, polished his leather shoes and ironed a stark white shirt twice. Other members were wearing Birkenstocks and cargo shorts, so he knew he'd stand out, but if he was going to pull off the role of serious scientist and AION believer, he had to act prepared for work. Dust was already turning his shoes from a shiny black to a matte gray when he got to the lab. A room full of eyes turned in his direction. Everyone was lounging around as if they were at a coffee shop. Given the large amount of plant-life and the opaque sky lights, it very well could have been. London tucked herself behind Taryn, and the others did their best not to look back and forth between them like it was a tennis match.

"Am I late?" Gable asked, looking at his watch.

"Nope, you're right on time," Dennis answered. "Please grab a seat and I'll get the briefing going. Did you want a muffin or something?" Myra was standing there with a tray of breakfast pastries. She beamed at him as if she were the rising sun itself.

"I made them," she said.

He leaned in and grabbed a blueberry muffin he didn't want in order to be polite and end the delay.

"Great," Dennis said. Myra nodded her head at him and left

the Laboratory. Dennis turned his attention to the group as a whole. "To start I want to cover everyone's role in this lab, just so we're clear," he announced. "I will be directing the experiment. I've been given certain liberties to make decisions and change the course if necessary, but we'll still be adhering to the outlined parameters and restrictions as provided by James, Siobhan, and Ruth." Siobhan was the only of the three leaders present. "Taryn is here to operate Clair in its standard mode. She is working on enhancements separately, but will not be exploring those new additions in this particular setting."

"You're no fun," Taryn said with a chuckle.

"Beth and London will have opposing roles as the psychic components of the experiment. Beth will be the recipient of the new compound being introduced. London will provide the readings.

"That brings us to Gable, who will be administering the compound. He will be recording its impact and making modifications as needed in collaboration with me.

"Ryan will serve as the non-psychic test subject for the compound."

"Word," Ryan responded. He was a skinny, disheveled-looking guy who wore an oversized hoodie despite it being at least ninety degrees outside already. He had his hands thrust into the front pocket and headphones snaking up underneath. He was kicked back in his chair so low, Gable thought he might just slide right out of it. He looked like the last person you'd find in a professional scientific setting. And even though this place was a far cry from the labs he'd practically lived in during college, Ryan looked more like a low-level drug dealer than someone involved with metaphysical, scientific research.

Dennis continued with the introductions.

"Amelia will be here to monitor vitals and make sure our

test subjects are all safe during their endeavors. And, of course, Siobhan will be coming and going to keep an eye on progress and ensure the stability of the experiment. Any questions?"

Gable had a million questions, but didn't want to draw attention. *How is any of this science? How can we guarantee results in a room that looks like a natural history museum? Is Ryan a test subject or an ex-member of a washed up punk band? What the hell is Siobhan's job? Can half the people in this room hear my thoughts?*

"Excellent. We'll be conducting two experiments a day. One will involve the enhancement of natural born gifts. Beth will be strapped into Clair to start. Taryn, using only the standard mode" —Dennis's tone shifted into a playful warning and Taryn rolled her eyes— "will help prepare Beth for travel. As a reminder, Gable, Clair helps bring to the surface the emotions and memories most predominantly represented in an individual's vast consciousness. Travel works best when it's connected to a strong feeling or recollection. Clair works like a magnet, drawing the most solid ones out. London will then perform a reading to help pinpoint a single destination that's relatively simple and safe for Beth. Finally, we'll administer a single dosage of the new compound and record the experience once Beth is back. Keep in mind that with a natural-born psychic, the influence of the compound could be minimal or even insignificant. Beth is already capable of opening herself up to the stream of consciousness, but we are still curious to see if it makes any noteworthy changes in psychics."

Gable tried to keep a concentrated look on his face, but he was struggling to restrain a laugh. These people believed all of this. They really believed they were inventing time travel. He genuinely couldn't believe it. They were as committed to this as any med student he'd ever seen hunched over a cadaver.

"If there aren't any questions, let's get started. Likely it will take some playing around with the dosage and the tactics, but the whole team is very hopeful that Gable's compound has the ability to start opening up opportunities for those of us who weren't born with the skillset necessary to travel."

"If everyone is good, let's go head and get started."

*G*able Matthew's didn't believe in a single word being spoken. His narrowed gaze implied that he was focused, but London was picking up on mocking, menacing vibrations pouring off him. There were too many people in the room to focus exclusively on Gable, but she was capable of at least detecting his skepticism. He handed Ryan a capsule of his compound and a glass of water while Taryn positioned Clair's receptors on his temples and Amelia took his blood pressure. Once everyone else stepped back, London pulled up a chair and sat in front of Ryan. She could smell stale cigarettes and cheap cologne. Ryan had always kept to himself unless he was a part of a lab. He never seemed to mind taking a mystery pill. As Clair purred, Ryan's internal world began to shuffle and a few distinct images come into focus on the screen and in London's mind. She started to name what she saw, hoping Ryan would hear something that appealed to him.

"Blue high-heel shoes," London said.

"Nope."

"The smell of lake water and pine trees."

"Errr." He made a sound like a game show buzzer.

"A dark garage. Maybe a basement."

"Not going to happen."

"Look, this isn't going to go very far if you don't hop on board a destination."

"You've plucked out some of the shittiest events in my life."

"I am not doing anything. This is what *your* consciousness is bringing out. These are places it wants to go. Or needs to go."

"If this works, I'm not having my first travel be to some fuckin' tragedy. I wanna go someplace good."

"Ryan, you agreed to be a part of this," Dennis reminded him.

"Yeah, I agreed to take a pill some dude invented in his apartment. Not to go exploring all my demons and shit."

London held up her hand to Dennis, closed her eyes and tried to look for a positive image.

"God. Is that burning man?" she asked.

"Oh, hell yeah. Let's do that!" Ryan squirmed with excitement in his chair like a kid waiting for an ice cream cone. London focused in on the memory for details that would help tether Ryan to that specific moment.

"We have about two minutes left on the release time of that pill," Gable inserted. "He'll be feeling the euphoric effect any second now."

As if on command, Ryan got a goofy smile on his face and his eyes drifted away from London.

"Ryan, you still with us?" London asked. He nodded slower than what would be considered normal. "I want you to think about the girl who was with you. She has on leather leggings and a crochet top. She's wearing a flower crown and her skin is covered in gold paint. Can you see her?"

"Emmmmily," he said in slow motion. His eyes closed and he slouched into his seat, his chin wresting on his chest.

Everyone was quiet, watching Ryan drift off. With the room hushed, London could concentrate on Gable. She was able to snag a single question drifting through his mind. *And we're just supposed to take this loser's word for it that he time traveled?*

"Do you have something you want to say Gable?" London asked. She was taken by surprise at her own boldness, but he was so rattled that the Folgers coffee theme song began playing on a loop in his mind. She had to fight to hold a serious face.

"No," was all he managed to spit out.

"You don't have any concerns with how we're conducting this?" she asked.

"I mean, I can't help, but feel like perhaps the results are a little manipulatable."

Dennis stepped in to answer, perhaps detecting the building tension. "One thing you'll have to get used to around here, Gable, is that we all work on something of an honor code. It's also hard to get away with lying if London and Beth are sitting in the room."

London continued to stare down Gable. Though she was trembling inside, she worked hard not to let it show. She may have some resentment for the way she was forced to be here, but these people were her whole world. This place, her home. And no matter who he was or what he invented, he didn't get to stride in here and dump on all the work they'd done.

"Sure. That makes sense. We're all just open books then, I guess," Gable said. It was hard to tell if he was being snarky or if he'd truly accepted the information. He immediately began singing the coffee song to himself, and London had to tune him out before she went insane.

For thirty-five minutes, Ryan's eyes remained closed. Amelia would occasionally check his pulse and his blood pressure. London would do her best to read him as he slept, looking for any indicators that he'd gone where they were trying to send him. The only elements she picked up on were the presence of fire and a thudding of drums. When Ryan began to stir, everyone turned toward him and waited, a collective breath all held in their mouths. Even Gable.

"Jesus. Anxious much?" he asked as they all crowded around him.

"Can you think about the last thing you saw while you were out?"

Ryan shrugged his shoulders. "I don't remember seeing anything."

"Nothing?"

"Nope. Like a dark sleep. No dreams. Just black."

London couldn't pick up on anything that would imply he was being untruthful.

The group groaned.

"No need to get frustrated," Dennis said. "This is day one, test one, people. It's taken us years to get to where we are now, and I wouldn't be surprised if it took as long to make the next leap. Relax. Go eat. We'll work with Beth next."

London grabbed two sandwiches and wheeled Beth out to a shaded bench. London took giant bites of ham and cheese as if she hadn't eaten in days.

"You're breathing through your nose really loud, babe." Beth looked concerned as she said it.

"Can you believe his audacity? Were you picking up on his...attitude?"

"You know I do better with the future than I do with the present or the past. Gable didn't seem so bad to me, though."

"Ugh. He just thinks he's so much better than us."

"That's just the college in him, honey. Give him some time to see what we can do."

"I don't have anything to prove to him."

"Don't you?"

London popped the remaining quarter of her sandwich in her mouth and gnashed hunks of bread and meat into something she might be able to swallow. She shook her head at Beth.

"What happened between us was a long time ago. And it wasn't my fault."

"I'm not sure either of you believes that."

"Do you know how long he'll be here for?"

Beth tilted her head and ran her fingers through her blonde hair. A few loose strands came out in her hand and she shooed them away into the wind. "He isn't going anywhere, babe. Might as well get comfy."

When they got back to the Laboratory, Taryn was recalibrating Clair and Gable was still missing. She heard two sentences slip from her friend's mind. *This will work. It has to.* London was caught off guard by the fact that she was perceiving Taryn's internal dialogue in English. She could sometimes pick up on feelings coming off of Taryn, but any actual words were always lost because they came through in Korean. Ruth had told London once that language, like everything else our brain constructs, is just a barrier capable of being broken down with the strengthening of her skills. She stared at Taryn in awe. She wasn't sure what the words meant and didn't even care. London was just fascinated she understood something happening inside Taryn's head.

"What?" Taryn asked.

"Nothing." The words running through Taryn's mind

returned to Korean and London was back in the dark. *Well, that was short lived*, she thought.

Gable entered with a bottle of water in his hand and sweat forming under his arms. His ridiculous office attire was betraying him in the midday heat of June.

"Looks like everyone is back. Beth, why don't you step right up."

Beth curtsied and flourished her hand as if she was an acrobat about to step onto a tightrope. The same collective effort to prep her took place before London sat down in front of her friend. Beth scrunched her nose at London.

"Try to send me backward," Beth whispered.

"You know that's not your strong suit," London replied in a hushed tone.

"Gable," Beth called and waved him over. "Please take note of any markings on my arms or legs."

He scanned her rosy skin and appeared to notate any occurrences of scars or scratches in his notebook.

"Write down the number three," Beth instructed. He did as he was asked. "Now go sit down, sweets."

She leaned into London's hair and spoke directly into her ear. "Send me to my aunt's again. We've done it before."

London nodded her head and looked over to Taryn for confirmation Clair was good to go. Seeing into Beth was so much easier than Ryan. She was a happy person. A light person. She wasn't trying to hide anything or bury trauma. People with simple lives were a simple read. The darker the history the muddier their consciousness. The brain wasn't just a filter. It was also a shield. The more damage it sustained the more it calcified in an attempt to protect itself.

It took little effort for London to pluck out visions of the farm Beth visited every summer.

"The smell of apples covered in cinnamon and sugar," London started.

"Mmm," Beth replied, a silly grin spreading across her face. She was apparently in the euphoric state.

"Sheep bleating."

"Baaah-aaah-ah." Beth giggled at her own attempt to sound like sheep.

"The weather channel."

Beth slumped to the side. Luckily, she was sitting in a large recliner that cradled her small frame.

She came-to only sixteen minutes later, shooting out of her seat seconds after opening her eyes and marching straight toward Gable. She threw her tan leg up and slammed her foot down on top of the desk Gable was sitting at. He leaned away from her at first and then got awkwardly close to her ankle. London could see him take a deep gulp and felt his stomach fill with panic.

"Is that enough proof for you, pumpkin? Did those when I was twelve. Or twelve minutes ago. Depends on how you look at it."

When she turned to face London again, she gave her a wink. London could see now that she had three long-healed scars on her leg. She'd traveled. But moreover, she'd taken over control of her preteen body to prove a point to Gable. *This place is real. We're not a joke. Eat that, college boy.*

22

*G*able had to unbutton the top of his shirt. He wasn't sure he'd be able to get in enough air to avoid passing out if he didn't. He marched away from the Laboratory without any idea where he was headed. First, London called him out for his internal doubts. He'd panicked and started singing the Folgers jingle in a last-ditch effort to throw off the reading. He hadn't heeded Taryn's warning and it was already biting him in the ass. Then Beth made three scars appear where there was once smooth flesh. Could she have possibly been hiding them with makeup? Had he simply missed them before the experiment? No one else in the room seemed to feel as utterly floored as he was. There had to be a rational explanation for it, though. A sleight of hand. An optical illusion maybe. He marched aimlessly through the scorching grounds, unable to stop moving. In his maddened pace, he failed to notice he wasn't alone.

"Gable." A deep, buttery voice called to him from the shade of a nearby tree. It had been a long time since he heard that voice, but there was no mistaking it.

Ruth Riley had white linen pants on with a matching white blouse. She looked like a mirage in the desert landscape. Untarnished by the harsh elements and the hellish temperature.

"Ms. Riley," he returned with a nod as he walked into the shade.

He stood facing her and she continued to stare off into the grimy breeze.

"How are you feeling?"

The question was so open-ended Gable didn't know where to begin. He also felt it was a little ridiculous for her to ask.

"Don't you already know?"

She gave him a closed mouth grin in nurturing acknowledgment. "You know almost everyone goes through the same phases when they come here. First, they're in denial about what we claim is possible. It's absurd even to the extraordinary people who come to this place. Then they're horrified as mounting evidence stacks up. Then they experience a bout of anxiety. They panic that every thought in their head and every feeling in their gut is splayed out on the table. And most of the psychics believe that is, in fact, their gift. But they're wrong. It matters just as much what a person *believes* they are feeling, even if it doesn't match what's inside. The lies we tell ourselves are sometimes the truest expression of who we are."

Gable had never been someone who was comfortable expressing his feelings. He'd much rather discuss facts than explore emotions. Emotions were complicated. Sticky. Misleading. They pinned you into corners and forced you in directions you wouldn't want to go if you were simply applying logic.

"It feels like there is no way to exist around here without revealing some deep dark secret."

"Maybe you should be concerned about why you're keeping secrets, Gable."

"I didn't say I was."

"Whatever you say." Ruth went back to staring at the line where open blue sky met hard beige Earth. She was so content with silence. He feared he was more exposed when neither of them were talking. "It's alright to just ask," she offered.

He cleared his throat. "Did she mean anything to you? Or was she just a client?"

"Your mother meant a great deal to me. The news broke my heart."

"Why didn't you see it coming?"

"I did. I just didn't know when it would happen. I was trying to guide her away. To keep her faith alive. It's why I asked her to bring you to a reading. I hoped the more connected to you she felt the harder it would be for her to go through with it. I'm still not sure she actually meant for it to happen. She just made a bad choice that became a permanent one faster than she or medical professionals could undo it."

Gable clenched his teeth and forced his eyes to stay open so his tears would evaporate before they could spill over. "Those pills didn't accidently slip down her throat. That was her decision."

Ruth set a hand on Gable's shoulder. "It's understandable to be angry with her and also forgive her."

"I forgave my mother a long time ago."

"I'm not just talking about her."

Gable rolled a rock under the sole of his shoe. He was already tired of feeling like someone had sliced him in half and pulled out all his guts. It had only been a day and he wasn't sure if he could handle it. He came here for closure. If he was able to expose them as frauds that was a bonus. But only twenty-four hours in and his determination was starting to fade. Things that shouldn't be possible seemed to be happening every few minutes, and he needed a chance to think without anyone trying to infiltrate him.

Ruth began to walk away, probably well aware of his desire to be alone.

"I'm not sure I can live like this," he admitted.

"There are worse things than being surrounded by people who know who you really are."

As she left, he felt a tingling warmth course through his body. Not the heat that was moistening his skin, but something comforting and delicate. He sat on the root of the tree where Ruth had been, watching the sun go down. He wasn't ready for forgiveness or peace, but his agitation had subsided for the time being. His phone buzzed in his pocket. It was a text from Taryn.

When you're done freaking out, meet us on the west patio for a drink. Seems like you could use it.

At this point, he shouldn't be surprised that Taryn had somehow obtained his phone number. If he was going to assimilate into the AION life, he needed to act like he wanted to be there. He wasn't sure what to expect, but he definitely needed a drink.

23

*L*ondon was wearing headphones to keep things quiet. The little buds were tucked under her hair, so no one noticed. She could hear some of what her friends were chatting about, but little else. As soon as her mind would drift from the conversation, the music would fill the quiet spaces. She needed a break from all the incoming information. It was getting harder and harder to slow the stream. Every time she used her ability it grew like a muscle. Each intentional reading meant more involuntary readings would occur. People were getting easier to crack and she felt crushed beneath the weight of their problems and worries. The last time she'd experienced a leap in abilities like this was when she finally accepted that AION was her home. Now, with Gable's arrival, she was feeling another upheaval.

This time, it was her skills as a medium that were sharpening. Spirits followed the living people around her all day, popping in and out of her peripheral without warning. She tried to ignore them, but they clung like dog hair to the ones they loved. And once she saw them, it was hard to unsee them. Her least favorite new visitor was Taryn's father.

Always an intimidating figure in real life, he was equally haunting in death. She could smell the booze that emanated off his ghostly remains. He never stood right next to Taryn, but instead lurked a few feet away, watching like a hawk. As they all sat around a fire, Taryn's dark eyes blazed. Over her shoulder London could see Mr. Trainor in the dim glow of the fire's light. He had a scar that cut across his forehead like a gruesome crown. London didn't remember that injury from when she knew him, but she'd never spent more than seconds in his company. His ghoulish figure would cough and spit into the dirt, but he never spoke. So many of the spirits didn't speak. They just hung nearby, watching a person they once knew. London closed her eyes, hoping he'd go away. She listened to her music and poured wine down her throat, desperate to disconnect.

When she opened her eyes, Mr. Trainor was gone, but someone equally intimidating approached. Gable had changed from his idiotic work attire into a t-shirt and jeans. He'd replaced his outdated wire-rimmed glasses with a pair of plastic hipster frames. There was something peaceful about him that went beyond his relaxed attire. He didn't have the fog of medication burying his emotions, but London could detect an ease even as she tried to repress her abilities. He gave a shy wave to the group as he entered her circle of friends.

"Gabe, good to see you've recovered." Dennis smiled, a purple haze on his teeth. "Consider yourself officially initiated. Not everyone has their 'shit your pants' moment on day one. You got lucky. Got it out of the way fast."

"You're welcome, honey," Beth said and raised her glass to him.

Gable ran his hand down the back of his head, a motion London remembered seeing him do when they were young. Often it happened while sitting in a class where he was eagerly taking notes and she sat many rows behind him, unnoticed and inconsequential.

"I feel like maybe we didn't get off on the right foot," Gable said to the group.

"Everyone needs time to adjust," Miles offered. "What can we get ya? Wine? Beer?"

"Beer's good," Gable said. Miles fetched him a brown bottle from the cooler and then sat next to London. He patted her leg and leaned back on the sofa, a frisky spring in his eyebrows. She caught Gable observing their closeness and wished she could explain there was nothing between them.

London unplugged one of her ear buds and listened as the group chatter moved from pleasant small talk to intoxicated exuberance. She stayed quiet and watched as Gable melted into the group's dynamic with relative ease. Despite the years since high school, she suddenly felt like the unpopular outsider watching the cool kids interact. Taryn would dip away from the circle to smoke a cigarette, and Beth threw her head back and laughed with her mouth wide open as Gable described a test-run gone wrong with his compound. Everyone was so vibrantly in the moment that she couldn't pick up much beyond the active conversations and collective cheerful vibrations. But now there was someone new. A small girl in a yellow dress, dancing just behind Gable. Her see-through skin sparkled in the beams of the bonfire and her hair flipped forward into her face. She panted and giggled as she spun around in delighted twirls.

As the wine bottles began to dry up and the fire died down, London knew what was coming next. Someone just had to suggest it.

She leaned closer to Taryn, who was seated on the arm of London's loveseat, and whispered, "He hasn't actually been all the way initiated."

"I think it's time to migrate," Taryn said to the group.

"He's been through enough today," Dennis said.

"Am I missing something?" Gable asked, an intoxicated glow in his cheeks.

"We have a little ritual for noobies," Taryn said. "It's customary for someone new to do a demonstration of their product or ability for the group in a more...casual, after-hours setting."

"By that do you mean unsanctioned?" Gable asked.

"We prefer the phrase 'off the books,'" Beth corrected.

"You don't have to do it if you've had too much today," Dennis said. "These lunatics don't know when to quit."

"Come on, Gable, let's see what you got," Miles said.

Gable ran both hands through his hair. London could tell he was nervous. His world view was already being shattered. Maybe it wasn't such a good idea to completely destroy his rigid foundation in one day.

"Yeah," he said. "I'm game. I'm not sure there will be much to see. You know the compound is just meant to unchain our attachment to negative emotions. Most people just pass out from it and wake in a slightly better mood."

"That's not what it does," London said. Everyone turned to look at her. It was the first words she'd spoken to the group since Gable sat down.

"Care to share your take?" Taryn asked. Gable had lost the cheery lightness in his face and now wore an accusing scowl that read, *How dare you presume to know what my compound does or doesn't do?*

"It doesn't clear out negative emotions or insert happy ones. It opens your mind to the truth. People walk around all day telling themselves to cheer up when they're hurting. Telling themselves to calm down when they're excited. The three times I've seen your compound at work, the person who took it isn't better, they're just living in their most unfiltered state. They are connected to raw consciousness without any of the limitations our brain tries to put on us. It's an opener. A tear in the façade that is our mind's instinct to protect us."

"Three times?" Miles asked. "I thought you guys only ran two tests today?"

"The third is when he gave it to his mother," Taryn said, unafraid of his reaction.

London held Gable's gaze. He was angry. Angry that she was speaking a truth he didn't want to hear. His compound was just as dangerous as London's abilities. And the two elements combined had the ability to produce catastrophic results.

"I'll do the demonstration," Gable said. "But only if we do it all the way. I want Taryn's machine. And a reading from London."

"I don't know if that's a good idea," Dennis said. "There's breaking the rules and then there's taking an actual shit on them."

"I'll do it," London said. He was challenging her. Daring her to prove herself. And she wasn't going to back down.

"I'll go grab Clair," Taryn said. "I left her in the lab."

"Can't you just use the one in your room?" Miles asked.

"Don't even look at that one," Taryn growled. Everyone was on edge all of a sudden, but no one had the sense to stop what was happening. They were all too curious. If Siobhan were there, she'd make them stop, London thought. But she hadn't surfaced since they were all in the Laboratory. With the group's voice of reason conspicuously missing, they marched to London and Taryn's shared apartment.

Taryn arrived shortly after with her metal briefcase in hand. She quietly set Gable up.

He took a pill and swallowed it dry. London's boldness was starting to waiver. A sinking in her gut poured icy liquid into her limbs. A growing dread pounded in her chest. Seconds later, Beth slipped from her chair and fell onto the ground. She was only out for a few seconds, but when she came to, her eyes were wide.

"I don't think you guys should go through with this," Beth said.

"What did you see?" Taryn asked.

"It's not super clear, but I'm worried. Gable, are you sure you're up for this?" she asked. "There's no shame in bowing out, honey."

"I'm ready," he said.

London pulled a chair up in front of where Gable was seated. Dennis, Miles, Beth, and Taryn were scattered around the small living room. Sitting face-to-face, London could see the gray and green tones mixed together in Gable's eyes. He had the habit of double blinking. The compound was already starting to clear the clutter from his mind and a single memory rose to the top.

"We don't have to do this," London said, giving him one last out.

"We're doing this," he said.

London took a few deep breaths. The compound was clearing Gable's mind of all the unimportant emotions that had been cluttering his brain throughout the day. His doubt in AION. His anger with London. An encounter with her mother she had just barely began to pick up on. It all dropped out of London's reading. It was all insignificant, muddied by the mind's need to constantly process the things happening all around. Gable's compound was incredible if she was being honest. It left only what was truly meaningful behind. If she could have given it a clever infomercial name it would have been "Bullshit Be Gone."

Taryn's machine was also doing its job. The memory that was most present in Gable's mind went from a shifting array of images and sensory details to a picture in London's mind that grew clearer and clearer with each passing second. She looked at the screen on Clair and saw a rose. A match for an image that was coming to her mind. There was nothing left to do but deliver the reading as it was coming in.

"Today's an anniversary," London said. "It's not necessarily a celebration. Anymore. It's important to you, though." The images and information kept coming in and she spoke as they did. "It's her day. One birthday wasn't enough. So they made another day to celebrate her."

"Who?" Dennis whispered to Beth.

"His sister," London said.

Gable sniffed and London opened her eyes. His exterior was calm. He had likely entered the euphoric phase of his compound's release, but nothing in his eyes read joyful.

"Her favorite color wasn't pink, even if that's what your mother dressed her in and decorated her room with. She actually loved yellow," London continued. "You had been mowing lawns all week. You were eleven, maybe twelve. You asked your dad to take you to the store so you could buy her flowers for her special day. You spent half of what you had earned on yellow roses."

His eyes began to water, but the look on his face remained the same.

"She was delighted. She carried the roses with her everywhere for days. She'd bring them down to breakfast and then back up to bed at night. Your mother told her to throw them out, but you showed her how to hang them upside down to dry so she could keep them forever. Those dry flowers are what you placed on her grave at her funeral."

London stopped speaking. Gable was sobbing uncontrollably, and she had run out memory to draw on. She'd tapped into his well, and buckets of heartache were being pulled to the surface. She looked at the others in the room. All of them had a mixture of horror and admiration as they watched the scene unfold.

She turned back to Gable, not sure if she should apologize or remind him that he asked for it.

Before she could think of what to say his eyes rolled back and he was on the floor. The convulsions from crying turned into seizure-like spasms and his body had a rigid, inhuman quality to it.

She was used to people passing out. As with Beth and even herself, tapping into raw consciousness was overwhelming and the body had a hard time sustaining motor functions while it processed unfiltered reality. It was in that moment that travels typically occurred. When the mind let go of the body, it was free to roam away from it. Some would wake with no memory. Other's had vivid recollections of occupying another time. What Gable was doing now, though, she hadn't seen before. His head jerked and his hands cramped until they looked more like bird talons. London shot back out of her chair, not sure what to do. Dennis was the only one in the room with medical training and he turned Gable onto his side. He cupped his head and checked his pulse while the rest of the group stared in terror.

His violent episode seemed to be ending, but his eyes didn't open.

The room was silent for a long time until Taryn grabbed London by the arm.

"What the fuck did you do?"

24

*G*able's eyes fluttered open and a room full of people stared down at him. For a moment, he was struggling to remember where he was and who these people were. The lights burned his eyes and pain pierced his temples. For some reason he was on the floor and had no idea how he got there.

"What's going on?" he asked.

Everyone exchanged concerned looks.

"What am I doing on the floor?"

The small crowd stared at London indicating she was the one with answers, but Dennis began to speak instead.

"You've been out for a little bit. You got sort of emotional during the reading and then you had an episode."

"An episode?"

"Looked kind of like a seizure. You have any history of epilepsy?"

"No, not at all. How long was I out for?" Gable blinked hard as he tried to clear his vision to see the clock on the microwave.

"About three hours," Dennis answered.

"Three hours?"

"Has this ever happened when you mix your compound with alcohol?" Dennis asked.

"No never."

Gable noticed he had a blood pressure cuff around his arm as Dennis pumped it until it tightened.

"Your blood pressure is looking pretty normal, but your heart rate is still high. Would you mind taking a few deep breaths for me?"

Gable inhaled and exhaled as Dennis pressed the cold, circular end of a stethoscope into his back and then his chest.

"I think you'll live," Dennis said. His smile was mellow and easy. It allowed Gable to feel relaxed for the first time since coming to. Beth rubbed his back in an effort to comfort him. Taryn was sitting on the kitchen countertop filing her nails trying to mask the fact that she was staring at him. And London sat at a desk chair, her knee bouncing in rhythmic spasms. She looked at the floor, then back at him, then to the floor again.

"Can anyone make a guess at what happened, at least? I've never had an experience like that on my own," Gable asked.

Everyone shifted in their spots.

"That was unusual even for us," Beth answered.

London closed her eyes and held her palms over them.

"I'm not seeing a whole lot," London said. "There's some fragments left behind from the reading. Pieces of memories, but I don't know what happened. One minute you were here. The next... nothing. Not an emotion or a memory or a dream to pick up on."

"Like I was brain dead?" Gable asked.

"Kind of."

"Or maybe his consciousness just wasn't here," Taryn chimed in.

"It seems pretty unlikely that we would get *that* lucky," Dennis added.

"What do you mean?" Gable asked.

"She's suggesting you just became the first non-psychic person to travel at AION," Beth said. "That would be pretty wild considering it's your first day."

"Wouldn't I know if I did?" Gable asked.

"None of us are sure. No one's done it yet. It's unchartered territory," London said. She seemed uncomfortable with even the possibility that it had worked.

"Maybe it was too much for him to process," Taryn said. "I mean, Beth has to roll around in a wheelchair and she's been popping in and out of time since she was a kid. Maybe it was just beyond what his brain could handle."

"Then it really wasn't much of a success at all, was it?" London said.

Gable stood up. He was dizzy, but he felt slightly more in control on his feet than he did on the floor.

"We did the same test on me that we tried with Ryan earlier. Taryn's machine, my compound, London's reading. Why would it have worked on me and not him?"

"Because everyone is different," London started. "My abilities are different from Beth's. The strength of your memories are different from Ryan's. Your willingness to accept what's happening and embrace even the possibility of travel could be the difference between nothing happening and changing the world forever. Consciousness is fickle. Every time we assume each person perceives it the same way, we get further from success. Maybe you traveled and maybe you didn't. All we can do is keep testing. And you don't believe in all of this anyway, so why do you care?"

With that she stood and left. Even though everyone was in her apartment, she slammed the door, leaving everyone in silence. But Gable wasn't done. He had more questions. The morning sun was just starting to rise, filling the sky with pink and orange clouds. The unpleasantly brown grounds took on a creamy glow at dawn. There was no temperature in the air. No heat. No crispness. Just indeterminate existence. They could have been anywhere and nowhere. He quickened his pace to catch up with London, who was only a hundred feet or so ahead.

"Hey," Gable said. "Hey." He grabbed her arm and spun her around. When her hair tossed, he could see she had headphones in. She didn't bother removing them just because he was standing in front of her. "Can you take those out please?" He tried to stay relaxed, but even he could hear the gruffness in his own voice.

She removed each bud slowly and stood staring at him. Her jaw was clenched shut and her forehead creased.

"Are you pissed at me?" he asked. "I'm not sure you have the right."

"I have the right to feel whatever I want, Gable. You have things to say to me. So say them."

He did have things to say to her, but his mind was foggy and, after everything that had just happened, he wasn't sure he could piece together a coherent sentence let alone carry a conversation he'd been waiting ten years to have.

"I'll start, then," she said. "When you showed up on my doorstep that day, I didn't have enough skills to do what you asked me. I was sixteen years old and you threw me into a fire. You couldn't have known that, so I'm not blaming you, but your mother was in deep trouble. I wanted to help her. I wanted to help you. I wanted you to like me. I wanted you to know that I wasn't some circus freak. I hoped if I could just help her feel calmer that it would be good for everyone. If I could give her a happy memory to hold on to, she'd make it at least until my mother got back."

The frown on her face cleared but her eyes welled up. A

quiver in her lip stopped her speech, and Gable looked away to the horizon. He didn't want to feel bad for her.

"Did you know? Did you see what was coming that day?" he asked.

"Not at all. I didn't know what I was doing. I shouldn't have even tried, and that's my fault. And I'm sorry, Gable. I'm so sorry."

"I don't need you to be sorry."

She wiped her cheek and straightened her back.

"You're volatile like she was. When I stand next to you I can feel what I felt in her."

"I'm not suicidal."

"I'm not saying you are. I'm saying you're a swirling storm of feeling just like she was."

"You don't know what I am. You don't know anything about me."

"Have I answered all your questions?"

"Not really."

"Do you want to ask me anything else?"

"Not really."

"Are you going to leave?"

He wasn't sure how to answer her. He had only just gotten there and instead of having to force her to answer to him, she freely gave up any information he'd been hoping to get. It hadn't helped at all. And whatever had just happened in her apartment was starting to form into thoughts and emotions he could perceive for split seconds at a time. Like being spontaneously triggered to remember a dream, he could all of a sudden picture himself sitting at his sister's funeral. The expression on London's face changed. He could only guess that she was picking up on whatever was entering his mind.

The memory was beginning to take on a life of its own. A moment he could only describe as new was racing through his mind. He remembered standing up in the middle of the ceremony, his mother crying and begging him to sit down. He raced down the aisle and looked into his little sister's casket. He had a dried bundle of roses in his hands that were crunching and crumbling as he frantically paced.

Whatever this recollection was, it felt tangible and vivid. It also didn't feel entirely real. He could also remember being at his sister's funeral and sobbing uncontrollably, never leaving his seat, not even when everyone else stood to leave. Both events were at war in his mind and he couldn't pick which one was true.

He looked at London for answers, but she offered nothing. She seemed as confused as he was.

"I have to go," he said. As he raced away from London Riley, he dialed his father's phone number. It rang so many times he figured his dad wouldn't answer. Then a weak scratchy voice said, "Hello?"

"Dad?"

"Gable? What time is it?"

"It's early. Really early." He was starting to regret making this phone call, but he had to know. "I have to ask you something."

"Sure. Is everything alright?"

"Yeah. I mean, kind of. I'm sorry to ask you this, but do you remember me doing anything weird at Abby's funeral?"

"Oh, son, I don't think we need to start the day talking about this."

"I'm sorry. And I know it's not something either of us like talking about, but please, can you just answer me? Did I act unusual during her service?"

"Well, we were all grieving Gable. It wasn't your fault. You were very young."

"Dad, please, just tell me what I did."

"Don't you remember it, bud? It was fairly dramatic. You

were sitting in your seat, very upset. Very upset. And all of a sudden you shot up and started running around. It was like... you didn't know where you were. We tried to calm you down and get you back to your seat, but you kept bolting all over the room. Finally you tired yourself out or something, because you collapsed on the floor. We had to call the paramedics. They never did find anything wrong with you. They said you were most likely in shock. You really don't remember?"

He could hear the worry in his father's voice. He hadn't wanted to upset him, but he needed information from the only person who could give it to him.

"I'm sorry, Dad. I didn't mean to— I'm sorry I ruined her ceremony, and I'm sorry I woke you up."

"Are you sure you're okay, Gable?"

"Yeah. I had a nightmare, I guess. Needed to check back in with reality."

"Oh."

"Try to go back to sleep. I'll call you later."

"Goodbye, Gabe. Take care of yourself."

As soon as he hung up the phone he vomited. There was no denying now what he had done.

25

*W*hen London got back to her room, everyone was gone. Even Taryn. The quiet emptiness was everything she could have hoped for. She wasn't sure she could take any more input.

The curtains on the windows were closed and London yanked them open. She let the sun stream on her face, warming her cheeks. There was a moment the night before where she was certain she'd killed Gable Matthews. Her stomach turned as she considered the possibility of being responsible for two deaths in the same family. *I have to get out of this*, she thought. It was one thing to give readings and tinker around in her own, trivial past. It was something entirely different to help another person travel.

She began a ferocious cleaning spree. Tossing every beer bottle. Scrubbing the dishes. Dusting every surface. As she made her way through her half of the room, she alphabetized a collection of books and watered each of her plants. When that was finished she moved to Taryn's side of the apartment. An eclectic collection of tools, jewelry and glass pipes were scattered on a floating shelf. London lifted and wiped under each item until she reached a clunky, unrefined heap of metal and wires. Taryn's first iteration of Clair hardly resembled the sleek technical marvel it was today. When London lifted it from its usual spot, the gadget stung her hand like a hot curling iron. The searing pain wasn't from actual heat but an intense emotional vibration that burned her skin. A series of images ripped through her mind.

Mr. Trainor yelling in pain.

Taryn, at an age younger than she was now, shouting, "I told you to stop."

The smell of burning flesh.

London threw the object onto the bed and let out an audible grunt. She was so tired of the flood. So done with not being able to move or talk or think or even clean without an intrusion. "Screw this," she said to no one. She took two sleeping pills and slid her headphones into her ears.

"London, wake up. London!"

When her eyes opened, there was still sunlight in the room, but her mother's silhouette cast a shadow on her face. She grabbed her phone and saw that it was after 2:00 p.m. She stretched and pulled a sheet over her face, in no way ready for her mother.

"Uh-uh," her mother said, and pulled the sheet down. "We need to talk."

"I would really rather not."

"Tough. What happened last night?"

London sat up and saw that Siobhan was sitting at the breakfast counter in the kitchen.

"Can I make a coffee or something before we get into this?" London asked.

Questions like *What happened?* and *Where have you been?* were silly formalities that overlooked the fact that Ruth almost certainly already had a good amount of the information she was asking her daughter to reveal. A relic of human conversation that London and Ruth had evolved passed, but still adhered to.

London stood up and stretched and shuffled toward the coffee maker in the kitchen.

"Sit down, London," Siobhan said. Stern but not unfriendly.

She exhaled louder than necessary and pulled a chair out from the bistro set next to the kitchen.

"You both already know what happened last night, so tell me what you came here to say." She'd been in trouble with them before. It never lasted long.

"How could you be so reckless?" Ruth asked. "You all think we don't know about your little underground testing parties, but we know. We let you blow off steam because for the most part, you haven't done any major harm yet. But last night was unacceptable. How long was Gable unconscious for?"

"About three hours," London answered.

"And you all just stood around and hoped for the best?"

"Dennis was there."

"Dennis isn't stable enough to be put in charge."

"He's in charge of our lab."

"He's an unreliable drunk," Ruth shouted.

"There's a fine line between taking your work home with you and trampling on everything that AION has built," Siobhan inserted.

"It went bad. I know that. We won't do it again," London said. She had a headache and she wanted the lecture to be over. Not to mention she really didn't want to attempt anything that created the situation she was in the night before.

"There's a problem with that promise," Ruth said. "Gable went to James this morning and explained to him what happened. Told him he thinks he traveled during an unauthorized experiment with *you*. I think he was trying to get kicked out. Instead, James wants you to try to do it again."

"That doesn't seem right. James always plays it safe."

Ruth and Siobhan exchanged looks. Both were more than capable of keeping London out most of the time so she wasn't able to read into the moment.

"James isn't quite himself lately," Ruth answered.

"What's wrong with him?"

"He needs things to progress faster than they are," Siobhan said.

It was an unusual peek behind the curtain. One that neither her mother nor Siobhan offered very often.

"What, is he running out of money?" London asked.

For a moment, silence was all the answer she got.

"He's not being as careful anymore, and I'm afraid you're about to get swept up in it," Ruth said.

"I'd argue that already happened when Gable was brought in."

"That wasn't personal," Siobhan answered.

"But this is," she said. "You two coming here. We didn't hurt anyone, so I'm not sure this is as big a deal as you two seem to be making it."

"You haven't hurt anyone *yet*," Ruth corrected. "There is something off balance between Gable, Taryn, and you."

Off balance was Ruth's favorite term. Anytime she sensed something unusual about people, this was how she described it. When she was younger, London could remember her mother describing a young man that lived down the street as "off balance." Three days later he killed himself in his garage.

London overheard Ruth tell a woman her husband was "off balance" during a reading. The next week that same woman returned, sobbing uncontrollably. Apparently, her husband had packed a suitcase and left without a word.

Ruth had never directed this phrase at her own daughter though.

26

*G*able hadn't had a plan when he walked into James's office. Early as it was, he didn't even know if he'd find him in there. But when he shoved open the door, there he was, elbows on his knees and forehead in his palms. It looked like he'd been sleeping on the couch. He was in a wrinkled button down and his hair was out of place, but he plastered on his sly smile, despite Gable entering unannounced.

"Gable," he said, looking him over. "Rough night?"

"To say the least. Do you already know what happened?"

"I have a pretty good idea. Why don't you tell me in your own words?"

"Do you have video surveillance in the rooms or something?"

"That would be pretty unethical. I don't spy on my members in their private residencies."

"So how do you know something happened?"

"For one, you're wearing the same clothes you were in last night. And you also know we have more technical ways of getting information."

Out of instinct, Gable reached for his phone. Was it tapped? Had he listened in on the call with his father? It didn't matter. He was owned by James in more ways than one now and trying to figure out how exposed he was seemed a fruitless task. Instead he divulged all the details of what he could remember and what he'd been told by the others.

"My history makes me vulnerable. London's connection to that history is clearly an issue," Gable finished. "I shouldn't be here. I'm not the right guy to do this."

"On the contrary, I think you may have proven last night that you are the only guy to do this. As for London, keep in mind that our ultimate goal is to phase out psychics. They are the original source we're modeling all of our science off of, and for now they give us a boost. But this wouldn't be a very good plan if it relied on always needing a psychic there to help. Try to take the day to relax. You have been through a lot in a very short amount of time. Are you trying to set some sort of AION record?" James chuckled, but it was a forced, exasperated sound.

Gable didn't want to relax. All he wanted was to run.

"Something happened last night that wasn't supposed to happen, James. I can't fix it, but I don't want to risk putting my family through anything else."

"Why can't you see the opportunity here? This place is a chance for making life better once all the bugs are worked out."

"I'm not sure anybody has the ability to wield it that way."

James stood and tucked his shirt in. He scratched at his stubble on the walk to his desk chair. When he sat, he'd resumed the authority he'd commanded the first time Gable met him.

"Please don't make me do this, Gable. The whole thing where I threaten to stop funding your father's medical care and I take ownership of your compound. And I cast you back out into the regular world where you're just the crazy guy mixing chemicals in his shitty apartment."

He was surprised by James's unfriendly shift. He had always given off an elitist vibe, but Gable wouldn't have guessed there was an intimidating figure under the salesman exterior.

"Aren't I allowed to leave when I want?"

"Sure, you can. You'll just be leaving with nothing." He covered his mouth, like he was trying to hold back the next words. "Look, Gable. I've spent my whole life trying to achieve what you stumbled into last night. Forgive me if I get a little touchy at the idea of someone wanting to throw that away."

"I just want to protect the only person I have left," Gable admitted, too tired to shield his heart.

"You protect your father by staying here, doing the work, and keeping him in good care. In the meantime, why not focus on protecting all the people you've lost? Keep moving forward, and there's no limit to what you can fix."

Gable had been trying not to think about the possibilities this place possessed. It was dangerous and volatile as the last twenty-four hours had proven. But also alluring. He could end up making things worse, not better, as he had done with his sister's funeral. It took everything to push his ego down and deny the temptation to daydream.

"What are you going to do with the technology if we're able to harness this ability into something anyone can use?"

"I'm going to do what any businessman does."

"Sell it?"

"Build an empire. Maybe with you at my side. This is going to change the world...with or without you."

There was no point in arguing. Gable was a speck in a

decades-long pursuit. He walked out knowing only a couple of things for sure: one, there was no quitting AION. Two, if he was stuck in this place, the only thing he could do was find a way to save his family.

*G*etting the lab started back up felt like a slow and tedious process. The first day there was a fog hanging over the group from the experiment with Gable. Ryan and Amelia were the only two who didn't see the event unfold or know about it second hand, but they were picking up on the discomfort.

"You guys all have a big orgy or something? Weird vibes in here," Ryan said.

Beth giggled and Amelia nodded.

Dennis took the lead.

"There was a little bit of after-hours experimenting that took place. It didn't go as well as intended and it has everyone on edge a bit. This will not inhibit how we conduct our experiments. We are moving forward as planned."

For a week they showed up each morning and administered the test on Ryan. Each time he refused London's urgings to focus on a memory that dominated the most space in his mind. Burning Man was a blip compared to the other scenes he held tight in his consciousness, but he shoved down anything that was uncomfortable.

Shy of the experiment that left Gable unconscious on London's bedroom floor for hours, London couldn't see any impact the compound was making other than filtering out some of the clutter for her readings. There was no traveling for Ryan and Beth did as she always had. Fainting, popping into the future, remaining for only seconds. The attempts to send her into the past as she had done on the first day were spotty at best. It was as if Gable's first day had brought with it a surge of energy and all of it was receding like a tide. Momentum was virtually non-existent.

London was grateful though. She didn't want to be there. She didn't want to spend any more time with Gable Matthews than she had to. She showed up out of obligation. To her mother, she supposed, but really to her friends who were all she had. What else was she supposed to do with her time if she didn't show up for the lab?

Gable tirelessly sang the Folgers song to himself during any down time. He was desperate to keep London out. She couldn't blame him.

But as soon as each gathering was over, she would head straight for home. The usual nighttime meetups fell by the wayside. Taryn also stopped sleeping in their apartment. She had come to her room to collect some clothes, her toothbrush, and a pillow. She didn't speak a word while she packed. As she was about to walk out the door, London stopped her.

"Are you breaking up with me?" she joked.

Taryn's mind was all over the place. Korean and English mashed up in her consciousness scattering words like hail on the ground. London would catch one or two phrases here and there, but they didn't make any sense.

I'm broken.

Damaged people can't do it.

She'll suspect.

It's for him.

"Are you alright?" London asked. "Where are you going?"

"I have a lot going on in the workshop. I'm just going to sleep there for a while."

"Do you need help?"

"No!" She screamed it at London, then immediately redirected her emotions. "This isn't really your area Lond-y. I just need some space to think."

After that, London was truly alone at night. Her mother stayed away. Taryn didn't come back. Even Beth stopped trying to drag her to dinner after being turned down too many times. She'd found the quiet she'd been seeking, yet her skin itched with the need to be around people. The abilities she resented were what defined her. She wasn't an artist or a writer. She didn't have any hobbies or skills to speak of. She was nothing if she wasn't psychic. On the eighth night of lying in bed hating herself, she decided to leave. She packed up what few things she had, mostly just clothes, and knew that in the morning she was going. It was time for her to be something other than this. And she may have to live in a car or work at a pawn shop or sell plasma to eat, but she was done being only this.

28

*I*t didn't require psychic ability to pick up on the weirdness in the air. All week, people had been coming to the lab, but there was no energy. Everyone was guarded and quiet. It was like they were nervous to succeed. Gable felt like he had introduced a toxin into their community. The idea that travel for the non-psychics wasn't all they had imagined made them surly and hesitant.

The worst was London. She hardly spoke except during a reading. She had virtually disappeared from campus. He wasn't entirely sure why, but over and over he felt compelled to track her down. He would stroll through the grounds under the guise of going on a walk, but he was really looking for her. After his travel, it was as if a piece of her was living inside him—or rather, she'd opened a void in him that only felt full when she was in the room. He was dreaming of her at night. Seeing into her eyes as they had stared into his own during the reading. In some nightmares, when he looked into the coffin at his sister's funeral he saw London instead of Abby. Other nights, he saw a little girl he didn't know, a shiny veneer of death coating her plump babyish cheeks.

It had been eight days since he traveled, and he was having a harder and harder time remembering the way events transpired at his sister's funeral the first time he'd attended it. He was losing details by the hour and every time he tried to picture that day it was more colored in with new details. He remembered the paramedics arriving at the funeral home. He remembered seeing his mother breathing into a paper bag as EMTs tended to him. He remembered his father clapping him on the back and saying, "It'll be fine, bud," over and over while he breathed into an oxygen mask. It was a strange thing. Like having someone tell you about an event in your life you had forgotten. Except you were telling it to yourself. It felt foreign at first. Like it didn't belong to him. But the more time passed the more it sunk itself into his memory and drew up other recollections and feelings.

As guilty as he felt for having hurt his family while irrationally flailing around during his first travel, he also had a craving to do it again that he couldn't explain. There was something powerful and magnetic in the experience, like runner's high. It was as if his mind was suddenly exposed to a new level of functionality and it wanted more. More opening. More traveling. More London.

He had been walking the grounds for almost an hour. He recorded his interpretation of the events into his phone. Details from the memory of his sister's funeral, old and new as they occurred to him, as well as dreams and other ruminations on what he believed was happening to his mind.

"A switch has been flipped," he spoke to his phone. "I don't know if it can be turned off, but it feels like it can be turned up. Perhaps with an increased dosage."

He could smell rain in the air and clouds were piling up in the east. The first monsoon of summer was brewing, and it made him feel alive. Gable closed his eyes and took in a nose-full. When he opened them, he saw Siobhan was walking directly toward him. They still hadn't spoken to one another since he arrived. She lingered in the back of the Laboratory. She hovered on the outside of crowds. If he was being honest, he was totally creeped out by her. As she glided toward him, her hands in her pockets and her eyes fixed on his, he shuffled and looked behind him, hoping she was headed for someone else.

Siobhan stopped in front of him and didn't speak for what felt like five minutes, but was probably only twenty seconds.

"What are you doing out here?" she asked. He couldn't tell if it was a passing inquiry or an accusation.

"Just walking. Getting some fresh air." He turned the recording app off on his phone and stowed it away in his pocket. "Looks like a storm is coming."

Siobhan looked into the clouds. She took a deep breath too. All native Arizonans welcomed the rain with gleeful embrace. It was a gift even in the modern age of irrigation and air conditioning.

"I need you to do something," Siobhan started.

"Yeah, sure."

"We're headed for disaster. I need you to interfere."

"I don't understand what you mean."

"Do you know what I do here, Gable?"

"Does anyone?"

She gave a closed-mouth grin. Gable had, in fact, tried to get some details on Siobhan. The more she lurked the more curious he got. When he'd asked Dennis, he'd said, *She's a witch. The good kind, though.* When he asked Beth, she told him, *Siobhan is a fixer.* When he asked for more specifics, Beth added, *Like in the mob. How someone always steps in when shit hits the fan.*

"They keep my role here pretty aloof," Siobhan said. "I do have psychic ability, but it's nothing like Ruth or London or

Beth's even. I can't just read a person or see into the future as I please. I have one specific skill. I can tell when something terrible is going to happen, as long as it impacts me in some way, and I have the ability to fix it no matter where in time the solution exists."

Gable tried to construct a picture of what that might mean. He couldn't get a clear image, but he had to assume she was able to travel through her consciousness as others did at AION. As he had only a week before.

"So why do you need me?"

"It used to be that when something bad happened to me, I'd go rocketing off into some other point in my life. I had no control over when I traveled or where I was going. It took years before I could hone it. There were consequences I've never been able to undo." Her voice got quiet and her face softened in a way he had never seen it. Beneath the square jaw and the pointed brows was a woman not much older than him, who had developed a callus that kept the world at a distance. "I try not to travel at all anymore. When I fix a problem, it has a tendency to create a new one. It's an endless loop. Instead, I've managed to develop my ability to detect trouble earlier, and if someone else can fix it, then I don't go shooting off into another timeline."

"There's something you think I can fix?"

"Yes."

He was hesitant to agree to anything. She didn't exactly make fixing the future sound all that appealing.

"What is it?"

"I need you to stop London from leaving."

"Leaving?"

"She's packed her bags and is planning to leave AION. She can't do that. She has to stay."

"Why?"

Siobhan looked surprised by the question.

"Don't you want her to stay?"

That felt like an impossible question to answer. Something was growing in his mind that screamed, *Yes!*

"I can't possibly be the best one for the job. Literally everyone else here seems more qualified."

"It needs to be you. If we were enough to keep her here, she wouldn't be leaving."

"Why do you need her to stay so badly?"

"She's a major piece of the puzzle."

"There are others like her."

"No, Gable. There aren't."

There was still a lot to learn. He didn't know what made each person significant. He wasn't even sure if *he* was. How many tests, how many members, how many machines and pills had it taken to get to this point?

"Do you already know how all of this turns out?" Gable asked.

"We've pieced together a lot through various visions from different psychic members. We just have to try to keep the train on its tracks until it actually happens."

"And London's a must?"

"As are you."

It was hard not to get pushed around at AION. How do you argue with people who claim they can see the past, predict the future, and hear the very thoughts running through your head?

"I'm not even sure what I would say to her."

"You're smart. You'll think of something."

Siobhan walked away without ever getting a confirmation that he would do what she asked. She was either very confident or had a back up plan.

ondon wondered if her mother already knew she was leaving. Would she even try to stop her? Ruth Riley was stubborn, but also smart. She knew not to push when there was no point. She could also see far enough ahead to know if London would come back soon. Was she not trying to stop her because she knew her daughter would be crawling back on her hands and knees in a matter of weeks? It was impossible not to get caught up in all the what ifs. Her mother was able to wage psychological warfare without even showing her face or uttering a word. Her lack of communication said more than any pleas to stay could have. She could go to Beth and ask her what she saw, but that was just another person who might try to stop her. Why had she been cursed with clairsentience, not clairvoyance? She could feel everything and see so little.

She grabbed her backpack and looked around the room to check if she was forgetting anything. A car was supposed to wait for her by the entrance with their headlights off. There wasn't a completely justified reason to treat it like she was running away, but she'd made secret arrangements, nonetheless. What she didn't want was to have to say good-bye. London knew she couldn't look into her friends' faces and feel their sadness and still justify leaving. A clean break was the only way out. Her first stop would be to Jerome to see if her grandmother would let her stay there for a few days while she looked for work and tried to come up with a plan. London had only been around her Grandma Nancy a handful of times in her childhood. Most of what she knew about her was from backhanded comments that her mother would let slip whenever she was mentioned. From what she had gathered, her Grandma Nancy was exceedingly hard on her own daughter—she'd resented Ruth's gifts while trying to find ways to profit off them.

When London was a young teenager she'd asked about their relationship.

"Why do you hate Grandma Nancy so much?"

Her mother didn't look up from the vegetables she was cutting. "I don't hate her. I just don't love her," Ruth had responded. "She's a user. And I was done being used. So, I was done with her."

London didn't have high hopes, but her estranged grandmother was her only connection to the outside world. She never knew her father. Her mother didn't have any siblings. Nancy was the only person she had any ties to who lived beyond the walls of AION.

As she said goodbye to her small condo a sensation began to seep in through the walls. A nervous energy. Though she was anxious herself, this feeling was external. As she walked toward the door, the emotion intensified. On the other side of the wall she could hear footsteps pacing back and forth. It was him. She opened the door and Gable's march came to a halt. His mind was racing. He spat clipped sentences off to himself. *What am I supposed to say? Why would she listen to me? Do I even want her to stay?*

"Gable?"

"London, uh, I was just out for a walk."

"Was your walk the six feet of space in front of my door?"

He let out a nervous laugh and rubbed the back of his neck. "Would you want to go on a walk with me?"

"I'm kind of busy right now. Maybe some other time."

"I know you're trying to leave." He almost yelled it at her. Instinctively she looked at the table where she had set her backpack.

"I'm not trying to leave. Just cleaning out some junk."

Her phone was ringing in her pocket. Likely the driver letting her know he was there.

"No, you're not. And I'm supposed to try to stop you, but I don't know what to say."

"Who sent you?"

"Siobhan."

London chewed on the side of her cheek. "Why didn't she come herself?"

"She thought you wouldn't listen."

Gable stuffed his hands in his pockets and rocked back and forth on his heels. London's stomach felt as if it were warming up. The spiritual remains of his mother rounded the corner. Mrs. Matthews looked London directly in the eye, her trademark sadness still drooping her face. Gable looked behind him in the direction of London's gaze. Though he could see nothing in the spot where Mrs. Matthews stood, his mind turned to her. His memories drifted to what his mother said to him when she caught him packing his bags, ready to flee after the death of his sister.

"How long will you be gone?" he asked.

The question threw her.

"I don't know."

"Are you leaving because of me?"

Strangely enough, she didn't quite know the answer. She'd felt betrayed when her mother and James brought Gable on board. Then, ever since he arrived, something had awakened that she feared would drive her mad. His presence, their interactions, just thinking about him pushed a piece of him deeper into her. Seeing his mother and sister floating around him broke her heart. So yes, it was because of him. But not because she hated him. Rather because she thought if she stayed by him too long she'd never be able to separate herself. Whatever they had done as kids left a mark on both of them, and the more time they spent together the more that mark opened up into a chasm. She had no way of telling him that, but it was the only thing she knew to be true.

"I'm leaving because I need a life that is about more than who I was born to be. I need to go be something because I've chosen it. Even if it's completely ordinary."

"Why the hell would you want to be ordinary?"

"Because what I am is dangerous. You of all people know that."

Gable began to walk away. He was getting frustrated with her for reasons she couldn't quite puzzle out. She assumed he'd be relieved that she was leaving. His head was hopping between so many different memories and ideas and emotions that she couldn't track what he was thinking. He spun around and charged toward her. When he stopped, he pointed a finger in her face.

"You're a coward."

The words cut into her like a razor blade, stinging as they pushed their way beneath her surface.

"Why? Because I won't stay here and be a lab rat?"

"No, because you have the ability to change the world and all you want is to run off and be a bartender or a fucking grocery store cashier. Don't talk to me about wanting to be ordinary. I'd kill to be able to do what you can do. You're just too weak to use it."

"Oh, so you're all bought in now, huh? Another of James's disciples? Going to fix the world by rewriting the past? Going to save your mother?"

He stood, unblinking, in front of her. She had struck a chord. She hadn't actually meant to hurl that dart at him, but it landed and there was no taking it back.

"Fine. Let's go for a walk," she said. London grabbed her keys and took off. The guilt she felt was only second to his anger. The lingering presence of Mrs. Matthews didn't follow them as they walked into the desert three feet apart from each other.

Both stomped along.

"Where are we going?" he asked.

"We're almost there."

It was pitch-black out except for a small paved trail illuminated by solar lights. The air smelled wet and muddy. Lightening flashed in the distance.

When the lights came to an end, there was a bench in the middle of nowhere.

"Why is this here?" Gable asked.

"James made it for my mother. She needed a place away from people. It's hard for her to find quiet so she comes here at night sometimes."

"How'd you know she wouldn't be here tonight?"

"I would have felt her long before we got here. Want to sit?" London asked.

The two scooted onto the bench. It wasn't just an ordinary park bench, it was carved from marble. There were birds etched into the arms and, even the darkness, the stark white stone seemed to glow.

"Quite the seat," Gable said, absentmindedly rubbing the cool surface.

"Whatever my mother wants, James delivers. Thinks it will keep her here forever."

"Are they…"

"Together?" London asked. "No. Only in his dreams."

"They seem close."

"They knew each other as kids, I guess. She doesn't talk about it much. That's a theme with my mother."

London could feel that Gable was still uneasy, but his anger was subsiding.

"There's Mars," he said, pointing to a faint red dot in the sky.

"Oh, yeah?"

"What are we doing out here?"

London pulled two capsules of Gable's compound out of her pocket. She placed one on her own tongue and handed him the other. He took the tablet and swallowed it. He looked confused, but went along with what she was asking. The initial sensation of the compound began to kick in and her chest swelled with warmth. Gable began to get a distant, dreamy look on his face. The stars, already iridescent, began to dance like a kaleidoscope. London closed her eyes, letting delightful vibrations wash over her.

"Remember Mrs. Buckley?" London asked.

She was a particularly unfriendly English teacher who London and Gable had in the ninth grade. Her breath reeked of coffee and she always had the same kind of sweater on as if she'd bought one style in nine varying shades of beige.

"Yeah," Gable said with a drunken chuckle.

"She'd say to you, 'Gable you are not in biology right now. The only thing we're putting under a microscope here…'"

"'Is literature,'" Gable said in unison with London. His head nodded off to the side and London's eyes closed a second later.

30

*A*s soon as the words left his mouth a tugging sensation pulled at his abdomen. When Gable opened his eyes, he was sitting at a desk. The room he occupied was lit by fluorescent bulbs and the floor was covered in an industrial blue carpet.

He looked to his right and a younger version of London was suppressing a smile.

"Mr. Matthews, am I interrupting you?"

Mrs. Buckley was standing over him with her arms folded.

"I asked if you could please start reading at the top of page 115," Mrs. Buckley repeated.

He scrambled to get his bearings, flipping through a book trying to find page 115, but he couldn't gather himself fast enough for Mrs. Buckley.

"Typical Gable. I'll see you after class. Melissa, please pick up the passage."

Gable turned back to London and could feel his face flushing. He tried to take in the scenery. Everything was too sharp to be a dream. Unlike the blackout in London's apartment, where details only flowed in after the fact, he felt fully in control and present. He touched his face and felt smooth skin instead of stubble. He could smell cafeteria food cooking. He was there. Really there. For all the things he could feel and see, he still couldn't quite believe what was happening.

There was a pocketknife in his jeans that his dad had given him for his twelfth birthday. It was supposed to be a signal he was entering manhood, but his dad fumbled through the moment and just ended the becoming-a-man speech by saying, "I just thought you'd think it was cool."

He pulled the knife out and saw London shaking her head, trying to get him to stop whatever it was he was about to do. He panicked and did the only thing he could think of. He slashed an *X* into his palm and, as the blood began to run onto his copy of *The Hobbit*, the tug in his stomach tightened again and he was back in the dark wilderness with London.

He looked at his hand. A scar in the faint shape of an *X* shone on his palm.

"Just had to have proof, didn't you?" she asked.

"I'm a scientist."

Memories of his hand being stitched up in an emergency room came rushing to the surface. He could see his mother pacing their living room feverishly asking, *What could you have possibly been thinking?* while his father sat dumbfounded in his recliner. And then an even worse memory came, where he was listening outside his parents' bedroom while his mother sobbed and asked his father if he thought this was because of Abigail.

"He never talks about her. He's so bottled up. Maybe this isn't the first time he cut himself," he recalled his mother saying.

"I'll talk to him," his father said to her and Gable could picture him putting a comforting arm around her shoulders as she slumped into him. He had no memory of his father actually having a talk with him about it.

Even knowing all that came after, he felt awful for making his mother worry. It all felt fresh as if it had just happened and the sudden nearness of his family made him queasy. As a kid, he could remember toiling after the event, thinking about that moment, trying to remember what compelled him to cut his hand in class. His younger self could remember the action, but not the motivation. Now he knows it's because his adult mind was driving his adolescent hands. But back then, he just assumed he was crazy.

"How did you do that?" he asked.

"It's hard to explain. I just had a feeling that if we were sharing a memory, we both might travel to the same spot. It's like all of a sudden I can see possibilities for what all of this can be." London waved her hands around in the air pointing to the universe around them. "Doesn't that happen in science? Like once you learn enough you can start to see a result before it has actually happened?"

"Yes, I suppose."

"I felt pretty sure if we both concentrated on a memory we shared, that your compound could open up a tunnel to get us both there. Almost like your consciousness could piggyback on mine."

"I didn't realize you had tried my compound."

"I've been sneaking samples."

"And?"

"It's like being on mental steroids."

"That's not what seems to be happening with Beth."

"Beth and I are different."

Gable rubbed the scar on his hand. It was hard to wrap his head around all the things that had changed in the short time he had spent at AION. His world was upside down.

"This was incredible," he said. "Are you going to tell anyone?"

"You think this was incredible? I can see the memories as they're hitting you. Your mother was worried sick. Things changed at school for you. People were afraid of you all of a sudden. I can remember what it was like before and what it's like now that this happened." She flipped his hand over and tossed it back to him. "You made what felt like a very small decision and it spiraled into all of these unforeseeable branches. Imagine if you changed something bigger."

Quiet filled the space around them and Gable felt certain they were both thinking of his mother.

"Don't leave," he said.

"If I stay, this just gets worse. You're right. I'm a coward. I'm scared that I could really hurt someone. And I'd rather leave than find out."

"What if someone gets hurt because you aren't here?"

He still didn't feel like he understood all her abilities, but he knew, sitting next to her, that he felt safer going forward with her in the room than he would if she left. She cared about people. She felt things others tried to deny about themselves. She wasn't just a piece of the puzzle, she was security.

"With or without me, this is going to end badly."

She stood up and walked away, leaving him in the dark. For a long time he watched flashes of light fill the clouds. London Riley had done it again. She'd dug deeper under his skin and he knew there was no getting her out.

The next morning, he walked into the lab unsure if London would be there or not. For all the time they spent together, he wasn't sure if he'd convinced her to stay. When he entered, everyone was crowded around Taryn. London wasn't among the group, but as he walked in, they turned to him.

"Today is gonna be a big day, man," Dennis said, clapping Gable on the back and inviting him into the circle. "Taryn's releasing a major update to Clair."

"We're testing bridging today," Taryn said.

"What does that entail?" Gable asked.

"Instead of using your pill and the machine and hoping a psychic can push someone into a travel, why not just borrow what our mystical friends already have?"

"I'm not sure I'm following," Gable admitted.

"Look, all this stuff we're doing is just trying to get normal people to a level that psychics are already on. Bridging is going to be like jumping a car. We're going to transfer what a person with abilities has into a person without them. Get it?"

"It doesn't look like London is—"

Before he could get the words out, London opened the door. He was glad to see her despite the fact that she didn't look entirely happy to be there. She nodded at him. It wasn't a thank you, just an acknowledgement that she'd at least decided to stay another day.

"Great, our little car battery has arrived," Taryn said as London joined in. She maintained her quiet demeanor and sat relatively silent as Taryn strung wires between London and Ryan. Ryan looked like he hadn't showered in a few days. His hair was shiny with grease.

Ryan took a pill and London held out her hand.

"Give me one too."

Gable did as he was asked and placed a tablet in her hand.

"You're going where I say you're going," London said to Ryan.

"Someone is bossy today," Taryn added.

Ryan nodded, perhaps unable to argue with her as the onset of the compound took over.

London began to speak what she was reading out loud.

"There's a river. You're fishing with someone. Whoever he is, he's important to you. A grandfather maybe. You feel a lot of guilt around this day. It's okay," she added. Always comforting.

His eyes closed and Taryn gave a silent thumbs up indicating everything looked good on her end.

His eyes rolled behind his lids. They watched as the tiny orbs danced absently like pinballs. As they waited, tears began to run down Ryan's temples and pool near his ears.

"Is he alright?" Gable asked Amelia.

She ran a thermometer across his forehead and held his wrist between two fingers and her thumb, staring at her watch.

"Seems fine," Amelia said.

Ryan let out a whimper, but no audible words.

After thirty-five minutes, Ryan's eyes batted open. He didn't say a word and only looked at London. She placed her hand on his knee and Ryan came apart. Not in a slow trickle of emotion, but an explosion of feeling. His shoulders bounced and his breath shook as he fought to draw in air through the tears. He sucked snot in through his nose until it honked with resistance.

London just stayed put, her hand on him in a way that was both delicate and stabilizing. As the onslaught subsided, Ryan pulled out his phone and begin scrolling rapidly. He sat for almost ten minutes flipping his thumb up the screen. Finally, he held out a photo, grainy from old, unrefined technology. The face staring at all of them was a much plumper, younger version of Ryan. Instead of a black button down, he wore a cartoonish superhero t-shirt that looked two sizes too small on his then-pudgy frame. Written down his forearm in mud was the name "London Riley."

Ryan popped a cigarette into his mouth and lit it before he'd left the room. Everyone looked to London for answers.

"Congratulations, Taryn," she said, and followed Ryan out the door.

31

When London left the Laboratory, she found Ryan perched under a tree, burning through a fresh cigarette. He had a memory humming on the surface. A young version of himself was standing with an older man. They were on a riverbank fishing. The older man was concentrated on his pole. He'd turn to Ryan occasionally to show him something with the reel. Ryan was upstream, releasing the fur from a cattail reed so it coated the older man in a cloud of fuzz and laughter. It was happy. Deeply happy. Yet now Ryan's eyes were puffed and distant.

"Everything alright?" she asked.

He nodded.

London didn't expect to get much out of him.

"He was my uncle," Ryan said.

"Oh."

"My dad OD'd when I was six. My mom was always working. I never got to go on field trips or vacations. We never had any money."

London stayed silent and let him talk.

"Once a year, though, my uncle would take me fishing.

He'd try to talk to me about 'man stuff,' but mostly we just sat and fished. It was my favorite thing to do. Pretty much the only thing I ever looked forward to.

"That day—that day I just went to—it was the last time we did that. I was acting like a shithead that day and wouldn't get off my phone. Some kids at school had posted embarrassing pictures of me online and I was reading all the comments over and over. My uncle…"

Ryan began to choke up again.

"My uncle asked me what was wrong. I told him nothing. Barely talked to him. Didn't even touch a fishing pole. He died two months later. Always felt really shitty for how I acted that last time."

"What did you change?" London asked.

"Not a lot. Just put my phone down after I took the picture and grabbed a pole. Sat with him like we usually did and listened to him tell stories about when he and my dad were kids."

"Sounds nice."

"It was."

"That was a good idea. Using your phone to take a picture. Better than cutting yourself."

"Yeah. I've only ever had the one phone." He laughed and held it up. "I don't take pictures very often. Guess it wouldn't work for most people."

"Well, it worked this time. Have a good night," London offered.

"Sure."

London felt relieved to know that not every travel ended in chaos. Small, whisper-like changes had the ability to bring closure without mayhem. Most people wouldn't have needs as simple as Ryan's. Her relief began to fade as she processed the fact that her abilities had just been successfully transferred into another person. She just went from an aspiration to a commodity.

She spent the break between experiments regretting her decision to stay. Gable had gotten in her head—an ironic turn in their relationship. He asked her to stay and she felt obligated to give him what he wanted. She knew she could never make up for what happened between them as teens, but something in her wanted to try. The team would try bridging between Beth and London next, and she had a feeling it would work. Though Beth had abilities of her own, they differed from London's, so the team wanted to test how much more potent Beth's skills would be if London was attached. James had once described discovery as having a snowball effect. *Once one thing starts clicking, the rest will come on quickly. As long as we're diligent, the rewards will be boundless.*

But it was more than James's reassurance that was guiding her. Since Gable's arrival, there had been a shift. As if something cosmic was coming together. It made her deeply uncomfortable and cautious, but London was beginning to believe that there truly weren't any coincidences and that she, Gable, and Taryn were more than accidental childhood peers. They were destined for this mission, and it was all coming to a head. Whether this was a gut feeling or a knack for clairvoyance emerging, she couldn't tell.

"Hey." Lost in thought, she didn't even see Miles approaching.

"Oh, hey." She hadn't seen him in over a week. Since Gable arrived and she'd self-quarantined, Miles hadn't even crossed her mind.

He had a trucker hat on backward and was looking more disheveled than she was used to seeing him. Still handsome, but scruffy. He clenched and released his jaw.

"Look, I've been instructed to back away from you indefinitely. If we don't see each other for a while, I just wanted you to know it isn't my choice." He looked around as if someone might be watching.

"Are you alright?" London was beginning to see a picture of Miles hunched over a computer late at night. Candy wrappers and energy drinks scattered across his desk. Page after page flashing in front of him on a computer screen.

"Look, it's no secret you guys are onto something. We need to make sure we can keep the doors open while you work out the kinks. I've been put in charge of finding bidders."

Something unsavory curdled in Miles stomach. He was agitated. A far cry from his typical, over-optimistic disposition.

"What do you mean bidders?"

"I mean crazy motherfuckers with a lot of money who want to be first in line to time travel."

London grabbed Miles arm and pulled him in close. "That can't happen."

"London, you coming?" Beth called from the Laboratory door.

She turned back to Miles for answers, but all she could pick up on was a sense of his frantic searching, some hacker terms she didn't understand, and hundreds of thousands of lines of code.

"We don't get to decide what happens from here. We're all in this now," he said.

Miles was scared and London got goosebumps as he walked away.

"Babe, you coming?"

London walked toward Beth. She wanted to tell the others what she had heard, but not in front of Siobhan.

32

*W*hen London walked back in, Gable noticed her eyes were darting back and forth when she held out her hand to him for another tablet of the compound. He placed it in her hand and brought one to Beth.

"You set, babe?" Beth asked.

London just nodded.

Taryn hooked the two women up to her machine. Bridging had already worked once that day. Could they really strike lightning twice? This wasn't how scientific discovery usually happened. It was usually years of agonizing, slow work, not an avalanche of advancements.

"It *has* been years," London answered, even though his question wasn't out loud. He wasn't sure he could ever get used to that. Beth and London took on an airy glow.

"Remember when we snuck off to Slide Rock?" London asked Beth.

Beth let out a high-induced snicker. "Yeah, we slept in the forest. We didn't come back for three days. Your mom called us 'hopeless.'"

"Do you remember what we ate that whole time?" London asked.

"Ew, yes. Seasoned tuna pouches."

As the memory seeped into both of them, Beth fainted and London followed quickly after.

Dennis gave Amelia a look and she raced over to check their pulses.

"What?" Gable asked.

"London doesn't usually faint when she's the one conducting a reading," Dennis said. "Just being overly cautious."

They all sat there staring at the two women. Siobhan didn't bother acknowledging Gable. She sat in her usual spot in the back as if they never spoke. He wasn't looking for a "well done" or anything for getting London to stay, but he thought they might exchange a casual hello.

Taryn walked away from the machine and sat next to Gable.

"How is the savior of AION today?"

Gable snorted, not even sure what she meant.

"Oh, you haven't heard? This place was about to go in the shitter. Then you show up with your mystery pill and day-one travel and bingo, all the lights turn back on."

"I didn't know I was boarding a sinking ship."

"James wasn't going to let me release this update. Said we might have to go underground for a bit. Then you travel and we get the green light across the board. No holding back."

"That's good, I guess."

"We'll see."

Gable watched London. There was nothing to see, but his eyes ran a line from her ear down her arm. "Do you every wonder if she's actually that good at it, or if we're just bad at hiding our bullshit?" Gable asked.

"I'm great at hiding my bullshit. Why, you let her in?"

"I can't seem to help it."

"Holy shit." Taryn stood up and was no longer paying attention to Gable.

When he followed her eyes he saw the same impossible sight. Beth's feet were vanishing. From the bottom up, her body was becoming immaterial. She didn't move or change positions; she just gradually grew more translucent. Taryn was running to her machine. Siobhan stood up and hurried toward the front of the lab.

"Everybody stay put," Dennis shouted.

The room froze.

"What's happening to her?" Amelia asked. She had panic in her eyes, but followed Dennis's orders.

"It's Divine Travel," Dennis said.

"How do we know?" Taryn asked.

Beth's fading physical appearance was spreading. And then she was gone. The band connected to Taryn's machine slapped down into her chair. London remained unmoved. Everyone's mouth hung open. Gable closed his eyes hard. *This can't be real,* he thought.

"What are we supposed to do?" Amelia asked.

"Call James," Dennis said to Siobhan. "And Ruth."

Siobhan stepped out and everybody remained in their places. Gable was beginning to suspect that no one at AION really believed in Divine Travel until this moment. They seemed as shocked as he was.

"Should we at least try to wake London up? See if she can get a read on Beth?" Taryn finally asked, after everyone had been silent for a long time.

"Don't do that," Ruth said, as she entered. "The two of them might still be connected. You have to ride this out."

Ruth sat next to her daughter. She grabbed her wrist and

gently brushed her face. Her auburn hair fell in front of her eyes.

"Just hang in there," she whispered to her daughter.

In the seat across from London, the air began to transform. It wasn't quite like smoke or fog. There was just the slightest distortion, like a gas leak. Soon that space began to fill with a diaphanous image of Beth. Particle by particle she returned, until her sleeping form occupied her chair once again.

"Now turn it off," Ruth said to Taryn. The whirring sound of Clair rolled to a quiet emptiness. Everyone was holding their breath.

"London," her mother whispered to her. "London, wake up." She shook her arm gently.

Beth began to blink first. Everyone rushed to be near them. London was still unconscious.

"Give them a little space," Dennis directed, never once losing the baritone coolness of his everyday voice.

Beth tried sitting herself up but seemed to struggle. London started to groan, but still couldn't open her eyes.

"London. Can you hear me?" Ruth asked.

London nodded, but still didn't open her eyes.

"What are feeling?" her mother continued.

"Nothing,"

"Nothing?"

"I mean, I can't feel anything coming off of any of you." She opened her eyes but stayed slouched. "I can't read anything."

"I'm running on empty, too," Beth said.

"Let's get them somewhere they can rest," Dennis suggested. Amelia had swooped in for vitals. She didn't seem alarmed, but no one knew exactly what they were looking for.

Everyone worked together to get Beth into her wheel-chair. Then they exchanged uncomfortable looks as they tried to decide what to do with London.

"Here," Gable said and scooped London into his arms.

"Mom?" was all she said before her eyes closed again.

33

When London's eyes opened, she saw her mother and Gable seated at the bistro table in her kitchen. They had coffees in front of them, but didn't appear to be engaged in conversation. When she tried to read them, a pain pierced her behind the eyes. She winced and let out a pathetic cry.

The two of them stood up and rushed over to her. Their solidarity told her that whatever happened, it must have been bad.

"How are you feeling?" Ruth asked.

London sat up stiffly, feeling like she'd been in a car accident.

"I'm not really sure. Sore," she admitted. "What happened?"

"We don't need to talk about it right now," Ruth said.

London looked at Gable. She needed answers.

He shuffled, looking to Ruth for approval. Her face said no, but he took another step toward London.

"It's looking like Beth experienced Divine Travel. After the two of you were out for a few minutes, her body started to fade away until it was just...gone. It came back, but you both have been having a hard time recovering. She's been up and moving for about an hour. She's asking about you."

Attached to the top of London's hand was an IV. Cold liquid was running into a tube and a chill went up her spine.

"If it was Beth who traveled, why am I so messed up?"

"Our best guess is that when you bridged, Beth's travel was so extensive that it drained you. Like a battery," Ruth said. "It's very hard for me to reach any part of you right now." Her mother's eyes were red and she didn't need her abilities to tell she was scared.

"Does Beth remember anything about where she went?"

"She remembers everything," Gable said. "Said she went to the destination you two talked about going to. But instead of being embodied within her past self, she was looking at you and her sitting on a rock from behind the trees."

"I want to see her."

In front of London's apartment, one of the campus golf carts was waiting. Gable drove them all to Beth's residence. London held on to Ruth's elbow to stabilize herself as they walked in.

"Oh, London," Beth said as soon as she saw her. She wrapped her arms around her friend, which hurt more than London was expecting, but she was glad to see her too. As Beth pulled away, London sank to her knees. The abilities that had eluded her since she woke up were suddenly returning with unrelenting force. She began to see Beth's life in astounding detail, as waves of memories crashed into her one after the other. From early childhood years to awkward middle-school life. From her aunt's farm to a lonely room in an opulent house, the memories streamed in back to back and at a speed that far exceeded their natural pace. Still, despite the volume of information, London was able to perceive it all.

"It's happening to you too," Beth said.

London placed her hands on the floor, trying to brace herself. Suddenly she could detect Gable's voice and a memory from Dennis of watching Beth fade away. Then an electric presence, one that was excited and volatile. James.

"What is this?" London asked Beth.

"I don't know, honey. About an hour after I woke up, I felt like *your* whole life flashed before my eyes."

"Two consciousnesses merging together," James said. He was standing near a window in the corner, a glint in his eyes.

"Explain," Ruth said. Her arms were crossed and she took on a scolding mother's tone.

"I mean, it should be obvious to everyone here. A reading isn't just a reading. A travel isn't a single event. Every time we explore, we are overlapping and interweaving with one another. We're all already connected. The things we're doing here are just opening the gates that our brains put up. This is a good thing."

"My daughter could have died!" Ruth yelled.

Gable was helping London off the floor.

"There's no such thing as death," James uttered like it was a casual afterthought. "You of all people should know that."

In the room, discomfort mixed with exhilaration. Now that she and Beth seemed relatively fine, London recognized the truth: they had just experienced phase one of the most significant discovery in the world.

"Where's Taryn?" London asked.

Everyone shrugged as if they hadn't noticed she was missing.

"I'll go look for her," Dennis offered. He kissed Beth on the forehead then came over and drew London in with his giant arms.

Dennis just go. And don't come back.

A memory of his wife was engulfing his mind. London knew he had been married and had a son. She would sometimes see images of them as a family or pick up on his sadness, but now he appeared to be fully existing in his past. Only his physical body was in the room.

"Are *you* okay?" London asked, her face stuck in his chest.

"I am now that I know you two are."

London knew it was a lie but let him go anyway.

"Everybody take a couple of days off," James said. "It's been an unprecedented week and you could all use some rest. Starting Monday, we'll be working harder than we ever have before. So enjoy this time."

Ruth eyed James as he walked out. She wasn't happy with him, but their fight would be continued in a more private setting. She turned back to her daughter.

"Why don't you stay with me for a few days? I can look after you."

"Oh, that's alright, Mom. I'm feeling better."

"Just for tonight then?" Ruth was rarely this maternal, and London felt like being taken care of for the night wouldn't be the worst thing.

"Yeah, alright. Just for tonight."

When they got to her mother's home London was finally starting to feel better. More like herself. She was feeling a return to stasis with her abilities, but her mother remained guarded as always. But she could feel Ruth's worry subsiding. There was a layer of regret woven in with her relief, but for the most part, London felt they were both recovering.

London flopped onto the couch and kicked her shoes off. A bruise was forming where the IV had been placed, and she rubbed it tenderly. Like she had their childhood home, her mother kept things flawlessly clean. Not a fingerprint on her glass table or a fleck of dust on the shelf. Ruth had paintings of a woman with a horse on the beach hung on the walls, something London always found odd considering they never lived on the beach or rode horses.

"Here," Ruth said, handing London a bowl of Thai noodles in a Tupperware. "You should eat something."

"I'm not sure I can."

"It'll help. Trust me."

London took the container and began shoveling forkfuls of slippery noodles and bean sprouts into her mouth.

Ruth fixed herself a gin and tonic without offering any to London. She stared at the wall, lost in contemplation.

"What are you thinking, Mom?"

"Do you hate me for bringing you here?"

"I've never hated you."

"You must be angry I dragged you here. Never gave you any other options."

"Did we have other options?"

"I could have tried harder."

"It's fine, Mom. I'm a grown woman. If I'd wanted to go, I could have."

Her face turned sad again and London could feel Ruth's mind drift. She was thinking about her own mother, wondering if she had turned into her.

"You're not like Grandma Nancy."

"That's what we all would like to think. That we won't turn out like our parents. But we always do."

London sat down her empty container of food and closed her eyes. She was feeling connected with her mom in a way she hadn't in years.

"Did you ever use your abilities in a way you regretted?" London asked.

"We all have regrets."

"I really messed up with Gable's mother. As soon as he got here, I put him in another dangerous position. And I'm afraid I'm going to mess up again the more I help other people travel."

"Sometimes, when you think you've made a mistake, you've actually just set a new course."

Ruth's mind opened up on a memory, one London could see as clear as the room around her. As she focused on the recollection racing through her mother's mind, she began to feel as if her stomach was being pulled through the couch. For a few seconds she couldn't even open her eyes. Then, when she did, she was no longer at her mother's home in AION.

London caught a glimpse of herself in a window reflection. Judging by the flatness of her chest, the braces, and her box-store-brand shoes, London had to guess she was around fourteen years old. There was no mistaking where she was. Jerome was as distinct a town as any. It was filled with funky little shops and perched on a mountainside, and the locals got their kicks from claiming every other spot was haunted. From hamburger joints to hotels, signs all over town claimed they had ghostly occupants.

Walking a few feet ahead of her was the unmistakable red head of her mother. And beside her, the broad-shouldered figure that distinguished her Grandma Nancy. Ruth and Nancy were locked in distracted, tense conversation. London couldn't hear what they were saying, but she could see her mother's one raised eyebrow, which suggested things were not going her way. For some reason, London couldn't recall this particular trip at all. Everything felt new and unfamiliar, so she quickened her pace to try to catch more of the conversation, pleased that she was mobile and able to move her own body in this travel.

She was able to catch snippets of the argument.

"...and whose fault is that?" Ruth said to her mother through gritted teeth.

"You never could just stay put. I didn't make you that way," Nancy returned.

London could see the similarities in the two women. Her grandma's hair was mostly white with only the slightest pink shade indicating it had ever been the vibrant red that Ruth's was. Both had deeply edged jaws, locked in frustration with one another.

London crept a little closer.

"If she asks, you are to say nothing, do you understand?" Ruth said.

She then stopped dead in her tracks, and London almost ran into her backside. She squared off with her daughter and narrowed her eyes, possibly detecting the stranger who was occupying her child.

London cowered under her mother's agitated gaze.

"London, go back to the shop with Grandma. I'm going for a walk."

The shop was what Nancy referred to as the "family business," though Ruth hadn't worked inside those walls since she was seventeen.

The sign on the door read Mystic Sisters. London could vaguely recall the layout of the store and felt a flood of giddy excitement as she retraced this almost-forgotten place. Candles were scattered absentmindedly on a wall of shelves, each with an alliterated name. Calming Cardamom, Lustful Lavender, Amicable Aloe. London picked the last one off the shelf and breathed in its artificial aroma.

"That one turns enemies into friends," Nancy said from the register.

London could recall Ruth referring to her grandmother's shop as a "shack that sells cheap tricks."

A revolving rack displayed a line of jewelry that had crystals dangling from a chain. Each with a word of empowerment written on a tag: *Confidence, Courage, Joy.* "I dare you try that one on and not feel happy," Nancy instructed to London.

London couldn't imagine what it would have been like to live there. With only a few hundred residents it felt more like an amusement park than an actual town.

"Where's Mom going?" London ventured to ask.

"Oh, up the hill to do Lord knows what."

London couldn't help but feel as if there was a reason she came here. She started to allow her surprise to subside and take control of the situation.

"Can I go grab a shake?"

"Sure, doll." Nancy pulled two dollars from the register and flicked her wrist as a sendoff.

Instead of going to the Creepy Creamery, London headed up the hill. There was only one main street, so if her mother was "up the hill" there was only one direction to head.

She came to the edge of the store-lined street and could feel her mother's presence as she had been able to most her life. It led her to an unassuming gate that served as the entrance to a run-down cemetery. The ground crunched beneath London's feet and dry weeds scratched against her ankles. Even at twenty-six, she felt a little unnerved as dusk's shadows stretched across the poorly kept burial sites. She rounded a corner and saw the scorching glow of her mother's hair beside a modest stone. Ruth's back was turned, but London could sense she was upset. London's blue velvet, platform sneakers slid in some gravel, and her mother's head jerked around.

"Damnit, London." Her mother wiped a tear away from her cheek.

"I'm sorry."

"Go back to Grandma's."

"I just wanted to check on you."

"Yeah? Is that what you're doing?" There was an exhausted smile on her face that was not meant to provide any warmth. She looked fed up to the point of delirium. "Go back to your own time. I know you're not my teenage daughter."

"Who's that?" London asked in deliberate opposition to her mother's request.

On the stone, a basic epitaph read John Parker January 8, 1967 – May 17, 1987.

Ruth stared London down and narrowed her vision. Then a look that said *I give up* swept across her face.

"He was your father."

London shook her head and let out a squeaky laugh. She looked at the stone again. Whoever's it was, he was only twenty when he died, so something wasn't adding up. "No. That's not right. I was born in December 1988."

"Yeah. You were."

London's intestines twisted into ropes and began yanking her adult mind from her childhood body. She shot up on her mother's couch and looked at her, begging for answers.

"You can ask anything you want," Ruth said, still sipping her gin and tonic. She was aware of what London had discovered. Maybe she had intentionally opened her mind to that memory, knowing her daughter could move forward from there.

"Did you know my father was going to die when you started a relationship with him?"

"I never even spoke to him until after he was already dead."

"You could Divine Travel even back then?"

"I didn't call it that. I didn't know what it was. All I knew was that if I laid down on top of someone's grave and concentrated my body could shift to another time. I know now that I was following someone else's consciousness, like a train on tracks. People leave doors open even after they are gone. Back then it was just something I did to escape."

"How long have you been able to Divine Travel?"

"Since I was fifteen."

"Do you still do it?

"No."

"Why not?"

"Because I had you."

London wasn't sure she was ready to find out how her father died or where their relationship started.

"James has seen you do it? That's what started this whole thing?"

"Yes."

"Why wait so long to tell me about him?"

"No time ever felt right. I was afraid you would think—" She paused to take a sip of her drink. "It's one thing to be a pregnant teenager. It's another thing to get pregnant by a man who I knew didn't have a future. I was afraid you would think I took something from you."

London was trying to block out the memories that were washing over her mother. A handsome young guy dressed in eighties attire. He had a big smile and hair that was dark and wavy like London's.

"I think I'm going to go."

"London, please stay."

"I'm not mad, Mom. I'm glad I know. But I think I just would rather absorb this without feeling what you feel about it. If that's okay?"

"Sure. I understand. Are you sure you're feeling well enough to go home?"

"Yeah."

Ruth hugged London for a long while and then held the door for her daughter. "Call me if you need anything."

There was nothing left to talk about. Ruth had an ability so explosive that before she could drive, she was able to transport her entire body into another time. No coaching, no chemistry, no machines, just raw, unfiltered power. And like London had around the same age, her mother made a horrible mistake. She fell for someone she couldn't have. She used her abilities to pursue her own heart's desire and time caught up with her, as it does with everyone. London felt an aching. Not for herself. She never expected a father to come walking through the door one day. Not for the man who likely never knew what he would be missing out on. But for her mother. It felt like Ruth Riley never got a single thing she desired. She always just survived. Adapted and survived. Was this all these gifts had to offer? A life of trying to correct a timeline that only ever sought to prove its inevitability?

London walked off in the direction of her apartment to throw off her mother's suspicion. Once she got out of sight from her, she turned toward Gable's building.

34

*G*able followed Dennis out of Beth's door. No one knew exactly what they were supposed to do for the "time off" James had given them.

"Where to?" Gable asked.

"Man, I'm not going anywhere." Dennis seemed exhausted. Very little of his usually jovial attitude was intact. "This place is all I've got. I'm going to spend some time analyzing these last couple of days. Shit's been moving so fast we haven't even had time to think about all the hows and whys."

"Do you think all of this is still right?"

Dennis ran a hand over his bald head. "Honestly, I don't believe in right or wrong anymore. There's just action. I'm going to keep moving forward and hope for the best."

"Good to see this hasn't robbed you of your optimism."

"Never." Dennis gave him a smile and a wave and walked off. Gable supposed he could just go to his apartment and sleep for a change. He felt like since he arrived at AION, all sense of normalcy had gone out the window. Meals were provided for him. He worked all day. And then at night he fell into bed for a few restless hours, dreaming of funerals and family and London Riley.

Sleep is no good, he thought. Instead, he walked to the kitchen. Sylvia, the AION Original who was in charge of dinner, was a bulbous Hispanic woman who reminded him of his great aunt. Her accent was thick and she smiled with her whole face, each wrinkle appearing at once.

"Hey, Mijo," she said as Gable entered. "Hungry?"

"Actually, I was wondering if I could sneak some ingredients away?"

"Oooh, handsome and he cooks? How are you not married?"

"I could marry you?" he teased.

Sylvia laughed from the center of her belly, jiggling with glee. "You stop flirting with me. What do you need?"

"Flour, salt, eggs, lemons, garlic, chicken, basil, and capers if you have it."

"You know Mama Sylvia has it all!"

She scooted away and collected all of Gable's requested items into a basket.

"Thank you," he said, grabbing the collection.

"I threw in a little white wine too… That's for cooking not for drinking, party boy?"

"No promises."

"Bad, bad," she said, giggling and waving him off.

When he got home, he went to work making a simple pasta dough. It was his mother's recipe. He hadn't made it in years, it was too simple to forget. He could picture her hands as he worked the dough with his own. He fastened the pasta maker he'd packed to his countertop. It was a small contraption and one of the few items he thought was worthy of taking with him when he left his apartment. Gable began hand-cranking the flattened dough into long noodles.

In one pan he sautéed some chicken, in another, he created the lemony sauce that would coat the pasta. For the first time since arriving, his felt focused and peaceful. Cooking and chemistry had a lot in common. Exacting measurements, appropriate application of heat, combining different elements to make a single creation that was better than the separated parts. His apartment began to fill with the smell of his childhood.

As all the components boiled and simmered, a knock came at the door.

"London."

"Hi."

"Is everything okay?"

"I think so."

She stood there, uneasy and awkward, reminding him of the shy girl he once knew her to be.

"Do you want to come in?"

"Yeah, thank you."

Surprisingly, his ease didn't disappear with her arrival. He went back to stirring and salting.

"It smells really good," she said. "What is it?"

"Chicken piccatta."

"I'm sorry, are you expecting someone? I should have asked."

"No. It's just me."

"This is a lot of work to just feed yourself."

"Cooking relaxes me."

She nodded her head and watched him as he squeezed lemons over a pan. He felt like she had something on her mind.

"Do you need any help?" she asked.

He didn't, but he showed her how to cut basil into ribbons and handed her the knife. She was clumsy with the blade, like a child who had only ever been told it was dangerous.

Their backs were turned to one another, each occupied by the meal preparations, but he felt soothed by her nearness. Gable plated the pasta, topped it with chicken, drizzled the sauce, then sprinkled the basil ribbons and parmesan cheese over the top. He cut an artistic twist of lemon to place on the side of each plate and motioned to the table.

"I don't really have anything to drink, want a water?" he asked.

"Sure."

They sat and ate in near silence, the only sound came from slurping noodles.

"This was amazing," she said.

"Thank you."

London cleared their plates and rinsed the dishes. A Phantogram album hummed in the background. He didn't want to break the bubble they were in. The quiet was nice. He wondered what she was reading inside him. Could she tell he was enjoying himself? At that thought, she smirked.

"I can't help but feel like you came here for a reason," he said.

"I needed some company. I didn't really think about it. I just walked straight here from my mother's."

"Did something happen?"

"Got some strange news."

She scoured a pot and let her words hang.

"I can't read your mind you know?"

"Reading minds isn't really what I do."

"Oh, it isn't? Well, then you're very perceptive."

She let out a soft laugh. "I can see why people would boil it down to mind reading. Sometimes it even feels like that to me. But it's actually all about feeling." She held a soapy hand to her heart. "People are just these walking piles of emotions. All day, every minute they are feeling. Sadness, joy, heartache, excitement, anger, regret. People believe they spend all day thinking, but they don't. They spend all day feeling."

"What am I feeling right now?" he asked.

"Happiness. Relief. Full."

"We did eat a lot."

Her eyes met his and a current ran through his system.

"I found out tonight that my father, who I never knew, wasn't even alive during the time of my conception." She waved her hands. "That sounds gross and weird. What I mean is, my mother Divine Traveled to the past and conceived me with someone who passed away in her present."

"Holy crap." Gable couldn't think of anything brilliant to say to soothe a revelation like that.

"It's kind of sad, I guess, but it doesn't make the reality any different. To some extent it's a relief. No better excuse for being a dead-beat dad."

He liked her dark sense of humor but wasn't sure if laughing was the right thing to do.

"That's a lot to process."

"When I found out, all I wanted to do was come here. I know that's weird. And I know that, at best, we have a complicated history. But something in me told me that this was where I needed to be. I'm sorry if I caught you off guard. I literally just showed up and dumped my life on your lap, so if you want me to go, I understand."

"You don't have to go."

She sunk into his couch and took a deep breath. He sat next to her and put on an old episode of Star Trek.

"Does this work?" he asked.

London shrugged her shoulders and tucked her knees up onto the couch. They watched the show, never touching, but connected, nonetheless. At some point he drifted off to sleep. A dreamless, deep sleep, like a child who had spent all day at the beach. When he woke in the early morning hours, London was gone.

35

The sun was cresting the horizon when London left Gable's apartment. The grounds were quiet and other than the early morning birds, there wasn't a sound for miles. She stretched her arms to the sky. Whatever that night with Gable was, it had been exactly what she needed.

Footsteps in the distance shook her from her makeshift meditation. As the person drew closer it was clear who it was. The Korean dialogue got louder as she approached. Taryn had the silver case that carried Clair in one hand and her phone in the other. By the time she saw London, she was nearly on top of her.

"Lond-y, what the hell?"

"Same to you, stranger."

"What are you doing out here?"

Taryn's eyes drew a line between London and Gable's apartment that was still only a few feet away. She frowned and waited for an answer.

"Nothing. What are you doing here?" There was no explaining that she had only fallen asleep at Gable's apartment after a night where they ate and hardly spoke.

"Looking for you, ya freak show." London rolled her eyes. Sometimes she wasn't exactly sure why Taryn said the things she did. "I need your help."

"With what?"

"Let's go to our place."

"Oh, it's still *our* place?" Taryn hadn't slept there in over a week.

"Stop being a baby."

The two women walked up to their shared domicile.

"Did you clean my shit?" Taryn asked, looking at her neatly made bed and dust-free shelves.

"I cleaned everything."

"A maid and a sorceress, how did I get so lucky to have you as my roomie?"

"Tell me what you want or I'm going to cast a spell on you." London was grateful to have playful banter with her friend. She'd missed her.

Taryn began assembling Clair. She hooked herself in and headed for London to attach her to the machine as well.

"What're you doing, T?"

"Bridge me."

"No. I'm not in the mood. I'm exhausted. We're supposed to be taking time off."

"Stop being such a whiner, it won't take that long."

"No!" London stepped back before Taryn could put the head piece on. "I don't want to."

Taryn took in a calculated breath. She was pacing the words in her mind and though London couldn't understand her, she felt Taryn was calming herself.

"London, please. I've spent years working on this. I need to feel what it's like." Taryn's shoulders slumped and she held the piece of Clair that London had just cast off as if it were a dead pet. "This thing is my whole life, and I haven't even got to experience it at its full potential." James had instituted a strict policy with Taryn that she not test the machine on herself. He told her she was too valuable to be lost in some experiment gone wrong. For whatever reason, she had agreed and listened to him until now.

London wasn't sure she had the strength to conduct another bridging test, but she hated disappointing people. And when Taryn was being vulnerable, she felt powerless to say no.

"Damnit. Where do you want to go?" London replaced the piece on her head.

Taryn took a capsule excitedly and gave one to London. "Remember the night we went to the lake with Gable and Derek?"

"Yes. Obviously. I'm not sure we should—" London started.

"Oh, don't worry, I won't change anything. I just figured it was a good memory. Kind of the last one we had together before this place. You've said shared ones are stronger."

"Fine. I'll try."

As Gable's compound began to kick in, Taryn's mind opened up fully to London in a way it never had before. Her thoughts were no longer in a foreign language, her feelings weren't buried beneath a tough, deliberate exterior. A memory began to pour into London's mind like black tar. It was dark and inescapable. No matter how hard London searched for any other memory or emotion, this one event smothered all others. Even as she tried to resist, images began to form in her head.

Taryn is hunched over a device with a screwdriver.

She was in her late teens or early twenties, London guessed.

. . .

Someone knocks at her door.
    "Go away," the younger Taryn yells.
    More knocks. And a jiggle of the doorknob.
    "Go away."

As the memory rushed in, London felt bile rise up in her mouth. Cigarettes took over her sense of smell. The memory was so vivid that London could have sworn she was in the room.

Present-day Taryn slumped over on the bed, her eyes closed and her face wrought into an agonized grimace.

"Open the door, goddamnit," the voice on the other side of the door lets out in muffled demand.
    Taryn connects two wires together and twists them.
    A key on the other side of the door turns.
    A large, but unstable figure enters the room.

London knew this man was Taryn's father, but he looked even worse than she remembered. He had an overgrown beard and his hands were covered in oily filth. London knew he was an auto mechanic, but it seemed as if he'd just given up washing away the day's residue.

"Get out of here," young Taryn demanded.
    "Who the fuck do you think you are talking to me like that?" her father asks. "I pay for the roof over this house, so I can go in whatever room I damn well please."

"I'm not going to say it again. You need to leave." She is insistent, but her voice quivers.

Her father doesn't even bother to respond this time. He simply begins undoing his belt and unzipping his pants.

As he reached a hand into his boxers in the memory, London instinctively clasped her hands over her mouth. She looked into her friend's sleeping face, begging it not to be true.

London wanted nothing to do with what came next. She couldn't turn away from it. The memory just kept invading.

London choked back the vomit in her throat.

Now younger Taryn was getting on all fours.

London couldn't imagine a version of her friend who would succumb to such horrors, but she was beginning to realize that she didn't know her at all. And this was not a place where she had any power.

As her father closed in on her from behind, Taryn's hand is wrapped around the device London saw her fidgeting with at the start of the memory. She flips a switch and the small object begins to buzz like telephone wires.

When her father gets close enough that his breath can be felt on the back of her neck, she spins around and hits him over the head with a hammer. He isn't unconscious, but the blow takes him off his feet and he begins to shout obscenities.

"Son of a bitch! You fucking whore. I'm gonna kill you for that."

His threatening distracts him, and he barely notices when she places a thick rubber band around his head. She places one similar around her own and flips a switch on her device.

Taryn screams in agony.

Her father curls into the fetal position and begins humming indecipherable sounds of sorrow. He weeps and babbles, "no, no, no, no," over and over.

Taryn rips the band off her head and flips the switch off.

She takes a few calculated steps away from him.

He remains a huddled mess on her bed. His moans get quieter and quieter as the seconds tick by.

The memory begins to turn into frantic clips.

Taryn uttering, "shit, shit, shit," as she checks his pulse.

Then they are in the hospital, London realized. The fluorescent light and the pastel patterned curtain indicate as much.

The words *"What happened here?"* kept popping up in Taryn's memory.

Then there was only blackness.

London ripped the device off her head and began shaking Taryn's shoulders.

"Taryn. Taryn? Come on wake up. Taryn!"

Taryn came to like she had just been underwater. She gasped for air and frantically looked around her for evidence that she was back.

"T. If I had known…"

"Jesus Christ. I just had to relive that night. I couldn't move. It was like I was paralyzed."

London was horrorstruck to find that her friend had traveled, but wasn't mobile. Just a frozen observer on what was likely one of the worst nights of her life.

"What the hell went wrong?"

"Taryn, I had no idea. I just started reading and it came on so strong I couldn't shake it, and then you passed out."

London wanted to be delicate about moving forward. "Why didn't you tell me?" London asked.

"I don't talk about that. And I sure as hell didn't want to relive it."

"What happened to him?"

Taryn bit at her nails and clenched her jaw. "That thing in my hand. What I used on my him... It's that." She pointed to the to the first version of Clair that was posted on her shelf. Taryn was panting like she'd just run a marathon.

"I still don't understand exactly what it did."

"In its rawest form, Clair takes one person's experiences —their thoughts, their memories, their pain, their everything —and it transmits it all into the other person. It's refined and complex now, but then, it was just raw consciousnesses pouring from one person into the other." Taryn bundled up her knees under her chin and squeezed her eyes shut.

"So when you put that band on your father—" London started

Taryn's head twitched at just the slightest reference to her father, and she cut her off. "That man was no father."

"When you put the band on him, he could feel what you felt?"

"Every fucking bit."

London tried to imagine what emotions Taryn returned to her rapist that day. Fear. Hatred. Disgust. Self-loathing. Betrayal. The kind of pain that seared you from the inside out. London had only been a bystander, and she'd felt the charge of detestation rushing through her veins.

"Did it kill him?"

"Not right away, but he never woke up again. He was in a coma for almost a year, and then his cirrhosis combined with his inactive state killed him."

"How did you end up here?"

"I told the police exactly what happened. I told them I had invented a machine that transmits one person's feelings into another and that my sick, pedophile father couldn't take the dose of his own medicine."

"And they believed you?"

"Of course not. Within twenty-four hours of my confession, James was at my side with what I'm assuming was the most expensive lawyer known to man.

"I don't know if he paid people off or used some legal crap to get me clear. Frankly, I didn't care enough to ask. We left the police station and drove straight here."

"I'm so sorry, T."

"Stop saying that. I don't need your sympathy. What I need is to clear this shit out of my head so I can actually use my own god damn invention."

"Have you tried—"

"Therapy, yes. They only know what I tell them. And honesty isn't exactly my top quality. I hoped you'd be able to reach in. Reach passed it."

"It completely overwhelmed anything else."

Taryn began to pack Clair away. She was angry, but her words had returned to Korean so London wasn't sure if the emotion was directed at her or herself.

"We're not going to talk about this day again, you understand?"

"Yes."

"I have to rethink everything."

"What do you mean?"

"Nothing, Lond-y."

As Taryn left, an image of Gable entered her memories. It was brief, but intense. London couldn't understand why, after everything, it was Gable on Taryn's mind.

*G*able couldn't fall back asleep once he was up. London was firmly placed in the front of his mind. Their night hadn't been romantic, but it was intimate. It had been a long time since he'd felt that close to someone. He decided to go get breakfast and found himself scanning the grounds for London. Instead, he ran into Taryn.

She had visible tears running down her face.

"Hey," he said. He tapped her arm to get her to look up. She dropped her case that held Clair and threw her arms around Gable. She sobbed and squeezed him. Her whole body was shaking and he didn't know what to do so he held her.

When she pulled away, she wiped her face with both hands and let out a guttural groan to push out what remained of her tears.

"Do you remember that day by the river?" she asked.

That day was impossible to forget. Gable had tested his compound dozens of times on himself, but he didn't talk to other people about his work, especially after what happened to his mother. It wasn't until he and Taryn started hanging out that he opened up to someone. He'd felt like a failure because as hard as he'd tried to make a pill that could heighten someone's positive emotions, all it ever seemed to do was give a brief euphoric lift followed by a crushing inflation of whatever negative feeling was occupying him that day. Loneliness. Disappointment. Anxiety.

What good was a compound that latched on to the parts of yourself you were trying to escape? On a particularly bad day, he poured out all his frustration to Taryn in the Riley's driveway. Endlessly fearless, she suggested they test it together. Gable began bringing a dose to their meetups, but each time they took the compound they walked away feeling dreadful. Both of them had more than enough hardship in their life and all his invention seemed to do was make it more prevalent.

On one occasion, they decided to try to create a perfect day so they could see if the compound could actually make them feel good for a change. The hope was that if their environment was flooded with positivity, the pill would enhance it.

They started the day eating breakfast at a diner. Then went and saw an over-the-top romantic comedy. Ate ice cream at a park. All the while popping some of the compound in their mouth. Every time they did it, the compound would just drive them right back into whatever abysmal emotional corner they had been trying to escape. The compound always exposed the lie that was their false attempt at happiness.

Finally, they went to the edge of a river just north of where they lived. They were feeling so awful after failing repeatedly and taking way too many doses, they could hardly speak.

"Maybe we're just too broken," Taryn said. Her shoulders drooped forward and her chest caved in.

She was probably right, he remembered thinking. Gable reached over and put his arm around her shoulders, he regretted having put her through that day.

Then the sun started to set. It was one of those brilliant, Arizona sunsets. Pink, orange, purple, blue. The colors stretched out in every direction. The air was warm, but the water on their feet was cold. Taryn put her hand on top of his. He remembered thinking it was the first time in a long time either of them had been touched in a way that was gentle and kind.

They took one more dose and then there it was. Just unending, undeniable peace.

"I remember that day," Gable answered.

"I want you to know it was one of the best days of my life," Taryn said. She stared him right in the face. He nodded, but before he could say anything she grabbed her case and walked away. While he agreed that it had ended on a good note, he didn't remember the day as pleasant. It was another day full of failures as far as he could recall. There was something sad about the fact that she enjoyed it even though they spent half the time languished by their own unpleasant thoughts.

When he got to the kitchen, the air was filled with the smell of eggs and bacon. Sylvia was wearing a hair net and deep maroon lipstick.

"Buenos dias Gable," she said with a wink.

"Buenos dias."

"Muy bien." She heaped more than enough eggs onto his plate and four pieces of bacon. "I gave you a little extra." He had apparently made a friend.

He found Dennis sitting alone at a table, a plate of food untouched in front of him. He wasn't reading or looking at his phone like everyone else who was sitting by themselves. He was simply staring out into the open desert.

"Mind if I join you?" Gable asked.

"Sure, have a seat."

Gable began to backtrack, feeling like he had imposed. "If you're busy…"

"No, don't be ridiculous. Sit."

Still, Dennis remained quiet as he forced bites of food into his mouth. Gable couldn't help but feel like there was something on his mind.

"Is everything cool?"

"Where do you plan to go?" Dennis asked.

Gable wasn't sure what he meant. "Uh, today?"

"I mean when all the bugs are worked out, and it's your turn at bat, and you get to travel to wherever you choose, where do you plan to go?"

"Still formulating, I guess."

"Bullshit. We all have something we would fix. Somewhere we would go. When we actually get this dialed in, what's your destination?"

"I guess if I was being honest, I'd try to go to the day my sister died. See if I could make it from my friend's house to home fast enough to stop what happened."

"And have you tried to plot all the changes that could then occur? It's impossible to catch them all, but surely you've considered the fallout."

"I mean, the hope would be that my mother would live. That life would be closer to normal."

"You probably wouldn't invent your compound. Wouldn't come here. The advancements we've made this week would cease to exist. Hell, you may never even have a noteworthy interaction with London," Dennis ruminated. He sipped his coffee. Gable couldn't tell if he was being manipulated or if they were just casually talking hypotheticals.

"What would you do?" Gable asked.

"Go back and buy courtside tickets to a Bulls game so I

could see Michael play up close and personal just once." Gable laughed; this was more of what he'd grown accustomed to with Dennis. But then the look on his face turned down again. "I'd fix things with my wife."

"Even if it means you don't end up here?"

"You just have to choose, Gable. No one gets to have their cake and eat it too. The luxury of time travel isn't real. We all just have to decide what we want. Whether it's in this timeline or another." This wasn't the hopeful idealist Gable was used to seeing. Dennis seemed fragmented, distant. He tried to force a smile, but it retreated before it took hold. "I'm sorry, man. Guess I'm a little down today. I'll bounce back. Maybe we all need some rest." He clapped Gable on the back with his giant hands and departed.

As Dennis's words began to sink in, Gable thought about how his two travels so far had been random and unplanned. He struggled to conceive of a world where traveling was in his control. That was almost scarier than his accidental trips. He'd have to claim full responsibility for what happened when it was his choice.

When he looked up from his plate, London was walking toward the breakfast line and Gable felt a spike in his system. She was several yards away, but all the air around him felt like it changed. As Dennis was passing by her, she reached out and grabbed his hand. They didn't speak, but he watched his friend's face change from agitated and distracted to pacified after seconds in her presence. Her effect on people was a wonder to behold.

As she walked toward him, he struggled to find a position to sit where he felt comfortable. He tried not to think of anything in particular, afraid of what signals he might be sending. Gable pondered how the sky was blue and the ground was brown and how his bacon was greasy in a desperate attempt to stay in the moment.

"I wanted to thank you," she said, setting her plate down, but not sitting. "I completely barged in on you last night and it was really nice of you to let me hang around."

"Yeah, of course. I'm glad it helped."

"Can I take you to this restaurant in Payson? As a repayment? I can't cook," she laughed. "But I'd like to return the favor, if that's alright?"

"Yeah, sure," he said.

"I'll get a car. Meet you at around seven?"

He nodded like an idiot. Happy to accept, but not sure what it all meant.

*L*ondon had never been bold enough to ask someone out on a date. She wasn't even sure if that was what she had done, but the end result was dinner with Gable. All of a sudden it was like a force not fully in her control was provoking her next moves.

She took the time to dry and curl her hair properly rather than letting the natural, frizzy ringlets fall where they chose. There was a fine line between dressing for a date and dressing for dinner with a friend or co-worker or former classmate or whatever Gable was to her. A pair of jeans and soft white blouse were neutral, she figured. She put on a gold necklace that had two coins dangling from different length chains. "One for you, and one for me," her mother had said when she gave it to her on her sixteenth birthday. They didn't always exchange gifts on special occasions. Sometimes Chinese food was all she got for Christmas. But when there was a little bit of extra money, her mother would try to find something meaningful to give her. The necklace was her favorite. It represented their life together. It had always been just the two of them.

When London neared the gates of AION, a black SUV was parked and waiting along with her mother.

"You look beautiful," she said.

"Thank you. What's this?" The large truck was not what she expected to drive.

"James hired you a driver." When Ruth looked back, the dark tinted window rolled down and a large man was sitting in the driver's seat.

"That is not a driver."

"Driver slash security."

"Why would I need a security guard?"

"I know it's a little over the top, but I have a bad feeling about tonight," Ruth admitted.

London wasn't sure if this was normal mother overprotectiveness or if Ruth was seeing something coming. Though her clairvoyance was more dialed in than London's, it still wasn't her sharpest strength.

"What is it you think will happen?"

"I don't know. I just want you to be careful."

She didn't want an armed escort to dinner, but nodded and agreed to take the ride being provided.

"Fine. Thank you."

"I love you, London."

"I love you too, Mom."

As Ruth walked away, Gable approached.

His face was shaved, and he had on a perfectly pressed shirt. The metal glasses had been replaced with his plastic ones again and his hair was combed with engineered precision.

"You like nice," he said.

"So do you."

"This is our ride?"

"Yeah, James hired us a driver." On cue, the drive exited his seat and opened the door for them.

"A driver or a secret agent?" Gable whispered. He was equally skeptical of the large muscular figure who was chauffeuring them to their destination.

The two got into the car but left a seat between them. If this was a date, London thought, it felt like the first one either of them had ever been on. She tried hard to stay out of his head and in the moment. He was trying equally hard to keep her out.

"Can I ask you something?" he asked.

"Sure."

"What was wrong with Dennis today?"

"It's his wedding anniversary. Tough day for him."

"Oh."

"See, you can 'read minds' too."

"Ha. I barely know what *I'm* thinking half the time."

"You have a kind mind. Lot of people waste time judging others and stockpiling things they can use against the ones around them. You're only really hard on yourself."

"And you?" he asked. "What are your thoughts like?"

"No one's ever asked me that before. Mine are boring. I think a lot about the future, but I have no idea what I'm going to do with it. I feel stuck a lot. Like I should be moving toward something, but I'm always on a treadmill. Walking, but going nowhere."

"Where do you think you'd be if you weren't here?"

"I don't know. I've always had this fantasy about being a painter. It would be nice to have a job that was all about feeling and sensation and observation, but had nothing to do with my abilities."

"Have you ever painted anything?"

"No." She began to laugh. "So stupid to have a dream and never even actually try it, right?"

"Well, maybe you *should* try it."

"Yeah, maybe."

They got quiet again. The drive wasn't long, but it was hard to hold a conversation without getting too personal, and London was afraid the deeper they got, the closer they'd get to talking about something difficult. His mother, traveling, Taryn, Dennis. So much heaviness. She just wanted the night to be light.

When they arrived at the restaurant, the atmosphere was lively and crowded. Brightly colored décor mixed with the smell of searing meat transported both of them. She could feel Gable relaxing, but tried to live on the outside, taking in only what her five senses could detect. He pulled out a chair for her and did something resembling a nerdy curtsy. The waiter approached and Gable ordered a pitcher of house margaritas and guacamole.

His clear comfort in this place made her feel a little sad for the Gable at AION. She couldn't help but feel like the bait that lured him into a trap. At that place he was stern and tense and agitated. Out here he looked like a normal guy on a weekend trip with his girlfriend.

The first pitcher of margaritas went down a little too easy and by the second they had fallen into comfortable banter over books and movies.

"There is absolutely no wiggle room on this," Gable insisted. "You can't say you're a Star Trek fan if you've only seen the Chris Pine movies."

"Bullshit," London said. "It doesn't matter what generation you love. If you know Kirk and Spock and Ohura, you're a Star Trek fan. End of story."

"I reject the entire premise."

"Agree to disagree."

"This is not over. We will resolve it over fried ice cream."

For a magical forty-five minutes, he was just a guy and London was just a girl. There was no weight or pressure to unlock the mysteries of the universe. They were so absorbed in each other's presence that it took a minute for either of them to realize the tone in the restaurant had shifted. The tables around them quieted down and a woman shouted.

"That's her. It's actually her." She was pointing her finger at London and getting closer to the table with each passing second. London's assigned security officer was quick to his feet and hooked the woman by the elbow. He tried to calmly coax her toward the front door of the restaurant.

"London Riley. Take me with you. Please, please!" The woman fell to her knees, slipping away from the security officer and crawling toward London now.

She hobbled toward her and was attempting to clutch her around the waist.

"Please, London. I have to go back. I have to go back. There's just one thing to fix. Just one thing and then my little Jane —" she was holding up a picture on her phone of a toddler "—I could save her. Just give me one chance."

London stood, allowing the woman to slide down to the floor again just in time for the strong-jawed guard to haul her less gently to the curb. He left her there, came back into the restaurant and threw a $100 bill on the table.

"Time to go," he said. Gable and London followed without question.

The two hopped in the vehicle, both out of breath.

"Did you know her?" Gable asked.

"No, I've never seen her in my life."

"She seemed to know you." He looked truly disturbed and London wasn't sure if she should comfort him or if he was supposed to comfort her.

"I mean, she was asking me to help her travel, right? I'm not just making that up in my head?"

"Sure seemed that way," Gable agreed.

London was baffled. "We're supposed to be anonymous. I've been there for years and nothing like that has ever happened when I went out. Sure people will shout as we leave the gate, but no one has ever called me by name."

Gable opened his phone and began typing and scrolling in a rapid pattern. He held up the bright screen to London and it took a second for her eyes to adjust. It was a news article with the headline, "Desert Cult Attempts to Discover Time Travel."

She began reading through the article that featured the last high-school photo that was ever taken of her, as well as an image that appeared to be captured by a drone. It was blurry and reminded her of a Bigfoot sighting.

There were some inconsequential bits of information about her childhood. Details about AION's history prior to James taking over. London skipped the bits that felt unimportant and then started reading out loud the sections of concern.

"'She and her mother, Ruth Riley, are believed to be two founding members of a cult that believes psychic ability is connected to time travel. Though the property is owned and operated by the rather mysterious millionaire, James Todd, he is believed to be only a funding entity. The mother-daughter duo lived in Apache Junction, Arizona for most of their lives prior to relocating to AION in 2004. Ruth Riley operated an illegal psychic readings business out of their home as their only source of income.'"

London looked at Gable, who was waiting patiently for her to continue.

"'It is believed that London claims to possess the same or similar abilities as her mother claimed she was capable of. An insider reported that many of the recruits claim to possess psychic ability.

According to our source, members use handmade machines, drugs, and psychic readings in their attempt to time travel.

Dr. Stephen Carter, a highly vocal debunker and an award-winning physicist had this to say: 'There never has been and there never will be an ability to time travel.'

Still, our insider has specifically named London Riley as a key element to the supposed breakthrough. 'She is the one. She's the one who will make it possible. There have already been a number of successful trials, and they are honing in on the finer points. Time travel is real. She's making it so.'

When the *Arizona Republic* reached out to local authorities, the sheriff had this to say of AION residents: 'They are a quiet bunch. Keep to themselves. Not a lot of traffic goes in or out of there.'

Will Arizona be home to the first time machine? Only **time** will tell.'"

The article was written in a mocking tone, but there were a shocking number of accurate statements.

"So do you think that lady read this and, what? Followed us out of there?"

"In all likelihood," the security guard answered.

"But who would report something like this?"

London flipped through the article again to see if she could find anything that would give away who betrayed her. She looked at the reporter's name: Aimes Odersall She clicked on it to find that this article was the only one Aimes had ever written. She searched the name and found no record of that person. No social media accounts, no phone book listing, no website. She stared at the name. It felt familiar, but she was certain she didn't know an Aimes.

"Holy shit," she said. "Oh, my god."

"What?" Gable asked.

"It's a word scramble. An anagram. For *Miles De La Rosa*."

"Miles wrote this?"

"Miles planted this."

a s they arrived on campus, London leapt out of the SUV before it even came to a full stop. She was moving so fast that Gable was having to jog to keep up with her.

"Are you confronting him now?" Gable asked.

"Mm-hmm."

They arrived at Miles's residence and the smell of stale popcorn wafted under the door. London pounded her fist again and again.

Finally, Miles answered. When he saw it was London, he tried to slam the door in her face, but Gable stopped it from shutting. Miles looked at him as if he were a parasite.

"What is this?" London asked, holding her phone in his face.

"I don't know," Miles responded. His hair was a mess and he had dark circles under his eyes.

"You're lying," London said. "I don't even need to read you to know that."

"Look, it wasn't my call. You got a problem, take it up

with James." He tried to close the door again, but Gable was holding steady.

"Why would James want this? Secrecy is his top priority."

"Not anymore, princess. Now that the ball is fully rolling, James needs the information to get out there. If he's going to get this to market, people have to know it actually exists. This is just the beginning. Step one in his plan to 'get the world on board.' There's articles and social media and blog posts planted all over the internet." Miles seemed crazed, and even though Gable hardly knew him, he felt pretty sure his wild rantings were accurate.

"Why me? Why name my mother and I specifically?"

Miles bit his lip.

"London, I tried to protect you. Tons of the information doesn't mention you at all. I wrote version after version and tried to leave you out of it, but he kept insisting I put you in some of the pieces. I did my best not to make it too... scathing. I'm not a total piece of shit."

"Did James say why he wanted her in the article?" Gable asked. "There're lots of people here. No one else was named."

He looked around as if he was watching for someone. Then he started to whisper. "Look, he caught wind that you were thinking about leaving. Thought maybe your mother would go after you if you did. He said you are both crucial, and that if we dragged your names through the mud you wouldn't have any options except to stay here."

"You're a fucking snake," London said, and she stormed away. Miles tossed Gable another look of disgust before slamming the door.

London was marching off in the direction of her apartment. Gable wasn't sure if he should follow or not, so he kept a safe distance while still heading toward her. When they got to the door, London struggled with her keys before letting out a scream.

"They've always told me I have a choice. That I'm not a prisoner here. That I can come and go as I please. They've always made it seem like I had freedom and chose not to exercise it."

Gable wasn't sure what to say. Her anger wasn't directed at him, but he didn't want to upset her further.

She huffed and when her door was finally open she walked in and looked around, leaving him outside. Then she returned to the door and pulled him in. She kissed him deep, but not desperately. He could feel the heat radiating off of her skin from racing around campus and confronting Miles. She was wounded and victorious, fragile and strong. For a minute, he didn't feel like an active participant in the kiss, he was so taken aback. Then as her hands dove into his hair he succumbed.

Gable grabbed her waist with both hands and lifted her off the ground. He sat her on her kitchen counter where she removed her own shirt and proceeded to take off his. There was a tattoo that danced its way up her hip and across her ribs. Flowers of some kind. He lifted her back up and they fell into bed. Was he betraying what he came here for? Was he losing himself to this mad place? Were they on a course that had been decided long before he arrived at AION? There was something inevitable about all of it. He let heartache and pleasure and confusion and certainty all mix together as they tumbled in the sheets. Any time an internal protest would arise, she'd find a way to electrify his senses back to the present.

As they fell apart, he experienced neither regret nor remorse. It was as if he had fulfilled some predestined purpose the second she was in his arms. The anger he'd felt all those years poured out and dissipated. Lying next to him was the person he'd spent years looking for, but perhaps not for the reasons he had thought.

39

*L*ondon could detect a cosmic shift in the world when she kissed Gable. It was impulsive and essential all at once. He could feel it too. Whatever it was that first brought them together, it was still in the room with them at that very moment, a force as tangible as a human being, and London could feel it all around her.

As they drifted off to sleep in each other's arms, London could see an image of Gable, older than he was now, beard grown in, sitting on a kitchen countertop she didn't recognize. Behind him there was a painting of different types of cacti, vibrant greens and pinks and purples, with a slight crescent moon hanging above them. His smile was wide. He was laughing at something outside of London's vision, but whatever it was it made her feel happy too.

When she woke in the morning, she sketched the cactus moon image as she saw it in her mind. Though she had never done much more than doodle, it came together fairly well.

"That's nice," Gable said, leaning over her shoulder. His shirtless chest grazing her arm.

"Thanks."

"Are you going to add paint?"

"I don't have any. Just pens."

He looked in her refrigerator as if he lived there. "You don't have eggs?"

"I don't think I have anything except mini cheese wheels and pickles."

He grabbed a cheese wheel and peeled the red wax off, then popped the entire thing in his mouth and smiled, cheese showing in between his teeth.

"I don't mean to put you on the spot, and I promise I am trying not to spend too much time in your head, but should we talk about what this is?" she asked. London did everything she could to play it cool, but she knew that, like her, he could feel they had started something far greater than a spontaneous romp.

She felt him reel. Not because he didn't have feelings forming too, but because any conversations around relationships made him uncomfortable.

"We don't have to talk about it right now," she said.

"No, we should talk about it. We live a quarter mile away from one another and work together every day. It would be weird not to."

His mind went to naked memories and unlit places. She felt her cheeks heat up and turned away from him.

"Maybe we should just…lay low about it. Keep it out of the lab. Not tell anyone?" London suggested.

"There will be some people who know no matter what we do." Her mother already knew before they did. Beth wasn't so good with reading in the present, but if Gable and London had a future, she would see that, if she hadn't already.

"I think we just keep it between the two of us as best as we can, and I'll try to stop our more mindful friends from spilling," she said.

Gable pulled his shirt on and shifted his feet by the door,

clearly debating whether he should kiss her goodbye or not.

London stood on her toes and kissed his cheek. "Thank you. For dinner and for backup with Miles and for…everything else."

London stayed in place after Gable left. It was their last rest day and she wasn't interested in facing the other members of AION. The idea of her mother seeing what happened the night before or running into James and being forced to confront the fact that he was holding her hostage by attaching her name to a "desert cult," was not something she wanted to deal with. She wanted to bask in the moment. Feel the joy without being reminded where she was. If she just stayed inside, where the smell of his cologne was on her pillows, it was easier to pretend life was simple.

All morning, she dosed in and out of sleep. Then a knock came at the door and she could feel his presence all around her. It wasn't what she was used to feeling. Gable had a lightness about him she could sense even through the wall. When she opened the door though, he was gone. On her doormat was a small collection of paints and paintbrushes.

She spent the afternoon coloring in her cactus sketch. With each stroke, she felt a sense of freedom she'd never known. The simple act of doing an activity only for herself felt more rebellious than confronting James or leaving AION in the night. London was beginning to decide who she would be.

It had been three months of testing and three months of quietly dating Gable Matthews. London was sure that many other members had caught on, but there was an unspoken agreement to keep quiet about it. There were enough distractions that it wasn't hard to do. Advancements were piling on at a rate that far exceeded anyone's expectations.

Taryn became something of a machine herself, often rolling out new updates multiple times a week. James had built out a living quarter attached to her workshop, and she spent little time anywhere else. On a night where London had been sleeping at Gable's, Taryn packed her belongings and moved out of their shared apartment for good. They would exchange quick greetings and be in labs together regularly, but most of what London knew about Taryn had become work related.

Clair was beginning to take on a mind of its own. The clarity with which it was able to read someone was beginning to rival the work of most psychics on campus. The display screen had gone from producing grainy, rudimentary images of what was running through a person's consciousness to unmistakable video where Taryn could actually capture a recording of someone's memory. Prototypes of Clair containing that feature were already being sold around the world to psychologists, law enforcement agencies, and neuroscientists. Further enhancements to Clair, exclusive to AION's mission, helped extend the length of a travel, stop someone mid-travel and bring them back, and even pinpoint where in time someone had gone.

Nearly everyone at AION had completed a successful mobile travel whereby they had managed to reach another time, past or future, with the ability to control their body. As of recently, all it took to travel was the exact right dosage of Gable's compound, Clair, and a technician who could help the subject focus on the memory as it displayed on the screen. Psychics were only brought in for mobile travels when the subject was enduring severe mental trauma. The machine struggled to navigate around emotionally significant wounds. Something about depression, anxiety, PTSD, and other injuries of the mind were too complex for it to navigate. Occasionally a bridge was necessary to overcome the event, but psychics, for the most part, weren't needed in that capacity anymore.

To London's knowledge, Taryn hadn't tried to travel again. If she had, she was attempting with the help of another psychic. She sometimes longed for the friendship, but Taryn had thrown herself so full-force into her work since the failed attempt to bridge that there wasn't really any time to spend together.

Psychics were now mostly used to explore Divine Travel. Since Beth's body faded in the lab that first time, it had become an obsession of James's to clear the next hurdle as fast as possible. He sat in on nearly every test, rarely speaking, but watching with hawk-like intensity. London's skin crawled when he was nearby. Selling the Clair prototypes had bought them some time and money, but he still didn't seem satisfied. James was having a harder time keeping London out, and when she caught glimpses of his memory, they were of late-night phone calls where he explained, "It's coming," "We're so close," and, "Your money has not gone to waste." Investors desperate to get their hands on what was inside the walls of AION were closing in around him. He'd promised them time travel and was expected to deliver.

Divine Travel was complicated. It was hard to do without bridging between two psychics—a draining effort for both subjects. No one without psychic ability had managed to do it, and the results were scattered at best. Beth had managed to fade away six times, but her mind was an unreliable map. It had always been in her nature to pop in and out of different times without much intention, and that continued to be her pattern with Divine Travel. Four of the six times she managed to fade away, she ended up somewhere in the future where she didn't recognize her surroundings.

As for London, she was starting to discover an eerie pattern. The first time she completed a Divine Travel was the day her Grandma Nancy passed away. Before she could even speak to her mother that day, she'd known it had happened because the spirit of her grandmother had been following her around campus. Nancy was in Gable's bathroom with London as she showered. She was next to her at breakfast. And she was standing in the corner of the Laboratory when London was testing. With Nancy's face being the last one she saw as Gable's compound took her over, London's body faded and reappeared in Ruth's childhood home. It was a decrepit little shack with paint chipping and cracks in the windows. She rushed to the bathroom and saw that it wasn't a child or a teenager staring at her in the grimy mirror. It was her twenty-six-year-old self. She could hear her Grandma Nancy's gravelly voice in the other room.

"Ruth, is that you? Ruth!"

London kept herself locked in the bathroom for the entire travel. Her grandmother gave up getting what she thought was her daughter's attention, and London faded from that time period before anyone noticed her.

Divine Travel, for London, was intricately tied to death. Spirits she witnessed around her acted as something of a guide to another time. Whenever she tried to explain it, James would boil over.

"That does nothing for the rest of us," he'd insist, trying unsuccessfully to keep his voice calm.

London would find herself spread all across time depending on who was near her. As a result, she'd begun insisting that Gable go elsewhere while she tested. His sister or his mother were still frequently nearby. She had lied to him, saying that she was too distracted by him to concentrate, but the truth was she was afraid of ending up in his childhood home.

40

*T*hings had been moving so fast, Gable hardly recognized his life before AION when he thought about it. His father's health was improving drastically and, aside from him, there was nothing to tie Gable to the person he'd been less than six months before. He and Dennis worked ten, sometimes twelve, hours a day refining and perfecting his compound. They had discovered a way to enable or disable mobile travel. Depending on the version of the compound that was given, the subject could either operate the body they traveled to or occupy it as strictly an observer. For psychics, they were still trying to dial in a dosage that supported Divine Travel without rendering the subject unconscious for hours. It was tireless work and yet Gable had never felt more invigorated.

When a day in the lab was done, he went home to London Riley. It still baffled him, but the more time they spent together, the more he came alive. She saw him in ways that went beyond her abilities. If he came home spun up from a day of failed attempts, she'd have ingredients for a meal waiting for him on the counter. She'd sit on a stool with a glass of wine and he'd disappear into mincing and seasoning. In the night, when agonizing nightmares would come for him, she'd run her hand down his face, reminding him he wasn't alone anymore. It was miraculous and horrifying to feel so interwoven with another person.

Gable walked into the lab to start another day with Dennis. He began to scrub his hands and prepare for the day.

"No need, man. I guess James has an announcement," Dennis said.

"Seriously?"

"Yeah, let's go."

The two went to the amphitheater together. London was already sitting with Beth, and in an effort to remain as discreet as possible, he stayed with Dennis rather than join her.

James appeared on stage. Lately he'd been dressed in casual clothes, but today, he was back in a suit.

"Hello, my friends," he said into a microphone. "It feels like every time we have these gatherings, we're ushering in a world we couldn't have imagined. I will try to be brief today, but I have a major announcement. As of today, we will no longer be testing on our own members. We have reached a point where each of you are far too valuable to risk a change that could occur during a travel and potentially alter our destiny."

The crowd began to protest with dissatisfied whispers amongst themselves.

"Who are we supposed to test on?" Dennis asked.

"Great question. We are going to be bringing in new subjects each week. These people have been pre-screened by Miles and one of our psychic members and have signed NDAs. It's time we expand our horizons and start seeing our creation's true potential.

"The one exception will be for those working on Divine

Travel. Since we still have a ways to go there, it only makes sense to allow those tests to proceed as planned. As for everyone else, your job now involves recording travels of these new subjects and working out any remaining bugs. Good luck."

As the crowd dispersed, Gable watched Taryn follow after James. Her fists were clenched and her jaw set forward.

London grabbed Gable by the elbow and pulled him behind a wall.

"This isn't about protecting members," she said. "He can't hold off his investors anymore. They want their chance to travel and he's run out of excuses."

"What are we supposed to do?"

"Be careful and be smart. Keep them immobile if we can. These people didn't pay to just go on a little trip. Who knows what they could change if given the chance."

"He's going to be watching."

"Just be safe, okay?" She kissed him quickly and took off toward the second lab that had been set up for Divine Travel testing only.

Gable walked back into his own lab and found Dennis pacing. Sweat was rolling down his head.

"Whoa," Gable said. "What's the matter?"

"That son of a bitch promised…" He kept pacing, then picked up a glass container and threw it across the room. It burst as it hit the wall, sending tiny shards of glass skittering around their feet.

"Jesus, promised what?"

"I guaranteed that man that I would set him up. Find him the right people, get him what he needed. He swore to me I'd get to go back when he had everything he needed. I've been careful. So fucking careful to make sure he was good. And then he closes the door?"

"Maybe this is just temporary? London said—"

"Nah," Dennis cut him off. "He never intended to give any of us the chance to really use this. Anything we did could mess up *his* plans."

Gable wasn't sure how to soothe his friend. He felt Dennis had every right to use the invention he was such an integral part of creating, but there was no saying what could happen if even one member changed something that kept them from ending up at AION.

Dennis walked out of the lab without another word, leaving Gable there alone. He began his day as he would have anyway. He wasn't sure how he felt about the announcement. Had something been taken from him too? Not a day went by that he didn't think about his sister and his mother, but his life had been occupied in a way that kept him distracted from the idea of traveling again. He supposed he always intended to use it to undo his family's tragedy, but the more fulfilled he was by his present life, the further away that intention felt. A swell of guilt consumed him and he suddenly felt panicked in a way he hadn't in months. Was he trading his real family for the new one he'd formed here? For the mission, AION, and London Riley?

Was he losing who he was?

41

*L*ondon shot up in the middle of the night. Her chest was tight and her palms sweaty. She reached her hand over to the spot next to her in bed and felt Gable's body. He was asleep, snoring faintly. The room was dark all around her. She got up to fill her glass of water. When she turned on the kitchen light, Dennis Locke was standing right in front of her. The glass slipped out of her hand and shattered on the floor, and then Dennis was gone.

Gable was in the kitchen before she could even think to start checking her feet for shards.

"What happened?"

"It's Dennis. Get your shoes. We need to go."

He didn't question her or pause. He grabbed both their shoes and was pulling pants up. She put her boots on with a long t-shirt and they rushed out the door, leaving it wide open. The two of them ran through campus, only the moonlight guiding them as them stumbled on rocks and scratched their legs on bushes.

Ruth and Siobhan were at the front gates when Gable and London arrived.

London could see their fear was directed at Dennis too.

"What's happening?" London asked.

"Dennis, Taryn, and Mallory are gone." Mallory was one of the newest psychics brought on board. She was shrewd and temperamental with nothing but contempt for authority, but she was an incredible psychic. London had struggled to bond with her and only occasionally overlapped with her during a lab.

"How do we stop them?" Gable asked.

"We don't know where they've gone. We were going to take a car and try to find them," Siobhan said.

"Why can't you just do what you do to fix things?" Gable asked her.

"I haven't been around any of them today. There are too many things going on—I can't be in every place at once. And if I wasn't there, my abilities won't send me to a place to fix it. That's why we have to get to them fast, before it happens and there's nothing I can do."

"I'm going too," Beth called, running up on them. "I know where they are."

Gable drove so fast London had to grip the door handle when he turned. Beth was up front, giving him directions to the place she'd seen in her mind as the trio's destination.

"Does James know?" London asked Ruth and Siobhan.

"No," Ruth answered. "He's gone off the rails. He will see this to the end, and it's hard to say what he'll do to make sure we get there. Let's just try to find them first."

The group pulled up on an abandoned barn with a truck parked out in front. There were lights shining inside, but no one came out at the sound of a car pulling in.

When Gable swung open the door, Taryn was seated on a stool in front of Dennis. He had the wired headpiece that attached to Clair secured to his temples. Mallory was standing over him, a flustered look on her face.

"What's going on here?" Ruth asked.

Neither Taryn nor Mallory would speak and Dennis was unconscious.

"Answer us," Siobhan insisted. London watched the look on Ruth's face go from demanding to perplexed. Just then, the same information hit London. They were both reading Mallory. Dennis had been under for two hours. He's taken way more compound than what was usually given and had told Taryn to max out the length of time he could stay. Taryn and Mallory started to panic when Clair began producing results they'd never seen before. They tried to stop the travel. Tried to read him to figure out where he'd gone when the machine could no longer locate him. But Taryn and Mallory's abilities were tapped. They couldn't reach Dennis through any of their tools, and neither, it seemed, could London.

Ruth knelt down next to Dennis and put her hands on him. She closed her eyes and the whole room went quiet. Minutes passed and nothing changed on Ruth's face, despite how anxious everyone around her was getting. Beth fell to the floor and London and Gable held her as her mind skipped out on an unsolicited travel. Beth woke before Ruth broke her concentration.

"Dennis," she screamed. She couldn't be consoled and yelled his name between tears over and over.

When Ruth's eyes opened, hers were filled with tears too. She glared at Mallory and Taryn.

"He went back to make amends with his wife," she told the group. "To change what happened so he could be with his family. There were so many layers of heartache that he couldn't do it with the usual procedure. He upped the dosage, demanded that Taryn push Clair to the brink, and brought Mallory for the extra nudge. It worked. He went. And was able to tell his wife he loved her and hug his son.

But it was too much. The mind can't handle being forced that quickly and that far. He's gone."

"What do you mean gone?" It was the first thing Taryn had said since everyone arrived.

"He's dead Taryn," Siobhan said.

"Well fix it! One of you travel and go get him," she demanded.

"It doesn't work like that," Ruth insisted. She turned to Siobhan. "Call James. He'll figure out what to do with them." Ruth began walking away as if everything was resolved.

Gable chased after Ruth and London followed.

"What do you mean it doesn't work like that?" Gable asked her. His heart was shattered at the loss of his friend.

Ruth's eyes were blazing, but she softened her face as Gable began to come apart.

"Dennis went back to change something in the past. He tried to start a new timeline that led him away from here. When Taryn and Mallory tried to pull him back, he was suspended between two realities. The person we knew as Dennis...his mind dropped into the stream, Gable, and got washed away. That—" she pointed to the barn where Dennis's lifeless body lay still "—is nothing but a shell anymore.".

London watched as Gable stormed off to the edge of the barn's property, where a wooden fence was crumbling. He shouted, "Fuck!" as loud as he could into the tree line. Siobhan had Beth's arm slung over her shoulders. Beth's feet barely stepped as she tried to get back to the car. Ruth turned to London.

"Get him back," she said. "And stay close to him. I'm going to stay here until James arrives."

"What's going to happen?" London asked.

"I wish I knew." Ruth must have been experiencing what

London was. So much heartache and fear and anger and confusion were swirling around it was hard to focus or grab on to any details. All she knew for sure was that Dennis was gone and none of them would ever be the same.

It was still night when they got back home. The grounds were quiet and a coyote could be heard yipping in the distance. Gable and London brought Beth to his apartment and laid her down on the couch. She pulled a blanket over herself and closed her eyes. Whether she was traveling or just trying to sleep, it was hard to tell.

Gable grabbed a bottle of whiskey from a cabinet, poured the amber liquid into a glass and threw it back. He held out the bottle to London, but she shook her head. He poured another glass for himself and swallowed it down in a single gulp.

"What can I do?" London asked. Obviously, she was reading every word that ran through his mind. Every sour, poisonous emotion that was filling him up.

"You can stay out of my head."

She nodded.

"You know what this is, don't you?" he asked her but didn't expect a response. "It's me. I'm a fucking disease. Everyone around me drops dead."

"That's not true." Her voice was strong even though her head hung in front of her chest.

"Oh, really? Well, then maybe it's me and you. We're like the two horseman of the god damn apocalypse."

"Dennis made a choice."

"Dennis took *my* compound and used a machine that was modeled off of *your* abilities, and it killed him."

London gave him a deadpan look. She could be thinking anything right now and he had no clue what it was. It didn't matter. Nothing could stop himself from saying all the ugly things in his heart.

"I should have just done what I could when I had the chance."

"And what is that?" she asked unflinching.

"I should have saved my sister as soon as I had the opportunity. Then I wouldn't even fucking be here."

"Is that what you want?" London was neither challenging him nor soothing him. Only asking point-blank questions.

"Trust me, you'd be better off. Just watch, you'll end up dead next if I stick around."

She stood up and walked over to him. They didn't make contact, but she stood only an inch away. Her face was like stone, but the smell of coconut in her hair almost brought him to his knees.

"If that's what you really want, I'll help you get there. Safely. Sleep on it and tell me in the morning." The door closed behind her and he burst into tears.

43

*I*n the morning, everything had changed for London, but AION felt utterly unaffected. Clouds rolled in and the wind whipped London's hair across her face. There was no call for an announcement from James. The AION Originals carried on with their usual chores. London searched for her mother's presence, but it was also conspicuously absent. London went to Taryn's shop and she was there, digging through her toolbox, Clair splayed open and in pieces on the table.

She looked up at London, but didn't say anything.

"What are you doing?" London asked.

"My job." A foreign language screamed in agony inside Taryn, and London could feel every bit of the pain that was filling her up, but her surface was calm as an untouched pond.

"Don't you think everyone should take a break from this right now?"

"Why would I do that?" Taryn shot back.

"Because you killed a man last night." Taryn slammed the wrench in her hand down on the table.

"I didn't kill anyone. Imperfect science killed him. I have to fucking fix this so no one else gets hurt."

"Or maybe we should just stop. Maybe this was never meant to be something the world had access to. More people could die or disappear or cease to exist."

"So that would be it then? Only a select few chosen ones get the chance to fix their mistakes and perfect their lives and the rest of us are just left with whatever shit circumstances we're dealt?"

"I don't think anyone gets a perfect life, no matter what they can do."

"That's real easy for you to say."

London didn't come here to fight with Taryn. She wanted to check on her, but there was no telling her that now. Her mind was made up and she was sticking to the course no matter what London said.

"Goodbye, T." London left the workshop with one destination in mind.

As she walked toward Gable's apartment, London caught sight of a pink wheelchair disappearing behind a building. She ran to catch up with Beth.

Beth's eyes were red and, though no tears were spilling out, she sobbed and gasped.

London didn't have any words for anyone. No one was okay. No one knew what to say or feel. She sat on a bench and pulled Beth up right next to her. Beth leaned her head on London's shoulder and placed her hand on her leg. She was as close to a little sister as London had ever had, and all she wanted to do was comfort her, but she needed someone to talk to.

"I told Gable I would help him travel to save his sister if that's what he wanted."

Beth shot up. "You can't do that."

"I know I could get him there without putting him in the place Dennis was in. Then he'd never have to come here. Maybe Dennis would even still be alive without all of Gable's advancements. James wouldn't be anywhere near where he's at now and maybe this would all just fall apart. And no one would have to get hurt."

"London, you can't do that."

"Why not? At a minimum a little girl and her mother wouldn't have to die. Gable's life would be better."

"You don't know that his life would be better."

"Well, it isn't good now."

Beth's face turned serious. "I have to tell you something I've seen."

"If Gable wants to go, I'm going to let him."

"He doesn't have all the information. Neither of you do!" Now Beth was yelling and standing. She wobbled on her feet, but London was beginning to see a picture form in Beth's mind. One where London's belly rounded and her feet swelled. One where Gable held a small bundle in a pink blanket. One where London brushed a plump cheek with the back of her index finger.

"You see?"

"When is this?" London asked.

"I'm not entirely sure. Sooner than later. I bought this when I saw it a week ago." Beth pulled out a pregnancy test from her backpack.

London began to breathe in and out in rapid succession. She was getting lightheaded. Beth placed a hand on her knee.

"There's nothing wrong with just taking things one moment at a time."

44

*G*able felt his head was going to explode. In bed with him was an empty bottle of bourbon. Some of it had spilled on his sheets, leaving an oaky, pungent stain. As memories of the night before came rushing in, he broke into cold sweats and his mouth filled with saliva. He turned on a cold shower and let the stream run down his head and over his body.

As he toweled off, feeling only moderately better, he was startled to find London on his couch. So many of the things he'd said to her were awful, but not actually untrue. He wasn't sure if he should apologize and take it all back or leave everything on the table.

"Have you decided?" London asked

"We should probably talk."

"I told you to have an answer for me. Are you traveling or not?" The same stoic look he vaguely remembered from the night before was still there. She didn't seem angry, just resolute.

"What would you do?"

"This isn't for me to decide. You have to make the choice. I'm not going to be the reason you don't try to help them."

Gable wanted to hold her. To kiss her. To bury his face into her neck. But he was afraid if he did that, he wouldn't be able to decide what he knew in his heart needed to be done.

"I'm going to try."

"I understand," she said.

"Can I ask something of you?"

"What?"

"Bridge with me. Come to that day too. If we're there together, then we'll both remember the original timeline and we can find each other again. If I go alone, everything could change and you would never know."

"We can only go back to the same day together if we have a shared memory. I'm sorry, Gable, but I don't remember that day. I remember the news reports about Abigail and a plaque being put up at school, but I don't have any memory of the actual day. If you go, you have to go alone."

"I promise, I will do everything in my power to make sure we still find each other." His heart couldn't take the thought of losing her. He had to find a way to make both worlds possible.

Her face finally softened and she looked up to the ceiling.

"Try not to forget me."

London had brought one of the copies of Clair with her—there were now multiple machines being used around AION. He didn't ask how she'd managed to get it out of Taryn's shop. Had she asked her for it? Had she stolen it? He supposed it didn't matter.

She hooked him up as they'd seen Taryn and the other technicians do on a number of occasions. He took a capsule and she took one too. "For good measure. Just so I can see as clearly as possible," she said. Her voice trembled, but not once did she try to stop him.

London let out a heavy breath.

"I need you to think about that day. Try your best to clear out the moments after you found out about Abby. You don't want to get there too late. Where were you before you got the news?"

"I was over at a Derek's house after school."

"What were you doing?"

"Watching Teenage Mutant Ninja Turtles."

London let out a chuckle and as Gable rolled into the euphoric state, his concentration broke for a moment. "I love you," he said.

She nodded. "Me too." Then swept her hands down his face to shut his eyes.

"Can you remember which movie it was?"

"Yeah."

"Where were you guys sitting?"

"In bean bag chairs."

Gable jolted like he was waking up after accidentally dosing off. He was wearing scuffed black and white sneakers and had dirt under his nails. His eleven-year-old best friend Derek was laughing at the screen, a mouthful of pizza on display. Gable started looking around for a phone, only to quickly realize he was too young to have a cell phone and it was still about five years before they went mainstream for adults.

"What time is it?" Gable asked.

"I don't know," Derek said, stuffing his mouth again.

"I gotta go."

"Wait, what?"

Gable ran down the stairs and out the front door. He

looked back and forth up the street trying to remember how to get out of Derek's neighborhood and on to the main road. He took off to the right and wove through parks and front yards until he was on the road that would lead him home. His chest thumped and his throat burned, but he didn't stop even once. He got to an intersection where the pedestrian sign was counting down and raced into the crosswalk. A driver turning left slammed on his breaks and stopped just inches shy of killing Gable. The horn honked and peopled yelled out their windows for him to get out of the street.

He made it to the other side and placed his hands on his knees, panting and shaking all over his body. Hysteria began to take over as he realized he almost just cost his parents both of their kids on the same day. He coughed and spit before picking up his sprint again.

As he rounded the corner to the street he grew up on, his heart sank. An ambulance and firefighters were already parked outside his house. No one was out front yet, but if the emergency crews were there, it meant he was too late. Not only that, but he had just delivered his preteen self to the scene immediately following his sister's death, something he never had to see the first time.

A twist and a yank to his stomach and his mind was back in the present. He kept his eyes closed as a new memory of watching them wheel Abby out came in. Though not much else had changed, it felt like it was a cruel punishment for failing.

London was stroking his hair. Her nails grazing his scalp. He focused on the sensation before rolling over into her. She pulled him in tight but didn't ask any questions. She already knew what happened and knew that all he needed was for her to be there.

After a glass of water and a few moments, she broke the silence.

"Did you want to try again? Aim for earlier?"

"I don't remember anything else specific from that day. I almost died, trying to save my sister. How is anyone supposed to use this without making things worse?"

She stared at him, a tight-lipped expression on her face. It had been her point all along. There wasn't right or wrong, better or worse. Just choices we all have to make.

"I have to tell you something," she said.

BOOK THREE

45

*C*offee was brewing. Pancakes were rising on the electric griddle. A tiny giggle echoed in the kitchen as a wild-haired toddler and her dad conspired to wake Mom from a late Sunday morning sleep. London kept her eyes closed against the morning sun, but couldn't suppress her grin as scheming little snickers filled the bedroom.

Tiny feet stuck to the wood floors and squeaked as their pace quickened.

"Mommy!"

Small hands squished into London's cheeks as her daughter pulled her mother's face into her own.

"Mommy, let's get up!"

This had become Marley's trademark request since she'd turned three and decided the whole house should be on toddler time. Gable was typically the first one up and could hold her off for forty-five minutes, maybe an hour if he agreed to put on *Harry Potter* for what felt like the thousandth time.

London pulled Marley under the sheets and rubbed noses with her child.

"But I don't want to get up," London whined playfully.

"Come on, Mommy. Let's get uuuuuuup." Marley tried to fake tears by sucking in exasperated air.

"Did you make Mommy coffee?"

"Yep. Come on."

London plopped the toddler onto her hip and carried her into the kitchen. Her waist had become a permanent saddle for the tiny jockey who demanded a ride into each room.

Gable was plopping blueberries into runny pancake batter.

"Morning," he said, and pushed the coffee creamer in her direction. Behind him was the framed cactus painting she'd created after their first night together.

London kissed his cheek and stole two blueberries from the carton in front of him. She popped one in her mouth and handed the other to Marley, who greedily inhaled the little treat.

"That will cost you two. I'm removing one blueberry from each of your pancakes," Gable said. He didn't crack a smile, but his girls knew it was a joke anyway.

Marley squirmed out of London's arms and back onto the couch. She held a blanket in one hand and sucked on two fingers from her other hand.

"Mars, hands out your mouth," London scolded. "You gotta make sure you catch her when she's doing it," London instructed Gable. They'd had this conversation about their daughter's slobbery habit more times than either of them could count.

"You staying in today?" Gable asked.

"I wish. I only have one appointment. It's at ten. Shouldn't take too long."

"W we have Liam's birthday party at noon."

"I'll be done by then. Need me to pick up a gift?"

"No, I'm just going to give him that drum set Marley got

from my dad for Christmas that we hid in her closet," Gable said.

"Savage. I like it," London said with a wink.

London took her coffee and her phone onto the back patio. Summer was close, but enough of spring still lingered that she could catch some crisp Arizona air in the morning. Desert citrus blooms made the breeze sweet, but tickled her throat.

She checked her calendar to make sure she hadn't just lied to Gable about her schedule. Just the one appointment, her calendar confirmed.

She opened the News app on her phone and tried to find anything worth reading that didn't involve James Todd or the work they'd done at AION.

When Gable and London decided to leave after she told him she was pregnant, James let them go without a fight. He'd dwindled the bulk of the members down to just six: Taryn, Mallory, Miles, a chemist that had trained under Gable, Siobhan and himself. He owned everything that had been produced within the community and, after the incident with Dennis, he decided not to take any more risks.

The public version of Clair that had been released before they left was already making its mark on the world. Memories were being captured that helped solve violent crimes and provided therapists with tools to truly help patients. A commercial version was also released that allowed people to record and capture happy memories to save as keepsakes for future generations. It was unprecedented technology, and at the time, most of the world didn't know it held any purpose beyond memory retrieval.

A year later, a new vitamin elixir hit the market that was intended to help users become more enlightened to their own state of being. Paired with a big push from the personal growth industry, a version of Gable's compound started to go mainstream.

London would obsessively read articles linked to AION and the products she knew were connected to their time there. She was glad to be free of the place and most the people, but she couldn't stop following the breadcrumbs it left behind. Gable told her she had Stockholm Syndrome. She told herself she was just keeping tabs.

Conspiracy theory forums talked about AION in terms of time travel from the beginning. She couldn't help but wonder how many of the threads had been started by Miles. More mainstream media viewed the releases of Clair and Gable's compound as miracle cures for some of society's top problems. By the time the combination of Gable's compound and Taryn's machine was introduced as a means for transporting consciousness, consumers had grown used to the idea of toying with their memories and manipulating their emotional state.

James's company, JT Enterprises, was among the top companies in the world. He rubbed elbows with billionaire CEOs and made a name for himself as the "Godfather of Consciousness." The same way Facebook made sharing your whole life with the world popular, James made exploring your consciousness commonplace. He never called it time travel. Instead, he referred to his centers that offered the procedures as Consciousness Exploration Clinics, where people could go and pay upwards of five thousand dollars per trip to relive moments of their life. The cost depended on how far back someone wanted to go and how long they wished to stay.

Some people used it as recreation. They'd go back to relive a vacation or feel what it was like to be a child again. Others used it for healing. Reliving moments spent with a lost loved one or processing trauma through immersion. It was the new white-collar adventure and everyone who could afford it, did it. Hundreds of thousands of personal accounts of travels flooded the Internet. James couldn't have bought that kind of PR. What the thousands of users didn't know was that they only had access to the version of the compound that kept consciousness explorers immobile.

The version that allowed for actual change and mobile travel was kept underground. An elite program for only the exceptionally wealthy and worthy. She discovered this when after two and a half years of barely making it outside AION, James came to her with an offer.

When the Consciousness Exploration Clinics, or CECs, first appeared—each with the words *You Own Your Past* emblazoned on the front of the building—the public was skeptical. They were sterile, small spaces that contained four pods for travelers. Each clinic employed a medic to administer Gable's compound and monitor vitals, a technician to operate Taryn's machine and an on-site pyschic, who had been rebranded and given the title "Travel Guide." None of the CEC visitors knew that psychic activity had been involved in the device they were about to be strapped into.

"His lack of creativity baffles the mind," Gable said as they watched the first TV commercial from their living room couch announcing the clinics' open date. James himself appeared on-screen in the broadcast that aired during the Super Bowl.

"For decades, it has been my passion to explore the bounds of consciousness," James said while music that sounded like it belonged in a Twilight Zone episode played. "Finally, that passion has paid off, and now I want to share it with all of you.

"This isn't a joke or a scam. This is real. Humans are able to visit different points in their life and view those moments with extreme clarity. Your mind is navigable terrain, and whether you wish to view a cherished memory or resolve a mystery that has haunted you for years, you now have that chance to see your life again through your own eyes."

That brief infomercial spread like wildfire, and people began sleeping outside the clinics for months hoping to get in. Since people were contained to just seeing their own past, regulators had a hard time shutting the clinics down. James had obtained or purchased FDA approval for the compound. His employees went through rigorous background checks. And a trained medical professional was on site at all times. Whenever he was taken to court, his team of lawyers shut down the opposition during very publicly held trials. His ironclad patents combined with his very broadcasted lifestyle made him hard to touch.

London and Gable watched on as the world debated if these clinics were legitimate. Throngs of reporters went undercover to trap the operation in a lie. Eventually though, news stations had to admit what Gable and London already knew to be true, which was that with a pill and a machine, humans could explore their memories to no end. Clair underwent several updates from the last version they knew, eventually leading to a point where the subject didn't even need to concentrate on a memory to relocate to it. Clair could find a memory if given a date or date range to work with. People who were willing to pay could browse their history and choose where to go.

What they didn't know is that the very technology they were using had world-changing capabilities that went far beyond a trip down memory lane. London learned that James kept mobile travel extremely secretive in order to keep it out of the hands of governments and terrorist organizations that would "throw the world into chaos." He handselected who had access to the mobile version. It wasn't just about price, though—which was astronomical—it was also about whom he deemed worthy. He couldn't decide that alone, so he sought his original psychic members for help.

Anyone eligible for the opportunity had to go to Beth to be screened. If their intent ended in calamity, she would see it and end their application there. Then there were those who had been accepted, but were deeply struggling to achieve a mobile travel due to trauma. Those clients went to London.

She and Gable fought about it for weeks before she accepted the offer. They needed the money, and what James proposed as an annual salary was more than either could earn in a decade combined. London argued that with or without her, the ability to travel was still out there. Ruth had no opinion. She shrugged her shoulders and said "Do what you must." while tickling Marley's sides as she sat cross-legged on the floor. Grandma suited her better than any other role London had ever seen her in. She lived nearby in an apartment, worked as an assistant at a doctor's office and tended a garden on her patio. She almost never spoke of James or AION anymore. She acted as if it never existed, brushing off most conversations London brought up about their time there.

So, with no pushback from her mother and Gable's feigning willingness to fight, London reluctantly joined JT Enterprises and had been meeting with mobile travel clients for the last six months, helping them navigate the pitfalls of their past so they could take a trip they'd paid an undisclosed amount for.

While she waited for pancakes to be ready, London read through her notes for the day's appointment.

Age: 47
    Name: Josh Anders

Number of attempts to travel: 6

History: Former U.S. Marine. Retired nine years. Widower. One child, boy, age 17.

Mental Health History: PTSD and depression

Purpose for travel: Wife's death.

Unintended Travel Destination(s): Afghanistan, Iraq, Camp Pendleton

"Do you want Nutella or syrup?" Gable called from inside.

"Both."

"Can't afford that," he joked.

She giggled and skimmed her notes one more time.

The gated community, the luxury preschool, the upgraded kitchen—all of it was bought and paid for by James Todd. The work actually turned out to be quite gratifying, to London's surprise. Working with people whose emotional baggage prevented them from traveling was not that different from what she'd been exploring at AION. Her innate ability to connect what someone was feeling to the memory it originated from was a puzzle that a lot of people wanted solved.

She would tinker around with someone's fears and sadness and joy and anger until she could get their mind to move fluidly through their individual history.

It was ironic, perhaps only to her, that she was making a living giving readings just as Ruth had. She liked to think that her mother also saw the humor in all that this ability had come to afford her daughter. They never talked about the work. They just pretended like the world hadn't changed at all.

"Babe, you're going to be late," Gable called.

46

*I*f five years ago, when he'd first arrived at AION, someone told Gable he'd be married with a daughter and that his wife would be London Riley, he would have never believed it.

Gable hadn't even been sure he wanted children. He felt certain he didn't have an adequate childhood that leant itself to solid parenting. And yet, he'd taken to it quite naturally.

London's pregnancy, while shocking, went smoothly. He read books, researched OB/GYN's and took a liking to the science of creating life.

When that life turned out to be a thing that his heart could hardly stand to behold, he found himself more bewildered by that bond than by any equation that had ever been laid before him. An unsolvable problem would usually spiral him into a research-filled stupor, but the problem of "How can you love something so deeply and infinitely whom you've just met?" was his favorite incalculable equation.

The older she got, the more fascinated he was by Marley's little quirks. Her lip tucked into her teeth when she smiled, just like her mom's. Her brow crinkled when she tried to figure something out, like Gable's father. These tiny shadows of the people she came from would appear in her face or in her words, and yet she was wholly her own person.

Gable grabbed a pair of socks from a laundry basket and wrestled his little girl into them.

"Daddy, no!"

"You have to wear shoes to the party."

"Those ones give me stinky feet," she squealed.

"All of your shoes give you stinky feet because you put your stinky little feet in them."

He tickled the bottom of one foot while she screamed with joy and tried to escape.

Gable still had serious scientific thoughts about complicated matters. Especially since James Todd hit the Go button and released his compound into the world. But there was something really soothing about falling completely into the role of fatherhood. His important work had become making sure this one human stayed alive and also turned into someone who other humans might one day want to be around. That was a monumentally imperative job and, though it felt off from how he'd pictured his thirties, there was a rightness about this life he couldn't argue.

Gable loaded Marley into her car seat, clicking each buckle into place and positioning the chest piece right on her breastbone. As they drove, they listened to Marley's playlist of songs—mostly Foo Fighters and Incubus. Another perk of parenthood, Gable had found, was that you got to shape whatever it was your children perceived as cool. Sure, she'd probably enjoy Disney soundtracks, but rock was what Dad liked, so rock was what she liked.

She sang the chorus to "Drive" wrong as he made his way to her preschool friend's home for an afternoon filled with cake and screaming.

"Is Mommy coming to the party?" Marley asked.

"She's going to try if she can finish up at work in time."

"I wish she was here now. Her car is better."

"Yeah, it is," he conceded.

He accepted the fact that James Todd paid for the roof he lived under, the food on his table, and the clothes on his child. He couldn't muster letting him buy his car though.

So instead of upgrading to a Lexus like London, he kept the Honda Civic he had driven to the hospital when they had Marley.

Gable didn't have any hold ups about his wife making the household income, but he still wasn't sure it was smart for them to have their names tied to James Todd.

As a condition of joining AION, the extent to which Gable and London were originally involved was never disclosed to the public. As far as most people knew, James was tinkering in a lab all those years, concocting the psychological, chemical, and mechanical factors that made travel possible. In a way, Gable was grateful not to have any notoriety around his involvement. A lot of people were skeptical about its introduction into the world. Some people were downright enraged by it.

When sixty-three members of a radical religious organization committed suicide because, they claimed, "mind travel" was the beginning of the end of the world, he was so glad not to be the one with cameras and microphones in his face. When two teenagers overdosed on a poor imitation of his compound, he felt a pang of guilt. Only a small group of people knew where the source of that drug originated, but all of them were bound by NDAs. Most of them had disappeared back into the regular world. Beth was a regular staple at their house. James had his council of five AION members leading teams. And most others simply fell by the wayside.

Not everything that came out of AION was negative. Gable listened to a podcast that interviewed travelers about how their experience helped them improve the world through revisiting the past. He heard stories about siblings finding each other after being separated as kids because they could retrieve the name of the social worker who had placed them in different foster homes. Or about people with Alzheimer's who took regular trips and began recuperating.

Like any major discovery, there was good and bad that came out of the release of AION's secrets. At least that was what London continuously reminded him. As was often the case, she had a neutral policy regarding James's decision to go public, meanwhile Gable spent a week in an anxious "what if" spiral after they'd watched the Super Bowl infomercial.

London taking the job had been a hard pill for Gable to swallow.

That was the second worst fight of their relationship.

The first was when Gable asked London if she thought they should give their child up for adoption. In a moment of weakness, when he felt his scientific future crumbling beneath his feet, he offered a tidy solution to what, at the time, seemed like the biggest problem he'd ever faced. She shoved his chest and said she would happily do this without him. He had never been more grateful for her instinctive ability to know when to push him, either physically or emotionally, than he was when he met his daughter.

Despite their history of London being right and Gable being less right more often, he still bucked against the idea of her working for James again.

"This thing will blow up in his face eventually, and you don't want to be on his list of paid employees when it does," Gable had insisted.

"I'm not afraid of the public. I want to help people. And we need the money."

That was a hard point to argue as they fanned themselves

with Chinese food menus because their air conditioning unit was broken again.

"It sounds like messy work," Gable pushed. "These people could be people who are severely mentally ill. I'm not sure that's the kind of environment I want the mother of my child working in."

At that generalization, she'd gently put a hand on his cheek and pressed her nose into his.

"We're all broken people, Gable—" she kissed his lips "—before we seek repair."

Sometimes he wondered if she read books of proverbs or if reading people all the time was what made her so profound. Either way, those were the last words they had on the subject. She went to work in a stylish downtown suite the following Monday.

Gable had to admit she seemed happy doing the work she was doing. London would come home from the office and her eyes would be on fire and her words were breathy from excitement.

"How was your day?" he'd ask out of domestic obligation.

"Amazing. I finally got Amanda to her destination. All she wanted in the world was to hug her mother again, but she just kept ending up in the time after her death. Or what was even stranger, a time where her mother was alive, but she wasn't physically with her in the period where she would arrive. It took us seven sessions of readings and talking and traveling. We finally figured out that she wasn't scared to see her mother. She was scared that her mother would be disappointed in how she turned out. The poor thing has debilitating anxiety," she explained as Gable poured her a glass of wine. She clinked her glass against his in a habitual cheers. "So we focused on a memory where her mother was proud of her. A dance recital. And boom, she went straight to it and got to hold her mom again."

"That sounds great, babe," Gable said.

And it really did. All these stories of delivering people to places they wanted to go by unlocking the trigger in their memories and emotions—it sounded great. He had no jealousy around her income or her fulfillment. At least, he didn't think he did. Still, he couldn't shake the feeling that something bad was going to come of all of this.

"You're just a person who's always waiting for the other shoe to drop," she scolded him.

She was probably right.

A text came into his phone.

Running a little long. I don't think I'll make it to Liam's.

"Just you and me today, kiddo," he said to his daughter

"Okay, daddy," Marley said.

---

47

*I*n London's plush, mid-century modern office, Josh Anders looked like a hand grenade in a field of daisies. His shoulders were square. His face darkened by the shadow of a beard that was cropping up on his cheeks. His legs tapped anxiously as he searched for vocabulary to define feelings he couldn't visualize.

This was the third appointment with the marine. All he wanted was to try to visit his wife before cancer ravaged her body and robbed her of her faculties, but after over a dozen travels he wasn't able to reach her in any memory he attempted to conjure up. When she read him, she learned that he'd taken out a second mortgage on his home to afford what JT Enterprises offered.

"I just want to remember her like she was, not like how she ended up. If I could visit her there a couple of times a year, I would stop dreaming of her in that god damn hospital bed," Josh insisted.

"Too often, it's less about where you want to go and more about where your mind feels you need to go."

"Well, I can sure as hell tell you it doesn't need to go back to the Middle East. That's the last place I want to be."

London could feel his insides churning up into a dusty windstorm. She tried to tow the line between fortuneteller and therapist, of which she was neither. A memory kept firing to the surface of Josh's emotional rampage. This man had experienced more than London felt she could ever absorb, but something was starting to find its way to the top of the pile. Something always did.

"Your father," London interrupted Josh mid speech. "What was the line your father used to say?"

"What?"

"Is there something your dad, maybe your grandfather, used to say to you? Like a mantra or a catchphrase? Something about protection?"

Josh gnashed his teeth.

"If you can't protect it, you can't possess it," he finally muttered out.

London let silence fill the room. There's nothing more powerful than the empty ring of a quiet space.

"I don't think I could have protected my wife from her illness," Josh starts explaining. "And she was never a possession."

"You've been saving people all your life, though. It's really unfair to have someone you love taken away and be powerless to stop it."

He nodded his head and jammed his fingers into his eye sockets to stop the flood of tears from coming.

"Did something ever happen where you did have to protect her?" London asked.

He racked his brain for a moment, then started telling a story.

"We went to a bar to celebrate a buddy's birthday once. She was pregnant. The place was pretty sketchy, but she wanted to go. She looked so silly. She had this giant pink dress on. It was the only thing her belly was fitting in anymore. Some cowboy type came up and sucker punched my friend and a fight broke out. I've never been one to run away from a fight. Usually I'm the one to start them, actually. Something switched in me that night, though. I turned to her and covered her with my whole body and shuffled her toward the door before anyone could come near her. I don't know if I protected her from anything. But I just remember that night feeling like I'd done right by her. I felt like I'd turned a corner and that maybe I wasn't actually going to be a total piece of shit husband."

London smiled. She could see the edges of that memory taking its place at the top of Josh's emotional pile. She handed him the compound. An assistant came in and placed a band around his head that was connected to a machine. An evolved version of the last one she'd seen Taryn operating. It was made from a reflective metal with blue lights that made the whole thing glow. London suspected these were just frills James added to make it look more futuristic.

"Josh," London said. "I want you to picture Emily's pink dress. Just her dress. The way it hugged her hips. The way her swollen belly showed through the material. Just think about that dress."

His eyes closed and she watched him leave. London stood next to the technician and an arrow moved along a timeline. It stopped moving when it landed on May 18, 2011.

The tech looked at her with an inquisitive eye.

"He was aiming for a time between 2006 and 2018. Hopefully he got to the right place," London said with a reserved grin. She stepped out of her office and let the large man burrow into her sofa. His eyes danced behind their lids as they opened in another year.

It took longer than she'd hoped for him to go down.

There was no way she would make it to Marley's birthday party so she sent her husband a text. Gable wouldn't be mad. He was never mad at a chance to spend time with his girl. She still felt a pang of guilt for being away on a Sunday, but this job kept odd hours.

The receptionist who occupied the desk in the main lobby approached her with a coffee in hand. It was exactly to her liking. Two vanilla creamers, one sugar. Too sweet for most, but thinking of the hot burst of candy-flavored liquid made London smile.

"Here you are, Mrs. Matthews."

"Thank you, Willow."

Willow had exceedingly long fake eyelashes that stood out on her otherwise plain and freckled face. "No problem whatsoever." She said everything with overexaggerated enthusiasm, as if London had anything to do with the hiring, promotion, or pay raises of people James Todd staffed. "I took a phone call from a woman who was desperate to get in and see you today, even though she has an appointment for tomorrow at nine. I fibbed and told her that you weren't going to be in until Monday.

London looked at her watch. The party was just starting and she had at least an hour and a half before Josh would wake up. If she took one more appointment today she wouldn't have to come in until noon the next day.

"That's fine, actually. Why don't you call her and see if she can be here by one."

"Alrighty. No problem," Willow said and bounded off back toward her desk.

London sent Gable another text.

Going to squeeze in another session today so I can stay home longer with you guys tomorrow. How's the party?

He responded quickly.

Your daughter has cake from nose to knees. She got that

from you.

London chuckled at an image Gable sent of Marley licking frosting off the back of her elbow.

What a mess, she responded. *I love you guys too much. I'll see you tonight.*

We love you too much, he said back with a heart emoji.

She looked at the picture one more time and went back to her office to look over the notes for her next appointment, who would be arriving shortly, Willow informed her. Since this was a new client, London only had the information that was required when filling out the automated form online.

Age: 30
Name: Lisa Green
Number of attempts to travel: 97

London did a double take at the number of attempts. *That can't be right,* she thought. Travel hadn't been around for a whole year, so at that rate, this person would have had to try multiple times a week. Not to mention the expense would be exorbitant.

She read on.

History: Mechanic. No spouse. No children. No siblings. Parents: Deceased.
Mental Health History: Nothing diagnosed.
Purpose for travel: Recovery.

Again, London paused. Whoever this person was, they weren't giving her much to go off of. Not that she ever went in fully prepared based on a person's paperwork, but she liked to have her bearings and this was giving her nothing.

Unintended Travel Destination(s): The same damn place every time.

There was little to do but wait. She stared at the number 97. It had to be a typo, she thought.

Josh woke up and burst into tears. *Success.* London allowed his eyes to adjust and greeted him with an unassuming gaze.

"She was beautiful," he said, his southern accent doubling. "Belly all big and her cheeks as pink as her dress." He wiped tears and wrapped London in a bear hug.

"I'm so glad, Mr. Anders."

"How do I see her again?" he asked.

"Remember the little things. It's not the big moments that take us back. It's digging down and finding those morsels that we can feel in our bones even if we can no longer see it with our eyes," she told him. As she recited her speech to him, it made her think of the one her mother used to make her deliver to the clients seeking Ruth's services.

Fifteen minutes passed and London reset the room for her next appointment. She was admittedly excited to meet this mysterious woman. A gruff knock rapped at the door. It sounded more like a man's knock from London's experience. *That's sexist*, she scolded herself.

"It's open," she called out.

The woman who walked in wasn't Lisa Green. She hadn't seen her face in years, but there was no denying that this was Taryn Trainor.

"Taryn?" was all London could muster.

"Yes. Hi. I'm sorry for all the cloak and dagger. I wasn't sure if you'd see me if I just made an appointment."

"You're 'Lisa Green?'"

"Yes. Can I sit?"

"Sure."

London couldn't say that the two ended things badly. After Dennis's death, everyone was raw and hurting. When Gable and London decided to leave AION, they didn't go around saying their goodbyes. They just packed and left.

"How are things?" London asked. She tried to get a read on Taryn, but all she got was Korean, like always. She wasn't sure what was being said, but the tone made London uneasy.

"Fine. Shitty. It doesn't really matter." Taryn was just as brash as ever.

"What have you been doing?"

"Working for James. Same as always. I run the factory in California."

She'd read that Taryn was in charge of manufacturing her machines on a global scale now. London waited for an explanation for why she was there but, as had always been the case, Taryn gave her nothing.

"What can I do for you, Taryn?"

"Everything on that form was true except my name."

London was surprised. "You *are* here because you're having trouble traveling?"

"Trouble is an understatement."

"Tell me what's going on."

"I need to speak to my mother. I've done a shit load of therapy and every quack I see tells me I should confront my mother about why she left me with my father. I need to know if she knew what he was capable of. I need to know why she didn't stop it or at least take me with her when she left."

"That's a lot to process."

"Yeah. My childhood was very sad and whatnot." Taryn hadn't lost her knock for sarcasm.

"I've had someone like you tap into my shit." She waved a hand all over her body. "They can't crack me."

"So you want me to try?"

"No. I want you to bridge with me again."

"What?"

"I want you to bridge with me. Try again to take me to a specific date where I know we were both together. I need to go to the day my mother left and you're the only one who can get me there."

"Bridging isn't really what I do."

"That's what makes it a favor. I don't need you for your psychic analysis. I need to hitch a ride with you to our childhood so I can sort all this shit out."

"It didn't work before, so why do you feel like it would now?" London asked.

"Because the products have gotten better. We've gotten older and more skilled. Instead of drawing on memories, we can just pick the date so I don't end up in a dark room with my pedophile father."

"Have you tried bridging with others?"

"Yes, but there isn't anyone else like you who I have a childhood history with."

London could feel her soft spot for Taryn returning.

"Let me try to help you like I've helped other people," London suggested.

"Nope. That's not what I want. I'm done poking around at this shit. I just want to jump back and get it resolved."

London bit her lip. This is not what she had planned to do today.

"What's the date?"

"Does it matter? It's a day in the fifth grade just before my mom left."

"If I do this, I am staying put at school or home or whatever feels natural for that day. I am not going to help you get out of class or walk home with you or do anything that would feel like changing my day," London said. "This is risky for me. I don't travel to dates before my daughter was born anymore."

At the mention of London's daughter, Taryn's back got rigid.

"Understood," she said.

"Fine. Let's do it," London agreed.

Taryn pulled a machine from her bag. Two cords extended off the back—one had a headband that would go on Taryn, the other had one for London. London placed a tab of the compound in Taryn's hand and put one in her mouth.

"How long will we be there?" London asked.

"A couple hours at most."

"Okay. Let's go be eleven again."

The corner of Taryn's mouth lifted into the slightest of grins.

*G*able hoisted his three-year-old into her car seat. Her body was heavy with sugar, and the length in her legs that was replacing the chubby rolls knocked into him as he buckled her.

"Did you have fun, bug?"

"Yeah. Daddy? Why do you call me bug? Devin says bugs are gross."

"Devin is gross."

"But why do you say it?"

"Well, when you were very little, you had this mark on your belly and it looked like a bug."

"What happened to it?"

"It's still there, it's just harder to see now."

She tried to lift her shirt, but the exhaustion of the party was already dragging her eyelids down.

"Daddy?"

"Yes."

"I like when you call me bug."

"Me too," Gable said.

He looked at his phone. London was staying at the office a little while longer.

"Let's go home and cook Mommy some scampi, bug."

She was already asleep, her chest rising and falling as her mouth fell open. Her curls, soft and springy like her mother's, sticking to her lips.

49

*W*hen London's eyes opened, she was sitting at a smaller than normal desk with a colored pencil in her hands. She looked around for Taryn, and it took a moment for her to remember that they didn't have the same fifth grade teacher.

There were children sitting around her whose faces looked familiar, but their names escaped her.

It was an odd sensation, just sitting there in an elementary class with no real purpose other than to just exist as her eleven-year-old self. She wasn't going to try to find Taryn to see if an adult mind was occupying the young version of her old friend. That would mean doing something she wouldn't have done.

So she sat there, dragging an orange pencil across a drawing of a sunset.

Minutes ticked by and soon everyone was shuffled out of their seats and into the cafeteria. It smelled like old pizza and feet.

A barely thawed chicken patty was placed on a bun with

two dried out carrot sticks beside it. Public education nutrition at its finest, she thought.

She chewed a couple of bites for appearances sake and looked around to see if she could find Taryn. The fact that she couldn't was probably a good sign that she made it and was now walking home to confront her mother.

How would she confront her mother about leaving if she hadn't left yet? Did Taryn's father abuse her when her mother was there or did that happen after she was gone?

London suddenly felt a little stupid for just diving into this without asking any questions. Her drive to help always leapt ahead of her instinct to be logical. Had Taryn actually thought through what she was about to do?

Would Taryn even end up at AION if she didn't live with her father beyond her preteen years? What did that mean for the current world?

Shit, shit, shit, London thought.

She tried to mentally yank herself out of the time period she was in, but felt magnetically stuck to 1999. London was stood in the cafeteria, frantically looking for Taryn.

"Ms. Uuuhh… Ms." She tried addressing a teacher whose name she couldn't remember. "Where's Taryn?"

"My name is Ms. Kelly, not Ms. Uh. And she had to go home because she wasn't feeling very good."

"Shit."

"Ms. Riley, that sort of language—"

Before the teacher could finish, London started running to the playground. She ran past slides and swings and through a game of four square. She slipped on sand-covered concrete, skinning her knees, but made it outside of the school gates.

London felt drag in her steps as her young body failed to keep up with her frantic adult pace. She was running toward their neighborhood even though she knew it would take a long time to get to Taryn's house at this pace.

She stopped at an intersection waiting for it to be safe to cross. Her hands were propped up on her knees and her lungs fought for air. Then suddenly there was no air. She couldn't breathe in or out. Her insides felt like they were turning to concrete and she dropped to her knees, no longer able to stay upright. The hot sidewalk singed her palms, but still no air would pass through her lips. The bright day began to darken around her and she knew she was about to pass out. London's head hit the cement and everything went black.

The first gasp of air she was able to take came screeching in so fast she choked. Tears formed in her eyes as she sputtered, trying to take in all the oxygen she could. Brightness returned to London's field of vision only this time it wasn't coming from daylight. Angry white fluorescents blurred her vision. She brought up her hand to block the light and felt unfamiliar resistance. An IV was taped to the top of her wrist, small tubes of liquid running to a bag behind her. Her nails were painted an unfamiliar pink, a much perkier color than what she'd typically wear.

She wondered if she was in another time. Maybe the day she'd had Marley. She felt her stomach and couldn't find any signs of the C-section that had extricated her daughter from the womb. There was no one in the room so she searched frantically for her phone. When she tried to open it, her password failed. She tried again. And again. And again. Until she was locked from trying anymore.

"Hello?" she yelled. "Hello?"

A girl walked in who looked too young to be a nurse. She

smiled, showing all her teeth. Way too happy for a hospital worker, London thought.

"Well, hello," she said. "I'm Jeanette. And while you can shout for me if you want, this little button right here will bring me right to you also." She pointed to a button on a tan remote that had a chord running into London's hospital bed.

"Where am I?"

"You're at Pheonix General Hospital."

"That can't be right."

Jeanette pulled her phone from her pocket, opened a map app and showed her the location.

"Now, Ms. Riley, I need to ask you—"

"Matthews."

"What's that?"

"Matthews. My name is Mrs. Matthews."

"Oh. Well, the ID we found on you had Riley listed as your last name. You should get that updated."

London frowned, trying to remember if she had done that after getting married.

"I need to ask you a few little questions. Could you please tell me your date of birth?"

"June 16, 1988."

"Very good. And your address?"

"1823 E. Jasper."

"Umm, nope. Did you also move when you got married?"

"I… What?"

"Do you have an emergency contact I can get a hold of?"

"My husband. Gable Matthews. His number is 480…"

Jeanette looked at London with wide, patient eyes and a soothing, less-toothy smile.

"480…"

No matter how hard she tried, she couldn't grab on to the next digits in his phone number. A searing pain shot through London's head as if someone had driven an ice pick through her temple. She clasped her hands to her scalp and let out a moan she couldn't suppress.

"What are you feeling right now?" Jeannette asked, her tone suddenly shifting into something much deeper and more serious than before.

London couldn't answer and could barely make out the words Jeanette was relaying to a doctor that just entered the room.

"We're going to give you something for the pain," the doctor said. "It's going to make you a little sleepy."

Like déjà vu, she woke again with nothing but the fluorescent lights to orient her. This time though, she wasn't alone. Sitting in a chair next to her bed with a book in her lap was her mother. London hadn't seen her in almost four months. Since Christmas, she guessed. Or was it longer?

"London?" Ruth asked, calm and even.

"Mom. What are you doing here?"

"Don't you think the question you should be asking is what *you* are doing here?" Ruth asked.

London hadn't even considered her own situation. She tried tracking her memory back to the most recent moment before she was in the hospital. The pain in her head returned.

She remembered running. Where was she going? Flashes of her childhood limbs and tattered tennis shoes came flooding into her mind. Then a secondary image that somehow felt sharper entered her memory. The adult version of herself jogging on a sidewalk. Not toward something, but for exercise. Wait. Which was it? The two scenarios battled for superiority. She looked to her mother for answers.

Ruth returned a cool gaze.

"I do not have the energy to beg right now, Mother. Tell me what you're seeing or what they told you or what you know before I throw the TV remote through the window."

"No. You need to look for the answer."

"Where is Gable?"

"You tell me, London."

"Jesus, Mom."

"Fine. Don't tell me where he is. Tell me who he is." Now Ruth's gaze was starting to turn frantic.

"He's…he's my…" For some reason, her mouth couldn't form the word husband. She tried again. "Mother, you know damn good and well that Gable is my…"

"Your what?"

If London couldn't grab on to the right words, surely she could hold the image of his face in her mind. His angled nose. Pain shot into her brain through the base of her skull. His sandy blonde beard. Her eyes winced under the pressure of the migraine. His blue eyes. Wait. Were they blue or green? A shrill ring began to echo in her ears and the image of his face blurred.

Panic began to erupt in London's chest. She took short, sporadic breaths.

"Husband. Gable is my husband," she spat out at her mother.

"London, you're not married," Ruth said. "Not that I know of, at least." She was standing now, her book sliding out of her lap and onto the floor.

"What the hell are you talking about?"

"London Riley, you are my daughter and I have been able to read just about every emotion, every memory, every dream you've ever produced. And right now, standing next to you, you feel like a stranger."

"Marley. Where is Marley?"

"Who?"

"My daughter. Your granddaughter. Where is she?"

"Stop this, London. I need you to think. How did you end up here?"

London took in steady, deliberate breaths. Her hands were shaking and her head was throbbing, but she tried to concentrate on what had brought her here.

"I was running. I was running and then I couldn't breathe."

"Did you take something? Were you hungover? What did you do last night?" Ruth persisted.

"I don't think so, I..." Something began to crystalize. "I was eleven. I was at school and then I was running home."

"That doesn't make sense."

London tried harder to remember.

"I had traveled. I had traveled there with..." She was having a hard time forming words again. "Tanya? Tiffany? Taryn! Taryn! She was in my office. She asked me to bridge with her to go back. So she could confront her mom. I felt bad so I said yes, and then I started to panic while we were there."

"Time travel? You're saying you time traveled?"

"Yes. That's what I'm saying."

"London. How could you be so stupid? That's illegal. And dangerous!"

Words were beginning to feel like they had no meaning at all. She was speaking and her mother was speaking back to her, but none of the words made any sense.

"Illegal? What are you talking about?"

"We have to get the doctor in here to do a toxicology test on you. How could you have been so stupid?" Ruth said again.

The doctor and Jeanette came back in the room and her mother relayed information London couldn't fully understand.

"She's on Chron," her mother said, not making eye contact, but casting a glare in London's direction all the same.

Jeanette and the doctor pulled masks over their mouths and offered one to her mother. She waved them off. Jeanette quickened her pace and swapped out the tubes connected to London's IV. First filling three vials with her blood, then reattaching the icy liquid. The doctor plunged a syringe filled with a black substance into the stream of fluid and London's blood began to thicken like syrup.

"This is going to make you ache all over, but it will keep the poison from penetrating your organs," the doctor said.

"Poison?"

"Chron is banned worldwide for a reason, hun," Jeanette said.

Ruth draped a hand over her mouth and just watched as tears streamed down London's cheeks, the pain of the medicine working its way into every nerve on her body. But despite the searing in her skin, nothing compared to the overwhelm of panic that suddenly filled her mind. What had she done? Where was her family?

50

*C*hron is the street name for Chronzaplan, a mind-altering chemical that never passed FDA standards, but is still produced on the black market. Chronzaplan is apparently the drug that once made time travel possible, but was banned nationally, and then internationally, six years ago. At least, that is what the social worker has been telling London. Eleanor has been unfolding pamphlets, patting London gently on the knee and making her watch health videos for an hour.

This is apparently standard protocol for someone who has taken Chron. Though she's tried explaining she doesn't know what Chron is, hasn't taken anything, and doesn't understand what a "temporal episode" means, Eleanor continues on with her speech as if someone pushed Play on a recording.

The end of the video she's being forced to watch has a placid older gentleman speaking in a docile tone.

"We know life can be hard sometimes. We know going back may seem like the best solution. But the best thing you can do for yourself and the ones who love you is to try to make the present better."

Eleanor hit the power button on the television remote.

"Do you have any questions, dear?" she asked, her wrinkles making her approachable and wise.

"No."

"You will need to go to six weeks of therapy. You will be assigned another social worker once you are released. That social worker will need to take a urine sample once a month for the next year. As long as you stay clean, life should pretty much go back to normal after that. Should you choose to attempt to time travel again, you could face jail time. This is very serious business, my dear."

London had no ability to process anything Eleanor was saying. She signed documents as they were pushed in front of her and then tinkered with her hospital bracelets as she waited for the gray-haired woman to leave the room.

Only seconds passed between Eleanor leaving and Ruth walking in with two coffees. She handed one to London. It was sweet, the way she liked it. It was the first thing to register as familiar since she got there.

"Mom, I need to find Gable."

"London, I don't know who Gable is. And, frankly, I'm too pissed off at you to help you track down some guy."

"Mom, look at me. Look inside me." She tried to push an image of Gable toward the surface and dug to find the outline of her daughter too. "Gable isn't a 'guy.' Something terrible has happened."

London searched for her mother's feelings using her own ability. What she found was a dulled, hazy read on Ruth. The ability to inhabit another person's mind, that itch that was so ever-present in London's life, felt like a muscle she hadn't used in a long time.

With drugs having been pumped into her hourly and pain

spreading across her body like ants on an apple, she'd yet to realize that her instinct to see someone from the inside out was virtually unreachable. Maybe the medicine was weakening everything. Her memory, her faculties, her mind.

"Look, Mom, you don't have to do anything. Please just help me open my phone."

"I don't know how to open your phone. Try 1-2-3-4-5-6."

London shook her head but tried it anyway. She felt a little embarrassed when it actually worked. Ruth's abilities were astounding even when she was being snarky and resistant.

She pulled up a browser window and typed his name into the search bar.

Gable Matthews

There were sparse details about anyone by that name, but she clicked on a social media profile, and there he was. His hair was cut shorter than she could ever remember seeing it, and she couldn't recognize the background in the image. The page was set to private, so other than his photo and the high school where he graduated, there was nothing to glean from her search other than the fact that he was real. And his eyes were in fact green.

She held the photo up to her mother.

"What am I supposed to do with that London?" It was a fair question. "Let's just get you home and then we can talk. I'm not actually angry, I'm just very worried and disoriented. We can talk once we're out of here," Ruth relented.

London's clothes were brought to her in a plastic bag. She didn't recognize any of the items. There was a pair of Lululemon leggings that looked way too small, a sports bra that crisscrossed in the back, a cropped t-shirt with the name of a band she didn't know written on it and a pair of tennis shoes.

She looked at her mother with pleading eyes. All Ruth did

was hold her hand up toward the bathroom, urging her to get on with it.

London peeled off the thick, oversized hospital socks that stuck to the bathroom floor. Next she slid off the gown, revealing a silky pair of underwear and breasts that had a little extra bounce to them. As she pulled her leggings up, staring at herself in the mirror, she froze. There was no scar. She pulled down the front of her underwear and ran her hand along the space between her hips, but nothing was there. The four-inch incision that had brought Marley Rose into the world didn't exist on this body.

Tears burst forth and she curled up onto the floor. Her mother either heard her or sensed that something was wrong.

Ruth gathered her half naked, adult daughter into her arms.

"I know, baby. We will find a way to fix this, but we can't talk about it here," Ruth whispered in her ear.

London perked up from her cradled position and made eye contact with her mother. Using what little ability she had left, she peered into her mother's soul and found a piece of her she recognized. She couldn't put a name to the feeling but, whatever it was, it gave her the strength to get off the bathroom floor and finish dressing in a world where Marley didn't exist.

When they walked out of the hospital, London wasn't sure where she was. It took a second for her to realize she was in downtown Phoenix, not the outlying suburbs where her home was.

Ruth drove her to a building rather than a neighborhood. They walked up a single flight of stairs to an apartment with the number 216 on it.

Inside, the décor was minimalistic. It was beautiful and clean, but there was no warmth in the room. Things like a glass bowl on the coffee table made London think of her daughter and how she would have broken it on day one. There weren't any framed pictures on the walls or magnets from travel destinations on the refrigerator. Literally anyone could have lived here. Male, female, old, young, any person could have lived here because it looked like no one specific lived here. But apparently this was her home.

"What am I supposed to do here?" London asked. Her mother looked exasperated, but sympathetic.

"Go take a shower. Try to clear your mind."

Even if her heart was breaking, she had to admit a shower sounded good. She tried to hold the roundness of her daughter's cheeks in her mind's eye, but a craving for something called a "green monster" kept creeping into her subconscious.

Shampoo lathered up in her hair and released the smell of coconut. The scent was familiar and comforting. The shower suddenly began to feel like it belonged to her. She rinsed quickly and dried off, trying not to pause to smell a different brand of laundry detergent on the linens. In her closet she picked out a pair of jeans and a sweatshirt that most looked like something she would usually wear, despite it being too warm for such thick clothing.

Ruth was searching the refrigerator when she walked out.

"There's not much in here," she said.

London reached in and grabbed a bag of spinach, an avocado, blueberries and a carton of coconut water. She opened a cabinet door and pulled out a blender. Her movements were so fluid and effortless, it felt like someone was remote controlling her in this stranger's apartment.

She offered a glass of green liquid to her mother who simply shook her head.

"I want you to tell me everything you can remember," Ruth said.

"That's easier said than done."

"What do you mean?"

"I mean I'm trying to patch together what I remember, and I can't put things on a straight line. It's like I have two boxes of puzzle pieces dumped onto one table."

"Just tell me what you know for sure."

London took a deep breath and reached for the memories she wanted to be her reality.

"I have a daughter. Her name is Marley. Her father, my husband, is Gable Matthews. We live in a home in Mesa. I work for JT Enterprises, which started out as AION, a place where we were trying to discover time travel."

"AION is the first thing you've said that I know."

London waited for her mother to elaborate, but instead, Ruth urged London to continue.

"During an assignment for work, an old friend, or colleague I guess, Taryn, came and asked if I would bridge with her so she could go back and confront her mother during our shared childhood."

"What's a bridge?"

"It's a function of a machine. People who can't travel by themselves are able to use this device and hook it up to someone like me and when we take the compound the person who can't travel can essentially hitch a ride through time with the one who can."

"Why couldn't she go back?"

"She has a traumatic past. That's what I do. Help people get over trauma so they can travel."

"Prior to that day, when was the last time you saw Taryn?"

"At AION. Where you, Gable, Taryn, and I all worked together. For James."

Ruth uncrossed her legs and positioned herself onto the edge of the couch. She leaned forward and spoke in a hushed tone.

"Here's what I know. When you were sixteen I took you out of school and brought you to AION. You were miserable. You hated me and at eighteen you left. We've seen each other less than a dozen times in the past decade.

"AION wasn't a place where time travel was released to the world. It's the place where time travel became universally banned. There is no device like you describe. There is just Chronzaplan and people like me."

Ruth opened her arms as if to showcase herself.

"Chronzaplan mixed with a fairly accurate reading could hurdle someone into a relative place in time. Never a specific time, but we did see some successes. James continued to have chemists tinker with the drug. It got really unstable. I refused to continue testing, but others charged forward."

She paused for a moment and turned her head to the side, trying to coax the next words out.

"Forty-five people died during testing. James kept it under wraps for almost three years, but eventually, loved ones started to come looking and everything imploded. AION was shut down. Any members tied to the deaths were found guilty of an array of crimes. James has been in prison for nine years with no chance of parole. Chronzaplan was made illegal. And anyone who claimed to be a psychic or operated a psychic business was targeted by law enforcement until they basically just went away. Time travel only happens underground, and there are consequences for anyone who is caught trying to do it."

London attempted to process all this information. She knew what Ruth was telling her was true because she could feel the threads of her own memory confirming it. The anger around her departure from AION. The news stories about a cult in the desert that had covered up dozens of murders. The slow quieting of her own abilities as she used them less and less out of shame and fear.

The more her mind focused on the events Ruth was describing, the further her daughter and Gable slipped away.

"Gable Matthews was never at AION?" London asked.

"Yesterday was the first time I heard that name."

A light bulb went on for London.

"His mother, Margaret Matthews. She used to come to you for readings all the time."

"I don't know that name."

"How could you not remember her at least? Her daughter drowned in their pool? She was at our house every week."

Ruth just shook her head. London could see the genuine lack of recognition.

"And no one named Taryn Trainor?" London asked.

"No."

"We have to find her," London said. "She's the only other person who knows what I know. She's trapped here too."

51

*L*ondon could still remember traveling in her timeline. When she made her first change during the trip to the beach with her mother, the events of the original event began to fade. Eventually the only way for her to remember her first experience was to read the notes she took in the days following the travel.

Then when she traveled to a shared memory with Gable and he'd cut an *X* into his palm, she could also remember the first timeline where nothing happened versus the second where he'd become an odd outcast. The original timeline started to fade then too, and without the journal of what happened, she would have had no memory of it. The point was that even though Gable made the change, she could remember two sets of history immediately following the travel, just by virtue of being there with him.

This meant two things: she had to write down everything she could remember about her real life. And she needed to find Taryn Trainor before she forgot where they came from.

Even as she thought about it, her recollection of events

grew foggier. She began to scribble down everything in her life she could remember that was significant. In giant letters she wrote *Gable = Husband, Marley = Daughter*. On a fresh page she began to sketch the cacti painting that she'd drawn on her first date with Gable. The same one that hung in their kitchen. Did that kitchen even exist, she wondered? Surely her body wasn't just sitting in an office in some other timeline.

"It was never there," she said aloud to no one. The events from this timeline would never have led her to that office. There were no CECs, there was no JT Enterprises, there was no London Matthews.

She had to physically shake her head to clear the idea. She taped the notes and the picture onto her wall. London refused to lose her family.

If Taryn had memories of the life London knew, she was the first person London needed to find. She may not be able to tell London the color of Marley's favorite bow or the way Gable's glasses slid down every time he checked messages on his phone, but she could confirm that a version of AION like the one London remembered truly existed. Maybe Taryn was desperate to get back too. In that world, she was a wealthy inventor. Who know what she was in this timeline?

Once she found her, they could work together to try to figure out exactly what had gone wrong to unravel her entire life. London reviewed the fuzzy facts she felt fairly certain were real.

She traveled to her fifth-grade class in 1999.

She and Taryn weren't in the same room together.

For some reason she can't grab on to, she'd run away from school.

She was looking for Taryn.

Then she couldn't run anymore.

Everything went black.

The next time her eyes opened, it was in this world.

This world where Gable was not her husband. There was no Marley. And no legitimate means of time travel.

London couldn't imagine how her running away from class could have snowballed into this timeline. Either the event was so infinitesimal that London feared she'd never be able to identify it or Taryn had done something. But what? She felt like neither of them had been in the past long enough to cause all of this.

The only thing that felt productive was trying to find Taryn to see if she could shed some light on the events that led them both here.

1-2-3-4-5-6

Her phone's home screen popped open using the world's most unoriginal passcode. At least in her timeline she used her daughter's birthday. Easy to crack, yes, but there was meaning behind it. She clearly wasn't connected like that to someone here. London found herself searching her new memories, trying to discover if she was close enough to anyone in this timeline who might be able to help. Faces that had a distant, dreamy quality to them started coming to mind and she had to force herself to return to the task at hand. Flipping through her new memories was like watching a stranger's home videos. She didn't want these memories from this life.

The only place to begin was with a search. Just as she looked for Gable, she began looking for Taryn. Like Gable, almost nothing came up. She couldn't help but feel like it was weird that the two people she needed to find most had zero online presence. No social media. No bios on a company website. No articles written about them. No addresses in a directory. Nothing.

There were two other Taryn Trainor's in the world, but neither were a match for who she was looking for.

"What the hell," she said out loud to no one since her mother had left to pick up some groceries.

London began to tear through the cabinets in the kitchen and the laundry room, most of which were stocked with all-natural cleaning supplies and pure white dishware. This house didn't have so much as a plastic movie cup, let alone an old phone book laying around.

Who was this version of herself? Clutter-free, identity-free, attachment-free. What did she even do for a living?

A vision of an equally neat and tailored office flooded into her mind. The title "Director of Marketing" appeared in her brain.

London physically shook her head to get the idea out her mind. She couldn't be sure, but she felt like any time she let memories from this life in, ones from her other life disappeared.

No phonebook and the internet was a dead end. What were her other options for finding Taryn?

She searched the contacts in her phone. There were a lot of names she didn't recognize at first glance, not in this set of memories or any other. When she reached the T's there were a lot of men's names. Terrence, Tony, Travis. No Taryn, though.

Ruth walked in with a bag full of groceries.

"Look I know you're vegan or vegetarian, but I don't know how to shop like that," she said, kicking the door closed. There was something a little sloppy and scatter-brained about this version of her mother that London liked. The poised, perfect idol she'd dopily followed behind all those years wasn't here. "I just bought a lot of pastas and produce," she said, hoisting the bags onto the kitchen counter.

"This is all just fine." She helped put away the groceries, again operating mechanically as she placed items in the spaces she somehow knew they belonged.

London stopped Ruth's shuffling to get dinner started and squared her shoulder's toward her mother.

"Mom. What do you see when you read me?"

Ruth rubbed her nose even though London doubted it itched.

"I don't know. I see a version of you that is recognizable. That undercurrent of agitation you always feel around me. The yearning to be somewhere else. But then there is this static."

"Static?"

"I literally feel as if I can't tune into the right station. I get little blips of images that I recognize, but the picture is never clear enough to see the whole thing."

This was not her mother. Ruth Riley was rarely unsure of anything. She could see more in another person than that person could ever hope to see in themselves. She was an emotional sniper, always able to home in on someone's weak spot.

"Can you see my other life?"

"All I can see is you. I can't see anything that orbits around you."

London tried to push an image of her daughter to the surface, but struggled to find a concrete visual in her own depleted memory.

"I have to find Taryn Trainor if I am ever going to get back to my life."

"Get back to your life? London, this is your life. There is no time travel here. Any attempt to try will get you thrown in jail or worse."

London burst into tears. "There is absolutely nothing I can think of that would be worse than living in a world where my child doesn't exist." Heavy, choking tears robbed her of her sight and robbed the room of sound. This was the first moment she felt like her old self. Only a mother could know love and pain and loss this deep.

52

*N*o matter how much London didn't want this life, she had to abide by some of its rules if she ever hoped to get back to her family.

When she opened her banking app, she was pleased to find that there was more than enough cash in there to survive on for a while, so she knew for a fact there would be no going to work in this world. London could only assume that the stream of incoming calls were people at her job wondering where she was. She was gone, London thought as she hit Decline. In fact, she was never supposed to be here to begin with.

On the other hand, giving a urine sample to a caseworker and attending mandatory therapy was something she couldn't skip. If she didn't do these things, she would be in violation of her probation and sent to jail, and she couldn't very well travel from there. Her abilities were so dulled in this timeline that she'd be lucky if she could read a fellow inmate enough to find protection, let alone hurl herself into the past.

She and Ruth had some sort of unspoken pact that they were now in this together. London didn't ask if there were other things Ruth needed to attend to, and Ruth didn't ask for permission when she turned the living room couch into a bed. Given the little snippets of information she received about their strained relationship, London guessed that Ruth was just happy to be around her daughter without a fight.

London rode in the passenger seat as Ruth followed the GPS to an aging church ten minutes away from her apartment.

"What am I even supposed to say?" London asked, speaking more to the car window than to Ruth. "Hi, I'm a time traveler from a different reality. This life isn't my own and I want out."

"London, these people are just like you."

"Crazy?"

"No. People who have time traveled or who have attempted to time travel and lived to talk about it."

It hadn't occurred to her that this was a program created specifically for Chron users and self-proclaimed travelers. She assumed she was going to narcotics anonymous or something similar. It hadn't even crossed her mind that she'd be listening to people talk about time travel.

"I made some calls and got you into this one," Ruth said, unlocking the doors and shooing her out.

The only guidance she had was a sign on the dead front lawn with sloppy chalk handwriting.

"Temporal Recovery"

London considered running until she reached a bar, but looked at the paper in her hand that needed signing and thought better. Other people were streaming into the building and so she joined the current.

There were plastic tables set up that had donuts, coffee,

and water bottles. She wanted a donut, but some subconscious instinct steered her toward the water.

There were three rows of chairs and as she approached them, aiming for a seat in the back, someone handed her a white piece of paper with a single, horizontal black line in the middle and a golf pencil.

"Name tag?" she asked, looking for a sticky side.

"No, honey. It's your timeline worksheet," the helper said with no further explanation as she handed a card to the next person approaching.

London took a seat in the back row. No one sat next to her, which felt like a relief as she saw other people exchanging subdued but courteous greetings.

The middle-aged black woman who had given her the card made a shushing sound. The crowd turned their attention to her.

"Does everyone have a timeline worksheet?" she asked. The crowd answered yes without making a sound. "If this is your first time here, I'm Yolanda. Nice to meet you. Please start filling out your worksheet by putting the date of your furthest travel destination in the past on the far left side of the line. Then put today's date on the far right side."

Everyone began to scratch letters onto their page. London did the same.

"Is everybody done with that part?" Again, the group silently confirmed.

"Now, above the line, please write everything you know to be true in this timeline. Below the line, if applicable, write everything you remember from your previous existence."

A young girl who barely looked like a legal adult raised her hand. Yolanda nodded in her direction.

"What if we only attempted to travel and never got anywhere?"

"Good question. If you are an F. TAP, sorry a 'failed traveler at present' please write down where you had hoped to go and why you were trying to go there."

London followed the instructions. Above the timeline she wrote:

I live alone in an apartment in Phoenix. I'm a Director of Marketing. I drink green smoothies. My home is too clean. I'm not married. I have no children.

Below the line she wrote:

My daughter is Marley. My husband is Gable. Those are the only things that matter.

"Is everybody finished?" The room nods.

"Moving on, then. Ms. Murphy is going to be leading today's discussion."

Yolanda sat down in a chair in the front row. London wondered where she had gone or tried to go. She looked like a woman just on the edge of becoming a grandmother. Soft creases in the corners of her eyes. The slightest whisper of grey in her locks. She seemed too content to be in this room full of chronological castaways.

An introduction broke London's fixation on Yolanda.

"I'm Bonnie Murphy," the woman at the head of the group announced. Her hair was sheered into a pixie cut and her hips were slimmer than London remembered, but this woman wasn't *Bonnie* Murphy. It was Siobhan Murphy. And while the woman she remembered would never go by a cutesy nickname like Bonnie, this was her. The aesthetic bits were all off. She was too put together. Her makeup dense and polished, her clothing couture. The way she hinged her jaw when she'd pause between sentences and the clasped hands draped in front of her waist made it clear that this was in fact a woman London knew.

Siobhan made eye contact with London and nodded.

Did they know each other in this reality? London flipped

through her memories like documents in a filing cabinet. They met the same way in both timelines. London and Ruth both met Siobhan when they arrived at AION.

London missed the welcoming introduction, but turned her full attention toward Siobhan as she dove into a story.

"I am a member of the psychic community. When I was ten I discovered that in moments of pain or sadness I could jump back to that moment's origin. If I had skinned my knee on my bicycle, I would return to the moments before I steered into a pothole and correct my path. When at seventeen I found my mother crying because our father left us, I was able to occupy my five-year-old body and watch the first moment where my mother chose not to confront my dad about his infidelity. Then when I was thirty-nine, I encountered a moment more devastating than any I had ever known before. My twelve-year-old son was diagnosed with terminal brain cancer. Without prompting, my consciousness leapt back to the night of his conception. At the time I didn't know when I was or why I was there and, because of that confusion, I didn't sleep with my husband when he made the attempt to stoke some romance. That night, my son vanished from existence entirely."

London had to cover her mouth with her hand to stifle a sharp inhalation. She spent years trying to find even just a fragment of a memory that would give her some insight into Siobhan's history. The little boy she occasionally had dancing through her memory now had a story.

The hurt that clung to Siobhan's clothes and darkened her eyes was the same hurt London was now living inside. Two mothers of children lost in time.

"I know my son was real," she continued. "I can't really see his face anymore or remember the sound of his laugh, but I can remember the weight of carrying him. The curve in my back when I was pregnant. The heaviness of his body when I'd lift him out of the tub. The gravity that love takes on when you create a person. I can still feel its mass even if I can't recall his first words. He didn't exist in this world. But my son was real."

Siobhan took a moment to look around the room. Some people shifted uncomfortably under her silence. Others nodded with recognition. London just let her jaw fall open and tears stream down her cheeks.

"Whether you are an organic traveler like me, a victim of Chronzaplan, or an F. TAP who took a leap for what they hoped would be somewhere better, I see you. I know you. And this is a place where you can feel at ease." She drew in a breath and looked around the room. "Who would like to share first?"

After a brief pause, a young man in a wheelchair rolled to the front. He had a harsh lean in his spine and his wrists bent in severe angles.

"I'm Carter," he said. London was glad when the room didn't respond with, "Hi, Carter," like she had been taught to expect from television depictions of AA meetings.

"I have taken Chronzaplan four times trying to get back to when my brother killed himself. Jacob, my little brother, was my favorite person in the world. He was sensitive and soft My dad was really hard on him. He didn't get how great Jacob was. My brother shot himself when he was sixteen after a girl broke up with him. I don't know if it was the girl or the fact that my dad told him to man up or if he was just always going to be too gentle for the world.

"He deserved to be alive. He deserved a chance to grow up and leave my dad's house and find another girl and get friends that didn't make him feel like a pussy for not smoking and drinking.

"I hoped if I could just get him to live long enough to see that the world is so much bigger than it feels at sixteen that he would make it. He would be okay. On my fourth trip back, I did it. I stopped him before he pulled the trigger. I woke up and immediately had the stroke that landed me here.

"Memories of my brother graduating high school and going to college and moving to New York flooded in, and I didn't even care that I was going to be in this chair for life. It worked and I was alive and so was he, so fuck it, who needs legs right?

"Then about a month and a half ago, they found my brother hanging in his apartment. Almost ten fucking years to the day after he killed himself the first time. Killed himself again. And it's not like I can handle another hit of Chron. Shit. Wouldn't even try if I could. Things just end up the way they are going to end up, ya know?"

He never dropped a tear or so much as sniffled. He just rolled back to the spot he'd been occupying before.

Four more people shared their stories of travel and loss and love and heartache. London kept waiting for a success story, but, she guessed, those people probably didn't need group therapy.

The session wrapped up and people flooded back to the refreshment tables. London couldn't move. She just stared at the card in her hand.

My daughter is Marley. My husband is Gable. Those are the only things that matter.

Despite the overarching lesson that time travel is futile and we should all just embrace the present, there was no way she could do that. She'd rather be dead than live in this empty timeline.

Siobhan approached her and asked to sit. London no longer felt surprised or delighted to see her. Bonnie was a bad omen. A relic of London's lost timeline. A symbol of time travel's immeasurable propensity for failure. AION or not, Siobhan had an ability like London's, probably stronger than London's, and she couldn't save her child.

"It's been a long time," Siobhan said.

"How long?"

"Over ten years according to my timeline. How long has it been according to yours?"

"About four."

"When did you lose her?" Siobhan pointed to the card.

"She isn't lost."

"She is, London."

She wasn't going to let this escalate into a paradoxical conversation about existence. If London started to believe that Marley was gone, then she would be forever.

London grabbed her purse and got up to leave. Siobhan grabbed her by the wrist.

"People who are lost can be found, but there is no going back to the way things were." Siobhan kissed London on the cheek and left her there to be haunted.

Ruth was twenty minutes late picking up London. She spent that time scrolling her Instagram account trying to get to know the woman whose life she was currently occupying. Fancy meals in San Francisco. Photos of essential oils. Selfies with motivational captions about loving yourself and strength from within. London tried to resist all temptations to roll her eyes at herself.

"This bitch," she said under her breath as she flipped through some photos of a much more toned version of herself on a sailboat in the Bahamas.

Ruth had to honk the horn to get London to break the scrolling spell she was under.

"I hope you at least picked up something that comes with French fries if you're going to be this late."

"I don't have any food. I did get some information on Taryn though."

London held her breath.

"Well, what is it?" she finally had to ask.

"I went through some of your old yearbooks and I didn't recognize the faces, but both of them, Taryn and Gable, are in them."

Why hadn't London thought to look there? She doubted that this overly organized version of herself would keep old photos or books, but was grateful that her mother had seen some value in nostalgic keepsakes.

"What did you find out?"

Ruth reached into the backseat and brought forth a hard-bound book. The year 2004 was emblazoned on the front. It was the last year London attended high school.

"Flip to page sixty-four," she instructed.

London did as she was told and almost choked when she opened on the page. There they were. Taryn and Gable at around sixteen years old, smiling and frozen like mannequins. The caption underneath read *Midnight in Paris* and a tacky purple backdrop with the silhouette of the Eiffel Tower hung limp behind them. Gable's hand rested on top of Taryn's and both of their hands rested on her hip.

Taryn was beaming in a way London didn't even know her face was capable of doing. Gable had his trademark, noncommittal smirk. London always told him that that smile made her crazy because she could never tell if it was genuine or sarcastic. That smile was the same one he wore in their wedding photos.

"So... I mean, this confirms that they are, in fact, real people. And I suppose it's kind of weird that they dated, but that's high school. People date and break up and are with someone new a week later. I'm glad you found it, but I don't think this gets us anywhere," London said.

"I saw this and I had an idea. I knew it was probably a

long shot, but I started looking for a 'Taryn Matthews' and I found one. Living in Scottsdale."

London's heart started to race.

"Did you find photos or social media or anything?"

"No," Ruth said. "Just an address."

53

*I*t was too late to rush over to the address that Ruth found. London was desperate to know more, but also realized that a late-night ambush was unlikely to result in anything productive.

Instead, she asked her mother to bring over more yearbooks.

The two of them flipped through every book from 1999 to 2004, scanning the background and foreground of every image looking for clues. Shy of the required school photo, London only found one or two images of herself. As it turns out, she was an awkward loner in both realities. *Lucky me,* she thought.

There was a lot more to learn about Gable and Taryn though. From junior high on they were inseparable. In one image they were shoulder to shoulder at a lunch table. In another, Gable wore a basketball jersey and Taryn had on a cheer outfit.

"A cheerleader?" London had yelled. "A fucking cheerleader!"

Gable was not an academic anomaly in this world, but

had instead risen to his father's hopes and joined the basketball team. And the track team, apparently. Taryn was a disturbingly preppy mirror image of her former self. In every photo where she wasn't with Gable, girls who wouldn't have bothered to spit on London and Taryn if they were on fire surrounded her. It was sad to think of a childhood without that friendship, but London mostly felt happy for Taryn. Knowing what Taryn had suffered in their original timeline, she assumed that this bright-eyed girl wasn't subjected to the same horrors.

As she turned the pages, flashes of memory cascaded in. Passing Taryn in the hall and shriveling under her popularity. Watching Gable play basketball, but never speaking a word to him. Working as her mother's sidekick. London tried to force away anything that felt like a false memory from this false world, but the new reality just kept pouring in.

She had to let the new information in if she was going to find Taryn or Gable.

A chill skittered up London's back, and the ability she had all but forgotten came creeping toward the surface. Her mother was flipping through a yearbook again, but had set down her wine in an abrupt and deliberate slam. London suddenly realized that the chill she was feeling was actually her mother's chill, vibrating in the air.

"London, what was the day you said you traveled back to?"

"I told you I don't know the exact date. Taryn said it was just a day when we were in the fifth grade."

"What did you say happened to Gable's sister?"

"Abigail? She drowned when we were..."

Her mother flipped the yearbook around, and London was staring at a picture of seven-year-old Abigail Matthews. She wasn't the only one in the photo though. Beside her was an eleven-year-old Taryn with her arm around Gable's little sister. Above the picture were the words *Hero of the Year*. A small paragraph below the picture told the story of Taryn Matthews walking home from school and hearing a splash in her neighbor's yard. Curious, she peeked over the fence and saw Abigail face down. She knocked on the front door and got the attention of Abigail's mother who quickly called 9-1-1 and began performing CPR. First responders said that seconds made the difference in these cases, and that if it wasn't for Taryn, Abigail would have died.

London's hands began to shake. She grabbed the 2000 yearbook and there was Abigail, grinning ear to ear in her second-grade photo. A photo that was never taken in the time London came from.

"This. This is what she went back to do? That doesn't make sense. When I saw Taryn in the present—in my present—she hadn't even seen Gable or I in years. Why would she use me to save his sister?"

London grabbed her car keys and pulled tennis shoes on without socks.

"What are you doing?" Ruth asked.

"I have to find out if they're married."

he truth was, she already knew the answer. As she was driving to the address her mother found, there was no doubt in her mind. Taryn was the most calculated person she knew. If she could figure out how to take London's abilities and implant them in a machine, she could do the math and figure out how to seriously alter her own miserable existence.

Why Gable though? Why London? Why were the three of them still so irrevocably intertwined?

London drove through intersections vaguely noting the color of the traffic lights.

She was angry. Angry at Taryn for her deliberate decision to majorly alter the past. Angry at Gable for being so malleable that he could go from a headstrong scientist to a junior prom-attending jock. But mostly mad at herself for being so unbelievably stupid. For diving into anything that Taryn had suggested without so much as a moment's pause for consideration. For being so god damn empathetic toward other people's heartache that she didn't consider her own safety. Or her daughter's.

"Fuuuuuuuuck!" she screamed to the heavens and at herself.

When she arrived at the address, the front porch lights were on and a few of the windows inside were lit up. The house was nice, but modest. It was probably a couple of decades old but had the signs of refurbishment etched into the details. Two cars were in the driveway.

London parked directly across from the home on the other side of the street.

What was her plan? Had she really driven over here to ring the doorbell?

She sat and waited for a better idea to come to her. She turned up the music and closed her eyes for a minute. She tried to find the place in the pit of her stomach that, in her own timeline, could have reached into that house and felt who was inside. Or could have at least felt if Gable was. She dug at her insides, trying to unearth the remnants of her once so deafening skills, but nothing came forth. Like any muscle, it atrophied from inactivity and she couldn't suddenly summon it up.

London opened her eyes and settled on going back home when the front door of Taryn Matthews's home opened. It was dark and she couldn't see anything other than shadowy figures moving toward the driveway. As they got closer to the streetlight, there was no denying the four people standing in front of her.

Taryn—without a doubt Taryn—was hugging Margaret Matthews. Gable's father leaned in and kissed Taryn on the cheek. And then Gable, coming up from behind Taryn hugged his mother before placing a casual arm around Taryn's waist. London felt her throat turn to metal. Mr. and Mrs. Matthews got in their car, and when they turned their headlights on, they shone directly into London's face.

She ducked down, hoping no one had seen her. She

stayed scrunched beneath the window until the light from their car turned away. Peering over the edge she inched her way up a little at a time. Taryn and Gable were walking back toward their home. She watched as Taryn made some sort of gesture to Gable that released her from his embrace. He walked inside and she stayed on the porch.

Once Gable closed the door Taryn turned and faced back toward the street. London was now certain she was staring directly at her, even though the tint on her windows, London guessed, would have made it really hard for her to see inside the vehicle.

Then Taryn started to walk toward the street. In a panic, London started her car and drove off.

55

"*W*here was your head tonight?" Taryn asked.

Gable hated that question. She always asked it when he was feeling off. It was like she could sense his emotions with an accuracy even he didn't possess. That's what happens when you've been with the same woman for two-thirds of your life, he supposed.

"I'm fine."

"Dinner was nice tonight. Your mom seems better."

His mother was never better, he thought. She was an exceedingly anxious woman, always certain someone—especially herself—was near death.

"Yeah, she seemed fine."

"You're fine. She's fine. Glad we're able to connect on such a deep, personal level," Taryn said, her eyebrow bucking up as it always did when she was being sarcastic.

"I'm sorry," he said. "You know how I get around her sometimes. I just can't stand the constant worrying over nothing."

"You know how she gets about Abby."

"Abby is a grown woman. She doesn't need to check in every day."

"Well, it's been two weeks."

She always did this. Took his mother's side. He understood why. Taryn might as well be her daughter. They were closer than his mom and Abby had ever been. Still, it would be nice if he won just one argument.

"Well, like I told Mom, I'll try to call her in the morning."

Taryn came up behind him and laid her cheek on his shoulder blade. She squeezed his chest as she had done hundreds of times before. The pressure of her hug relaxed the tension he was carrying in his neck as he'd sat for hours, jaw clenched, listening to his mother fret over mundane texts his sister had sent and odd Tweets she posted in the middle of the night.

He spun around and kissed Taryn. Her lips took what was left of his irritation, and he lifted her tiny frame off the floor, her feet dangling and bouncing off his shins.

"Don't worry about it, babe. She'll turn up. Your mom will cool down for a couple of months. And then the whole thing will start again."

Gable let out a snort. He agreed, but didn't want to talk about it anymore.

He brushed his teeth next to his wife. Grazed her butt as she changed into pajamas. Took his melatonin so he could fade into a dreamless sleep.

Starting three years ago, visions of a little girl were all he could dream of. Every night, without fail, a curly-haired child would dance around in his head while he slept. When they were in the throes of in vitro, it felt like a sign of things to come. He didn't even believe in things like dream state premonitions, but something about her was so tangible and so real that he couldn't help but get hopeful.

In the last year, however, he and Taryn had decided to

stop trying. To stop thinking of it. To stop dreaming of it. She was devastated but had shifted her focus toward plans of travel, dog ownership, and a life without restrictions. He'd started taking something at night so that he was no longer dreaming in secret. Most nights it worked, but on the days where his life felt out of focus, his mind would go to the little girl.

Sticky hands on his face. Static-filled hair under a blanket. Deep, peaceful breaths from a small figure curled under his arm. Gable knew better than to share the dreams with Taryn. When he'd tried in the past, she'd told him that the child wasn't their child and that he needed to stop pretending and focus on the present. Her reaction was so visceral, fueled by hormone injections and heartbreak, so he just stopped talking about it.

But he never stopped thinking about it.

56

*L*ondon barely slept. There were too many thoughts flooding her mind. She started writing down everything from her own timeline she could remember in feverish bursts, starting from 1999 and moving forward. Given how much time she'd spent living in and focusing on her own memories in the timeline she came from, she was shocked at the large swaths of time from her childhood where she couldn't differentiate between her original past and this reconstructed one.

Had she been carried out of a party after smoking weed for the first time in timeline A or timeline B? Had Brian Palmer been her first kiss or Kyle Lorne? Her head throbbed as she mined the two streams of data cycling through her consciousness.

First concert?

Last movie she'd seen with friends?

The coffee she usually ordered at Starbucks?

There were just fragments of information she knew for certain.

Marley's birthday, her wedding anniversary. London

wrote down the exact dates of any major event from her first timeline she could think. She thought about the people from AION. Beth, Dennis, even Miles. She didn't know any of them in this timeline.

She searched for Dennis Locke first. He was easy to find. Dennis was one of the forty-five people who died as test subjects at AION. She closed her phone, unable to bare it if Beth was one of them too.

London put her head in her hands. She felt so far away from anything that resembled her life. Her mother had gone home to get some fresh clothes and clear out anything that might be spoiling in her refrigerator. There was nothing she could do here anyway.

A knock on the front door broke London from the pitiful spell she was under.

"Mom, you can just come in," she yelled.

The knock came again.

She pulled herself off the floor and went to answer it, then stood in the open doorframe in total shock.

In front of her was Taryn.

"Hey, Lond-y."

London was paralyzed and could only hold the door open while Taryn strode in like she owned the place.

"Sit," Taryn instructed.

London did as she was told.

"I'm sorry," Taryn said. "I know everything feels a little fucked up right now."

The posh, refined woman in front of her didn't look like Taryn, but she sure sounded like her.

"I knew we'd come face-to-face sometime soon. To be honest, it took you a couple more days to figure it out than it should have. Systems not quite firing on all cylinders?" Taryn asked, pointing a circling finger at London's head. How did she know London's abilities had faded? "I did my research on you too, Lond-y."

"Stop calling me that. Do you have any idea what you've done?"

"I am fully aware."

"How could you take everything from me? I have a child."

"No, you don't. And I took nothing from you. I took back what was mine and then gave to everyone around me."

"What does that mean?"

"That life you're thinking of, it didn't belong to you. When you left Gable and I at sixteen, we were happy. We were two fucked up people with a common thread. I loved him. He loved me. I got him into AION so we could have a chance. And then what happened? You. With all your quirky readings and all his open wounds, you just wedged yourself right in. *You* took the life that should have been *mine*. All I did was take it back."

"This isn't right," London said, desperately grasping for an answer to Taryn's blatant confession. "You can't just take away my whole life and expect me to sit here idly."

Taryn stood up and walked into the kitchen, helping herself to a water bottle from the refrigerator.

"Who gets to say which life is right? That was your whole time-traveling motto wasn't it? That there is no right and wrong to any of this, just the choices we make. Every day we could make a choice that seriously alters the future. What does it matter if it happens today or in the past?"

"If you think I'm just going to lay down and let my daughter disappear forever, let you take my husband—"

"What are you going to do, London? Go back and keep me from saving his sister? Let her die in that pool? Let his mother kill herself? Let me get raped by my father for nearly a decade?"

London grabbed at her temples. She couldn't solve every problem right here. She couldn't even concoct a response.

Taryn had made such intentional choices, and this version of London was just a byproduct of the world she created. A left-over from a distant timeline.

"Look, I didn't want you to remember any of this. I tried for so many years to fix what was wrong with me and the gaps in my machine so that you would wake up blissfully unaware that anything had happened. It just wasn't in the cards, London. I was too messed up. I needed help, and I only knew one person who would help anyone who was hurting."

London's insides began to boil again.

"This is the last time we will ever speak," Taryn said firmly but calmly. "I needed to come and make it clear to you that the life you think is yours is gone. And unless you are willing to kill to get it back, you might as well get comfy in this cushy little life of yours. It's really not a bad one," she said, peering into the rooms of London's apartment and running her hand along the bookshelves beside her. "Just let go. You'll forget that you were ever with Gable or that you ever had a kid, and then you can be happy. It's what I'm going to do."

Taryn came over to the couch and sat down right next to London. Their shoulders were touching and London didn't even try to summon her abilities to read what was inside Taryn. She was saying exactly what she felt.

"One more thing," Taryn said. "If you come anywhere near Gable, I'll kill you."

Taryn stood and walked out of the door. Not another word or glance in London's direction.

London released the breath she was holding in. A panic attack overwhelmed her body and she panted, trying to regain control of her intake of oxygen before she passed out.

Ruth walked in as London fell to her knees. She felt her mother's arms gather her around the shoulders, and then someone else was talking. London looked behind her and found Siobhan standing dumbstruck in her living room.

"Did you take anything?" Ruth was shouting. "London, answer me!"

London shook her head and waved a limp hand.

"Taryn. She planned it all perfectly."

57

"*D*o you want some coffee?" Gable asked. Taryn had just returned from the gym, which meant now it was time for coffee, croissants, and aimless conversation about whatever podcast they were listening to or whatever headlines were in the news. They did the same thing every Saturday and there was a lot of comfort in that consistency.

"Yeah, I'll take coffee," she replied.

Gable sifted through the cabinet of coffee mugs, then opened the dishwasher searching for the right one.

"Where's my 'Carpe Caffeine' mug?" he shouted into the other room.

"Your what?"

"The tall black mug that says 'Carpe Caffeine.' Have you seen it?"

Taryn walked in pushing her hair into a ponytail. "Your what?"

"My favorite mug. It's like twice the size of a regular one. It says 'Carpe Caffeine' on it."

"I have no idea what you're talking about."

Gable shrugged and grabbed another cup. "How was your workout?"

"It was great," she said, tucking a lose strand into her hair tie. "Did you call your sister?"

"No, I forgot," he said, feeling a little guilty.

"You know your mom is going to ask."

"I'll text her right now." He held up his phone as evidence. *Hey freak. Where are you?* Gable sent it off to his sister.

Taryn leaned into him and pressed her body against his. She kissed his mouth and her fruit flavored lip-gloss grazed his tongue.

"Feeling a little saucy this morning?" he asked.

"Feeling victorious."

"What does that mean?"

"Come into the bedroom and find out."

Gable peeled the yoga pants from his wife's smooth legs. She pulled her tank top over her head and leapt into his arms. He couldn't help but chuckle as she pounced on him like they were teenagers again.

"Remind me to thank your Pilates instructor," he said.

They tumbled into bed. He knew he should be turned on, a familiar aversion crept up. He kissed her with tight lips and couldn't coax his hands into sliding down her body with ease. When he was younger, he wondered if he was gay. In his twenties she'd talked him into getting his testosterone checked out. They had done sex therapy and even hypnotism. They never found a source for the issue. Sometimes he just couldn't.

"Seriously, Gable?" she asked, letting out a low growl of dissatisfaction.

"I'm sorry. I'm distracted by work things."

"It's always something isn't it?"

Taryn left him lying there naked and ashamed, and strode off to take a shower. He knew this would result in the usual two-day communication freeze between them. She'd spiral into an alcohol-fueled depression, where she and her two best friends would begin drinking bottomless mimosas at ten a.m. and she'd only come home to change from day to night clothes.

At first, these episodes made him feel humiliated and angry with himself for not being able to give his beautiful wife something as simple as an erection. But after almost two decades of having an average performance rate of 70%, he just took these other times as opportunities to get caught up on some of his own to-dos. In the next forty-eight hours he might finish a book, reorganize his dresser drawers, and get to the bottom of his inbox. It maybe wasn't the healthiest means to productivity, but there was no use sitting around waiting for her to come home so he could console her. By the start of next week, she'd act like nothing had happened, he'd take a Viagra to guarantee his performance for makeup sex, and all would be forgotten until the next time his flaccid failure showed up.

Between the conversations about his sister, the bottle and a half of wine he'd drank to cope with his mother's worrying, and last night's dream of the little girl, he should have known better than to even attempt it. Nevertheless, this was an opportunity for him to live inside his own head for once instead of having Taryn dig around for what was missing.

The truth was, there *was* something missing. He had felt "off" for days, but couldn't put his finger on it. And then last night his dream of the little girl took on some new elements. Usually, the only frame he could hold on to was the vague outline of her face. There was never anything familiar about the setting or the scenarios, just the obvious fact that it was always the same little girl in each dream.

Last night, there were more details. She was sitting in a highchair, and behind her there was a painting of cacti. Also, there had been another person. Someone who was vaguely recognizable, but whose identity he couldn't quite put his finger on. Not that any of it mattered, but he did find it strange that the woman acting like the little girl's mother wasn't Taryn. Wasn't even close to what Taryn looked like. Wasn't even one of those odd dream state scenarios where a person looks nothing like they do in real life, but you still somehow know it's them.

There was a warmth to her presence, and she called the little girl "Bug."

58

*I*t took an hour for London to recover enough to explain to Ruth and Siobhan what Taryn had said. It took an hour for the three of them to fetter out all the reasons why Taryn's plan was so ironclad.

"She was always meticulous, but this is a whole new level of obsessive detail," London said. "She thought of everything. The more I let in from this timeline the more I can see her plan in action. Taryn tortured me in junior high and high school. We were not friends. She made every effort to dull my abilities by making me feel shame for having a psychic mother. Every time I would so much as look at another person, she'd ask, 'Are you reading his mind, psycho?' And like a switch, it would turn off any attempt to read the people around me. By the time we got to AION, there was barely anything even left. Makes sense that I hated being there. I didn't have anything to do."

"And you didn't have your friend," Siobhan added.

London couldn't stand thinking of Taryn as a friend. Was any of it ever real?

"How could she occupy her past self for so long?" Ruth

asked. "In this timeline, there were only minutes of travel. Maybe a couple hours. Not days and months and certainly not years. Are we saying that the adult from your timeline occupied this Taryn from childhood to now?"

"It feels that way based on what she said and how she treated me. In my time, we made a lot of advancements beyond what you have here. There were always new iterations turning out. It's possible Taryn built something into her machine or had access to a form of the compound that made her move permanent," London guessed. "I wasn't involved in the development side of things after I left AION. I just held appointments and helped people that were sent to me. It's hard to say how far James and Taryn were able to take things after I left. They always saved the best inventions for their black-market clientele. If she had that kind of ability to travel long term, all she would have had to do was record her memories from our first timeline while they were fresh and she could steer every moment to get what she wanted."

"What were you like at AION in your timeline?" Ruth asked, ignoring the revelation. Her mother seemed less concerned about the means by which Taryn was able to steal her daughter's life and more curious about a version of London who held abilities closer resembling her own.

"Still living in your shadows, but sharp. And I got sharper every day I was there. By the time we were doing serious testing, I could travel without anyone's help. I could bring someone with me just using Gable's compound. And with Taryn's machine, I could go anywhere I wanted. I even was starting to Divine Travel."

Both of them apparently knew that phrase from their time at AION and with James.

"Wow," Siobhan said. In her world, no one had even come close to managing an accurate travel. There were just bodies being hurled through time, never knowing when they would land or how long they would be stuck there. Psychics refused to even use Chron after AION discovered that it was fatal in over half of them. Someone with organic abilities, Siobhan explained, would basically overdose on time travel. The few who made it through said they were stuck in their past bodies for years, even decades. The others left a cold shell of a body on a table in the current timeline to which their consciousness would never return to.

"Is there any way you could replicate Gable's compound? Or at least come close?" Siobhan asked.

"I don't know how he made it. I know what it did. I even heard him talk about a number of the components and their effects. Same as hearing someone talk about building an engine, though. I could listen to the fragmented details for years and still have no idea where to start assembling one myself."

Siobhan bit her lip. She was genuinely trying to solve the problems at hand. Ruth, however, remained silent and detached.

"Do you think Taryn built her machine anyway?" Siobhan asked.

"Why would she do that?"

"I don't know. Insurance maybe. In case she had to go back and fix something again. Maybe the world didn't actually go perfectly her way on the first attempt. I mean, she still has the same original memories you do, so she would know how to do it in this time."

That was actually an interesting idea. It would be a huge risk for Taryn to hold on to her device, but even if she had, it wasn't much good to London since there would be no way for her to travel without Gable's compound.

"She seemed to have considered everything else. Isn't it possible she also memorized the recipe for that?"

The more they talked about it the more it seemed like a

real possibility. And even if there was no compound, maybe London could rebuild her own skills so that she wouldn't need any of it. She had no idea what time she'd travel to or how she would go about fixing the royal disaster that had become her life, but it was a glimmer of hope.

"How am I supposed to find out if she did rebuild it?"

"I guess you have to break into their house."

"You think she'd just leave it lying around?" London asked.

Siobhan shrugged her shoulders. These ideas, while heading in a more positive direction, were just guesses on top of guesses that would likely lead nowhere.

"You have to at least try to snoop around their place. If anyone has any of the pieces for time travel with them, those two are it right?"

She wasn't wrong.

"Care to add anything, Mom?"

Ruth had been staring out the window, paying little attention to the conversation happening around her.

"If you get caught breaking and entering, you'll be violating your probation and sent to jail. If you get caught by Taryn, something worse might happen to you."

"I can't just do nothing."

London sometimes had a hard time embracing the fact that this woman was the same Ruth Riley she'd known in her other timeline. This Ruth, disheveled and dressed in an ill-fitting kaftan, barely even looked like a relative of her real mother. The slow, uncertain cadence of her voice didn't even echo the crisp, solid tone of the woman who was second in command at AION. Could this version of her mother even offer her anything?

The idea made her chuckle out loud as she came to the realization that the other Ruth, while capable, likely wouldn't have offered much in terms of help either.

"All I want to do is help you, London," Ruth said, replying to a conversation that wasn't being had out loud. Her abilities were so dim that she forgot Ruth might still be firing on all cylinders.

"In your timeline, did you know anything about your father?"

"I knew the only details that mattered. When he lived and how you reached him."

"Those are far from the only details that mattered, but in this instance, they matter a great deal," Ruth said.

"As always, I have no patience for mystery," London complained.

Ruth got up and stood an inch from London's face. "Read me."

"What?"

"Read me. Where is my heart right now? What emotions are right here on my surface?" Ruth asked. She took London's hands and placed them on her own chest. "Read me, London."

"I can't. There's nothing left in here."

"If that's true then you will never reach them."

"Ruth, maybe give her a moment. It's been a long day," Siobhan suggested. The two of them seemed to be communicating in a way that was lost on London.

"Read me now, or I'm leaving and I'm never coming back."

"Jesus, Mom. What does that mean?"

"I will not stay and watch things fall apart."

London tried to storm off, but Siobhan grabbed her by the wrist.

"Read her," she insisted, suddenly switching teams. London felt as if her last ally had fallen. "Just try, London."

London turned back toward her mother. She didn't touch her or even look directly at her, but she stood in front of her, searching for just a whisper of the ability she once possessed.

Instead of trying to rouse something in this empty vessel, she focused on taking her mind back to who she was. She thought only in terms of the memories from her original timeline. She tried to feel her body and her mind in that other place. When she felt she had a grip on it, she turned that sensation outward.

At first what came up didn't make sense, and she felt like a projector whose light had gone out. Everything was functioning except for the only piece she actually needed in order to see. She could hear her mother's voice, but couldn't see her face. She could feel the butterflies in her mother's stomach, but couldn't identify the source.

"I'll come back, John. I promise," she heard her mother say. But her mother's voice wasn't in the room. It was distant, like they were in an open field or a meadow.

"I'll come back, John. I promise," London echoed, saying her father's name for the first time in either lifetime.

"Good girl," Ruth said, putting a hand on her cheek.

London felt a surge of energy as her dormant skill rose to the surface in timid waves. It was hard to hold on to, but there it was.

She turned her focus toward Siobhan, but was met with deafening silence.

"Are you able to read her?" London asked her mother, nodding toward Siobhan.

"No one can," Siobhan answered.

"I'm not sure how much good it will do to resurrect my abilities. Even if I can get to a point where I can travel again, where would I even go? This entire timeline is screwed unless I go back to the day Taryn saved Abigail. And I'm not sure I have it in me to let a little girl die."

"We're not going to bring back your abilities," Ruth said. "We're going to try to make you capable of mine."

London chased the idea around in her mind. "Divine Travel?" London asked.

"You said you did it before."

"I'm nowhere near being the person I was then."

"You're the same person," Ruth said.

London still wasn't sure where she'd go, but at least she had a plan for how to get there.

"You can do this. You've never had a better reason."

59

*T*aryn had already come and gone, doing a silent outfit change and reapplication of makeup. Gable attempted to greet her, but didn't dare touch her.

"I'll be late," was all she offered as she let the door slam behind her. She was wearing a tight electric blue dress and a leather jacket. Her heels were twice the height of the shoes she wore to work and Gable felt some movement below the belt when she clicked passed him. There was no sense telling her though. She was off to prove to herself and him that lots of guys could get it up for her if given the chance. Or at least that's what he always felt the goals of these party binges were. They never really talked about the weekends where she'd stumble in hours passed closing time and sleep in their spare bedroom. Both accepted that this was the punishment he deserved for being an impotent loser.

His laundry was done, and his desire to catch up on work had long since passed. He checked his phone for a response from Abigail. Nothing. There were three texts from his mother asking if he'd called or texted or heard anything.

He tapped his phone on his forehead and spoke into the speaker.

"Call Abby."

"Calling Abby," his phone responded.

It rang five times before she answered. When she did, her voice was slow and she drew out her vowels with raspy indifference.

"Hello."

"It lives," Gable said.

"What do you want, big bro?"

"Just proof of life."

"Sorry to be the bearer of bad news, but no one with a life here."

"Can you just text Mom and tell her you're alive?"

"How can I tell her that when I'm not?"

"What's wrong with you?" He didn't have it in him to perk up his voice into a more convincing impersonation of sincerity.

"I'm drowning."

He waited, but she didn't expand on her claim.

"You're drowning?"

"Yeah. I just feel like I'm under water all the time."

"Well, that's probably the copious amounts of weed you smoke and pills you take."

"Probably."

"Can you at least text Mom and tell her you're breathing?"

"Are you sure that I am?"

"God, Abby. It was good talking to you."

He hung up the phone and sent a message to his mother.

Abby is fine. Just talked to her.

Three dots appeared in the message chain, but after thirty seconds he shut down the screen to his phone. He had no doubt a slew of questions, concerns, and appreciation was about to flood his phone, and he didn't care enough to even open the text when he felt his phone finally buzz.

Food. Food was all he had on his mind.

He could order takeout and commit to not leaving his house or his tattered basketball shorts all day, but that felt a little too pathetic.

Instead, he showered, shaved, and traded his basketball shorts for some board shorts and a clean t-shirt. He could at least grab wings and a beer and watch what was left of the Suns game.

When Gable backed out of his driveway he almost hit her.

He wasn't sure who it was, but there was a woman standing in his driveway, inches from his bumper.

"Christ!" he yelled to himself.

He put the car in Park and flung open his door.

"I'm sorry, I didn't see you. Can I help you?"

The sun was setting behind her so even just a few feet away he couldn't make out the features of the person he almost flattened.

"Gable?"

He held a hand up to his forehead to shade his eyes. "Yes. I'm Gable."

The woman drew in a sharp inhale.

When he got closer, he began to realize that this wasn't just some woman walking her dog or a solicitor offering cleaning services. He recognized her. This was the woman he saw in his dreams the night before. And that woman wasn't just some figment of his imagination. That woman was London Riley. An adult version of a girl he hadn't seen since he was a teenager. Now that she was in front of him and not inside some indistinct dreamscape, her identity was unmistakable.

60

*L*ondon didn't know what she was doing here. She didn't tell her mother or Siobhan where she was going when she left the house. She didn't devise a plan on the way over. She hadn't even concocted an opening sentence.

Taryn's warning didn't feel like it mattered. She'd already robbed her of everything she loved. Dying sounded easy compared to the infinite landscape of what if's that laid out in front of her now.

"London Riley?" Gable asked, his hand hovering over his eyes. She hadn't expected him to recognize her.

"Yes."

"I'm…geeze. How are you? Do you live over here?" He looked up and down his street as if there should be some sort of obvious answer for why she was in his driveway.

"No. I don't live here."

She should have planned for what she was going to say, she thought. Now she was standing in front of him dazed and off balance. She reached down deep in search of the ability that would help her see who he was in this world.

"Do you need help or something?"

Perfect. She was coming off like an escaped patient from a mental institution.

"Is your wife home?"

"Umm…how do you know I'm married?"

"You're wearing a ring."

"Oh, yeah. I'm actually married to Taryn Trainor. From school." He laughed as if this revelation should be something that she might also find amusing.

"Oh," was all she could offer.

"She's not here. She's out for the night. I was just about to head out for some dinner."

"Can I join you?" London asked. She knew it was weird. This whole thing was weird. Why not lean into it?

She could see his eyes searching for a way out of this conversation and way out of bringing her along.

"I…I guess."

She climbed into the passenger seat of his car. The cologne he was wearing didn't smell familiar and she hated that he was in board shorts and a t-shirt. Her Gable would not have gone out to dinner looking like this. And his glasses were gone. Along with the beard. She couldn't stand how naked his face was.

Still, there were some similarities. He hummed a nonsensical tune every time the car turned a corner. The air conditioning in the car was turned down too low, chilling her exposed arms and face.

And then she found it. That storm inside his chest. That crushing combination of chaos and beauty. Her skills were nothing like they used to be, but that sensation she felt every time she was near him was still there. Despite his sister and his mother surviving. Despite a childhood lived in relative peace. Despite a nice home with a wife who would cross time and space to be with him, he still churned from the inside out, unsettled and full of raw, furious potential.

"So, what have you been up to?" Gable asked. Too much time had passed since she got in the car without a word spoken, and she wondered if he was maybe driving her to a police station.

"I'm not sure."

"What do you do for a living?"

"I was a Director of Marketing somewhere, but I've decided not to go anymore."

"Not to go?"

"No. It doesn't fit me. What do you do?" she asked.

"I'm in IT."

"Pfffft." London couldn't help but let out a sound of ridicule. Her husband, a brilliant chemist and a co-inventor of time travel living his life as an ordinary man doing ordinary work.

"You have a problem with IT?"

"No. It is a perfectly acceptable occupation."

"Boring as shit is what it is."

She laughed. Less at his obvious joke and more at the casual rhythm she felt herself falling into.

"I know it's really strange, me showing up at your house and getting into your car like this. Do you ever just feel you have to do something?"

"We haven't seen each other in almost twenty years. Why do you feel like you needed to see me? We never even talked in school."

"No. We didn't."

"Are you here to murder me?" That noncommittal smile crept onto his face and she couldn't hold it back anymore. Tears sprang forward.

She didn't apologize or explain herself. What did it matter if *this* Gable thought she was crazy or if he told Taryn what she had done. Nothing seemed to matter at all in this timeline and so, right or wrong, she just reacted.

London was surprised when they pulled up in front of a sports bar. This was another sign that her Gable was still in there. For all his straight lines and seriousness in her reality, Gable Matthews was a man who valued good wings above all other forms of dining.

"Should we at least get a beer and some food before you kill me?"

"Sure," London said.

They drank their first beers in perfect silence. He asked nothing of her. Maybe he was afraid to. Maybe he could detect that there was some greater purpose to her arrival.

He ordered another round by holding up two fingers. He turned to her, his green eyes starting to swim under the comfort of a first-beer buzz.

"Do you want to hear something crazy?" he asked. "I feel like I can share this with you given that I currently have the mental high ground in terms of sanity." London nodded in agreement. "I had a dream about you. Last night."

"That can't possibly be true."

"No. It is. I know it sounds impossible and I didn't even realize it was you until you showed up."

"Are you messing with me?" she asked in disbelief.

"Hand to God I am not. I dreamt of you and a little girl."

An icy sweat formed in all of London's creases. Chills hollowed out her thighs.

"What was the child's name?"

"I don't know."

"Well, what did she look like?"

"Why?"

"Just answer me!"

"Umm, she's small, has curly hair. Blondish-brown hair."

"What color were her eyes?"

"I don't know. It's a dream. Who notices those things about a dream?"

"Did she have any distinguishing marks or did she say anything?"

"Well, it looks like you're reclaiming your Queen Crazy crown." He moved a detectable two inches away from London.

"Gable, I need you to think. What else do you know?"

"You called her Bug. In my dream you called her Bug." Now he was shouting a little and putting his hands up in a defensive motion that told her she better stay back.

"Marley." London clasped shaking hands over her mouth. "I have to go."

She got up from her seat and left Gable sitting there. She used her phone to order a car service. She couldn't stay here and drink with her imitation husband. Her daughter was slipping further and further away, and yet she had somehow found a way to reach him. In this place, where Marley was so far from existence, she'd found him. If Marley could reach that far, London could find a way to reach her daughter.

61

*G*able couldn't piece together exactly what happened. It all seemed too strange to even explain to himself. A girl from high school shows up in the driveway. Asks to get in the car. She gets in. They drive together to a bar. Drink. Talk. He confesses he dreamt about her and she freaks out and leaves.

She's probably some sort of stalker who has been following him for years and now he's upset her. *Real smart*, he says to himself out loud on the car ride home. He's probably seen her and not even realized it and that's why she's in his dreams.

As he approached his house he looked around the front yard. He turned on his brights expecting to see London Riley tucked into the hedge. Instead he saw that the lights were on inside and Taryn's car was in the garage.

His wife was sitting on the couch, no longer dressed for a nightclub. Taryn was in a pair of sweatpants holding a glass of wine. She offered a hesitant smile.

"Hey, babe."

"Hey." There was no way he could tell her what happened.

"Out for wings?"

"Yeah. I'm surprised to see you home."

Taryn got up off the couch and laid her head on his chest. "I'm sorry."

"Don't be."

Gable held her tight and then pulled her in tighter, glad to see the person he'd shared every moment with for most his life and relieved that she didn't seem to want to do much talking.

They make love with no equipment failure. Their bodies collided in the dark and she moaned under his weight. He grabbed at her hair and rubbed his cheek alongside hers, but in the darkness, he wasn't seeing his wife. He was seeing London Riley. He tried to shake loose the thoughts of the strange woman from the bar, but the image of London spread through every nerve of his body and Taryn murmured, "Oh, my god" as he pressed into her.

They fell apart, breathing in desperate unison.

"That was incredible," she whispered.

When he fell asleep, the images of London and the little girl were sharper than ever. They were in the kitchen making breakfast. London was holding the little girl and stole two blueberries from a basket in front of him. She popped one in her mouth and handed one to the child. He pretended to be angry, but couldn't suppress his grin. When he sips his coffee, it's from a tall, black mug that says "Carpe Caffeine."

62

*T*raining to travel through time using an inherent ability passed down from your mother wasn't exactly something people build dojos for, London thought as she and her mother and Siobhan sat on the floor in her living room.

"We're just going to do it here?" London asked.

"Do you have another suggestion?" Ruth was already agitated. "We're not going to go far. And you're not going to try to take your whole body. Just try to get your mind to go back a day or two."

The last thing London wanted was to end up back in that bar with Gable. She needed to just contain herself to this apartment, so she tried to hold a less impactful memory in her mind.

Yearbooks on the floor. Wine in her hand. Her mother sitting at the counter. She tried to picture the moments just before she found out about Taryn and Gable.

"I'm not sure that's going to be strong enough," Ruth said, referring to London's memory. Ruth was peering into London like a fish bowl.

"Let's just try it."

"London, place your hands in Ruth's," Siobhan instructed.

"This feels a little séance-y," London admitted.

"The power of touch is not something to underestimate. There's a reason it's used in séances London." The icy exterior that was Siobhan's trademark in London's world crossed over into this one.

"Sorry," was all she could say, feeling as if she had maybe hit a nerve.

"London, you need to try to call upon your abilities. Don't try to think of how you would do it in this time. Try to think of how you would do it in your own," Ruth suggested.

London tried to think about the first time she'd felt her abilities course through her veins. She was six and thought she heard her mother crying. London ran through the house looking for her, but when she found her, Ruth's eyes were dry and her face set to its normal pallor. Inside though, London could feel her sadness. She felt like she could hold it in her hand and roll it around if she wanted to.

"Mama, what's wrong?" she'd asked.

Ruth looked at her with an exhausted droop in her eyes. "Sometimes mommies just feel sad."

From that moment on, London began to notice it in people all around her. At the grocery store, she'd say something like "that man isn't very nice to the little boy." Ruth would hush her and move them to the next aisle. Getting down on her knees she'd point her finger in London's face and tell her not to say things about people she doesn't know.

As she got older, it was students in school. Not just students, actually. Teachers, janitors, parents in the pick-up line. If she met two or three members from a single family she could pretty quickly piece together the makeup of their household.

There were exceptions. Ruth was always good at keeping

her out. Taryn's bilingual upbringing kept London from digging. And Siobhan. Siobhan was a brick wall. Almost everyone else was open season. Their memories and emotions, radiating off of them like body odor. Some she could detect more intensely than others. Gable most of all. It drove him crazy how good she was at reading him. He told her over and over again that she made him feel so exposed. London loved that about him. She loved that his heart was splayed out on a table. It's what she fell in love with.

"You have to get out of that headspace," Ruth interrupted. "We can't even attempt this with you focused on your husband."

"You told me to think of my ability, and he's a huge part of it."

"Let's try something else." Siobhan went into the kitchen and uncorked an already open bottle of wine. "Slam this," she said, handing it to London.

"It's ten o'clock in the morning."

"I've seen your Instagram. Looks like you do your best drinking before noon, Miss 'Hashtag Sunday Brunch Crew.'"

"I hate you a little for that," London returned with a scowl. Still, she followed orders and drank down the bitter leftover wine in three gulps. London tried to remember what she would tell her own traumatized travelers who were desperate to jump into another timeline. *It's in the small details.* She held the image of the dress her mother had been wearing on the night they flipped through yearbooks. It was so unlike anything Ruth would have worn. Small, springtime flowers with a light blue backdrop. It was loose, oversized, and showed none of Ruth's shape.

Ruth's lips pursed as she perceived London's reaction to her clothes, but she grabbed her daughter's hands nonetheless.

London closed her eyes and tried to reach inward for the spot at her center that would tingle and tug as it ripped her into the past. Nothing. She closed her eyes tighter and squeezed Ruth's hands harder. She pictured the blue dress. Tried to count the petals on the flowers. After what felt like an hour, but was really just minutes, London opened her eyes.

Siobhan was standing exactly where she had been. Her mother sat across from her on the floor. The room was unchanged. The time on the clock only changed by the standard passage of seconds into minutes.

"Well, we didn't think it would actually work the first time right?" Siobhan asked.

From the look on her face, London guessed that Ruth also believed they could make this work on the first try.

She released Ruth's hands and unclenched her fingers.

"How do you do it?" London asked Siobhan.

"How do I do what?"

"How do you travel?"

"It's not usually voluntary. Like I said in group, I go in moments of extreme emotion or pain. I get hurled back to wherever the problem started. It's like a simultaneous flight and fight reaction."

"How does it feel for you?"

Siobhan cracked her knuckles and bit her lip. "It feels like falling from a really high point. Like the cables were cut on an elevator shaft. I get this dropping sensation. My eyes close, and when they open I can be seconds into the past or decades."

"Have you ever traveled on purpose?"

"I've only learned to stop a travel when I don't wish to go. I can't seem to get it to happen on my own, though, no."

"Mom. What about you?"

"It's hard to remember. It's been a very, very long time."

"How long?"

"Thirty-two years."

It was no coincidence that London's age and the time it had been since Ruth Riley last traveled through time were nearly the same, give or take a few months.

"You haven't traveled since you got pregnant with me?"

"No."

"Why not?"

Ruth hesitated and shook her head.

"Tell me why not."

Tears filled up in her mother's eyes. "I was afraid I might lose my daughter."

London nodded her head. Ruth was wise enough to know when to quit. To know that what she was risking was far greater than what she had to gain. Why had London been so reckless?

"So you haven't traveled in three decades, and you have never been able to control your destination. I was another person the last time I did it. How are we ever supposed to figure this out?"

The room was silent.

"Right. I'm going to find someone who deals Chronzaplan."

"You can't do—" Siobhan started to say. London held up a hand.

"What would you have done to get your son back, Bonnie?"

She swallowed hard. "Anything. But, London, I tried Chron nine times. And I did travel. Never to anywhere I wanted to go. Never to any time where I could fix anything. I spent three months in a coma and was lucky to survive it. Why do you think I lead those groups? No one has tried more than me, London. It's not the answer."

"I won't just sit here and hope." London looked back and forth between her mother and Siobhan. Neither had an argument to offer.

*S*undays were the days Gable and Derek got together to play one-on-one at the courts in his neighborhood. Sweaty and aggressive, they would throw elbows, shoot hoops and coax their bodies into teenage movements that their thirty-plus-year-old bodies weren't as skilled at performing.

"You suck ass today, dude," Derek taunted. He wasn't wrong. Gable felt off like he'd never held a ball before. He had no follow-through on his shot and was barely even managing to push it high enough to hit the rim.

"I can't find my rhythm."

"You don't have any rhythm." Derek continued to throw jabs, but Gable wasn't in the mood.

"I think I have to call it for the day," Gable said.

"We've only been out here for like a half an hour."

"I don't know, man. It's just not clicking."

"You alright? Things with Taryn cool and shit?" Derek was not known for being a deep guy. Taryn once said that their friendship was based exclusively on beer, basketball, and Will Ferrell quotes. She wasn't wrong, but he decided to dive into the deep end anyway.

"Hey, do you remember London Riley? We went to school with her."

Derek got a look on his face like he'd been asked to find the square root of something. Then a light bulb went on.

"The psychic's daughter?"

"Yeah."

"I don't remember much about her other than that she was really weird."

"Right," Gable agreed.

"Why are you asking?"

"I ran into her the other day." Gable decided it was better to leave out the part about literally almost running into her in his driveway.

"No shit. You talk to her?"

"A little."

"What's she like?"

"Still kind of strange. But she looked good and was sort of interesting. I've thought about her a lot since I saw her."

Derek jerked his head back, obviously feeling the sudden shift from idle chitchat to serious conversation.

"What do you mean you've thought a lot about her?"

"I keep having these weird dreams." Gable rubbed the back of his neck. It was hard to say these things out loud without sounding like he was having an affair.

"Dreams? Are you saying you're wanting to hook up with her or something?"

"No. I'm married."

"Yeah. To Taryn. The same girl you've been with all your life."

"I don't want to cheat on my wife."

"I'm not saying you should. I'm just saying it would make

sense if at some point you started fantasizing about other chicks."

"That's not what this is."

"Whatever. No judgment."

"Do you ever just feel like everything about your life is off?"

"I'm a thirty-two-year-old bartender. I feel like that every day."

Gable let the conversation die in half-hearted laughter. Derek wasn't the guy to have existential conversations with. He attempted to play for fifteen more minutes before leaving Derek on the court alone. His head wasn't in the right space, he'd decided.

When he got home, Taryn was packing up a box in the middle of the living room.

"Hey, hun. I didn't expect you to be back already."

Gable shrugged. "Not on my A-game."

"Sore loser." Taryn smiled but didn't look up from the packaging tape she was layering over the box.

"What's all that?"

"Oh, nothing. Your mom wanted me to send some of my old clothes to Abby so she could use them for job interviews."

"She's just going to sell that stuff."

"I'm not wearing them. She can do whatever she wants with the clothes."

"You're not getting rid of that yellow dress I love that you hate are you?" He playfully tried to peel up a corner of the box and she slammed it down.

"Don't!" she yelled, aand the tone in the room shifted.

"Geez, I was just kidding." Gable put his hands in the air in surrender.

"Sorry. I'm just trying to wrap this up so I can start getting ready."

"Ready for what?"

"Good lord, Gable. It's your mom's birthday. Have you not even called her?"

He hadn't. He hadn't even remembered it was her birthday. His mind was out of sorts, but forgetting his own mother's birthday was a new low.

"What's the matter with you lately?" Taryn asked.

"I'm just having a hard time keeping things straight."

"I don't know what that means, but go take a shower and shave your face, you look homeless."

*L*ondon wasn't sure where to even start buying an illegal, time travel street drug. She felt resolute about her decision when she told Siobhan and Ruth that this was what she was doing. Now, sitting alone in her room, it felt less like a solution and more like suicide.

Was it worth the risk? She felt her choices slipping through her fingers. Anger and heat and agony and loss bubbled up underneath her clothes. She latched her focus onto the feeling and closed her body around it like a white blood cell attacking a virus. The pain felt solid, like a blade between her ribs. She concentrated on what she'd sacrificed by trusting Taryn and let the blade twist.

"Take me back," she whispered to the wound. "Let me choose again."

A familiar tug pulled at her insides.

The room began to darken.

Her eyes closed, and when they opened again she wasn't in her apartment. She was in her apartment at AION. She looked at her hands and saw chipped polish instead of a perfect manicure. Her clothes were familiar and delightfully ordinary instead of the tight athletic wear she'd been occupying for days.

No one else was in the room, but on the table was her drawing. It was the morning following her first date with Gable.

She shook out of her daze and realized that she was in a place where Gable was. Her Gable. And Taryn. Before she'd destroyed London's life. When London tried to go to the door, she couldn't move. Her body glided toward the bathroom. She was immobile, but she was in her time. That was a start.

The wrenching feeling in her stomach returned, and she was ripped back to the present. Not her present, but the alternate one where she has nothing.

Not nothing anymore. Now she had a twinge of hope. She could still travel. Not with any accuracy or intention, but it was still there, buried under layers of fake reality. And she could do more than travel. She could travel to her old timeline. As long as she held on to the memories of her real life, she could navigate her way back.

London slammed her fist against her mother's front door and waited for Ruth to open up. She'd found her mother's address in her phone and decided to drive over. She couldn't stand her four walls any longer and needed to tell Ruth what had just happened. She wasn't entirely sure how to recreate the travel, but it felt like a success.

She was surprised to see Siobhan was there too. Both women had a guarded hush in their voice.

"Are you alright, London?" asked Siobhan.

"What happened?" asked Ruth.

"I traveled. I managed to summon something up from

deep inside and not only did I go back. I went back to my time. My world."

Neither woman responded. She didn't expect a roaring round of applause, but there was absolutely no celebration or follow-up questions.

"I thought this was pretty good news," London said, trying to lead them toward at least acknowledging her proclamation.

London began to detect agitation in her mother. She could tell that Ruth was trying to mask something. London tried to wrap her head around the emotion that was being held at a distance.

Guilt.

It slithered into London's skin a little at a time, but soon her body was filled with Ruth's guilt.

"What did you do? Mom, answer me. What did you do?"

"I'm sorry, London. I can't lose you."

Another knock came to the door. London could have asked who it was, but in the heat of the moment, Ruth's guard was all the way down and London's abilities were sharpening by the second.

"You called my probation officer?"

"We were afraid you were going to hurt yourself or someone else, London," Siobhan inserted.

"I can't lose you." Ruth looked at the floor as she opened the door.

A man entered the room. He was in slacks and a flawless, pressed button down. She hadn't met her probation officer, but already she could tell he was no one to mess with.

"London Riley?"

"Mike?"

"That's me. We got a call from your mother. She's worried about you. You doing alright?"

"I'm fine."

"Have you obtained or attempted to solicit Chronzaplan?"

"No."

"Did you have any intentions of seeking it out?"

London shrugged her shoulders. She had never been a good liar.

"Protocol dictates that I take you in for a 48-hour hold."

"Are you serious? Can't you just test me and see that I'm not on it?"

"Unfortunately, we have to take it a little more seriously than that."

"I'm going to jail?"

"You're going to a psychiatric facility that specializes in temporal dysphoria."

"I have a disorder now?" London was getting more indignant by the second.

"I have rules I have to follow. What you do or don't call yourself is up to you and a therapist."

"If I refuse to go?"

"You don't have that option, London."

The guilt in the room took on a stench that was making it hard to breathe. London walked out the front door without looking at her mother or Siobhan. They had made their decision. She could perceive that they both hated themselves for it, but that they felt it was necessary. There was no point in punishing them with a scowl. Something about traveling back to her own timeline put her back in touch with the essence of her makeup. It was as if someone had plugged her back into a power source.

The car ride with Mike was silent. The hard part of his hair and the perfect edge of his beard told London all she needed to know about him. There was a steady, circulatory feel to his insides like a bike chain. Everything was done with precision in his life. He turned on the blinker precisely four seconds before every turn. He held the gas at the exact speed limit. When they parked, there was equal space on each side of his vehicle. If he weren't ushering her to a two-day lock-down, London might like Mike for all his exactitudes.

The two of them approached a desk intended for check-ing-in patients. The Medical Center for Temporal Dysphoria looked like any other healthcare institution. The workers were wearing scrubs. There was a patient in a hospital gown being pushed around in a wheelchair. Family members with hearts full of concern visited with a teenage boy in the lobby.

Mike did all the talking for London. He gave her name, address, date of birth, and a summary of the events as described to him. The young woman entering in the data gave London a gentle smile. Inside, London could feel how little care was behind that practiced expression. It didn't matter, though. She didn't need an admittance worker to feel for her.

"Just take a couple days and get yourself on track," Mike said, placing a practiced hand on London's shoulder. "I don't want to have to take you to jail, or worse."

London gave an awkward thumbs up and a tight-lipped smile. The gesture was enough for Mike to nod and leave through sliding glass doors.

"Miss Riley? Would you like us to get you a wheelchair?"

"No."

"Alright, then. Miles will be right over to collect you and show you to your room."

London followed the administrator's gaze to a familiar face. The most familiar face she'd seen since she entered this timeline. Everyone else she knew had different hair, different clothes, a different way of carrying themselves. Somehow Miles looked strikingly the same as he always had.

Feelings of betrayal and warmth swirled together inside her. She never quite got over the way he would do James's bidding, but she knew that at his core he wasn't a bad person.

He was just someone who was easily pushed around. He walked up with a wide smile on his face, blissfully unaware that London had seen him naked several times. What they had was only ever casual, but she felt a deep-seated affection for the glorious sameness that hummed inside Miles.

"Miss Riley?" he asked. She nodded, too quick and too eager. "Hi, there," he continued, like he was talking to a child. "My name is Miles. I'm a nurse working on the floor where you'll be staying. Can I show you the way to your room?"

She agreed to follow him but kept staring at his face, looking for even one eyebrow hair that was different. How had he managed to stay so like himself? How was it that all these people in her other life were spilling into this one? There was so much about time travel that made absolutely no sense, but she felt comfort in this reality's attempt at familiarity. Maybe everyone she ever knew was meant to intersect with her life no matter the timeline. Maybe her accidental skew into this timeline was drawing pieces of her old life toward her like a magnet.

He showed her to a white-walled room with a single window opposite the door. There were two beds and two nightstands, one closet, and one bathroom. The space was somewhere between a hospital room and dorm. There weren't any heart monitoring machines and the beds were just beds, not rolling stretchers.

"You have a roommate, but she's in group right now. You'll like her. She's been here a long time and can help you get acclimated."

"Oh, I'm only here for two days."

"Yes. Of course. Still, she can at least let you know which foods to avoid at lunchtime. Hint, it's anything in the pork family." Miles smiled, amused at himself and careless about whether anyone else was entertained. "You're on a forty-eight-hour hold for now. No cell phone, no TV, no computers. You'll attend two group sessions and two private sessions, and then you'll be evaluated for release."

"Wait, are you saying there is a chance I could get stuck here longer?"

"It doesn't always happen that way. If your therapist feels you're able to go without the potential to harm yourself or others, then you'll be released at the end of that forty-eigh-hour hold."

"And if my therapist determines something else?"

"That's not really for me to say. That's up to you and your therapist. Again, my name is Miles. I'll be here until eight tonight, so let me know if you need anything or if you're feeling crummy."

London nodded her head again, bewildered once more at just how terribly she'd managed to make everything in so few days. Not only had she lost her own reality, but now her control over this one was being taken away.

She sat on the bed and picked at the small balls of fabric that textured the surface of her comforter. The linens felt like they'd been overwashed and were coming apart one tiny thread at a time.

The door opened, and she hoped it was Miles again with his unassuming smile. Instead, it was another face she knew. Skewed almost beyond the point of recognition, but still a face she knew.

"Beth?"

65

"*H*e's playing like garbage this year."

Gable wasn't sure which player his father was talking about but nodded as he stared at the television screen.

"You alright, Gabe?"

"Huh? Oh, yeah. Just tired."

"Trouble sleeping?"

"A little."

"Everything okay with the Mrs.?"

"Sure."

"Worried about your sister?"

"You know Abby. She always turns up more or less unscathed."

"Yes. She always does."

His father let the conversation die there. Gable appreciated his simplicity. Everything about his dad was on the surface. Their talks only ever involved the weather, sports, his immediate family, or work. They never got into political or philosophical debates. His father hadn't even bothered to bring up how Gable had forgotten to contact his own mother all day on her birthday. He and Taryn were here now for dinner, so as far as his dad was concerned, the issue was settled.

Taryn and his mother were preparing lasagna in the kitchen. In all likelihood, they were talking about Abby's physical distance from them and Gable's mental distance as of lately. He couldn't describe it, but seeing Taryn and his mother so close made him uneasy at times. He would wonder if the reason Taryn was with him was as much about being with his mother as it was about being with him.

Even after twenty years together, Gable still couldn't get Taryn to talk much about her own family. On the day she saved his sister, Taryn became an honorary Matthews kid until she became an official daughter-in-law when they got married at twenty-four. There were signs of abuse when she was younger, bruises and cuts, and his mother closed in around her. Taryn spent all her days at their house and at least half the nights as a teenager. Gable felt pretty certain his parents knew she was sleeping over, but everyone kept up the pretenses around her sneaking in at night. What were they going to do? Banish the girl who kept their daughter from drowning?

Yet even back then, Gable felt like Taryn loved all of them equally instead of loving him especially. He would try to lure her to a movie so they could make out in a dark corner and she'd push for staying in and watching *Law & Order* with his parents. Almost all of their vacations included his mom and dad. The cruise to the Bahamas. The European trek. The California beach house. Sure, Gable loved his folks, but he often felt guilty because he was pretty sure Taryn loved them more.

Of all his family, Abby was actually the one he felt the most related to. Had Taryn not always been there to draw him in, he might have also been living at some undisclosed address touching base only once or twice a month to keep his mother from reporting him missing. Abby used to tell him she didn't belong here. She never gave much detail, but he couldn't help but agree. He wasn't even sure *he* belonged here.

Taryn slid her arms down his chest as she approached him from behind the recliner he was sunk into. She placed her mouth close to his ear so only he could hear her. "Want to go for another roll tonight?"

His stomach dropped.

She was becoming insatiable lately and, given his track record, there was always some performance anxiety associated with it. He forced a smile and squeezed her wrists. From what he could tell, she didn't detect his hesitation.

They passed the time drinking wine. His father drifted out of the conversation toward the basketball game on TV. Taryn and his mother talked about books they had both read and plans for the next big trip. Gable couldn't think of much else to do so he drank. And then drank a little bit more.

By the time they sat down for dinner he was well beyond buzzed. He gulped down water and began shoveling in bread to help counter the ebb and flow of the room around him.

His mother reached for his hand to say a prayer and Taryn batted the bread out of his grip to get him to join in.

"Thank you, God, for this beautiful meal and the gift of another year. Thank you for my husband, always strong and sturdy by my side. Thank you for my son, whose sharp mind keeps me focused. Thank you for my beautiful daughter-in-law, whose heart is always full. And, God, please look after my sweet Abby. Though she is lost, I know she will be found."

At this Gable let a snort escape his nostrils.

Taryn elbowed him in the ribs, but it wasn't enough. The alcohol was already starting to choose his words for him.

"She isn't lost. She just doesn't give a damn."

"I don't think that language is necessary at the table," his mother protested.

"I'm just saying. Why do we always have to talk about Abby like she has any interest in being a part of this family? She's gone ninety-five percent of the time. When she is here she clearly hates it. Does she really deserve a spot in the prayer or the hundreds of conversations we have about where she might be and what she's doing?"

"Gable, that's enough," Taryn scolded.

"It is enough, babe. This is more than enough. Can we just all finally say it? That the second Abby was revived after being found in the pool she was a different kid. That the sweet little girl she once was drowned in that pool and never came back."

"Gable, how could you say something like that?" Now his mother was doing the fake weeping that was so typical of an Abby-talk. He knew he should stop. He knew it was wrong. But something inside him had cracked open, and the truth poured onto the table in hot, liquid bursts.

"Mom, maybe you would have more of a life if you didn't tie up fifteen of your sixteen waking hours worrying about Abigail. Let her go. Let her be whatever the hell it is that she's out there being and let her go."

"Gable, it's your mother's birthday," his father interjected, still maintaining his role as the most unimposing man alive.

"You're telling me you're happy, Dad? That twenty years of 'Do you think she's alright?' 'Why did she say that?' 'Where is she going?' 'Who are her friends?' hasn't driven you up the fucking wall?"

"Gable, that's enough!" Now Taryn was yelling. And standing. Here would have been where he stopped in any other scenario. His mother was a doormat. His dad was the concrete slab beneath the doormat. His wife, however, was not one to be messed with. Yet something about this night pushed him to his limit, and there was no turning back now.

"And you. Sending her clothes for job interviews? What job interviews? We all know that, best-case scenario, Abby is stripping at some dive."

"Go walk whatever this is off, Gable. Get the hell out," his wife demanded.

Taryn was done with him. And, frankly. he was done with himself. Years of holding that back and now it was all on the table. He felt good. He felt free. And there was nothing he wanted more than to leave this room full of dumbstruck faces.

Gable shoved his chair out and threw his napkin on the plate. He slammed the front door as he stepped into the dry desert air. He inhaled deeply and felt like it was the first breath he'd taken in days.

He knew he shouldn't drive, but he hopped into his car anyway, stranding Taryn with his parents. She and his mother could toil over his mental breakdown for hours and he could enjoy the peace of his own home.

Door to door, his home was less than seven minutes away from his parent's. So even though the stoplights were blurry and he was certain he wasn't holding his lane, he made it to his garage without a major incident.

Gable headed straight for his closet and began ripping his button down over his head in search of a loose-fitting t-shirt. He stumbled around the closet, looking for one among the dirty clothes on the floor.

His finger jammed on a box tucked behind a rack holding Taryn's clothes. He swept the hanging pants aside, knocking some onto the floor. The box he stubbed his thumb on was the same one he saw Taryn taping up earlier. The box of clothes for his sister.

Well aware the alcohol was driving him, he picked up the

box, fully intending to throw it in the garbage. It would be the climactic finish to his temper tantrum, he thought. When he lifted it, he was surprised that the contents didn't have the quiet dense feel of a box of clothing. Instead, items shifted around inside. Some sounded metallic and heavy. He studied the box again and was sure it was the one he had seen.

On his knees, he ripped at the excessive layers of tape and shredded a piece of the cardboard. When he finally got to the box's contents, he wasn't sure what he was looking at. A rectangular machine with wires coming out the end was placed to one side. An unlabeled bottle containing some sort of pills was also there. There were also at least a dozen notebooks. He reached for the top notebook and immediately recognized Taryn's handwriting. His eyes swam in his drunken state so he couldn't quite comprehend the words he was reading. It seemed like journal entries from the last couple days. Then all it once his vision came into focus and he saw a name: *London Riley.*

Written in Taryn's handwriting was the name of the woman he couldn't shake from his brain. He frantically began trying to read backward from the name to figure out why it was written in the first place.

Before he could make sense of what he was reading, something hit him on the head with a thud. Searing pain spread at the base of his skull and he fell face forward onto the box without seeing where the blow came from.

66

"*Y*eah, I'm Beth. Who are you?"

London tried to coax words out of her mouth, but she was too stricken. There are chance encounters and then there's fate beyond reason. Beth was one of her closest friends in her timeline, and while so many people from AION were from Arizona originally, to have two members in one place here seemed impossible.

If she thought about it, though, this *was* a place for time travelers. With or without AION as she remembered it, London, Siobhan, Ruth, and Beth were all psychics capable of at least some level of travel without Gable's compound or Taryn's machine. London had to get used to the fact that the refugees of her timeline would parade into this life. It still didn't ease the shock of seeing Beth in the condition she was in. Her hair looked like she cut it herself. Her cheeks were hollowed out. Her forehead had a large bruise spread across it.

"I'm London. I'm your roommate for a couple days, I guess."

"No, you're not."

"Excuse me?"

"You're not just my roommate. We know each other."

"I'm not sure I understand."

Beth tapped her finger on the side of her head.

"You know what I am," Beth insisted.

She wasn't sure why, but London felt the urge to whisper.

"Wait, do you remember things? How they used to be? How they're supposed to be?" London asked.

"Used to be? I can't go back. I can only go forward."

London knew this about her. Knew Beth's capabilities were more centered around clairvoyance.

"Right. So if you can only go forward what makes you think we know each other?"

"I'm just seeing us talking about things that two-day roommates don't talk about."

"Yeah. We know each other."

Beth let the conversation hang. She went to a drawer and pulled out a notebook. She began scribbling something down. Occasionally she would look up at the clock and then go back to writing.

"Do you want to know how we know each other?" London asked.

"You're in some sort of messed up version of reality, right? In this other , you and I were friends or lovers or something?"

"We were friends. How do you know that?"

"Look around you."

London looked around the room. Her face must have read confused because Beth rolled her eyes and continued to explain.

"We're at a place where they send people who have time traveled, think they can time travel, or are desperate to time travel. So it's pretty obvious that your timeline is all out of whack and you're from some other reality where you and I are connected.

"That happens all the time here. It's why so many people just stay. We may not be who we were in other timelines, but there's comfort in familiar faces."

London couldn't argue with that.

"Why are you here? You couldn't have messed up a timeline if you can only go forward."

"You haven't seen *Back to the Future 2*?"

London let out a breathy laugh.

"I'm here because I'm one of the remaining members of AION. I was lucky enough to be sent here instead of prison."

London had so many questions, but wasn't sure if any of the answers mattered.

"Do you and Miles know each other from AION?"

"Miles? He has no gifts other than the ability to remember movie quotes beyond a reasonable amount. Plus, James never let tourists on campus."

"Tourists?"

"People with zero to contribute to our Temporal Destiny."

Even the language Beth was using was completely disconnected from her own experience. Whatever happened at AION between London leaving at eighteen and its demise was a world apart from the place she spent most of her twenties. She couldn't help but be morbidly fascinated.

Beth went back to scribbling in her notebook. This was all new to London, but talks of alternate timelines and friends lost to another reality were apparently second nature to her.

"What are you writing?"

"I'm not writing. I'm tracking."

"Tracking what?"

"Time. Obviously. If I don't write down the time and a quick summary of what is going on then I'm not sure when I've gone forward or when I'm in the present."

"What happened at AION?"

Beth was growing tired of this conversation. London could feel it, and she didn't want to annoy her friend and risk opportunities to talk more.

"You can read about most of it online."

London laid back on her bed, allowing the conversation to end.

"I don't know everything that happened," Beth began with reluctance in her voice. "What happened to me was that for almost six weeks I had Chronzaplan fed intravenously 24/7. I saw myself at almost every stage in my life. As an old woman. Middle aged. One day ahead, three thousand days ahead. I spent a month and a half hopping around my future, unable to stop, and you know what I found?"

London turned her head and looked Beth in the eyes.

"That I was screwed. Not just for a few years, but for the rest of my life. It's all garbage."

London returned her eyes to the ceiling tiles. She spent a lot of time resenting her own abilities. Wishing she could just have some peace and quiet instead of always picking up on what others were feeling. To know everything that was ahead of you and be unable to stop what was coming sounded worse.

Inside Beth was a meat grinder full of coins just chomping angrily down on a reality that she wasn't supposed to have. The vivacious woman who radiated light in her time looked like a cancer patient who had been decimated by treatment.

The door opened and Miles stepped in.

"Glad to see you two have met. London, it's time for your first appointment with a therapist."

She rolled off the bed and tried to catch Beth's attention so she could leave her with at least a warm smile of gratitude, but her roommate was back to scribbling in her notebook.

The therapist was a lean man in his forties, London guessed. He had pictures of himself running marathons on the walls and she fought the urge to immediately dislike him.

"Not a fan of runners?" he asked.

She jerked her head back.

"Don't panic. Most psychics aren't used to having someone read us for a change."

"Wait you're...?"

"I am."

"So am I good to just sit here, then, and let you decide if I'm staying or going?"

"You can. It will make for a sort of awkward session though."

London shrugged her shoulders. At this point nothing felt particularly strange anymore because everything was strange.

"Let's start by pretending like we aren't digging around in each other's subconscious first, what do you say?"

"Fine."

"I'm Brian."

"I'm London."

"That's a fun name."

"I guess. People always ask if I'm British."

"That's dumb."

She let a smile crack. Despite being a runner who hung pictures of himself on the walls, he was actually pleasant to be around.

"Seems a little unfair to have a psychic therapist."

"It's actually pretty necessary around here. We have

people who don't know where or when they are. Others who can't piece together their own reality because of how many times they've tinkered with the past. Not to mention, it serves as a good safeguard for determining if people have the potential to repeat their offense."

"Well, where I come from, traveling isn't an offense."

"We have many like you. Who have a reality where time travel wasn't discovered publicly or where it's out in the open and positively received. Unfortunately, in this reality, it is illegal."

"So, am I going to repeat offend?"

"Without a doubt."

"Are you going to keep me here then?"

"We'll see. Tell me about your daughter."

"I can't."

"Why not?"

"Because I'm having a hard time remembering her right now."

"Well, she's still in there. I can see her."

London's eyes welled up, but she refused to let the tears spill over.

"You went and saw your husband."

"He isn't my husband here."

"Didn't stop you from going to see him."

London counted how many photos were on the wall then counted how many books were on the shelf.

"You can spend the whole session counting, or we can try to get somewhere, but I can't let you go if we don't have any real conversation," Brian said.

He never broke his pleasant tone or made London feel she was being judged. When she would try to read him, all she could see was inside herself. His ability was cross polluting her own.

"I want my life back. I know that's probably not possible,

but I want it. I don't know when I would have to travel to or how I would even get there. The tools I had in my reality don't exist here, and so I'm stuck."

"You didn't actually ever take Chronzaplan did you?"

"No. I took a compound from my time. One that was safe. My husband is actually the one who invented it."

"And he isn't involved with time travel in this reality?"

"No. His wife made sure of that."

As thoughts of Taryn flooded London's mind, Brian's passive face turned downward.

"What she did to you was horrible," he said.

At that, London could no longer hold back her tears. He saw everything she'd been through, everything she'd lost, and knowing that just one other person truly saw her for what she was—a wife and a mother who lost everything—was both comforting and devastating.

"I've never been to therapy before," she said, laughing manically through tears.

"Well, you're doing a great job." The airy smile returned to Brian's face. He explained a little more about what the next two days would look like and sent her on her way.

It wasn't Miles who walked her back to her room, but when she got there something in Beth had changed. She looked eager, but waited for the nurse to leave before she began talking.

"What's the matter?" London asked.

"You want to travel again, don't you?"

Taken aback, London nodded. "I do."

"Where are you trying to go?"

"Back to my time."

Beth waved for her to come over to her bed. She opened her notebook and pointed to a line on the page.

London disappears from the bed.

London read it again to make sure she wasn't making things up.

"What does this mean?"

"I flashed forward, and this is what I saw," Beth replied.

She had no idea how, but Beth had recorded what seemed to her like a Divine Travel.

hen Gable came to, his head was splitting and Taryn was holding an ice pack against his scalp.

"What the hell," Gable said, reaching back for the cold spot.

"Oh, thank God you're alright," Taryn said.

Alright isn't exactly how he would describe his current state.

"What happened?"

"I don't know. I came home and you were lying face down on the floor in the closet. I figured you blacked out from drinking and then I noticed this lump on your head."

"You didn't think to call the cops or something?"

"Call the cops? Why would I have done that?"

"Because someone attacked me."

"No one attacked you, Gable. You fell down drunk and hit your head."

He squeezed his eyelids tight and tried to remember the blurry details.

"Someone hit me."

"Who?"

"I don't know. It was from behind."

"Well, no one was here. Nothing is stolen. I think you just fell and hit your head."

"The back of my head?"

"Apparently."

Taryn was using a tone that towed the line between annoyed and concerned.

Gable scrambled to his feet and headed for their bedroom closet. He tossed clothes aside and unhooked Taryn's hung pants from the rack.

"Where is it?" he asked.

"Where's what?"

"The box?"

"What box, Gable? God, you're still acting crazy."

"The box. There was a box. The one you were going to send to Abby. It was right here." He pointed with two hands to a blank spot on the floor. "It was right here, but there weren't any clothes in it."

"You have lost it." Taryn threw her hands in the air and stormed out of the room.

Gable tried to unpack the hazy details of the night before. He remembered yelling at his mother at the dinner table. *Classy move*, he thought to himself. He did not remember how he got home, but he did remember being in the closet. There was the box and it had something in it. What was it?

He took off in a half run, half limp toward the living room.

"There was a notebook, Taryn. A notebook."

"You know what, why don't we focus less on this box and more on the fact that you completely eviscerated your mother on her birthday."

"Oh hell, Taryn, it's nothing you and I haven't talked about a thousand times. This Abby worship has got to stop."

"And you thought the best way to do that was to throw a drunken fit at the dinner table? What is the matter with you lately?"

"I don't know. Nothing feels right."

"Care to explain?"

"I don't know how. I just know that I feel like I was on a track for a long time and that I've completely come off the rails."

"We can both agree there."

Gable stared at his wife, wishing for answers. He could feel he was hurting her. For a minute he considered telling her everything. Telling her about the dreams and the encounter with London and the notebook. Maybe she knew about London already. She could have seen him with her or maybe he said her name in his sleep or maybe Derek ratted him out. Taryn kept journals their whole life, and it made enough sense that she was on to him and holding it back for fear of what it all meant.

"I just want to get back to feeling like us again," Taryn said, exasperation in her voice.

"Me too," he admitted, and pulled her toward him.

The dreams were just dreams. This was his place. Here, with the woman who spent her life loving him despite just how often he disappointed her.

"You need to apologize to your mom."

"I know. Can we just go out, you and me, first?"

"Sure. I'll get ready."

Taryn and Gable drove in silence to the farmer's market. Her hand was in his and he felt centered for the first time in days. The routine of their weekend ritual helped settle the roller coaster that had been his recent pace.

His wife hummed along to the song playing on the radio and the cold air conditioning helped ease what was left of his hangover. He squeezed her hand even tighter. It wasn't fair, keeping everything from her. They never lied to each other. He hadn't done anything wrong necessarily, but guilt hung over him nonetheless.

"Do you remember a girl named London from school?"

When she didn't respond Gable glanced over at Taryn, her face was ghostly white.

"Babe?"

"No. Not really. The name sounds familiar."

"You kind of picked on her."

"Why are you asking me this?"

"I saw her the other day."

"You what?"

"I saw her. Bumped into her when I went out for wings."

He was still lying, but at least part of the truth was getting out.

"Did she say anything to you?"

"Not really. We just said hi. Asked how each other were doing."

"And what did she say?"

"Nothing much. Are you okay?"

"Fine."

The car cabin was silent again. He hoped he'd feel better after coming at least part of the way clean, but instead the feeling shifted from guilt to regret.

Over the next three hours London hovered around Beth watching her pop back and forth between the present and future. Her departures were brief and almost seamless to the untrained eye. She'd occasionally collapse to the floor as she used to do, explaining the bumps and bruises.

One minute she'd be engaged in conversation, and then she'd pause, almost as if she was gathering her thoughts, and then she would scribble in her notebook. More than ninety percent of her travels were either too brief to assess or had nothing to do with London, but occasionally she would get flashes that included London. All signs were pointing to a Divine Travel, but it felt so far out of reach.

"I mean, it sounds like I traveled, but even in my own time, relocating my mind and body was extremely difficult. I don't feel like I have the abilities I'd need."

"You need to talk to Hopper," Beth said.

"Who?"

"She's traveled back like a hundred times and changes things like crazy. Claims she can hop to any timeline she puts her mind to. Just a heads up—she's...quirky."

. . .

At group, Beth pointed Hopper out. She was a petite Latina who looked more likely to be a YouTube star than a time travel expert. The majority of the eyes in the room were on her as she finished a story. Those closest to her laughed, while Beth and London talked under their breath.

"How is she supposed to help?"

"She likes to brag. Just pick her brain."

Group passed by and London barely heard what anyone had to say. She was too distracted trying to come up with ways to talk to and leverage "Hopper."

When the collective therapy ended Beth grabbed London by the hand and dragged her toward the big-eyed woman picking at a donut with her painted nails.

"Hey, Hop," Beth said.

"Elizabeth. What's up, girl? How's the future looking?"

"Terrible, per the usual." Beth was relaxed and friendly with Hopper, which just made London feel even more out of the mix.

"Well, maybe for you." Hopper smacked her lips like she didn't have a care in the world.

"This is London. We were friends in another line. She needs some help."

"Luuhn-din? You British?"

"Nope." London forced a smile. "I don't really know where to start, but Beth says you've been everywhere and I have somewhere I need to go."

"This about a dude or a kid?"

"Both."

Hopper sucked air in through her teeth. "Poor girl."

"I lost my husband and daughter in another timeline. And now Beth is seeing me Divine Traveling, but I don't think I have the skills to do that here."

"What the hell is a...'Divine Travel'?" she asked in a mocking tone.

"Where your mind and your body travel. I wasn't mobile when I tried to mind leap, I could only watch things play out. And I'm losing memories fast."

"Gotcha. So you wanna jump?"

"I guess. I need to get to another reality and fix it so I don't end up here."

"You ever done it?"

"I did a lot of things before I came here. This body and this mind are rusty though."

"Well, it's not that hard, but if you've never done it with this vessel before, you might need some—" she looked around the room "—prescribed help, if you know what I mean."

"You can jump?" London asked.

"Why do you think they call me Hopper?"

"I want to go to a timeline other than the one I'm currently on."

"That don't matter." Hopper waved her hand in London's face. "Our minds, our consciousness, it's like all one big map. As long as you have the destination up here you can jump around anywhere."

"So how do I get my body to come with me without my usual abilities?"

Hopper beckoned her in with a finger and got up close to her ear. "Love and sacrifice. And some good Chron."

Hopper started to walk away, but London had one more question.

"If you can do all this, why stay here?"

Hopper's brow creased and London was afraid she'd just started a fight.

"Understand this, London. There are worse places to be than right now."

London and Beth went back to their room and she told her what Hopper had said.

"The love and sacrifice part is on you," Beth said. "But I know who can get you the Chron."

"You do?"

"Yeah, but you understand this could work or it could kill you, right? And at a bare minimum, if you end up back here and they test you, you're going to prison. You only get one shot at this. And you still have to decide where you're going."

"Therein lies the sacrifice I suppose."

69

*I*nstead of relieving the tension, the farmer's market became a nightmarish game of who could act the most normal in the least confrontational setting on the planet. Taryn and Gable stuffed samples into their mouths and spent too much time talking to vendors in order to avoid the collapsing façade that everything between them was all right.

Gable wasn't exactly sure what it was about bringing up London Riley that had set his wife on edge, but from the moment her name left his mouth, Taryn appeared to be adrift, lost in a sea of contemplation.

He didn't dare approach the conversation again. There was just a glacial acceptance that he'd made the wrong choice in telling her.

When they got home, she headed for the guest room and slammed the door shut.

Gable pulled his phone out of his pocket and sent his mother a text apologizing for his behavior. Taryn's anger could have just been the accumulation of his many mistakes over the last few days. Impotence. Forgetfulness. Drunken tirades. He had hit the shitty husband trifecta, and then he'd tossed running into a girl from their past onto the heap.

He paced his kitchen, waiting for some sign that she wanted to see him.

Instead he heard the ripping sound of tape being torn from a box.

Gable stormed down the hall and jiggled the handle to the room Taryn was in. The door was locked, and he slammed his fist into the wood.

"Taryn. Taryn."

Silence.

"Let me in there now!"

Silence.

He went to the kitchen and rummaged through a junk drawer until he found a small screwdriver meant for fixing eyeglasses. He jammed the tool into the tiny hole and twisted until he found an edge. He turned and the lock clicked. When he opened the door Taryn was crouched on her knees. Two sticky pads were adhered to her temples and connected to wires that were plugged into a rectangular machine. The one he had seen the night before. She looked at him with tears in her eyes and put something in her mouth.

"I love you," she said. Then her eyes closed and she fell to the floor. No matter how much he shook her, she wouldn't wake up.

When he called 9-1-1, her heart rate was slowing down. They asked him questions like "What is this on her head?"

"I don't know," he answered, eyes fixed on his wife.

"Did she take anything?"

"I think so."

"What was it?"

"I don't know."

When they arrived at the hospital, doctors informed him that they couldn't find any brain activity. A toxicology report suggested that she had taken Chronzaplan. He had heard about people using an illegal time travel drug but couldn't imagine a world where his wife would do it. They talked about how crazy those people in the desert cult were and how stupid the idea was that anyone could fix anything with time travel.

"This can't be right. This isn't right." He repeated it over and over to her unconscious body. His mother cried in a chair next to her. His father didn't even attempt to turn the television onto a sports channel. A ventilator breathed air into Taryn's lungs. Tubes and machines all around her were keeping her body alive, but everything that made Taryn Taryn was in her mind, and according to doctors, that was gone.

Gable made the decision to remove her from life support. They had promised to pull the plug on each other if every they ended up in that position. He could at least do one last thing right by her. When he went home, her clothes in a plastic bag, he drifted down the hall and looked into the room where he'd last seen her. The cardboard box was there, and in it were volumes of notebooks.

There was one marked *#1*. He opened it, and on the first page was his wife's sloppy handwriting. The first line read, *Gable, if you're reading this, know that I did it all for you.*

70

*A*s it turned out, Miles was Beth's hook up for the Chronzaplan. He dropped it off in their room the next morning when he was doing rounds. London didn't ask how she got in touch with him without a phone or how he was able to get it so quick, she just accepted it and gave him the password to her bank account so he could transfer five thousand dollars out of it.

"Are you sure you're ready?"

"No," London said. "But I do know that after talking to Hopper, if I go into Brian's office for therapy today he's going to see what I have planned, and then it will be too late. I'll be locked down and I may never get out."

"I haven't seen anything involving you in the future since you talked to Hopper."

"That doesn't necessarily mean I'm not there."

Beth paced the room biting her thumbnail. "So, what, you're just going to go then?"

"I don't think I have a choice. My session is in an hour."

London was panicked, but she needed to find a way to shift her focus.

"Where are you going?"

"I think it makes the most sense to try to get back to the day where Taryn showed up in my office and asked me to bridge with her. If I can just stop her from coming in or stop myself from agreeing to do it, then all of this should go away."

Beth shrugged and ran her tongue back and forth across her teeth. There was nothing else she could do to help.

Her hand shook as she picked up the dose of Chronzaplan. She stood up and hugged Beth.

"There's a note in my drawer for my mom if something happens. Just make sure she gets it, please?"

Beth nodded and her shoulder twitched upward.

London sat down on the bed and pictured the layout of her office. A vision of Marley's face popped into her mind. She thought of the color and shape of the couch where travelers would sit seeking her counsel. Gable's smile. London placed the pill on her tongue and swallowed. She held the image of the diagonal angle of her office's tiles beneath her favorite pair of boots in her mind. Taryn asking to bridge with her.

When her eyes opened she knew immediately that she had failed. She wasn't in her office the day Taryn arrived. She wasn't anywhere near that date or place. She was pretty sure she'd hit the right timeline, but the completely wrong target. She was back at AION.

Clearly, though, her body had come with her. She was wearing the clothes from the new timeline. Her nails were still manicured to perfection. London looked around and tried to get her bearings. She was on the east side of campus and began to run toward Gable's apartment. She was making up her plan as she went. Was she going to try to tell him everything? Was she hoping to find her past self and warn her of what was to come?

It was early in the morning, and the residents at AION were still tucked away. She bolted through the grounds as fast as she could. As she closed in on Gable's apartment, she nearly knocked someone over.

"What the hell?"

London looked at who she collided with. It was Taryn, a metal case containing Clair in her hands.

They stared at each other, locked in a confused staring contest.

"Lond-y, I was looking for you."

London was dumbstruck. She couldn't find the words.

"I need your help," she said and hooked her by the arm, leading her toward their shared apartment.

"I can't, I have to…" As she looked back at Gable's apartment, a younger version of herself was leaving his apartment. It was the night he'd cooked for her. Which meant this was the first time she tried to help Taryn bridge. Now she knew why the Chron brought her here.

When they reached their apartment, a million things were racing through her mind. Her Korean dialect was turned up high. Taryn locked their door and turned to face London.

"Looking a little old, Lond-y."

She wasn't sure how to respond. London knew the version of herself standing in front of Taryn was about five years older than the one who was her roommate. Her clothes were unusual, but what did Taryn think the explanation for this was?

"Do you know who I am?" London asked.

"Oh, I know who you are. I've been waiting a long time for this."

"How could you possibly have been waiting for me?"

"It's me. Taryn Matthews."

London felt her heart rate double. The pounding in her chest was ringing through her ears.

"How is that possible?"

"Well, when I realized you didn't listen to me and had been fucking around in my perfect life, I knew I had to come back here and make some changes. What I didn't expect was to get stuck here. I've been in this timeline for four years. That Chronzaplan shit is messed up. On the bright side, without all my abuse, traveling was easier. Time travel trade-offs, am I right? Like you—you got this hot bod, but no husband and kid."

"You stole my life. How could you do that to me?"

"I didn't do anything to you. I told you that. I did something for me. I did something for Gable. You saw that time. I was happy. He was happy. His mom and his sister were alive. Everyone was better. Even you."

"My daughter."

"It wasn't personal. And it's not like I drowned her in a bucket. She was just collateral damage. Gable didn't know any different, and if you had just given it some time, you would have forgotten about her too and everyone would have been fine."

"I can't let you do this."

"What are you going to do? Kill me? Stop me from travel-ing? Let Abigail and Margaret die? All so you can have your life back?"

London put her hands over her ears. She couldn't let Taryn manipulate her. "I'm not killing anyone. This is the correct timeline. That other life isn't real. *This* is what is real."

"Oh now, Lond-y, that's not the speech you feed people. We all just make choices, right? Well, I made mine, and everyone was better for it."

Her hurt and her anger bubbled over, and she lunged at

Taryn. They knocked into the wall, landed on the bed and rolled, Taryn landing on top. She had her hands on London's throat.

"Don't worry, it won't be as bad this time. I'm going to find a way to help Gable and change everything before you two ever have a chance to get together. That way, you never have to feel this loss. I can give you that, London." She squeezed tighter around London's neck.

Drumming up her last bit of strength, her hurt from deep below, London slammed her fist into Taryn's elbows and freed her airway. She grabbed a wrench from Taryn's shelf and hit her in the head with it. Taryn began to bleed and held her head. While she was distracted by her wound, London grabbed the scrappy, first version of Clair that Taryn always kept nearby. The one Taryn used on her father. The one that unloaded pure, unfiltered consciousness into the two people plugged in. London fastened a headband to herself then slipped the other onto Taryn.

"No," Taryn said.

Then London flipped the switch.

Both women wailed in agony. Pain and heartache pouring from one mind into the other. They felt everything the other had lost. Everything the other desired. London ripped the band off herself and flipped off the switch. Taryn was huddled on the floor, unmoving, her eyes unblinking and locked on a distant point.

London looked down and her hands started to fade. The door opened and she saw her younger self entering the room, rushing over to her friend as the last of her dissipated.

71

*W*hen she opened her eyes, London experienced some panic. She was in a hospital bed again, just as she had been after Taryn bridged with her in her office. Was she in some sort of inescapable loop? Destined to always come right back here?

A nurse entered the room. Not the same nurse from her last visit, though.

"Oh, my god. You're awake! I'm sorry. This is not how I'm supposed to react. I need to get a doctor."

London looked at her hands and tried to assess the damage she'd done this time. There was absolutely nothing personal in the room. No clothes. No phone. No people.

On the white board that was meant to keep the hospital staff organized, a date was written down, but it didn't make sense. She was back to 2019, but it was three months beyond the date it was when she left the facility and Beth.

A doctor entered the room.

"Ms. Riley. How are you?"

"I don't know."

"Understandable. I'm Dr. Navuluri. You're at Phoenix

Samaritan Hospital. You've been here for eighty-seven days in a coma. When you arrived, you had an abnormally high dose of medication in your system. We weren't able to identify exactly what it was. Can you remember taking something?"

"Yes."

London wasn't concerned with imprisonment or consequences at the moment.

"It has taken a real toll on your body."

"Toll?"

"I know this is a lot to take in, but I would like to explain a few things to you about your current condition if that's alright."

"Sure."

London tried to adjust herself in her bed, but found it difficult to get repositioned.

"You were brought into us unconscious. At the time when you arrived, you were showing very little brain activity. You were legally dead, but paramedics resuscitated you and brought you here. We believe you did incur brain damage due to a lack of oxygen, but as the days passed, your brain activity began to tick up. It was a very unusual and unexpected anomaly. Most people in your condition would never wake up again. Yet, here you are. However, these events caused the formation of lesions on your brain. We've conducted three surgeries since you've been here in an attempt to remove them. We couldn't get them all, but we're hoping we got enough to help with your mobility and motor functions."

"Am I paralyzed?"

"We're not sure what your abilities are. We needed you to wake up first. You will need to take it slow and be patient as we assess the damage. That being said, the fact that you are speaking is remarkable."

"Am I going to prison?"

No one spoke for a long time. Dr. Navuluri looked at the nurse confused.

"Why would you be going to prison?"

"I time travelled illegally. I took Chronzaplan."

The team exchanged uncomfortable looks.

"We're going to give you some time to rest. We've already called your husband and he's on his way."

"My husband?"

The doctor nodded and went to leave.

"Who's my husband?"

Again he got a confused look on his face. He flipped through her chart.

"I have Gable Matthews written down here. He's the one who called 9-1-1 when you passed out at your home."

London began to weep hysterically.

Within the hour, Gable entered the room. Holding his hand and trailing a little behind him was a curly-headed toddler, two fingers in her mouth.

It took months before London could walk again. Her body felt like it had aged decades. Little by little, her physical faculties returned, but her psychic functions never fully recovered. No matter how hard she tried to summon up the abilities that had defined her all her life, they were nowhere to be found. Not even a whisper.

She did, however, keep both sets of memories: the original timeline and the horrifically skewed one Taryn created. It was as if the two had merged into one and just made up who she was now. London could remember life at AION, testing and creating alongside Gable and Taryn. She could also remember a life where she left that place at eighteen and never looked back. It was as if her consciousness held on to whatever was necessary to keep her alive and intact.

The timeline she was in now wasn't an exact replica of the original. Some things had changed when she left her alternate reality and tried to hop back into this one.

Taryn was alive, but never fully recovered from the encounter with her first version of Clair. Seeing all she'd stripped London of in full color had damaged her too. AION didn't reach its full potential without her, and there was no JT Enterprises. London suspected James still operated underground, but they didn't hear from him again once they'd left.

Gable worked as a chemistry teacher at a community college. London had a small but loyal fanbase who bought her paintings, all depictions of this world and the others she'd occupied. Beth was Marley's godmother. Fairy Godmother, as she preferred to be called. And, once a month, London would go see Taryn.

Every time London walked through the doors of the Scottsdale Adult Care facility, she had to summon up courage from deep down to make it to Taryn's room. When she entered, Taryn made no effort to acknowledge her. Sometimes Taryn spoke, other times she just stared out the window.

"Lond-y," she said. Her voice dry and scratchy.

"Hey, T."

London sat a Diet Coke, a bag of French fries, and two cups of Ranch dressing on the nightstand next to her. Taryn stared at her through the corners of her eyes. With her one properly functioning arm, she lifted the bed that had become her permanent home and reached over for a fry.

"You tell him yet?" Taryn asked.

It was always the first thing she asked. London shook her head softly.

"He deserves to know."

London nodded.

She wasn't sure why she came to see Taryn. Perhaps it was a form of penance for landing her here. Maybe it was an acknowledgement that there wasn't much difference between them. Both had fought for what they wanted, made a choice, and there were consequences. Each time, Taryn asked if she'd told Gable what it took to get their life back. Did he know who really attacked Taryn that day at AION? Did he know there was a world where his sister and his mother were alive? Did he know Taryn had also been his wife?

They were thoughts that haunted her all the time. She knew what she did wasn't right. It was just what happened when she was fighting to get her daughter back. She had succeeded, but it cost more than she could have ever imagined.

72

"*H*ow's Taryn?" Gable asked when his wife returned home.

London just nodded. She was always down after visiting Taryn. It was hard to see her like that.

They tucked Marley into bed, each of them taking one cheek to kiss.

"Night, Bug," Gable said as they left her in the soft glow of her flower nightlight.

Gable grabbed his pills from the cabinet.

"Trouble sleeping again?" London asked.

"Yeah. Same dreams. My mom and sister being alive. Can't shake them."

He left out the part about how, in those dreams, Taryn was his wife. It didn't seem like a necessary detail. They were just dreams.

AFTERWORD

I have always been obsessed with time travel and the idea that our memories are the closest thing we have to this ability. How someone remembers an event or how they hold onto the past shapes their whole being. But memory is flexible, moldable and sometimes an outright lie. How we *choose* to apply our memories can save us or destroy us. I wanted to explore this in fiction and thus, London, Gable and Taryn were born. Three imperfect people with imperfect histories who just want a good life. At their core, they are trying to do what all of us try to do: live a good, satisfying life.

When naming my debut novel, I was thinking about what a luxury time itself is. I'm a mom of four, a freelance writer and a hopeless dreamer who is always wishing for just a few more hours in the day. So time travel feels like the ultimate extravagance. The truth is though, we all just have the time we're given and the abundant gift of being able to choose what we do with that time. As my three main characters show over and over, you can do what you think is best and still end up on the edge of a cliff. So try to treasure your "now" and consider every day a luxury.

ACKNOWLEDGMENTS

Over a decade ago I had the wild idea that I might like to write books for a living. At the time, I couldn't have imagined all the hours and, more importantly, all the people it would take to finally arrive here. To every person who asked me "How's the book coming?" after years and years and years of knowing I was working on it, thank you. Thank you for your patience and your belief in me. It meant more than you can imagine.

To my husband, who else in the whole world could have so many nerdy time travel conversations with me and never get sick of it. You get who I am at my core and you never doubted me. I love you.

To my mom, it's not every daughter who has a parent who will watch her kids, help pay for editing, listen while she cries for the 100th time because she isn't sure she'll ever cross the finish line and then shares about the publication on every social media site she has. This couldn't have happened without you.

To my children, I hope one day you can see this book for what it is. I know the days where my head was down or my door was closed were sometimes tough, but Maddison, Maxwell, Cooper and Jack... I did this with the hope that in the future, when you have a dream, you understand what's possible and you go for it with all of your heart.

To my editor, Michelle Meade, girl you get me. You understood what my story was before I even fully understood what my story was. I could not have asked for better guidance as I unearthed my first novel. Your love of science fiction and your care for budding authors is extraordinary.

To Sara Chambers, my cover designer, web designer, brand strategist and dear, dear friend, your vision is a freaking Earth-shattering wonder.

There are too many people to name who have been there for me all the way, but I am going to try to drop a few more. Dad, thanks for telling me to keep a journal and reminding me to write, write, write whenever I felt anything. Crystal Patriarche, who gave me my first job in publishing, and allowed me to keep a career surrounded by books no matter what phase of life I was in, thank you. Neely, Kristin, Paige, Victoria, Ashley, Michelle, Stacy, Megan, Britt, Val and the countless additional powerhouse women and sisters and mothers in my life who encouraged me every step, I feel honored to call you my circle.

ABOUT THE AUTHOR

Christelle Lujan is an author who has spent her whole life making up stories in her head. She mostly writes Sci-Fi... some may describe her work as Sci-Fantasy, she's okay with that. (But also totally willing to debate you on the idea that psychics are a scientific topic and not a magic-based one.) Christelle calls her work Science Fiction with a Soft Center. She likes a whole lot of heart mixed in with time travel, aliens, parallel universes, experiments gone wrong, and AI with attitude.

Stories like *The Handmaid's Tale*, *Dark Matter*, *Arrival*, and *The OA* leave her breathless. Her favorite movie growing up was *Honey, I Shrunk the Kids* (name drop, street cred).

Christelle is married to the love of her life and fellow nerd who she met in seventh grade science. The two live on a homestead in Arizona with their four children.

If you'd like to learn more about Christelle's other stories or are if you're a mom trying to write her own book and struggling to find the time, head over to ChristelleLujan.com. She has free fiction and fun advice for fellow writer moms.

facebook.com/ChristelleLujan
twitter.com/ChristelleLujan
instagram.com/christellelujan

FREE NOVELETTE

If you enjoyed *The Luxury of Time Travel*, check out my free
novelette for a quick time travel read.

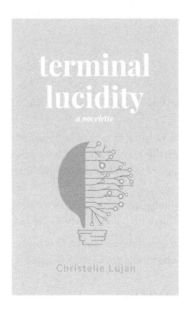

Terminal Lucidity

**"What would you do to get your son back? Leave your husband?
Drain your bank account? Risk your own life?"**

Ophelia paused for what felt like an appropriate few seconds to
think, even though she didn't need to. The answer was simple. she'd
give it all up for Luke.

With a single "Yes", Ophelia goes from a grieving mother to the
subject of a bizarre experiment held in the back offices of a family

counseling center. Her naked body is ushered into a machine by a doctor she just met, searing pain rips through every fiber in her body and she's thrown two years into the past.

Back to when her son was alive. Back to when she thought the world was fair and kind. But the fate she meets during her second chance is another testament to just how cruel this world can be.

As she unlocks the potential of her mind, time, and space, she races against the forces that seek to take her son once more. With the ferocity of a mother who has felt unimaginable loss, she fights to keep her family, and her memories, intact before both are lost forever.

Download here! or at ChristelleLujan.com/lucidity

THE ORIGINS OF TIME TRAVEL

If like me, you felt satisfied by where London and Gable ended up, but couldn't stop thinking of Ruth… I have news. I'm writing a prequel covering her story. Her amazing abilities, her troubled childhood in a creepy, Arizona ghosttown, and how she fell in love with London's father *after* he died. Not to mention a peek into her relationship with James before AION came to be.

Be the first to hear about the release of *The Origins of Time Travel* by subscribing at ChristelleLujan.com

CHAPTER ONE SAMPLE

Her back was damp from the grass. She could feel the sun baking her into wakefulness, but didn't have the energy to open her eyes. Ruth stretched her hands above her head and stubbed her fingers on cold, hard stone.

She let out a groan, but squeezed her eyebrows towards her lips to keep the morning out for just a few seconds longer.

Something hard jabbed into her side, forcing her into a seated position.

The figure of a man blocked the sun so all she could see was a black silhouette, haloed in rays of sunlight. It wasn't a man though. It was a boy. James.

"Get up! You gotta get out of here," he said, poking the end of his rake into her ribs again.

"Stop it," she said, swatting the rake away.

"I'm serious Ruth. I'm going to get in trouble if someone sees you and complains."

Ruth brushed bits of grass and leaves from her clothes. She looked back at the headstone she'd fallen asleep in front of then turned a one-eyed squint back to James.

"Okay, okay."

"There's a burial happening in five minutes. If you're not out of here by then I'm gonna get fired."

"You know, you could just stop being such a coward all the time. Who else are they going to find to work nights at a cemetery in this town?"

"Just go," James insisted, conceiting her point, but not acknowledging her jab.

"Fine, I'll leave, but only if you tell me who kicked it," she nodded her head to the prepared site awaiting a coffin and its inhabitant. "Was it Mr. Meyers? He was what, 102?"

"Shhh," James looked around the cemetery, but no one was there. "No, it isn't Mr. Meyers. It's John Parker."

"John Parker? He died weeks ago."

"Yeah well, when you're Jerome's first murder victim in years, things can take a little while before they get to the funeral."

Ruth's eyes fixed on the gravesite.

"Don't even think about it," James scolded.

She flashed him a teasing grin, a deep dimple sinking into her right cheek.

"Get the hell out of here." James grabbed her beneath the armpits and hoisted Ruth to her feet. She waved him off and made her way toward the gate. Not fast enough though. As she reached the entrance of the cemetery, mourners began to pour out of cars, spilling like ink onto the pavement in their black frocks. Ruth ducked behind a bush. The first two to pass her were John's parents. She didn't personally know the family, but had seen them on the news, begging for anyone with information to come forward. Then a young boy, no older than thirteen with John's teeming dark eyes and waved black hair followed, his hands in his pockets and his gaze on his shoes.

There was no sound other than the crack of formal shoes on gravel and the occasional sniffle. Four solid men bore the weight of a casket on their shoulders. The heft of their unfortunate load drew sweat to their temples. Ruth assumed the arrival of the body marked the end of the procession and bolted out from behind the bush to make a fast exit. Instead, she collided with a young woman. Blonde and bony, she had her face buried in a tissue before Ruth disrupted her slow march. The grieving attendee stood rigid, eyeing Ruth's disheveled appearance from head to toe.

Ruth was suddenly overtaken with the young woman's sorrow. In every nerve, she could feel the pain of loss filling her up like a bucket in the rain. She had to grit her teeth to keep tears from erupting.

"I'm so sorry," Ruth managed as she dropped her head and pushed herself out of the cemetery. When she looked back, the woman was still staring at her and she could hear a shrill scream echo in her head, though the onlooker's lips didn't move.

Jerome was built on a mountain, so anywhere you went you were either hoofing up Cleopatra Hill, or avoiding skidding down it. As Ruth dissented towards her home, she took back streets and cut through yards to avoid the main drag where she might be forced to interact with other people. Her tolerance for the unwelcome flood of information that poured out from anyone she passed was dwindling to nearly zero.

"You should be grateful for your abilities Ruth Ann. Stop acting like a child," her mother would chide if she noticed her daughter wincing in a public setting. It had skipped a generation, so her mother had never felt an ounce of sympathy around Ruth's ever-developing psychic abilities. Only jealousy.

By the time Ruth reached her home, the choking sensation of sadness and the ringing from an inaudible scream was cleared from her mind. Distance usually did the trick.

The only place she'd ever lived could be described by most as a shack. Two bedrooms, one bathroom, a kitchen only one person could occupy at once. She spent as little time here as possible to avoid suffocation. Even with just the two of them living there, Ruth felt the strangling effects of an inescapable space any time she was there. Paint chipped from every beam on the exterior and overgrown brush threatened to claim the tiny patio for itself. Ruth placed a hand on the door to enter, but as she did, could detect the presence of more than one person inside the walls.

"Shit," she whispered. She took a reversed step away from the door, but an unforgiving creak let out. Pinching her eyes shut, she held her breath and waited, frozen in space. Her mother opened the door, a look of anticipated disappointment draped on her face.

"Good lord Ruth." Her mother began running her hands through her scattered red curls to smooth out the spots that had been matted by wet grass. "Well come on then, you're fifteen minutes late." Ruth was shooed into the house like a cat who had been missing for days. Everyone knew it would return, but wasn't sure what to expect when it did.

Sitting on the couch in their cramped living room was Emerald Webb, a particularly unstable menopausal mother of four and wife to one of the drunkest men in town. Though Ruth never advertised it, her mother had been letting anyone who walked into her store know that "her little Ruthy" was developing the gift. She told anyone who cared, and some who didn't, that her abilities were on track to "far exceed" her own mother's. Ruth's grandmother was Jerome's most sought psychic once upon time, and though she died when Ruth was just a kid, her reputation remained.

So on any given day, Ruth could expect her mother to be waiting for her with a client seeking a reading. She never bothered to ask if it was something Ruth wanted. Anything that could earn a few dollars was expected and when she would refuse to show up for an appointment, her mother would only stock the house with foods she knew her daughter despised.

"Hello Mrs. Webb," Ruth said, a sigh escaped with her greeting. In truth, she had forgotten the appointment, but the element of surprise didn't keep her from feeling a deep sense of dread. Ruth found little joy in having access to everybody's internal dialogue, thoughts, emotions, and memories. Whispers from the living and the dead confirmed that people were mostly a constant stream of suffering as far as Ruth could tell. Emerald Webb was a special brand of pitiful though. Always chastising herself for aging and gaining weight. Constantly on the hunt for a solution that couldn't resolve the obvious problem in her life: that her husband was an asshole. Adding to it was a hedonistic obsession with daytime television that rotted her mind into believing tragedy was the best version of life she could hope for.

"Oh Ruth thank goodness, I was beginning to worry," Emerald said, fanning herself with a magazine.

"Sorry to keep you waiting," Ruth said, looking at the clock seeing that it was 8:15. Emerald always came right after dropping her children off at school.

"Well, let's get to it, I have errands."

Ruth held up her hand, ushering Emerald to dive into whatever nonsense she was seeking counsel on.

"I've been thinking, perhaps some of my issues could be resolved if I tackled my history with my mother." After knowing Emerald for years, Ruth couldn't help but agree. A dozen memories from a childhood filled with an abusive father and a complicit mother had carved Emerald into a person who knew only shame and anger in male relationships. "Could you help me unpack some of my baggage around that?"

Ruth blinked her eyes tight and pressed her knuckles into her lids. Her mother elbowed her, always watching and critiquing as she did a reading.

"Mrs. Webb, I think you understand that having a father as cruel as yours has complicated your marriage." Ruth tried to be delicate even though she knew it would be only seconds before Emerald was in tears.

"Yes. Yes, it's true that he was a mean ol' son of a bitch."

"Maybe, you sought something similar in your own husband."

Tears burst forward.

"No. No I would never have wanted for my own children what I was raised with."

"I don't think you did it on purpose Mrs. Webb, but there are some striking similarities."

"Andrew has never laid a hand on me," Emerald insisted, pointing her index finger while the rest of her hand clutched a tissue.

"No. That's true. But the drinking…"

"I've asked him to get help. Told him he should go to one of the meetings at the church."

"He's never been particularly receptive to your suggestions," Ruth tried her best to lead her gently. She could see the argument they had over AA playing out in Emerald's mind. He'd smashed her favorite rooster figurine on the kitchen floor and shouted "No way in hell you'll catch me dead there."

"Maybe if I offered to go with him…"

"Mrs. Webb, he seems pretty unflinching. What if instead you did something nice for yourself, last time you were here we talked about possibly getting a job or taking up knitting."

"I tried Ruthy, I really tried. No one wants to hire an old gal like me who's never worked a day in her life."

"And the knitting?"

"My hands cramped up."

"Have you ever thought of seeking a counselor?" Ruth asked.

"What do you think I'm doing *here* sweetheart?"

"I'm not a counselor Mrs. Webb. I can only tell you the things that are already inside of you. I can't tell you how to fix them." Her mother darted a damning look in her direction. "Look, I think maybe it would just be good for you to spend less time focusing on how to make him happy and more time on how to make yourself happier. Maybe your positivity would spill over into him." Ruth looked over at her mother to see if she'd recovered the session.

"Yes, perhaps you're right. I'm sure it isn't easy for him to come home to a wife who behaves the way I do." Ruth clenched her jaw at the notion that she'd made Mrs. Webb feel responsible for her pig of a husband's behavior. What she really wanted to say was "Why don't you leave him?" "Maybe, you should let him get behind the wheel drunk and see if he doesn't just drive right over the edge of Cleopatra and solve all your problems?" When she'd jokingly brought that up to her mother though, she was told that curing clients wasn't good for business.

"Well Ruth, thank you dear. I'm sure you have school or something to get to."

"I actually graduated in May."

"Oh that's right. So forgetful these days." Emerald pulled out a compact mirror and blotted the tears from her cheeks before she brushed powder onto them. She fluffed her permed coils and clapped the makeup container shut. "Same time next week?"

"Same time Mrs. Webb."

"Nancy, I'll come by the store with the cash after I've run to get groceries, wouldn't want Andrew catching the money missing. That man has no idea what a roast costs, thank goodness."

Her mother walked Emerald to the door then moved to the kitchen without making eye contact.

"Were you in the cemetery again?"

Ruth froze on her walk to the bedroom. She'd hoped they wouldn't have to speak again until it was time to open the store.

"Yes."

"Get anything good?"

"Not really. He was pretty boring to be honest."

Her mother sucked air through her teeth. "Go get cleaned up. I'll let you know who to visit next when we're on our way to open up. "

Made in the USA
Monee, IL
20 October 2020

45695319R00233